First Edition
Copyright © 2022 Jill Berry
All rights reserved
ISBN: 979-8-82-825668-6

The Dresser
#OneWord
The Button Box

Jill Berry

DEDICATION

...to all those who have read and offered me feedback on earlier versions of each novel. I have been able to use your responses to revise and review, and I hope to improve, what I've written, and I am very appreciative of your support and encouragement.

Thank you all.

REFLECTIONS

I have been a voracious reader for most of my life. I love fiction, especially fiction which makes me think, and which engages my emotions. I've been a member of several Book Clubs and enjoy reading and discussing, and often disagreeing about, what we have all read.

I am a resilient reader. I rarely start a book and fail to finish it, and I ALWAYS - whatever I think of it - finish a Book Club read, but even I sometimes find I'm flagging in the final third or so. When did novels grow so long? Does anyone else ever feel: this is good, but it would be even better if it were a few thousand words shorter?

Each of these novels is under 60,000 words, which is why I'm publishing them all together. I don't want any potential reader to feel short-changed. But I think a more concise read might be MORE successful - including for Book Clubs. They don't take too long to get through, so everyone should manage to finish the novel and not arrive for the discussion with it half-read. I've also included possible discussion questions on each one at the back of the book (but note that they contain spoilers, so I wouldn't advise reading the questions first!) in case they're helpful.

And even if Book Clubs aren't your thing, I'm hoping these will be stories you want to share, and talk about, with other readers.

I'd love to know what you think, and even to engage in discussion with you – whatever you think! Do feel free to contact me on Twitter @jillberry102.

Thanks for your interest in my three short novels.

Jill Berry
May 2022

THE DRESSER

CONTENTS:

Prologue: January 2020

Laura looks round the kitchen for one last time. It is empty and echoing, the quarry tile floor swept clean and the harsh winter light coming through the small windows, now without curtains. Only the dresser remains, the one piece of furniture she and James inherited from the previous owners when they moved into the house as a young married couple sixty years before. Laura's eyes settle on it, and she remembers. It had been painted black then, and loomed over the low-ceilinged room. It occupied most of the end wall, and was already quite battered and worn when it became theirs. But they had little furniture in those days; in fact they had little of anything. They were grateful for its shelves and cupboards. They were grateful for everything at that time, starting out on married life together and thrilled to be moving into The Old Vicarage, their new home - next to the church in a small village on the banks of a river. They had loved the village from the moment they saw it – the warm stone of the cottages, the village green, the single shop and the inn – and a short walk along the river to the small primary school in the next village where Laura was to begin her teaching career. They had been delighted to find the house, within their means as it needed considerable renovation, which energised, rather than deterred, them. They were looking forward to putting their own stamp on the place. They were happy, healthy and excited about the future. They were young.

Laura moves slowly now, as she prepares to leave the house in which she has made her home, lived her life, raised her children. She is leaving the village, and the country in which she was born, to travel at the age of eighty-four to the other side of the world. She will join her son and his family, to live near her grandchildren and to spend what time remains to her basking in the warmth of the southern sun. She will never see snow again, she reflects, remembering winters when the villages were snow-bound, the school was closed, and the children, beside themselves with joy, played in the white garden and relished their freedom. She will never again spend days baking, gathering produce and flowers and decorating the church for the Harvest Festival. And she will no longer have to worry about flood, when the waters of the river rose perilously following heavy rains combined with high tides, surrounding the house and on several occasions, memorably, encroaching into the property.

The dresser will remain for the new owners to use or to dispose of as they wish. Over the years it has been painted lighter, brighter colours, and finally dipped and stripped down to its original wood. Laura touches it lightly, blinks and shakes her head a little, before moving gingerly to the door, stepping through it and closing it softly behind her, making her careful way down the path to join her son John at the car.

PART I: 1900

Chapter One: *early days*

Alice bustled into the kitchen, her arms full of produce from the garden, the youngest children milling around her skirts. Edward sat in his accustomed chair, poring over his latest sermon. He peered at her over his spectacles and gave a faint smile.

"I do believe this might be my best yet, my dear. Let us hope the villagers appreciate it."

Alice returned his smile as she moved to deposit the vegetables on the broad, scrubbed table.

"A good crop today!" she said. "I shall set aside some for the collection, of course, but we shall enjoy a feast of fresh vegetables, Edward. We are, indeed, fortunate that the Harrisons kept such an abundant kitchen garden."

Alice was appreciative of the fact that her family was benefiting from the labours of the previous owners of The Vicarage, although some of this bounty was earmarked for the Harvest Festival rather than for her own table. She reflected on how their life had changed since they had taken the place of Reverend Harrison and his family a month before. She was gratified that Edward was enjoying his new role and that the children clearly loved their new home, the village, the riverbank. Alice was pleased to have moved into The Vicarage too, although she was less sure of herself than others often realised. As the wife of the incoming minister she knew she had a position to maintain within this community, but she did not yet feel fully confident about what her role would be and how best to establish herself with her neighbours, who nodded and smiled but seemed a little distant and circumspect. The birth of her last child had left her drained, and the demands of six growing children meant that she was constantly required to attend to one or other of them, with little time for herself. She missed her family and the close friends they had left behind when they moved. She often felt weary. Perhaps this was the lot of a married woman with children at the beginning of the new century, she reflected.

Alice began to prepare the midday meal, with the help of Martha and Betsy, the eldest girls. She mused as she worked.

"Edward, have you given further thought to our conversation about a dresser? It would be useful to be able to display those few, precious pieces I have from grandmama somewhere out of the reach of small fingers," smiling at the upturned faces as she spoke.

"I have indeed!" exclaimed Edward with some satisfaction, pleased to show that he was responsive to Alice's needs. "A local carpenter will call on Monday to discuss it with you. I have been told he is a good man. He lives with his wife on the edge of village, I believe. I shall be on parish visits, but as the kitchen is your domain I know you are fully capable of explaining to him what you have in mind."

Edward unfolded his long limbs and stretched himself to his full height, his thinning hair brushing the ceiling as he did so. He swooped forward and, gathering the youngest children in his outstretched arms, ushered them out of the kitchen into the garden, shrieking as they went.

Alice paused in her work and turned to face the wall where, in her imagination, she could already see the dresser – broad, tall, substantial – a safe repository for her few treasures, with serviceable space to store other goods below. She felt a little nervous at the prospect of meeting the carpenter by herself and explaining to him what she envisaged. But then she found herself wondering whether working with the carpenter to create the piece she could already see in her mind's eye might help her to feel more settled and comfortable, and a little more at home here. At least it would give her the opportunity to get to know one of the villagers better, and perhaps that would ease the building of further relationships across this new community.

Alice could hear the children's laughter from the garden, which always lifted her spirits. Through the window she could see that Edward had settled himself in a garden chair and was dozing in the weak autumn sun, while Molly and the twins played a complex game around him, and the baby gurgled from the blanket which was stretched out in the shade of the tree. After a while, she sent Martha and Betsy outside to gather them all, and when the meal was ready, the family took their places at the kitchen table, where Edward said grace.

The children chatted as they ate; the twins, Matthew and Benjamin, were especially lively and vocal, and inevitably entertained the others.

"This afternoon, when we go down to the river again…"

"…we're planning on building a jetty!"

The twins had a slightly disconcerting habit of completing each other's sentences.

Throughout the meal, the older girls helped their mother, and Molly, the youngest girl, kept a watchful eye on baby Jack, feeding him and quietly murmuring to him from time to time. When all had eaten their fill, Martha and Betsy cleared the dishes from the table and washed and dried them in the scullery, before returning to the garden. Molly settled Jack for his afternoon sleep, after which she went to join her sisters, and the boys left to continue their exploration of the river bank, their current favourite occupation, looking for pieces of wood from which they planned to construct their jetty. Tomorrow would mean church services and restricted freedom, and on Monday the four eldest children would walk together down the path by the river to the school in the neighbouring village. Alice and Edward were content to give the children latitude on this mild autumn Saturday.

The couple settled in their chairs on either side of the kitchen range. Edward lit his pipe which he smoked contentedly while looking over his sermon once more. Alice attended to her sewing, and they lapsed into a companionable silence.

After a while, Alice looked up to find Edward peering at her over his spectacles.

"What is it, dearest?"

Edward hesitated before replying, and Alice set aside her basket of work and regarded him steadily.

"I was reflecting on my good fortune," said Edward, with a wry smile. Alice waited, and in due course he continued. "It is ten years since we wed, Alice, and I still thank the Lord each day that you accepted an old man like me. You have brought such bounty into my life, and you make it possible for me to do the Lord's work with joy and peace in my heart."

"Edward!" Alice had never known her husband to speak in this way, and she blushed as she sought for an appropriate response. "The difference in our ages is not so great, and I count myself fortunate to have made such a good match – you have given me a secure home, six healthy children and, of course, your love…" Alice felt the colour continue to rise to her cheeks, as this was not a word she and Edward were accustomed to using, even though there was affection and warmth between them. They had never, she realised, exchanged an angry word, and she knew from her family and other close acquaintances that this was not necessarily something to be guaranteed in a marriage.

"You are happy, then – and content to be in our new home, away from all that was familiar in our last place?" asked Edward hesitantly. "At times you seem thoughtful and, perhaps, quieter than you were of old…"

Alice reflected carefully before she replied.

"It is true that we have left close family and friends behind, of course. And as yet I know few people in the village. The children keep me occupied, but I do appreciate that, as the wife of the new minister I shall have a role to play within this community and this is something to which I need to give careful thought. I recognise I am very different from Mrs Harrison. She seemed so confident and capable. She clearly knew everyone, and it is evident that they held her in high esteem."

Alice remembered vividly their visit to the village shortly before the Harrisons vacated the vicarage. Emily Harrison had shown her round the neighbourhood while Edward accompanied Reverend Harrison to the church. The villagers the women had met on their slow stroll had shown respect and deference for the minister's wife, who was much older than Alice, her children long grown and living their own lives in other places. Alice had felt almost a child as she walked in her shadow.

She looked steadily at Edward, now, and continued. "I do wonder exactly what will be expected of me and how I shall establish myself among these villagers, many of whose families, it seems, have lived here for several generations. However, I know my duty, Edward, and I am determined to do what I can to support you and to build relationships within your congregation."

Edward mused for a short while.

"The Harvest Festival will be our first significant event, and I understand there is a group of women in the village who take on the responsibility of gathering and arranging the offerings in the church for the service, and after that they pack the produce in boxes which are distributed amongst the less fortunate members of our community. Reverend Harrison's wife has co-ordinated their efforts in the past, I understand, so it may be that they will now look to you for leadership."

Alice found herself blushing again.

"I do not think I have ever seen myself as a leader, Edward – unlike you. However, I shall certainly be willing to play my part and it may, as you say, be an opportunity to get to know others and to help me to find my place here."

After a while, Alice added, "I might perhaps ask the carpenter on Monday whether his wife is one of this group, and that might be a way of introducing myself to her and even beginning to form a friendship."

"That is an excellent plan, my dear. And I feel I have perhaps been remiss that after the services on Sunday I have not yet endeavoured to introduce you to others. But I have been mindful that you are looking after the children, and I fear I have been focussing on building my own relationships with members of my new flock, rather than considering your position."

Alice smiled and was quick to reassure him.

"It is still early days, Edward – we have been here but a few weeks. As you say, the Harvest Festival will give us an opportunity to begin to get to know others better. I am sure that we will make friends and establish ourselves increasingly in the months ahead. Christmas will soon be upon us, I have no doubt! Now it is beginning to grow gloomy, I see, and it looks set to rain. I shall step outside to call Benjamin and Matthew home, and see how the girls are faring. And Jack will be ready to be fed, I am sure."

Alice rose and gathered herself, but looked back at Edward before she moved away.

"You are a good man, Edward. Thank you for thinking of my comfort and contentment. All shall be well," and Alice smiled as she crossed the kitchen and opened the door into the garden.

In bed that evening, Alice listened to Edward's regular breathing and, not for the first time, envied him his ability to fall into a deep sleep within minutes of their extinguishing the lamp. She reviewed their earlier conversation and recognised that Edward's concern for her, and his halting attempt to express his appreciation of her, had helped her to feel a little less anxious. It was, as she had claimed, early days, and she would, no doubt, in time form friendships and feel increasingly settled in her new home and role. Presumably Emily Harrison had felt as Alice did when she had moved into the vicarage with her husband and young family several decades before.

In church the next day she would ensure she spoke to some of the congregation, rather than simply smiling and nodding, as had been her custom. She might ask about the group of women who had in the past organised the harvest offerings, and this would give her an opening to begin to introduce herself to individuals with whom she might be able to strike up a friendship in time. Perhaps it would be possible to identify the carpenter and his wife, and speak to them in advance of meeting with him on Monday. She thought, too, about how she should explain her plans for the dresser. When she closed her eyes she could see it: could she articulate what she hoped for, and how probable was it that the craftsman would be able to construct it to her specifications?

Jack snuffled quietly in his cradle next to the bed. He would wake in a few hours, Alice knew, and she would feed and rock him to soothe him back to sleep. Edward, as was his custom, would continue to snore gently throughout this interlude. For now, Alice concentrated on breathing deeply and evenly in an attempt to steady her own thoughts and find the calm necessary before she could drift into a sleep of her own.

Chapter Two: *a piece of furniture I shall grow to love*

Alice opened the kitchen door on the following Monday morning to find the doorframe filled with the broad, smiling figure of Tom Weatherbury. He removed his cap and bobbed his head slightly in greeting.

"Morning, missus. The minister said I should call today?"

By way of credentials he raised his heavy carpenter's bag, and looked expectantly at her. Alice returned his smile and stepped back to allow him to enter the kitchen, dipping his head to clear the doorframe with the ease of someone who was often called upon to do so in the houses and cottages where he worked.

The kitchen was peaceful at this time of day. The eldest children were at school. Molly was playing quietly with baby Jack in the corner by the range, and the autumn sun slanted through the windows, lending a glow to the copper pans and catching the light in Alice's fair hair as she bent to make tea. Tom thought of angels with halos as he watched her, slight of figure but somehow still substantial, strong, he decided.

"Hello, young lady," Tom smiled at Molly. "And who have we here?"

"This is Jack," lisped Molly, tilting her head to look up at him. "He's our baby. And I'm Molly. I'm nearly five!" and she gave him her best smile.

Tom edged slowly into the room.

"Do take a seat, Mr Weatherbury. You will take tea with me?"

"Thank you – I'd be happy to." And Tom lowered himself into Edward's chair by the range.

"Reverend Jensen is out making visits, I'm afraid, but I hope I can explain to you what I have in mind. You are the craftsman, and I have little knowledge of the detail of construction, but I can see this piece of furniture when I close my eyes," and Alice did so, as if to demonstrate, laughing softly and a little nervously. "So I hope that perhaps with my imagination and your skill we will be able to bring it into being!"

"I will certainly do my best, missus."

Tom looked round the kitchen while Alice prepared the tea, and then handed him the china cup and saucer which seemed incongruously delicate in his broad workman's hands.

"I hoped perhaps to introduce myself to you and your wife at church yesterday, but wasn't able to find you."

Tom shifted a little uneasily.

"I'm usually there, but Mary, my wife, was badly this Sunday and I was uneasy about leaving her at home on her own."

Alice felt uncomfortable. Had she appeared to be chastising him for his failure to attend the service? That certainly had not been her intention.

"I am so sorry she is unwell. I do hope she is feeling better today?"

Tom could not meet her gaze, and both of them felt discomfited at the turn the conversation had taken.

"She has been unwell for some time, now. She isn't strong..."

There was a pause, and Alice realised Tom was searching for the right words to describe his wife's condition. She spoke gently.

"Perhaps I can visit her to offer my sympathy and support. I could bring her something.... Vegetables, perhaps? We have a thriving kitchen garden, thanks to the Harrisons' stewardship. Or I could make up a soup. Do let me know of anything I can do which might help."

Tom smiled faintly.

"Thank you. You're very kind. And I appreciate you offering me work, which is always welcome. Can you tell me what you have in mind?"

He is changing the subject, thought Alice, and is much more comfortable talking about carpentry than his home situation. She wondered whether Tom and Mary had children, but realised it was inappropriate to ask. If describing her plans for the dresser helped to ease the atmosphere – and this was in any case a topic about which she grew increasingly energised – she was happy to oblige.

Alice was animated as she explained her hopes for the dresser – shelves at the top for displaying the china she treasured, drawers and cupboards below which would provide useful storage. A warm wood which she hoped would catch the sunlight and contribute to the cosiness of the room, which was where the family spent most of their time. A plain and simple design, she thought. Something, perhaps, to complement the large kitchen table and the eight chairs ranged around it. Alice hoped for something both serviceable and attractive: "A piece of furniture I shall grow to love!"

She laughed a little self-consciously at this point.

"Is that sentimental of me, Mr Weatherbury?"

"Not at all – and please call me Tom."

Alice smiled and nodded, wondering whether it would be fitting if he were to use her Christian name in return. She hoped, at least, to move him on from "missus". She should, perhaps, consult Edward about this. It was one of the many aspects of her role within this community about which she was unsure. Was she to be known as "Mrs Jensen" throughout the village? Was her relationship with a workman employed by them to perform a service inevitably more distant and formal than the relationship she hoped to build with the group of women she would work alongside to prepare the harvest boxes, and with whom she desired in time to form friendships? And how would her interaction with Mary Weatherbury align with this? Presumably if the health of the carpenter's wife was poor, she might not be one of the group. Alice still felt she knew so little about the villagers.

As Alice continued to outline her plans and hopes for the dresser, Tom listened carefully, nodding from time to time and thinking how clear-sighted and definite Alice seemed. Alice herself felt far less assured than she tried to sound. Giving instruction to a capable working man like Tom was a new experience for her, and she had to remind herself that she was the minister's wife, in her own home, at the centre of her family and working to carve out a life for them all, here. She paused and smiled. Tom grinned back, and nodded again.

"That all sounds capital. I'll start today by measuring up, shall I, if that's convenient? I expect I can have it finished within a few weeks – I hope, perhaps, by the time of the Harvest Festival. It should look just right along that wall," and they both turned to gaze at the wall in question, each seeing in their mind's eye the finished dresser with its smooth shelves, useful cupboards, and honey coloured wood catching the autumn sunlight.

Baby Jack had fallen asleep while Alice had been talking, soothed, perhaps, by her measured tones, and Molly, relieved of her supervisory responsibilities, had gradually edged her way closer to Tom, where she now sat cross-legged at his feet and gazed up at him. He smiled down at her.

"What do you think, Miss Molly? Does this plan meet with your approval?"

"Will you be here every day?"

Tom gave a short laugh.

"Perhaps not every day. I will need to prepare the larger pieces at home in my workshop, but I will bring them over here and assemble it so that you can see it slowly take shape. Will you enjoy that?"

Molly nodded seriously at him.

"I'll just do some measuring, then, shall I, Mrs Jensen? I won't be in your way?"

"That will be wonderful, Tom – thank you. I am so pleased you are able to share my vision, and that you have the confidence and the skill to turn a dream into reality!" When Alice smiled, a single dimple appeared in one cheek, Tom saw.

Tom stood, and the chair on which he had been sitting scraped on the flagstones, waking the baby who started to grizzle, so Alice scooped him from the cradle.

"Molly, will you keep Mr Weatherbury company while I take Jack for his feed? Be sure not to get in his way, mind." And Alice left the room with the baby.

Tom moved to the wall and began to take his measurements, pausing from time to time to record numbers in a small notebook. Molly watched him with fascination. He worked for several minutes while Molly looked on, wide-eyed.

After some time, Tom realised that Molly would not speak to him unless he addressed her directly, and once he had completed measuring and returned his notebook and pencil to his pocket, he turned to her and smiled.

"So, young lady. Tell me something of yourself and your family, and whether you all like living in The Vicarage."

Molly was very happy to have Tom's attention and she chatted comfortably with him.

"It's very different from where we used to live but we all like it here. We do miss seeing grandmama and the family and friends we had when we were in our last house, but papa says we will all make new friends, and I have started that already. I like playing in the garden – it's much bigger than our last garden. Matthew and Benjamin – they're my brothers and they are twins - especially like the river, but I'm not allowed to go there with them because they might forget to watch me and I might fall in the water, mama says. I go there with Martha and Betsy sometimes, though – they're very careful. Martha and Betsy like their new school. They are learning lots of new things and they tell me about it every day when they get home. We don't know what baby Jack likes yet because he's too little to say. I look after Jack and mama says I am a very good big sister."

Molly took a breath.

"Papa likes writing his sermons and we all go and listen on a Sunday. I like Sunday school too – we paint pictures and listen to stories out of the Bible with the other children from the village. Annie is my special friend..."

Molly paused for a moment, thoughtful.

"Do you have little girls and boys?"

Tom stiffened slightly, and there was a pause.

"No. We're not as lucky as your mama and papa, I am sad to say. Tell me what you do when your brothers and sisters are at school."

"I look after Jack – did I tell you that? – we play and I nurse him. Sometimes when it doesn't rain we can play in the garden and sometimes mama takes us for a walk along the river and we meet the others walking home from school. I will go to school soon and then I will learn to read and when I am big I want to be a teacher. Martha and Betsy tell me all about what their teacher does."

Molly looked up and saw Alice standing still in the doorway with Jack in her arms. Tom became aware of her presence, too, and wondered how long she had been there and how much she had heard. The expression on her face betrayed nothing.

"Well, I think I have what I need for now," Tom said, briskly. "I will make a start cutting the wood as soon as I get home, and I will let you know when I need to come back to begin to put the frame together."

"Thank you, Tom."

"And I will see you, Missy, then, and you can tell me more about what you get up to, and your plans for the future. I can see you will be a good teacher – look how well you look after your baby brother already."

He smiled warmly at the little girl who returned his gaze earnestly and basked in the glow of his compliment.

Alice settled Jack in his cradle in the warmth of the range, and spoke to Tom as she did so, her back to him so that he was unable to see her face. "Please give my best wishes to your wife, Tom, and, when you next visit, let me know if she would be happy for me to call on her, and what I might take with me which she would find useful."

"I'm grateful, missus." Tom dipped his head as he returned his measure to his bag, gathered his belongings and prepared to leave. "Thank you for the tea – and the company," he smiled at Molly, "and I will be in touch again soon."

Alice opened the door and Tom passed through it. She watched as he lifted the latch on the gate and then looked back and touched the brim of his cap before he turned towards home.

"There's a sad man," Alice reflected to herself, as she quietly closed the door.

That evening, when the children were settled in bed and Alice was nursing Jack, in her customary chair with Edward seated across from her, she told her husband about the visit, the progress they had made and the plans for the construction of the dresser.

"And what did you make of Tom Weatherbury, my dear?"

Alice thought for a few moments before she replied.

"I liked him," she said carefully. "He seems to me to be a capable craftsman who takes pride in his work and who is committed to doing a good job. He seems to be troubled in some way, however. He told Molly that he and his wife weren't sufficiently fortunate to have children, and he strikes me as a man who would be a very loving father. He was very good with Molly, and she was clearly taken with him. His wife is unwell, he told me – something unspecific, but it sounds like a permanent condition rather than a temporary illness. Were you aware?"

"I don't recall having heard anything about this," Edward mused. "But I will enquire. Perhaps you could visit her?"

"Yes. I suggested I would. I am reluctant to intrude, but want to help if I can. I shall discuss it again with Tom when he returns."

Alice looked down at Jack in her arms.

"We are lucky, Edward, aren't we? I hope we never take that for granted."

"Praise the Lord." Edward smiled at his wife and child.

They sat quietly for some time, listening to the ticking of the clock and the soft crackling from the range, and Alice thought of Tom and Mary Weatherbury in their cottage on the far side of the village.

Chapter Three: *until I am a little stronger*

At home that evening, Tom's wife Mary had asked him about the new minister's family. He was careful in his answers, for Mary was a fragile, vulnerable creature whose health had never recovered following their last still-born child. Without discussing it openly, husband and wife had reached a tacit agreement that there should be no more child-bearing – the pain of three unsuccessful confinements was sufficient, and the Weatherburys accepted, sadly, that their home would not be graced with children.

Tom was fond of Mary, protective and solicitous. She seemed to him in some ways like a small bird – easily hurt and in need of careful nurturing. They were not incompatible, as man and wife. In some respects their shared pain had brought them closer, and they certainly never quarrelled. In addition, Tom was mindful of all he had to feel grateful for in his life, including his love of the craft which brought him sufficient and satisfying employment; a comfortable home inherited from his parents, with the workshop off the garden in which his father had taught him his skills; a secure place within a community where he was respected and liked. But talking to Mary about Alice, her children and The Vicarage required him to weigh his words carefully. He recalled the woman he had met and to whom he had listened as she spoke with enthusiasm about the work she wished him to do for her. Her obvious energy, her glow, and her chattering, healthy daughter were not easy to put into words for Mary, who sat in her accustomed chair with her blankets around her, her thin, pale face turned up to him and her bird-like eyes watching him. After a time he found it easier to alter the subject.

"Will you feel well enough to make the Harvest Festival service this year, Mary, do you think? You'd be able to see the minister and his family for yourself, then, and hear him preach – I don't doubt but he will have thoughtful words to share.

And you always say the church looks grand with the flowers and the offerings?"

Mary smiled wanly at him, but made no commitment. He would, he suspected, be going alone again this year.

Tom continued brightly, "Mrs Jensen suggested she might call upon you to introduce herself and to offer her support. She said she would bring you something – she wondered about bringing vegetables, as they are benefiting from the Harrisons' kitchen garden. Do you remember how we used to admire it on our walks?" Tom reflected that it had been a long time since he and Mary had taken a walk together. "Or some soup, Mrs Jensen thought. That was kind of her, do you not agree?"

Mary did not respond immediately. She looked into the fire, and Tom wondered what she was thinking.

"I accept it is a kind offer, Tom," she said slowly, after a pause, "but I am unsure I have the energy to strike up a new acquaintance just now. Would you be willing to ask her to leave it a while, until I am a little stronger?"

Tom had heard Mary use that phrase, 'until I am a little stronger', increasingly frequently in the last year. In truth, Mary never felt any stronger, and so was unable to commit herself to anything that required greater energy. Tom would, he realised, have to explain to Alice that Mary was not able to accommodate a visitor at the present time.

In the early days of Mary's current indisposition, various friends, family members and neighbours had called at the cottage, offering support and bringing food, or flowers, or other small gifts to cheer the home and its occupants. But Mary had increasingly found these visits draining, and had implored Tom to let the well-wishers know that she needed quiet, and rest, and would call upon them if there were any way in which they could help. Tom had found these to be uncomfortable conversations, but Mary's plaintive words, "Do it for me, Tom, please," rang in his ears and gave him the strength to communicate the unpalatable message to all who wished to visit. Mary had not left the cottage for many months, now, and as a consequence, she seldom saw anyone other than Tom.

Whenever Tom was out and about, working, or at the church, or the village shop – he never, these days, frequented the village inn – the same friends and neighbours always asked after Mary, sent their good wishes, and made clear they would support the couple in any way they could. Tom was not too proud to ask for help, but he found it difficult to see how anyone could do anything which would make Mary feel any better. The previous minister, Reverend Harrison, had called from time to time, but, although an affable man, he had seemed at a loss to know what to say that was fitting and positive. He always reassured Mary of God's love, and she would look up at him with her watery eyes and faint smile, which he clearly found rather unnerving. Finally his visits had become less frequent, and Mary had been patently relieved. Tom realised he was not looking forward to Reverend Jensen's first visit, which was sure to happen soon. Perhaps this was something he should broach with Alice, too, although he expected her husband would see this as one of his important parish duties, and might not be easily deterred.

At least Tom was never short of work, and he sometimes wondered whether the villagers recognised that offering him regular employment was the most effective way in which they could support and sustain the family. But he was also the only carpenter living in this village or the next one along the river, and he was a very capable craftsman, conscientious as well as skilled, and he was a popular, personable man, so even before Mary became unwell, work was plentiful. Working locally meant that he could call in on Mary during the day, especially on those days when she seemed particularly low in spirits – something which had been happening more often of late.

Tom wondered from time to time whether he should consult the nearest doctor, who lived in the town several miles away. This doctor had attended Mary following the most recent still birth, and had quietly reassured Tom that he would return at any stage if the couple required advice or his wife was in need of treatment. But Mary was even more reluctant to consult a medical specialist than she was a pastoral adviser.

"There is nothing he can do," she had announced to her husband, the last time he had raised the subject. Mary spoke with uncharacteristic conviction on that occasion, and Tom had not argued.

This evening they sat in silence by the fireside for some time. Eventually, Mary levered herself slowly from her chair.

"I will go up, then, Tom. Goodnight."

Mary's lean hand lightly touched his shoulder as she passed his chair. The clock had not long since chimed seven. It seemed that Mary retired a little earlier each evening, Tom reflected. She did not sleep well, but she lay, very still, in the bed with her quivering eyelids closed and her breath shallow. Tom usually sat up by the fire and read for a while before quietly making his way upstairs some time later. Mary was invariably still awake as he climbed in beside her, but usually neither of them spoke.

Tonight, Tom's book lay open on his knee, but he found it difficult to concentrate on the words. He stared into the embers of the fire and thought back to the early days of his courtship with Mary. It was only fourteen years earlier, but it seemed to be a different lifetime.

In such a small community, where the children in every generation walked along the riverbank to the tiny school in the adjacent village, most of the married couples had known each other since they were small. Tom's earliest memory of Mary was of freckles and pigtails, frequent laughter as she played skipping games with her friends in the summer, or strapped on skates to dance on the pond's thick ice in the depths of winter. As younger children, the girls and the boys had seemed to be different species, and there was little interaction between them. Inevitably, around the time that these children left school, they became self-consciously aware of, and suddenly interested in, each other.

At the age of 13, Tom began working with his father, learning the trade to which he was well-suited and which would support and sustain him throughout his working life. Mary was kept on at school as a pupil-teacher, supervising the small children, and during the hours when she was at home her mother took seriously her responsibility for continuing Mary's domestic education, fitting her for the time when she would marry, begin a family and manage a home of her own.

Tom had a vivid memory of Mary dancing round the maypole on the village green on May Day of the year in which they had both reached the age of 16. He could still see her in the slim-fitting white dress which showed her figure to great advantage, with flowers in her hair. She and the other village girls skipped and twirled, plaiting the coloured ribbons and laughing with delight at their own grace and skill. He had watched her carefully, recalling the early freckles and the pigtails, the skipping games and the ice-skating. He had never, to his knowledge, exchanged a single word with her. He determined that this would change, today.

After the maypole dancing, still laughing and a little out of breath, the girls dispersed, and Tom waited patiently until the opportunity arose for him to saunter close to Mary, catch her eye and smile.

"Tom Weatherbury," she said, looking up at the tall, broad-shouldered young man she remembered as a tousle-haired, grinning boy with scratched legs from tree-climbing.

Tom suddenly realised that he had no notion of what he should say in return. He was holding a fruit cup which he had just poured for himself, but had not yet touched. He held it hesitantly out to her, and, after a short pause, Mary reached out and took it, and began to sip it carefully, all the time looking at him over the rim with her bright eyes.

And so it began.

Tom recalled walking along the river, holding Mary's hand, the day on which he had decided to ask her to wed him. It was a year into the courtship, and their mood was sombre, as Tom's parents had, only the month before, contracted scarlet fever and died within a few days of each other. Tom was adjusting to his independence. His elder sisters were all married and had moved into homes of their own. Tom had inherited the cottage, with its workshop, and the business. He was continuing to master his craft and to build his reputation across the community.

"I know I still have much to learn," he told her. "But I love the work and I believe I am skilled at it."

"That is certainly true, Tom."

"You know I love you, Mary."

They both blushed at this. It was not the first time they had spoken of love, but this was not a language which came easily to them.

"I think the time may be right for me to ask for your hand."

"And I think the time might be right to accept your kind offer," returned Mary with a shy smile.

They stopped and exchanged a chaste kiss, after which Tom blew out his breath in relief.

"I'll call to talk to your father this afternoon, if you think that's fitting. He will be pleased, I hope?"

"So he will, Tom. He knows you for a good and steady man, who will make a good and steady husband. They will be well pleased at home. When shall the wedding be?"

When Tom closed his eyes now he could see the two of them, standing holding hands on the riverbank. He could recall every word of the conversation, his trembling hands, his relief when Mary said yes, his slight feeling of nervousness at the prospect of speaking to her father. He could remember, too, the anticipation of all that lay ahead.

They married on a warm spring day when the village was full of blossom. Mary moved into the cottage with him and supported him as he learnt and grew ever more confident in his role as the local carpenter. She was a capable home-maker, and the cottage soon felt like theirs, rather than Tom's parental home. Then the babies came. And the babies died.

Tom shivered and, looking up, he saw that the fire had burnt itself out. His book lay unread on his lap. He should go up, but did not relish the thought of lying silently beside a still wakeful Mary in the darkness. He allowed himself just a few moments to think of Alice and Molly in the kitchen of The Vicarage that morning: the autumn sun shining on the copper pans and Alice's golden hair; Alice's single dimple when she smiled at a comment she had made which might be seen as foolish; the child's intent gaze and cheerful chatter.

Molly, Tom could not help thinking, was the kind of child he would have hoped for had Mary and he been blessed.

He shook his head as if to clear the thoughts, which seemed in some way disloyal, and a betrayal of his wife, and even of his life. He rose slowly, lit a single candle and then extinguished the lamp before taking the candle and climbing the dark, narrow staircase, finding his way with the aid of its flickering flame.

Chapter Four: *a secret*

"We plough the fields and scatter
The good seed on the land…"

In the front pew with the children, watching Edward at the lectern, Alice could hear Tom Weatherbury's rich baritone voice from the other side of the aisle, and a row behind her. She was aware of the contrast with Edward's reedy tenor.

Over the last few weeks Alice had watched the dresser take shape beneath Tom's capable hands. She was delighted to see the piece she had imagined gradually come into being and to turn out, in fact, even more impressive than she had expected. It took up the whole of the wall, stretched to the ceiling, and exuded a warm, golden glow. She recognised this was fanciful but found herself thinking that the wood appeared to respect Tom's authority and confident skill. She was already deciding how she would fill the shelves and cupboards: which of her most precious possessions would take pride of place and how the populated dresser would add to the comfort and homeliness of The Vicarage.

The twins Matthew and Benjamin were fidgeting, and she stilled them with a look. She realised that Edward was now part way through his Harvest Festival address, and she had not in fact heard a word of it. She felt a twinge of guilt as she smiled encouragingly up at him. He was a good man. Although their means were modest he was a conscientious provider, a loving father and a well-meaning and willing minister who cared about his congregation and who would, she knew, relish his duties in distributing the harvest packages amongst those families who needed them the most.

The church looked impressive. Alice had worked alongside the women from the village to arrange the flowers, fruit and vegetables which had been donated by every household. They filled all the window sills in the church – shaggy bronze chrysanthemums jostling against the plumpest pumpkins, well-polished apples and small baskets of horse chestnuts (which the children eyed with interest, already planning their conker contests). A huge display of colourful produce graced the steps up to the altar, and greenery laced the railings of the pulpit where Edward now stood.

Working to collect and arrange the offerings had given Alice the opportunity to get to know her neighbours better. She felt she was beginning to find her place in this new community, as Edward had hoped, although "I am most definitely not 'leading' them, Edward – as you suggested Mrs Harrison had, and I might! Dora Willetts, the postmistress, has most certainly assumed that mantle!" Alice had enjoyed the women's company and conversation as they worked together, and having something to occupy her hands and eyes as she spoke had enabled her to chat to them more easily than might have been the case over tea in a parlour, she realised. She had nodded and smiled to the women as they all filed into the church today, and stopped to exchange a few words with those she knew best, asking after a sick child, a lost kitten (safely found in the nearby barn) and the progress of a planned wedding.

"I am beginning to feel properly at home here," she reflected, and her confidence was building as a consequence.

After the service, leaving the church with her children, Alice paused to greet Tom, and he fussed over the children, especially Molly, who was the one he knew best. Molly had invariably crept close to Tom as he worked outside preparing the wood he had laboured over in his workshop, and then assembling the dresser in the kitchen. She was drawn to his quiet strength and ready smile, and he found her curiosity and eagerness to learn refreshing. Jack was a little too young to be interesting, and the older children - the twins, and the eldest girls, Martha and Betsy - were only to be seen at the end of the school day when their arrival home often coincided with Tom's leaving The Vicarage. But Molly and Tom had struck up a friendship, and on the days he walked to The Vicarage he recognised how much he was looking forward to seeing her. And Alice.

"So, missy – what will you be up to this afternoon?"

"It's a secret!" lisped Molly with a twinkle in her eye.

Tom knew her well enough by this stage to recognise how much Molly savoured her secrets. In a household with five siblings it was perhaps not surprising that she was keen to carve out some privacy. When Jack was asleep, her mother was occupied and her older brothers and sisters not yet returned from school, Tom had seen Molly assembling, sorting and rearranging her small collection of treasures – a few interesting and unusual pebbles, a feather, a marble, a pearly shell, two bright buttons and – the pride of the collection – a brand new shiny farthing. Whenever Molly explored the garden or along the riverbank, she was always alert to the possibility of finding something that took her interest which she could add to her treasures. She had begun to collect things, she had told Tom, when the family were sweeping out The Vicarage after the Harrisons had left, the day they moved in, and she had unearthed the two beautifully-coloured buttons in a corner of a little-used room. She had slipped them quietly into her pinafore pocket, recognising that they held little value for anyone else, and this was the beginning. She kept all of her special possessions in a small, battered tin, and Tom had already decided that, before he finished the work and left The Vicarage, he would craft for her a beautiful, carved wooden box which would be a more fitting receptacle for her precious things. He was not unaware of the fact that, by allowing him to watch her sift through her treasures, and by talking to him about them (usually in a whisper), she was showing great trust and confidence in him. He suspected that he was the only person alive who knew about this particular secret.

Watching her now, as Molly and her siblings made their way through the back gate of the churchyard into their own garden, Martha carrying baby Jack, he had an even better idea.

Alice stood by him, waiting for Edward and also watching her children, and when she turned to him with a smile, Tom said, "I fear I owe you an apology, Mrs Jensen."

"Why ever would that be, Tom?"

"The day I first called at The Vicarage to see you about the dresser, when you explained so well what you had in mind..." Tim paused to await the single dimple which he knew would appear in Alice's cheek at the compliment, "I promised you the work would be done by the time of the Harvest Festival. I must have vastly over-estimated my own speed. Here we are, and my work is not yet finished."

Alice thought for a moment.

"If I remember rightly, you did not in fact promise that the dresser would be finished before the Harvest Festival. I think your words were that you hoped, perhaps, it would be. That does not, to my view, constitute a broken promise."

Tom looked at the twinkle in Alice's eye, which definitely mirrored Molly's, and he felt his stomach react to the suggestion that she had remembered his exact words.

"Your memory is clearly much better than mine, Mrs Jensen. And I can safely say we are not far off completion, now. Two more visits should see it done, I reckon."

Alice tilted her head and nodded slightly.

"Though we must make a decision about the mouse," Tom continued.

Over the past weeks, she and Tom had had earnest conversation about how much decoration was appropriate for the dresser. Alice favoured something very plain, but Tom was attempting to persuade her to allow him at least to carve a small, running fieldmouse in the bottom left-hand corner, something which he assured her would delight the children.

Alice laughed.

"You are very persistent, Tom!"

"One of my finer qualities, I have been told – although 'stubborn' is the word Mary has tended to use in the past."

At the mention of his sick wife, the playful tone of their conversation faltered.

"How is Mary?"

This was a question Tom had been asked often, and he had initially struggled to find an appropriate response. The villagers who knew him best had given up asking, as they recognised his discomfort.

"About the same," was becoming Tom's stock response.

"I am sorry."

And she was, Tom knew.

On his second visit to the Vicarage Tom had explained diligently to Alice that Mary did not feel up to visitors at the moment, but he would most certainly let her know if that changed. He wondered, he asked hesitantly, whether Alice might mention that to the minister, too. He recognised that Reverend Jensen would no doubt feel honour bound to call upon a sick parishioner, but, in truth, visits – especially from someone unfamiliar – exhausted Mary and had the unfortunate effect of making her feel considerably worse. Might he respectfully suggest that this initial visit be postponed for the present?

Alice had duly reported this conversation to Edward, who was sympathetic, though he felt a little uneasy at the prospect of neglecting a duty he considered important. His intention was to deliver one of the harvest packages to the Weatherburys' home – they kept no vegetable garden and so should, he knew, appreciate the gift of produce. This would at least give him the opportunity to introduce himself and to see Mary for the first time.

Tom, as he usually did when the conversation turned to Mary, was skilful at changing the subject.

"The harvest offerings looked grand, I thought – even more impressive than in Mrs Harrison's day. I expect you feel proud of your handiwork."

"That is most definitely unmerited, Tom. I played my part, but it was a minor one. You have to thank our postmistress for the creativity, I fear, rather than me. But I was happy to have the opportunity to contribute, and to begin to know my neighbours a little better – and for them to start to know me." Alice blushed slightly at this, and Tom had sudden insight.

"She is shy. I hadn't realised that," he thought to himself.

"So – the mouse," Alice said more brightly. "Whatever shall we do?"

"My suggestion is that you gracefully give in to this master craftsman and accept my judgment on the subject."

"I think I shall have to do that! I rely on you to create something which the children will be so thrilled with – Molly especially, as she is such a champion of yours - that I never regret it!"

"I accept the challenge. I hope to call to continue the work on Tuesday, and, after that, one final day should be enough for me to finish the task. Good day, Mrs Jensen. Good day, Reverend..." Tom turned as Edward approached them, "and thank you for the service." With a final tip of his (best Sunday) cap, Tom withdrew, and Edward joined his wife and took her arm.

Alice and Edward watched Tom make his way steadily through the churchyard, and then Alice turned to her husband.

"It was an excellent address, Edward. Your first Harvest Festival in your own church."

"It was a pleasure to plan and deliver it. And the church looked magnificent, Alice. I had a word with Dora Willetts, who appeared suitably gratified, but could you, too, pass on my appreciation to all the village women who worked together on it?"

"I certainly shall. And what happens to the produce now?"

"A group of us shall carry it all into the village hall so that the women can gather again to pack it into boxes – beautiful wooden boxes which Tom has donated to the village for this very purpose over the years. That is his contribution to the success of the event. After this I shall deliver them to the families in the village which we consider will be most grateful for the gift – the church wardens will assist with the transportation. The recipients include Mary Weatherbury, in fact. I hoped, my dear, that you would agree to accompany me on these visits. I thought it would be a further opportunity for you to meet my parishioners and to take your rightful place by my side."

Alice blushed, but she was pleased to be asked and could see the good sense of Edward's suggestion. She felt uneasy about visiting Tom's wife, but could see that they must meet at some stage. And she recognised that a part of her was curious to see Mary for herself, having heard something of her from Tom.

She thought about Tom as she and Edward walked slowly back to the house, enjoying the autumn sunshine and the colours of the trees around the church. She had relished Tom's company and conversation in the weeks during which he had worked on the dresser. They were easy with each other – there was a gentle teasing in his approach which was something that made her think of her elder brothers, whom she missed. She sometimes felt that this was perhaps not strictly appropriate between the lady of the house and a craftsman her husband was paying for his services, but she had become adept at brushing that thought aside, and simply relaxing into Tom's presence in her home.

After two more days' working in the kitchen of The Vicarage, Tom would have finished the dresser and would have no further reason to return. Of course, in a village such as this one she would continue to see him from time to time. But she realised she would miss the closeness of contact which had become the pattern of recent weeks. Molly would certainly miss him – she had described him only this week to her mother as "my best friend, Tom. Tom, and Annie – my two best friends." He may be the closest friend I have in the village, too, Alice mused. That may be a little irregular, but it is, without doubt, true.

"You are an artist, as well as a craftsman!" smiled Alice. She had watched as Tom carved his running fieldmouse – he was intent, focussed, completely absorbed in the work, and the small mouse was, indeed, perfect. Alice knew it would be very well-received by the youngest members of the household. The older children were at school, but Molly's delight at its creation clearly mirrored the reaction Alice could expect from Matthew, Benjamin, Martha and Betsy later that day. She turned to her youngest daughter.

"Molly – may I suggest we say nothing to the others about the mouse? Let them discover it for themselves, and we shall watch their response when they do! Who do you think is most likely to notice it first?"

Molly was thoughtful for a moment, but then announced with conviction, "Benjamin!" Benjamin was the livelier of the twins, and as curious and observant as Molly herself.

"We shall see! And, Tom – you were, of course, right. It is the perfect addition to your masterpiece. Now we should be leaving, Edward. We have many calls to make. Tom, we are extremely thankful that you have agreed to mind Molly and the baby while we are out."

"I'm content to do it, Mrs Jensen. There's a little more work to do before the masterpiece, as you're kind enough to call it, is finished. And I always enjoy the little lass's company and conversation."

The child beamed at him.

Alice and Edward were donning their outer coats and preparing to deliver the harvest packages throughout the parish, helped by the two church wardens who would walk with them, transporting the boxes on a wooden cart. When Tom had agreed to watch over Molly and Jack while the visits took place, Edward and Alice had both expressed their gratitude. In truth, Tom was delighted to have the opportunity to complete his work on the final panel, at the bottom right-hand corner of the dresser, in the parents' absence.

As Tom had walked through the misty village that morning he was acutely aware of the fact that this would be his penultimate visit to The Vicarage. He accepted that he would continue to see Alice and Molly from time to time – at the church, at special village events, occasionally at the village shop, perhaps. However, he knew he would miss the intimacy of the warm kitchen, and his conversation with this vibrant, good-humoured woman and her lively, interested little girl. He had enjoyed watching Alice with all her children, and had given thought to exactly what it was that she said, and did, which made her such a capable, loving mother.

Tom wondered whether he might find other work to do for the Jensens, but he was mindful of the fact that the family's means were modest, and that the commission to build the dresser was an exceptional event. He had watched Edward and Alice together on several occasions in the past few weeks and saw that Reverend Jensen was thoughtful and solicitous where his wife was concerned. Edward had encouraged, and been prepared to invest in, the dresser project because it meant a good deal to Alice, and was one way in which she could put her stamp on her new home.

Tom thought back to the early days of his own marriage, when Mary had joined him in his parents' home and, over time, made it *their* home – comfortable and welcoming when he returned at the end of a day's work. Sadly, Mary's interest in home-making had waned as her health deteriorated following the tragically unsuccessful confinements. This was unsurprising, and Tom was understanding and sympathetic. But during the last few weeks he had been painfully conscious of the difference as he left the warm, homely Vicarage with its smiling inhabitants and entered his own cold, grey cottage with its single, unhappy soul.

Tom had stood for a few moments by the village green as the early morning mist dissipated, gathering his thoughts and summoning his resolution. This was his life - his life with Mary. Was there any way in which he could cheer and brighten it, he wondered? Perhaps, despite Mary's reluctance, he should encourage visits from well-wishers, and be more gently insistent that Mary ventured out of the cottage to re-establish contact with the village community. We could take it slowly, he thought, but if I were more assertive about helping her to begin to live again, rather than simply existing, as she presently seems to do, it might help us to find some joy in our lives, or, at the least, contentment. Should he talk to someone about this – the doctor, his sisters, the minister – Alice?

He shrank from raising the issue, however, especially with Alice. He could not shake the sense that it would be disloyal to speak about Mary in these terms – she would be mortified if she knew he was even considering it. But if it were to help her – to help them both – would that not justify his actions? He felt torn.

Alice and Edward had sought Tom out the day before to explain about the delivery of the harvest packages and to ask if he were willing to mind the youngest children while they made their visits. Tom had already arranged to work on the dresser that day and agreed that keeping a watchful eye on Molly and Jack while he worked would be no trouble to him. Alice had added, a little hesitantly, that one of their visits would be to his own cottage, as they knew that the Weatherburys did not cultivate their own vegetable patch, or have fruit trees and bushes, and Reverend Jensen was very much looking forward to meeting Mary. Tom inclined his head in mute acceptance. He was unsure exactly how Mary would react to the visit, though he knew it would be something of a trial to her. But he recognised he was powerless to stop it. He had known that, at some stage, Reverend Jensen would feel duty bound to pay a call on a parishioner he knew to be unwell and in need of succour. The distribution of the harvest produce had given him a good reason to do so.

Tom realised he was looking forward to spending time with the youngest children. He knew that Molly, despite her tender age, was skilful and confident in her care of the baby – he had marvelled at how well she managed Jack and had said as much to Alice in one of his early visits to The Vicarage. He well remembered her response.

Alice had laughed. "This is one of the advantages of having six children, Tom! The oldest learn to manage the younger ones. Martha and Betsy, for example, have been well-trained in the arts of motherhood and should take it in their stride when the time comes!"

As soon as she had spoken, Tom saw that Alice went still. She had been busying herself chopping vegetables at the kitchen table while Tom worked, and she had her back turned. He saw her pause in her work, and he observed a sudden, slight stiffness in her back. Then she spoke softly, still facing away from him.

"I am sorry, Tom. That was an insensitive thing for me to say."

And Tom realised that the villagers had informed Alice, and no doubt Edward, about his family history and the children they had lost, though it was not something he and Alice had ever openly discussed.

There was an awkward silence, and then Tom, turning his back, too, and beginning slowly to plane a piece of wood, said, "Not at all, Mrs Jensen. No call for an apology," and the moment had passed.

Tom reflected on this exchange as he stood by the village green. He sighed deeply, picked up his carpenter's bag and continued on his way. He could, at least, relish his final visits to The Vicarage which did, he recognised, bring him a feeling of joy – though at times, joy mixed with pain. He loved his work. He had found a great sense of satisfaction in designing and constructing the dresser to Alice's specifications – it was, he knew, a beautiful piece of furniture, and it should last for many years – substantial and solid and well-made. He wondered whether Alice would think of him when she removed and returned the items she displayed and stored there. Then he shook himself.

"That is fanciful of me. It is a piece of furniture to her – serviceable and convenient. She may well feel a sense of pride at the part she played in creating it. She will not think of you, Tom Weatherbury."

He had reached the gate at The Vicarage, unlatched it and walked down the path, knocking at the door with his broad knuckles, waiting to be let in.

Now, several hours later, he was working on the bottom right-hand panel of the dresser, while Molly chatted brightly to the baby who gurgled in response. Tom wondered how the Jensens' visit to Mary had gone. He had forewarned his wife the previous evening that they would call with a harvest box, and Mary had said little, accepting, Tom felt, the inevitability of the meeting at some stage. He knew that it would be only a brief visit, the wardens waiting outside with the remaining harvest boxes. He asked himself whether, in some ways, Mary might be curious to meet the couple, about whom he had talked from time to time in recent weeks. He knew Edward and Alice would be sympathetic and kind, willing to help if Mary would permit it. He could not imagine what the three might say to each other, however. Perhaps they would mention him? Mary would, no doubt, reprise the exchange for him that evening.

What he would never know was that, as Alice and Edward had walked away from the Weatherburys' cottage to rejoin the church wardens with the remaining boxes, Alice had turned to her husband and said, "What makes it especially sad, is that, having seen Tom with our children in the last few weeks – especially with Molly, who he sees the most and knows best - I am mindful of what a good father he would have been. We are blessed to have heathy children, Edward. Many others are not so fortunate." Edward smiled gently at her and squeezed her arm as they walked on.

By this time, Jack was dozing in his crib, and Molly, as was her custom, drew nearer to Tom and watched in fascination as he worked. She was a bright, alert little girl, and she realised immediately that there was something special about Tom's attention to detail in this final panel.

"What are you doing?" she asked.

"It's a secret!" Tom replied in a low voice.

Molly beamed, and her smile grew even wider when Tom added, "A secret just between you and me."

He finally stepped back and critically examined his handiwork. The bottom right-hand panel looked, in fact, just like the others – with the exception of its left-hand counterpart with the scampering fieldmouse. But Tom beckoned to Molly to join him as he sat on the floor next to it, and when he guided her small fingers she discovered a tiny, hidden catch beneath it. And when she pressed the catch gently, the panel moved, and a slim, narrow drawer slid out.

Molly gasped, and then giggled.

"A secret hiding place!"

"Yes – for special treasure!" Tom added with a twinkle, and, understanding completely, Molly scuttled into her bedroom to retrieve the battered tin.

When she returned, clutching the tin tightly to her chest, Tom sat her down at the kitchen table.

"I made this just for you," he announced, softly. "No one else knows about it, and, if you don't say anything, no one ever will."

"It will be my secret place – my secret hiding place for all my treasures?"

Tom nodded and smiled.

"Our secret."

And Tom watched as Molly moved to crouch on the floor and transfer her treasures – several pebbles, the feather, the marble and the shell, two brightly-coloured buttons and, her favourite find, her shiny 1900 farthing. He had considered giving her something to add to her collection, but he recognised that these were all things Molly had found for herself as she explored her new surroundings. A gift would not necessarily have the same meaning for her, he felt. So he had decided that his gift, using his craftsman's skill, would be to create a safe repository for her secret collection. A carved wooden box would have been far better than the battered tin, but a hidden drawer in the dresser, of which only the two of them were aware, was a much better prospect, knowing Molly's love of secrets, as he did.

Molly carefully closed the hidden drawer and then practised opening and closing it, with delight on her face. Each of them would remember this moment for the rest of their lives.

Chapter Six: *to our dresser*

The following day was Tom's last visit to The Vicarage. He had spent the early morning applying the final coat of varnish to the wood, with patience and loving care, Alice thought. As he began to gather up his things, he asked, a little shyly, if he could return in the evening to check that the varnish was dry and to ensure all was well.

"Of course you may!" exclaimed Alice. "I should love for you to be present when I use the dresser for the first time, if you are sure that the varnish is sufficiently dry for me to do so. We are making a small family party of it, and it would not be fitting for you to miss the moment. I was about to invite you, but you pre-empted me! We thought seven o'clock?"

Tom nodded, and smiled at Molly as he moved to the door. "I'll see you later, then, young lady." Molly beamed back at him.

As Tom and Mary shared their modest meal, he said, "I am going out this evening to call at The Vicarage, only briefly. The varnish should be dry, and Mrs Jensen wants to make a small ceremony of the moment when she uses the dresser for the first time. She has asked me to be present."

Mary looked levelly at him, but said nothing. How often, Tom wondered, had he been called upon to interpret a silence from his wife?

As the time approached for him to leave, Tom hesitated.

"It's a quarter of seven, Mary, so I should set off for The Vicarage. But should I perhaps stay?" he asked. "I like not to leave you when it is dark."

Mary rose from her chair slowly.

"Go, Tom. I am going up, in any case."

And Tom watched her move gingerly across the kitchen to the staircase.

"I will not be long."

"It matters little."

Tom's heart sank at the despair in Mary's voice.

When he arrived at The Vicarage, all the family members were assembled. Jack was awake and alert in his crib by the range, and Molly had been allowed to stay up a little later than usual in recognition of the special occasion. Matthew and Benjamin were uncharacteristically quiet and sober, appreciating the importance of the moment. Martha and Betsy had sought permission to change into their best Sunday dresses, and Alice had agreed, with a smile. Edward stood by his wife, with an air of quiet pride, Tom thought.

"And here is our invited Guest of Honour!" Alice announced, her dimple showing. Tom bowed his head and blushed a little. There was a definite sense of ceremony as they gathered to watch Alice prepare to use the dresser for the first time, once Tom had confirmed that the varnish was, in fact, completely dry.

"It seems like a christening!" she laughed.

"We might perhaps have cut a ribbon!" smiled Edward.

"Like the opening..."

"...of the village fete!"

"I feel as if I should make a speech!" laughed Alice, a little self-consciously. "I just want to say how thrilled I am with your creation, Tom – even the little fieldmouse, about which you were so insistent, and which, I agree, was a perfect touch, and which Benjamin, as Molly predicted, spotted as soon as he came in from school that day!"

"It is your creation as much as mine," Tom insisted. "You dreamed it..."

"And you made my dream come true!" Alice laughed, and then, more soberly, "Thank you, Mr Weatherbury. It is everything I hoped for."

And Alice, helped by Martha and Betsy, carefully placed the precious china she had inherited from her grandmother on the grooved shelves, and then went on to decide how she would organise the cupboards, arranging their possessions, and occasionally changing her mind and repositioning different items.

Afterwards, Edward served glasses of port wine to the adults, and the children joined the toast, "To our dresser!" with glasses of home-made lemon water. It felt like a party. But Tom prepared to leave as soon as the toast was made.

"I'd better be getting off home. I don't like to leave Mary once the darkness draws in," he said, and then immediately felt guilty. "I'm using my sick wife as an excuse," he thought, "when really I just can't breathe and I have to get out – out of this kitchen and away from this loving, happy family. A family and a home where I have no part."

"Must you leave so soon?" Alice looked sad and sorry to see him go, but then she, too, felt guilty. Of course he needed to return to his wife, who would be alone in the silent cottage, unwell and, clearly, unhappy. Alice thought back to their visit with the harvest box, and realised she had felt haunted ever since by the vision of this shrunken, forever-grieving woman, who had never recovered from the loss of her children. It was selfish of Alice even to suggest that Tom should stay longer when Mary was suffering alone. She turned and picked up the baby – to cover her momentary discomfort and to give her a task to occupy herself.

"Say goodnight to Mr Weatherbury, children."

"Goodnight!" they all chorused, but Molly, to everyone's surprise, instead of joining in with the rest, launched herself towards Tom and tightly hugged his legs. He looked down at her, taken aback, and pained, rather than pleased, at this sudden demonstration of affection.

"Now, little miss...What is this in aid of?" he began.

"Will you come here no more?" Molly looked up at him, her face pale and her tone plaintive.

Alice gave a short laugh, but it sounded forced and unnatural.

"Goodness, Molly – we will see Mr Weatherbury all the time, I'm sure. We live in a tiny village, after all."

"But will you not come here, to our kitchen, to make our dresser every day?"

Tom found that words failed him.

Alice passed baby Jack to Martha so that she could crouch down and draw Molly towards her. She gently unwound Molly's small arms from where they had clutched onto Tom, and spoke softly.

"The dresser is finished, Molly. Look how handsome it is - tall and strong and solid." Like Tom himself, Alice thought, the realisation coming suddenly into her mind, unbidden. "Now we must thank Mr Weatherbury for all his excellent work. This dresser will grace our kitchen for many years to come – perhaps until you are a lady grown, and a mother yourself. And we will use it every day, as the years pass. What do you think to that?"

"I will use it every day," said Molly, almost to herself, but Tom caught the words and understood them.

A slow smile appeared on his face, and he said, "I know you will, Missy. I know you will look after it." And he gave a short bow. "I trust this dresser to you, Miss Molly."

Edward followed Tom to the door, shook his hand, and thanked him again.

"I shall visit you in your workshop tomorrow to settle up, Tom, if that is acceptable."

Tom nodded shortly.

"Goodnight, all."

And he was gone.

Alice took Molly's hand and led her up to the children's bedroom.

When Molly was settled in bed, Alice sat beside her and gently stroked her hair.

"I know you will miss seeing Tom almost every day, but he will always be our friend, Molly. A very special friend."

"My best friend," Molly whispered.

"Yes. Tom and Annie - your two best friends," Alice smiled. "I am sure we will see him often – at all the Christmas festivities, for example, in the church and in the village hall.

Christmas will soon be upon us. And on the days when perhaps you don't see him, you will have the dresser to remind you of him."

"I will use it every day," Molly said again.

"Perhaps you will. I will give you special permission to be the one who fetches things from the cupboards for me, and puts them away again afterwards – very carefully. I know how good you are at looking after things and taking great care. And you have watched every day as the dresser was made, which gives you a particular relationship with it, and with Tom, who made it. Now sleep, my love."

And Molly slept.

Tom walked home slowly, and his heart was full. Within a few days of meeting Alice he had realised that he was captivated by the warmth of this home and this family, and the woman at the centre of it. Alice was in some ways shy and lacking in self-assurance, he saw, but she was cheerful and friendly towards him, loving towards her husband and her children. There was an energy here, colour, life – a wholesomeness, Tom realised. When he returned home each day, he had been acutely aware of the contrast between his own home and The Vicarage. He loved his wife, but could see that life's blows had left her pale, and chill, and lacking in any animation. How different life could be, he thought, if he had had Alice as a life partner. And then he felt the agony of his betrayal, and of the helplessness of this situation.

And Alice, as she sat beside her sleeping daughter, knew that she, like Molly, would miss the regular contact with this man of whom her daughter had grown so fond. Alice realised that in the last few weeks she had become increasingly conscious of Tom's strength, combined with his gentleness and the power of his presence. She was a loving mother and a dutiful wife, but she recognised that there had never been any passion in her marriage, and she felt for the first time the lack of it. Since Jack's birth she and Edward had ceased any physical intimacy. Alice was reluctant to have more children – six was exhausting enough, although she adored them all – and Edward respected that and may not have been unwilling to retreat into his books and his sermons. His family was complete. His work was fulfilling. His home was well-kept and comfortable. Edward was not a passionate man. What would life be like, Alice reflected, if it were lived alongside a man such as Tom Weatherbury? And then she felt appalled at the fact that she was asking herself such a question.

Tom and Alice, each absorbed in their own thoughts, were unaware that these thoughts were, in fact, aligned. Neither of them was sufficiently confident to recognise that what they thought and felt was reciprocated. But each of them knew that nothing would happen to change their life's course – the future was plotted and they would not deviate from what was expected – what was, in fact, their duty and their destiny. The attraction they felt would never be acted on.

The next time Tom and Alice saw each other was on the following Sunday, at the church. Tom tipped his hat to Alice and the family. He winked at Molly, who grinned back at him. As everyone filed in to take their seats, Tom saw Molly hang back, and he did the same. She slipped up to him and whispered, "I have a new treasure!"

"Can you show me?"

Looking around to check that no one was watching, Molly extracted from her pinafore pocket an object which she handled carefully and passed to Tom.

"But I don't know what it is," Molly frowned.

"It's an old buckle, Molly. Made of brass, I think – though it's tarnished – dirty," he corrected, as he caught sight of her expression. "I'm betting that if you polish it up – keep rubbing it with an old rag – in no time it will gleam like gold."

Molly's delight at this was evident.

"Where was it found?"

"In the field by the river. Martha took me for a walk. She didn't see me find it, though."

"It may be from a horse's harness – a horse that pulled a plough. And do you have a safe place to keep this treasure, Miss?" Tom asked in a low voice.

"I do!" Molly whispered back. "A special, secret place my best friend made."

At this point Alice turned to look for her daughter, who quickly scuttled off to join her family in their pew. Tom took his accustomed place on the other side of the aisle.

The service proceeded, with a short, thoughtful sermon from Edward, hymns and prayers culminating in the congregation's incantation of the Lord's Prayer. At the words "and lead us not into temptation…" Alice opened her eyes and looked across the aisle to find Tom's eyes fixed on hers.

Chapter Seven: *the coming of flood*

And then the rains came. November was always the time when there was the risk of flood in the village as the increase in rainfall combined with the high tides to swell the river, which overflowed into the water meadows and then, if heavy rain continued, began to encroach on the gardens and then the cottages.

Tom had known several floods in his thirty-year lifetime, having lived in this village, in the very same house in fact, since he was born. Whatever measures the villagers took to keep the waters at bay – digging out the dykes or building up the banks - every few years the river water invaded the properties. No villagers left their homes – where would they go? - but families carried up to the higher floors what possessions they could, and then they kept to the upstairs rooms until the waters receded. Local rowing boats were used to bring in provisions and to ferry passengers where required. The school closed and church services were suspended. Once the water had returned to its usual level, the clean-up operations began, and Tom and the other workmen in the community were fully occupied making good any damage which had resulted, before village life resumed its accustomed rhythms.

Reverend Jensen and his family heard all this from their neighbours. Edward, Alice and the children had never experienced flood, and they were amazed at the calmness of those villagers for whom it was a fact of life. The children were over-excited at the novelty.

"Imagine rowing through the village…"
"…lanes in a boat!"

The twins were beside themselves with delight at the prospect. The adults felt differently. Edward was unsettled by the likely disruption to his familiar routines. Alice was fearful about the safety of the children, and of the possibility of damage to the house.

"What about my dresser?" she asked Edward, wringing her hands. "It cannot be moved, although I can empty it. Will the wood not warp if it is standing in water?"

"I am afraid I do not know, dearest. But surely Tom would never have constructed it as he has if there were significant likelihood of irreversible damage from flood water. I suggest you go to see him to ask for advice and reassurance – or perhaps send a message to him and ask him to call here."

Alice was thoughtful. She had seen Tom each Sunday at the church services, and occasionally during the week as she went about her errands in the village. He was always friendly and respectful; he invariably smiled broadly and they spoke briefly – he usually asked about the children, Molly in particular, when he saw Alice out and about without them. They had not, however, had a proper conversation since the time of the dresser's construction. In those days they chatted easily while he worked and she busied herself in the kitchen. Since the dresser had been finished, Alice felt considerably less comfortable about the prospect of engaging Tom in conversation, though she could not easily articulate, even to herself, why this should be.

But these were exceptional circumstances. She needed to understand how best to prepare for the possibility of flood – the rain had not abated for several days by this point, and the river was set to overflow. In particular, she needed to know how best to protect her dresser. She remembered describing it to Tom, perhaps a little fancifully, as "a piece of furniture I shall grow to love". She accepted that this was a material possession, and that it was not wholly appropriate to think of it in these terms. However, love it she did. She recognised that one of the reasons she felt so attached to the dresser was because she had dreamed of it, and Tom had constructed it. It was bound up with the time she and Tom had spent together, of which she would always have memories which conjured up a sense of warmth, energy and happiness – together with a slight undercurrent of guilt and pain.

"I think I shall send a message to him, and ask him to come to call. I have confidence in his judgement and am sure he will be able to inform us of what we need to do to protect ourselves, and our home and its contents. I know Molly will certainly enjoy seeing him in our kitchen again," and she smiled down at Molly, who was following the conversation intently.

Tom responded promptly to Alice's request and called the day after he received it. Alice was aware of feeling nervous as she opened the door to him – how odd that was, she thought, when she had never felt nervous in his company before. What, exactly, had changed?

Tom shook the rain from his coat and cap before he dipped his head to clear the doorframe, and at Alice's invitation, seated himself in Edward's chair by the range while she made tea for them both. It made Tom think of his very first visit to The Vicarage, the first time he had met Alice. So much had altered since then, he reflected – and yet, so little.

"Thank you for coming today, Tom. I understand you are busy and I do appreciate your taking the time," Alice said as she handed him his tea and seated herself opposite him holding hers. Molly, playing on the rag rug with Jack, edged closer to them and, although ostensibly occupied with her baby brother, was clearly listening carefully to the conversation.

"May I ask after Mrs Weatherbury's health?"

"About the same, I'd say."

"I am sorry she's no better. I am sure this must be a worry to you, especially with the rising waters and the possibility of flood."

Tom looked steadily at her.

"It is a trouble when the water comes, but we have weathered the storm before, so to speak, and will again, I am sure. There are many reasons to love living in this village, I know, but the coming of flood can be a trial. I understand it may be especially worrisome to you as this is something you have never experienced before, I think?"

Alice shook her head.

"We have never lived so close to a river. We love that we do – Matthew and Benjamin especially – but we feel considerably easier when it remains within its banks!" and she gave a faint smile.

Tom began to relax a little in her company. In recent weeks he had tried steadfastly, though not always successfully, to resist thinking of Alice and how it felt to spend time in this warm, comfortable kitchen. Now he was back here, it felt easy and natural to be with her, and, despite himself, he found he was beginning to relish the opportunity to talk to and listen to her.

"I understand that if the water is likely to encroach into our homes we need to move what we can to the upper floor," she continued.

Tom nodded.

"But I am mindful that my beautiful dresser is fixed to the wall and cannot be moved. Will the flood water harm it, Tom?"

"Not seriously. The dresser will withstand the water. You will, of course, need to empty the lower cupboards," and Tom shot a quick glance at Molly as he said this. She returned his glance with equanimity. "From previous years' experience, the water should rise no higher than a foot or two before it begins to recede – this has been the usual pattern – although it does, of course, depend on when the heavy rain abates. When the flood water drains away, there is usually sand left behind, and the village community pulls together to manage the cleaning up. Everyone helps everyone else. I will come back then to check the wood. Depending on how long the water has been in the house, I may need to rub down and revarnish, but that is but a day's work."

Tom thought momentarily how it might feel to return to The Vicarage to work in the kitchen again. He was a reliable and trustworthy craftsman who would never spin out a task for longer than it needed to take, but he found himself wishing that revarnishing were a more time-consuming process.

Alice, too, reflected privately on how she would feel were Tom's visits to The Vicarage to resume. How is it possible, she thought, to want and not to want something in equal measure?

"Thank you, Tom – I hoped you would reassure me, and you have." Alice rose to her feet as Tom drained his teacup, and he prepared to take his leave.

"Do give my best wishes to your wife."

Tom nodded, and then bent down to ruffle Molly's hair before he moved to the door.

"I hope you're behaving yourself, Missy. I see you're looking after Jack as well as ever. He's growing into a proper little boy. You be careful when the flood comes – take care of yourself and of him."

"I will – I do!" answered Molly proudly.

Tom stood in the open doorway and looked up at the rain.

"They say the river is likely to overtop its banks tonight, and the water meadows will fill quickly. But it will take a few more days before we know whether our homes are at risk."

"In the meantime we will hope and pray," murmured Alice. "Goodbye, Tom – and thank you again."

The rains continued and the water level rose.

Edward was agitated when he returned home, three days later.

"The villagers are saying that the water meadows are full, and, in their experience, this means that the flood is likely to reach the houses tomorrow," he explained, to Alice's dismay and the children's barely-concealed excitement.

Despite her consternation, Alice was organised and capable when faced with a challenge.

"Betsy and Martha, Matthew and Benjamin, I want you to help papa and me to carry upstairs all we can. Molly, you will take Jack and settle him to sleep before you go to your own bed. You need to stay out of the way, please. When we rise tomorrow the kitchen may still be dry, but we cannot guarantee that it will remain so as the day progresses. We will have to make the best of things. The rest of the villagers appear quite calm about what is to happen and we must take the same approach – remember what I told you Tom Weatherbury said, when he came to visit. We must trust his judgement." Alice spoke briskly and the older children immediately moved to obey her instruction.

Edward looked thoughtful. "It is, after all, God's will," and he retreated into his reflections about whether he could frame his next sermon around Psalm 137, "By the rivers of Babylon we sat and wept", when the church services resumed.

Molly glanced towards the dresser but she obediently picked up Jack, as she frequently did, and carried him with care up the narrow staircase to the bedroom he shared with his parents, and soothed and rocked him until he slept. She had heard her father say that the river water would reach the kitchen tomorrow. If she rose early, she should be able to rescue her treasures from their secret hiding place before the rest of the family stirred.

From her own bed Molly heard her brothers and sisters, under Alice's guidance, moving to and fro, bringing what possessions they could into the upstairs rooms where they should be safely above the water level. She had kept the battered tin secreted under her bed, and she could transfer her treasures into it. She counted them off in her head, as she often did – it was a night-time ritual which helped her to relax into sleep:

three unusually-shaped pebbles,

a soft white feather,

a marble with a piercing blue eye,

a smooth, pink shell,

two buttons, one bright red and one a beautiful sea-green

a bright farthing, dated 1900

and, lastly, a brass buckle from a horse's harness, now polished to a dull gold.

Molly lay quietly listening to the heavy rain continuing to drum on the roof of the house. Despite its sober significance, which she did understand, she found it an oddly comforting sound: a sound which, eventually, lulled her into sleep.

Chapter Eight: *my punishment*

Molly woke to hear the house in silence but the rain continuing to hammer down. In the gloom she could still see her brothers and sisters as they slept, Martha and Betsy sharing her own bed and the twins together on the other side of the room. She could also make out the unfamiliar dark shapes of some of the family's possessions which had been moved up from the ground floor. She lay there listening to her siblings' quiet breathing and tried to identify which of the items the Jensens possessed were represented by these looming, dark masses. She was more excited than frightened at the prospect of the flood. The break from the usual routine and the sense of novelty, together with the heightened emotions of their parents, were thrilling to the children.

However, Molly was concerned at the thought of her treasures in their secret place being threatened by the flood water. She found it difficult to imagine the water in the house, but knew from all she had overheard that this was what the adults feared, with the mess and the damage it would inevitably cause. Her father had said that the kitchen would be dry until the morning, but what if he were mistaken, and the water was, even now, lapping at the dresser? Would her treasures be safe?

Moving slowly and cautiously, careful not to disturb Betsy who slept beside her, Molly stretched out and reached under the bed for the old tin which had originally housed her collection. She could transfer her treasures back to the tin, and hide it safely until the water receded and she was able, once again, to make use of her secret drawer. This was an adventure, and she would be able to tell Tom all about it when next she saw him – how she stole downstairs in the middle of the night and rescued her prized possessions. She clutched the tin to her and felt a shiver of excitement pulse through her.

Very quietly, she crept from the bed and padded across the bare boards to the door, holding the tin and her breath as she moved, careful not to wake her sisters and brothers. As she descended the narrow staircase she thought she could hear the sound of water, and as she reached the last few steps she knew she was right. Her foot touched flood water as she stepped out into the darkness.

Tom had also woken in the night, and as he listened to the rain beating on the roof of his cottage, he thought of Alice and her family in The Vicarage. He had lived through sufficient floods not to be unnerved by the experience. It was inconvenient but not disastrous. As long as no lives were lost, the damage done was only to things which could be repaired or replaced. In truth, most of the villagers owned very little, and what they possessed was practical and serviceable. Anything more precious – and he thought of the china which Alice had carefully, and with some pride, displayed on her new dresser – could be moved out of harm's way. Quarry tile floors or flagstones would withstand the water; kitchen ranges would be cleaned up and would work just as well once the water level had subsided. The walls of the houses would be damp for a while, but, in fact, many of the cottages were a little damp anyway. Over time, the ranges and the woodfires would dry out their homes. Until the next flood, of course.

Tom knew how the village community pulled together at such times, with every family supporting its neighbours. As a physically strong man and a capable workman he would be busy in the weeks ahead, but he had a clear sense of purpose, enjoyed his work and was always happy to help those among whom he had lived all his life.

And he was very willing to offer his services and to lend his strength to the newcomers, too, of course. He realised, uncomfortably, how much he was looking forward to having an excuse to return to The Vicarage. He recognised that he felt anticipation and guilt in equal parts.

Tom could clearly appreciate that the prospect of flood was far more worrying for those who had never experienced it. He sympathised with the Jensens who, unlike the villagers, had not grown up knowing that this would inevitably happen from time to time. Facing any challenge was always easier when you had the memory of similar challenges faced and survived before, and, in Tom's case, he remembered the floods his family had lived through when he was a boy. He recalled the joy of weeks without school, and being carried in a rowing boat, helping to deliver packages of food and to offer encouraging messages of support to the more remote cottages. He thought of seeing familiar sights transformed by the water level: a new perspective on the world he knew so well. And he could still see himself, when the water finally receded, walking the village lanes with his friends and exclaiming over the detritus high in the trees, showing how far the flood had reached. Perhaps living through the novelty and excitement of this as a child had helped him to develop the resilience and the sense of acceptance and equanimity he was able to muster as an adult?

Mary stirred beside him. She never slept well, and often rose in the middle of the night to sit in the chill kitchen so as not to disturb his rest, especially when he was rising early to work. She was a good wife, and reflecting on this had latterly made Tom feel uneasy. But Mary did not, on this occasion, wake fully. She settled again into her fitful sleep, leaving Tom to lie awake thinking of Alice.

He realised that this was something he had done increasingly in the last few weeks, despite his intention to resist the impulse. He knew it to be wrong, but found himself helpless to break the habit. He first of all remembered scenes from the kitchen of The Vicarage, what Alice had said, how she had laughed. He thought of her with Molly, and baby Jack. She was always tender and gentle with all her children, but at the same time she was firm and clear in her expectations of them, and high standards of conduct were always expected. He remembered her welcoming the older children home at the end of their school day – giving instructions to Betsy and Martha, and occasionally having to quell the boys' high spirits and remind them of how they should behave. He marvelled at how she always managed to do this in a loving way, but in a way that brooked no dissent. Alice was, he reflected, a natural mother.

Tom had seen her, from time to time, with Edward, too. They were so different in many ways – Tom was always acutely aware of the difference in their ages, and the fact that he himself was a much closer contemporary of Alice than her husband was. And the physical difference between the couple always struck Tom. He saw Edward, stooping and bony, with thinning hair and sharp, pale features, reaching out to touch the arm of his wife, who was fair and, although slight of stature, appealingly rounded, with colour in her cheeks and a twinkle in her eye, her hair shining. He could, of course, understand why she had agreed to marry Edward, and how much Alice must appreciate the comfortable existence this marriage afforded her. Edward was always solicitous of her – Tom knew with certainty that, whether in company or when they were alone together, Reverend Jensen would treat his wife with consideration and respect. Tom was deeply thankful for this; he could not imagine how he would feel, were Alice ill-treated by her husband.

And then sometimes, as he did this night, Tom allowed himself to imagine what his life could be like, if he were the one coming home each evening to this wife, and these children. He closed his eyes and could visualise this family filling his home with life, with colour and with joy. In his mind's eye he saw his cottage transformed, and he, himself, at the centre of it, basking in the warm glow.

Mary coughed in her sleep, and Tom felt the now familiar pang of pain and guilt. Was thinking warmly of Alice just as sinful as acting on his impulses, he wondered? Did the Bible not make clear that we will be held accountable for our thoughts as for our deeds? Tom recalled the words from Matthew: "But I say to you that everyone who looks at a woman with lustful intent has already committed adultery with her in his heart", and his spirits sank.

As dawn broke, Tom still lay wakeful, and, taking care not to disturb Mary, he slipped from the bed and dressed quietly in the half light. When he reached the ground floor of the cottage, he saw that the water had already encroached into the kitchen. He waded carefully through to the door, which, in common with the rest of the village, they never locked or bolted, and made his way out into the garden.

As he looked around he thought, not for the first time, how impressive the expanse of water appeared. The heavy overnight rain had finally stopped and the village looked peaceful, as if being in flood lent it a particular sense of calm. The gently lapping water reflected the grey of the sky. A displaced swan sculled slowly across the village green, and it turned its graceful head and caught his eye. Soon the village would be waking and rising and there would be purposeful but unhurried activity as everyone checked on their neighbours and adjusted their routines to accommodate this new, temporary reality. But for now only he seemed to be abroad. Tom had moved what he could to the first floor of the cottage the evening before. There was nothing more he could do at this stage to protect his own home or possessions. Mary would, he hoped, sleep a while longer. He would not wake her – let her rest. Tom, instead, found himself drawn towards The Vicarage.

"I should check on the Jensens, who will find the invasion of water into their home much more disconcerting than the rest of us do. Perhaps I can reassure and support them." Tom knew he was justifying himself. He wanted, simply, to see Alice.

As Tom approached The Vicarage he realised that the inhabitants had not yet stirred – there was no sound and no sign of human activity. Something impelled him to open the door and to step into the kitchen. Tom had never before crossed the threshold without knocking on the door and waiting to be invited in. This morning he excused himself for his presumption by telling himself that he should check on the family to ensure all was well. He was sure that they would pardon this intrusion upon their privacy under these exceptional circumstances.

The interior of the kitchen was dim after the grey morning light outdoors. The first thing Tom became aware of was something white, floating at the base of the staircase, and as his eyes adjusted to the gloom he tried to establish what it might be. He waded slowly towards it. His leg made contact with something floating in the water, and Tom looked down to see a battered tin, which he scooped up gently. Tom experienced a deepening sense of foreboding, and, inches away from the floating white shape, everything became clear to him. He groaned deeply, and bent to scoop the small body from the water. He looked at the child's face, a contusion at the temple. As he straightened, holding the child in his arms, Alice was making her tentative way down the staircase. Tom realised that Molly would have risen in the night to retrieve her treasures. She had lost her footing in the dark and slipped into the water, striking her head against the table as she did so. He looked down at the frail corpse in his arms and up at the terror-stricken face of the woman he knew he loved. When their glances met, each was thinking the same thing.

"This is my punishment."

PART II: 1960

Chapter Nine: *idyllic*

Shortly before they married, Laura had secured her first teaching post at the primary school in the next village, to begin at the start of the new academic year, in the autumn. She would have a mixed class of six to eight year olds; numbers at the school were small, and combining age groups the norm. Laura was keen to begin her career, though she also looked forward to starting a family in the not-too-distant future. She and James often talked about the children they would have.

James travelled each day to an office in the city, and loved making the journey home through the suburbs and out into the country in the early evening, feeling a rush of joy as he turned into the village, the lane, and then saw The Old Vicarage ahead of him. They had moved into the house in the spring immediately after the wedding, when every lane was bordered by the bright, bobbing heads of the daffodils planted by earlier generations. Now it was early summer and the village was lush and colourful, and they sat in the shade of the oak tree in the garden on this warm Saturday afternoon, listening to the sounds from the cricket match being played on the village green.

"This is idyllic!" James said, and Laura smiled back at him, deeply happy, her eyes closed against the sun which filtered through the leaves. He watched the play of light on her face and felt how lucky he was – his elegant, slender wife, her fair hair swept up in a knot at the back of her head, and her smooth, well-defined features in repose. I have a beautiful wife, James reflected, and an attractive home; I am at the beginning of my professional journey and, although we have relatively little money at this point, I know I have excellent prospects and considerable self-confidence. And one day we will have children. There is so much to look forward to.

"You don't mind too much not taking a holiday this year?" James asked, and his wife opened her eyes and smiled across at him.

"I don't mind at all. I'd much rather we spent the money we have on the house. There is so much we could do – so much I want to do to make it ours. And we need to make the most of this summer at home and the time I have before school starts in September."

"You're looking forward to that, though, aren't you?"

"I am! Very much, in fact. I loved the school when I visited, and standing in the room which will become my own classroom – it felt just right, I think. I have some preparation to do, but I feel excited rather than nervous. I look at every small child I see in the village and wonder whether they will be in my class. Teaching will be such a good way of getting to know our neighbours and their families. I sometimes feel very mindful of the fact that we are one of the few households here that hasn't lived in the village for generations."

James grinned at her. "But this is just the start of our dynasty! Perhaps our children's children's children will be here well into the 21st century!"

"The house has so much potential," Laura mused, as she looked back at it from her seat in the shade of the large tree which dominated the garden. "It's a shame it was empty and neglected for some time before we moved in."

"Though remember that's why we bought it for a snip, my love. If it hadn't needed so much attention I doubt we could have afforded it. But it is structurally sound, and will be wonderful when we've spent some time on it. With your skill, and my graft, we will make it a beautiful home where we can raise our family."

In the first weeks after moving in they had worked to clean the house thoroughly, and repair everything that required it, and they had further plans for the summer months. That black-painted dresser, for example, needed to be rubbed down and then repainted a lighter, softer colour, they thought – one of the jobs James had ear-marked for when he was on annual leave in a few weeks' time. The garden, too, was overgrown and in need of some taming – a neglected kitchen garden could be made fertile and productive again. James saw the repairs, decoration and gardening as his responsibilities. Meanwhile Laura was busying herself with sewing soft furnishings, making their home as cosy and comfortable as she could. She was the one with the good eye, and the taste. James thought of nest-building.

They listened to the soft tock of ball on bat, drifting across from the village green.

"Might you play cricket with the other villagers at some stage, James, do you think?"

"I was just thinking the same thing," James smiled. Increasingly often, he found his young wife voicing a thought which had been half forming in his own mind. "I thought we might wander across before we have tea and watch for a while. If the standard of play is such that I don't think I will embarrass myself, I will ask how I might go about joining them."

"I do want us to be part of the village - to get involved and to make friends. I want us to make a contribution, here," said Laura with conviction. She had already struck up a friendship with the woman who ran the village shop, Maisie Hamilton, and was keen to do more to establish their place in this community.

Laura knew this was something she needed to work at, however. She lacked the easy self-assurance she often observed in her husband; she was, in fact, quite shy, and had never found it easy to form strong friendships. She hoped that it would help to commit herself to supporting the local church, too. From their arrival she had attended the Sunday services. James himself was not religiously observant, but Laura could see that she would be able to develop her relationship with her neighbours, and to find a sense of purpose, beyond her roles as wife and teacher, through the church and village hall community.

Laura loved sitting in the church's quiet interior as the soft light fell through the stained-glass windows and she reflected on the peace her belief in God brought into her life. She enjoyed the services, and felt lifted when, as she readied herself in her kitchen, the single church bell began to toll to welcome worshippers.

"I forgot to tell you – I had a conversation with Maisie last week about how I might be added to the rota for arranging the flowers in the church. She said she thought the other women would be delighted to have my help."

"I'm sure they will. It's one of your many talents, my love."

Laura felt the warmth of the compliment.

"Maisie told me they hold a summer fete in August, and I said I would be happy to do some baking for that, too."

"You're certainly making the most of all your skills! They will be lucky to have you. As am I, of course!" and James rose from his garden chair and stooped to kiss her nose before he headed for the house. "Shall I bring out a pitcher of lemonade and some biscuits?"

"Yes, please, to the lemonade. No biscuits for me though, James, or I won't be hungry at teatime."

Left alone, Laura lent back in her chair and closed her eyes again, feeling the warmth on her face and thinking ahead to what their life in the village might be like. Maisie had talked to her about the cycle of the village year which helped her to anticipate all that might be to come. Laura remembered their conversation.

"The village is attractive in all seasons, you know? Spring bulbs and blossom, the summer colours and the autumn leaves, and then the crisp frosts in winter!" Maisie had told her. "You'll love it too, I'm sure. And the different village events, like the Harvest Festival – well, they kind of mark the seasons. For the Harvest service, we decorate the church with all the produce and flowers and then take it all to the village hall afterwards where we pack it into boxes. There are these beautiful Victorian wooden boxes which we use to make up packages and then they're distributed to any family that might be in need, such as the older folk. It's one of the village traditions I enjoy the most." Maisie had been born in the village, and she talked of how she had spent her childhood there, and what it was like to grow up in this community. She had attended the very school where Laura was to embark on her teaching career. Joe's parents had run the shop, and Maisie had started work there as soon as she had left school. Joe was fifteen years her senior.

"Once he saw how good I was behind the counter, he courted, married and impregnated me inside a year!" Maisie laughed. Two more children had quickly followed their first. Now Maisie ran the shop with her husband ("though I do the lion's share of the work, mind!"), and his parents lived with them in contented retirement.

Maisie seemed happy enough, as she enthused to Laura about the shape of the village year.

"And Christmas – well. I've always enjoyed Christmas, and a village Christmas is something special – the tree on the green, carol singing, the Christmas services. From time to time, when it's cold enough, the pond freezes and the ice is thick enough for us to skate on it. One of my earliest childhood memories is being on the ice at Christmas. Do you skate?"

"Badly!" smiled Laura. "But James is good at it. He's one of those men who seems able to make a good fist of any sport or physical activity. I'm afraid I don't have his talent or his confidence!"

"Oh, Joe is hopeless!" laughed Maisie. "No sense of balance at all. I'm really hoping our children take after me, not him, in that department. I loved sport as a girl. I'm probably a bit like James - I just assume I can do anything until I have evidence I can't!"

Laura marvelled at Maisie's self-belief. They were very different from each other, she recognised, and yet they had connected. Their conversation flowed easily – although Maisie usually dominated, Laura realised – and they clearly enjoyed each other's company.

"To be honest, it's refreshing to have somebody new to talk to," Maise had reflected. "I do love living in the village, but sometimes yearn to spend time with someone when I can't already predict what they're going to say next! That's one thing about growing up in a community where everyone knows everyone else so well."

"I'm really looking forward to being part of this community," Laura told her. "I grew up in the suburbs and have to say we didn't really know our neighbours very well. My family believed in keeping themselves to themselves, which didn't help. I was an only child, and I think my parents and I were all quite shy," Laura blushed at the admission. "Meeting James through a mutual friend transformed my life, I think! I want my children to have a different kind of experience. I want my family to have friends, and happy memories, and to feel part of something bigger."

"I think you already fit right in!" said Maisie, with energy. "I know I don't know James yet, but from what you've told me I think the pair of you are going to turn out to be a great addition to village life. And I hope you're really happy living here."

"We already are, I'd say. And your friendship is helping, Maisie – thank you!"

And Maisie reached over to squeeze Laura's arm, in response.

"Here you go, madam – a cool pitcher of home-made lemonade (though not made by me, I admit) and no biscuits."

James set the tray down on the rickety garden table – something else he needed to repair, he reflected, as it wobbled.

"Drink up, and then we'll wander over to look at the cricket. Perhaps you'll have the chance to introduce me to the infamous Maisie, who I've heard so much about."

Laura sipped her lemonade. The summer fete in August, the Harvest Festival in the autumn. And Christmas in the village would be magical, she thought, hoping for snow.

Chapter Ten: *life was hard*

As the next few weeks passed, Laura's appreciation of her friendship with Maisie grew. She found Maisie's cheerful confidence and enthusiasm refreshing. She also recognised that Maisie's knowledge of this rural community, its customs and rhythms, was very helpful to her as she settled into village life and sought to establish herself and her place in it. They had stalls next to each other at the summer fete, Laura selling cakes and Maisie supervising the tea urn. Laura loved her friend's company and conversation.

James inevitably had fewer opportunities to build his relationships with their neighbours in these early months. At weekends he was often working on the house or in the garden. He had not, yet, joined in with cricket on the village green. "Perhaps next summer," he suggested. During the week he worked long hours at his office in the city, and in the evening once he was back at The Old Vicarage he was content to relax at home with Laura. He would sit with a glass of wine and gently quiz Laura about how she had spent her day. She often talked about "what Maisie said" and he occasionally teased her good-humouredly about this.

"But you may not understand, James! You have always found it easy to make friends – you are a skilful communicator and you're easy with people. I've always been reticent and have found it much more difficult to open up, especially to those I've only just met. I think I just find Maisie disarming - I love the fact that she is so quick to laugh, and never takes herself too seriously. I know I have a tendency to overthink things, and I sometimes wish I were more like her. I'm a serious soul, I think."

James reached out and drew Laura to him. He settled her comfortably on his lap and spoke softly to her.

"I don't wish you any different from how you are, my love – my beautiful wife, who has all the graces, and a good dose of modesty thrown in!"

Laura relaxed against him.

"I think Maisie and I complement each other, and that's perhaps why we get on so well. She makes me feel more relaxed, I think. It's been lovely to get to know Sally, her daughter, too. Sally is seven, so she'll be in my class when the new term starts. I feel pleased there will be at least one friendly face in my classroom from the outset."

"Did you say Maisie and Joe have three children?"

"Yes – there are two boys, too – younger than Sally. Daniel and Robbie, they're called. Maisie was a very young mother. We're about the same age, and she has had three children already."

There was a pause, and then Laura slowly disentangled herself and rose to her feet.

"Do you know, I think Maisie is the first really close friend I've ever had, James – is that sad? It's taken me until my twenties to find a best friend. Most young children seem to manage that quite effortlessly," she mused.

"Ah – speaking of best friends, that reminds me," James said brightly. "You remember we talked briefly about how we might like to get a dog, now we're settled? There are so many attractive country walks in this area, and if we had a dog to walk that would encourage us to make the most of them."

"I remember the conversation. Have you made some progress?"

"Yes – if you're in agreement. Peter at work has a terrier bitch who has had her first litter. They're about ready to be weaned and he's looking for homes for them. I thought I might call after work tomorrow and have a look. I've even thought of a name!"

"Can you name a pet before you've even met it?" Laura smiled. "Don't you have to wait and see what he or she looks like?"

"Well, I thought we would go for a 'he', and I'd like to name him Angus, after my very first boyhood pet. He was a terrier too. So if I call at Pete's tomorrow, look through the litter and see if I can find a puppy who is clearly an Angus, would you be happy with that?"

"I would be very happy. I like the prospect of walking through the country lanes with my handsome husband on my arm and an adoring dog at our feet. You will be sure to choose one who is likely to adore us, won't you?"

James leapt to his feet and took his young wife in his arms.

"Who, my love, could fail to adore you?"

The next day, Laura and Maisie had contrived to share the same duty on the church flowers rota. Since they had met the month before, they had enjoyed sitting at their respective kitchen tables, drinking tea and sharing stories of past experiences and future hopes, while Maisie's three children played around them. But with Maisie's family commitments and her work in the store, her life was busier than Laura's, currently, and Laura also realised that once the new school year started she would have more to occupy her, too. It might be harder to find time to spend in each other's company once September arrived. So engineering the church flowers rota would give them an additional opportunity to see each other, and they were both content to chat as they worked.

"Time for a break," announced Maisie, heading out into the churchyard with her packet of cigarettes, after they had worked companionably on the flowers for an hour or so. Laura trailed behind her. She wasn't a smoker, but she was happy to take a breather, and she enjoyed sitting with Maisie in the summer sunshine. They perched on the churchyard wall.

Laura loved the church, and she also found the churchyard a restful place to be, with its well-established trees and weathered headstones. A willing parishioner cut the grass and worked to keep the place tidy, and he was occupied now at the far end of the plot. He raised his hand in greeting when he caught sight of them.

Maisie lit up and smoked peacefully for a few minutes. Although smoking had never appealed to Laura, she felt Maisie looked stylish with a cigarette in her hand. And Maisie always said she found smoking relaxed and 'centred' her.

"Have you ever looked closely at the gravestones around here?" asked Maisie. Laura shook her head.

"There's a family I think must have lived in your home, fifty years or so ago, because the father was the local minister, so I assume the vicarage was theirs." Maisie pointed with her cigarette to the far corner of the churchyard, where a family grave stood in the shade of a yew. "Come and have a look". Laura followed her, unsure whether she really did want to think about those who had lived and died in her current home, but unable to think of a valid reason why she shouldn't show some curiosity. Maisie clearly found this interesting.

"See?" Maisie read out the inscription. " 'Reverend Edward Jensen, who served this parish faithfully from 1900 to 1920. Born 1850, departed this life October 1920, aged 70.' Looks like he died while still in the job. Maybe he keeled over in the pulpit? His wife wasn't long after, but she was a fair bit younger than him: 'Alice May Jensen, beloved wife of Edward, 1873 to 1922'. She was still in her forties when she died. But I supposed they aged faster in those days. Village life wouldn't have been easy, would it?"

"And she had three children," added Laura, looking at the other names and later dates inscribed on the stone.

"More," corrected Maisie, pointing to a small headstone near to the larger family plot. They walked across to look at it more closely. "A little girl, Molly, died at the age of four in 1900."

"How terrible! Can you imagine losing a child even younger than your Robbie?" Laura shuddered at the very thought of it.

Maisie paused for a moment.

"It's even worse than that," she said. "Have you ever read the names on the war memorial?"

Laura shook her head.

"Come and have a look." Maisie led the way out of the churchyard, towards and then across the village green to the memorial which bore the date of 1918.

"To the members of the village who gave their lives in the Great War," Laura read. Among the twelve names listed were Matthew and Benjamin Jensen, who died at 22 years old.

Laura found her eyes filling with tears.

"So dreadful – to lose a child of four and then her two boys in the war. They must have been twins, as they died in the same year and were the same age. What a loss for the village. In fact, for a village this size, to lose twelve boys and men..." She scanned the names, which ended with Thomas Weatherbury, aged 48.

Maisie hugged Laura as they walked slowly back towards the church.

"I actually remember the Jensens' youngest child, when he was an old man – well, in fact, not actually that old, though he always seemed ancient to us, as children. We all called him 'Old Jack' – not disrespectfully, but he was something of a fixture in the village. He'd lived here all his life, I think. He must have lived in your house when he was little, but by the time I'm remembering he lived alone in the very last cottage, Stone House."

"Yes – I've seen it. I think it's unoccupied now? It's very small, I think?"

"It is. But it was big enough for Old Jack. He lived there on his own all through my childhood – no wife, no children. But he had an old dog, a border collie – what was it called? Tom, was it? - and Jack would be out in all weathers, walking the lanes with his dog, his stick and his flat cap. He wore the same clothes, winter and summer – I remember him in an old tweed jacket - and he smoked a pipe, I remember. I don't think he ever left the village. He wasn't unfriendly, exactly, and we children weren't afraid of him or anything, though I don't remember him speaking much, or smiling very often. He always gave you the impression that life was hard."

"I suppose it would have been – losing his sister, his parents and his twin brothers by the time he was – what? – still in his 20s, it looks like?"

"Yes. And I think he'd only have been in his fifties when I remember him, but he was stooped and grey and seemed like an old man. He was an expert when it came to the floods, though. I remember, as a child, when the waters started to rise, people would always consult Old Jack. Sometimes he'd say, "Not this year," and we would know that, although the river might burst its banks and the water meadows would fill, the levels would start to drop before the flood reached the houses. And then on a couple of occasions when I was growing up, he said something along the lines of, "This will be a bad 'un." And everyone knew to start moving their furniture upstairs."

"So how did he know, do you think?"

"No idea! He just seemed to have a sixth sense for it."

"We know The Old Vicarage has flooded in the past," mused Laura, "And no doubt it will flood again. But it was one of the factors that made the house affordable for us. And we loved it, and the village, so much, it seemed worth the risk."

"It's not easy, when it happens, but at least you're surrounded by people who have experience and who know how to minimise the damage when it comes."

Laura and Maisie had turned round and were making their way slowly back to the church. Neither spoke for a few moments, but then Laura asked, "Do you remember how Old Jack died?"

"I do. He collapsed one day while he was out walking his dog. A heart attack, I think. It was the dog's howling that alerted the village, and some of the men found him and brought back the body. I do remember his parents' grave was opened so that he could be buried there with them, and his name was added to the headstone."

Laura, thinking of the Jensens and their troubles over the years, found her eyes once more pricking with tears.

Maisie saw this and reached out and tucked Laura's arm inside her own.

"Sorry to upset you – I know how sensitive you are. I'm a tough old bird, compared to you," with a rueful grin. "Let's go and make ourselves a cup of tea before we start again on the flowers."

And they walked slowly back into the dim coolness of the church.

Angus, did, indeed, adore them, and the feeling was definitely mutual. James brought the puppy home the day after he had chosen him, and both he and Laura were immediately smitten by the enthusiastic tan and grey bundle of fur.

"He does, indeed, look like an Angus!" Laura conceded, as the puppy tried to climb into her lap and lick her face. She leant away from him and laughed.

"I'm happy to take responsibility for walking him," James announced.

"But I thought the idea was that we'd walk him together?"

"I suspect that once school starts you'll have enough to do, my love. And it will do me good – to get more exercise, and to blow away the cobwebs at the end of a day in the office and the long drive home."

So James began to rise half an hour earlier each morning, to take Angus out for a walk before he left for work. And in the evening, they went out for a longer stroll, whatever the weather.

Then James' annual leave began. He had arranged his two weeks' break from work to coincide with Laura's last fortnight at home before she began her new job.

"We need to do some intensive house-training with this boy before school starts," suggested James, glancing down at Angus who looked expectantly up at him. "I find I'm discovering a new reason to be pleased that we have a quarry tiled kitchen floor." James bent to mop up yet another puppy puddle. "Do you think after you start work you might be able to come home at lunchtime to let him out? Or should we ask your best friend Maisie to pop round and do that during the day?"

"Maisie might be too busy in the shop, but there are other neighbours we could perhaps ask," mused Laura. "I don't know whether I will be able to come home in the middle of the day – I expect I will have duties at lunchtime. I will find out."

Laura had a meeting at the school with the headmistress later that week, prior to the start of term in two weeks' time.

In addition to house-training the new addition to their household, they wanted to press on with work in the house and garden, including, finally, tackling the kitchen dresser. They were working together on rubbing it down in order to remove the chipped black paint, which was hard work.

"Whoever thought to cover the wood in this thick black paint?" James muttered as they worked away at it.

Eventually, they got through this arduous task, and then primed the wood in preparation for applying their own choice of paint. Laura had suggested that a few coats of duck-egg blue would transform the dresser and significantly brighten the kitchen.

James was on his hands and knees working on the base of the dresser when he suddenly exclaimed, "I'd never noticed this! There's a small mouse carved on the bottom left-hand panel. Nice touch!" Laura knelt beside him and they examined the carving together. It had been unnoticeable when the dresser was covered in the black paint.

"I wonder whether it was carved there especially for the children in the family," offered Laura, thinking, as she quite frequently did, of four-year old Molly who had died in 1900. Laura had taken James to the churchyard to see the gravestones for himself, and then they'd walked slowly across the village green to examine the war memorial together. Laura had also told James Maisie's stories about Old Jack, the last remaining member of the Jensen family, who must have been only a baby in The Old Vicarage ("although I expect it would have been just called 'The Vicarage' then...") in 1900. Like Laura, James found this a sad and sobering history associated with their new home.

"But we will fill this house with joy, my love," James had reassured his wife. And now they were starting with the substantial piece of furniture they had inherited, and preparing to paint it a much more cheerful colour.

James was looking forward to tackling the actual painting. Laura was happy to help with the preparation, but James was far more skilful than she at decorating, so she would leave him to it and continue with her own work, sewing curtains and cushions in a co-ordinating delicate floral print. Laura recognised that James's skill at practical tasks was something of which he was proud. Once the dresser was finished, he planned to repaint the kitchen walls a pale cream which they knew would lighten and lift the room considerably.

"With the low ceiling and small windows in here, we need pale colours to keep the gloom at bay," Laura suggested.

"As I always say, you're the one with the taste! I'm happy to be the labourer and just follow your direction, my lady!" and he tugged an imaginary forelock in deference.

They made a good team, Laura reflected.

The little terrier proved to be a positive, affectionate addition to their household. James enjoyed taking Angus out round the fields and along the river, and during his leave he had more time to do so, and said how much he appreciated the fresh air. Laura watched him whistle to Angus who darted ahead of him on the path, and then she turned back to her own work.

In addition to their activity on the house and in the garden, Laura was preparing herself for the start of term by reading and planning. She had compiled a list of questions to ask the headmistress, Miss Willoughby. And she was collecting things for her classroom, considering how she could make the space her own and put a distinctive stamp on it. "I feel like I'm home-making in both places," she mused.

On the Thursday, Laura filled her basket with the things she had collected for her classroom and walked along the river bank for her meeting with Miss Willoughby. The headmistress, rosy-cheeked and broadly smiling, welcomed her at the school house door.

"Mrs Williams. Welcome. I am very pleased to see you again!"

Laura relaxed a little as she returned Miss Willoughby's smile.

They sat in the small staffroom where they sipped tea and chatted companionably. Miss Willoughby taught the oldest children in the school, a mixed class of nine to eleven year olds. A third teacher, Miss Johnson, took responsibility for the smallest ones.

"So that's the team, the three of us – though we do have a handyman and caretaker, Bill Davies, who helps with everything not to do with actual education. He is a godsend, I have to say!"

"How many children are there altogether?"

"Currently we're expecting 39 to start with us next term. The number fluctuates a little from year to year. A family leaving one of the villages, or a new family moving in – as you have done – can make a difference. But the local council seems quite happy with our modest numbers as long as we provide a good education for the children we have. We are small, but perfectly-formed, I sometimes think! You will have a group of about 12, I'm expecting, ranging from age six to age eight. Some are from your own village and some from this one. You may know some of the children already, I imagine?"

"Only Sally Hamilton at the moment, I think – she's the daughter of Maisie, who runs the village shop, and who is a friend."

"Yes – I know Maisie. A lively soul! You will become accustomed to the fact that everyone knows everyone in these parts, I'm sure!"

Laura smiled. "I have to admit I'm quite a shy person, but I'm slowly getting to know my neighbours – through the church and the events in our village hall. And I don't feel shy about meeting the children. I loved training to be a teacher, and feel I can somehow be my best self in the classroom." Laura blushed a little self-consciously, but Miss Willoughby simply smiled.

"That was the impression I gained when I first met you – and after teaching for thirty years and being a head for fifteen, I consider myself to be a good judge of such things! Now, as we've finished our tea, shall I give you the full tour – that really doesn't take long! - and then we can go and look at your classroom? I see you've brought some things to start to make the space your own - capital!"

And the two women rose and left the staffroom. Laura found herself feeling increasingly comfortable, in the school and with Miss Willoughby ("Please call me Hester, if I may call you Laura?") and she could feel excitement building at the prospect of taking up her position here.

Two hours later, having had the tour, the opportunity to ask all the questions she had planned, and then time alone in her own classroom – "I'll leave you to get settled, Laura" – she was on her way home, feeling quite elated and looking forward to telling James all about her day. It was a bright, late summer afternoon, and she enjoyed the walk along the river, watching the light reflect on the water, and anticipating the autumn. She saw leaves whose colours were just beginning to turn, with some drifting lazily from the trees.

She called at The Old Vicarage to release Angus into the garden and then clipped the lead onto his collar. She crossed to the village store where she popped her head round the door, Angus straining on the leash outside.

"Are you busy, Maisie? Can you be spared, do you think?"

At Maisie's insistence, Joe had recently engaged a local village girl, Clara, to help her at the counter. Maisie had complained that she had so little time to herself, between the shop and her family, the church rota and village hall duties. She accused Joe of not pulling his weight, and insisted that he either changed his ways, or hired help. Enter Clara, who was a willing girl ("though not over-bright…" Maisie had confided to Laura), and now Maisie turned to her.

"Can you manage, do you think, Clara? It isn't too busy at this time of day. I'll slip out for a break. If you get in a pickle with anything, Joe is in the back, though he'll be snoozing behind his newspaper and you might have to give him a prod."

Collecting her cigarettes and slipping off her shop coat, Maisie joined Laura and they stepped out into the open air, Maisie drawing in a deep breath and then letting out a sigh.

"Freedom!" she exclaimed, and linked Laura's arm.

They walked for a while without speaking, Maisie smoking and Angus enthusiastically pulling ahead.

"Does he need proper training, do you think?" Laura asked her friend.

"I wouldn't worry about it – he'll learn. Once we get away from the cottages, you can let him off the leash."

"Yes – that's what James says he does."

"So – tell me how today went." Maisie knew that Laura had visited the school.

"I really enjoyed it. Miss Willoughby - Hester - was lovely: warm and welcoming and helpful. I'm looking forward to starting. Is Sally excited about going back to school?"

"She's beside herself – especially with the arrival of an exciting new teacher who she's already half in love with!" Maisie squeezed Laura's arm. "And how are the home improvements coming along?"

"Very well, I'd say. James should have finished painting the dresser while I've been out this afternoon. The sewing is done now – I was determined to get that out of the way before the start of term. The garden is tidy, and we've planted our spring bulbs already and started to prepare the ground where we want to establish the vegetable plot eventually. I'm feeling – calm and in control, I think!" Laura laughed.

"Lots to be proud of. Lots to look forward to!" Maisie smiled. "Now give Angus his freedom – share the joy!"

Back at The Old Vicarage, Laura admired James's handiwork.

"It looks terrific. Just as I'd hoped!" Laura enthused.

"Keep your distance – it's still drying. And I'd better take this young man out or he'll be brushing up against it."

"But he's just had a walk with me and Maisie. We've just got back."

James looked down at Angus, who was leaping up at him with apparently boundless energy.

"I wouldn't say there's any lack of enthusiasm on his part. And I think I need some fresh air after breathing in paint fumes all afternoon. I'll leave you in peace for an hour or so."

"I wanted to tell you all about my visit to the school..."

"And you shall, my love," and James bent to kiss the top of the head, "Over our meal when I get back. Come on, boy!" and James clipped on the lead and followed Angus out through the doorway, leaving the door open to help get rid of the smell of the paint.

Laura made herself a cup of tea and sat at the kitchen table, listening to the quiet ticking of the clock and relishing the peace. She glanced at the newspaper, and at the reading she had been doing for school, but decided just to sit for a while before she started to think about making their meal. She closed her eyes and allowed herself a few moments to reflect on the day – her visit to the school, her friendship with Maisie, her love for her husband and her home. She looked at the dresser and congratulated herself on her choice of colour. James would start work on the walls tomorrow – that shouldn't take too long. She looked around the kitchen, and saw that James had not yet cleaned his paintbrushes – he had been in such a rush to take Angus out as soon as she came home.

She rose slowly to clean the brushes and to dispose of the paper and rags James had used. Opening the kitchen bin, she saw something catch the light coming in from the doorway. She looked more closely, and then reached forward to pick it out. On the top was a marble – a marble with, she saw, once she had rubbed it with the cloth in her hand, a bright blue eye: the kind of marble a child might treasure.

Laura polished the marble gently, and then popped it into her pocket. Later, when the dresser had fully dried, she placed it carefully on one of the grooved shelves, where it winked at her daily. James never mentioned it.

Chapter Twelve: *an amateur at friendship*

On the day of the Harvest Festival, Laura arrived home from school and bent to retrieve the door key they kept hidden. It was customary in the village that neighbours seldom locked or bolted their doors, but James and Laura, having both grown up in the town, had always had the habit of locking the kitchen door, and bolting it securely when they went to bed. They shared one, old but sturdy, key which they kept in the log shed when they were both out.

Laura had, it turned out, never been able to return home at lunchtime to let Angus into the garden, as she shared playground duties with her fellow teachers, but their near neighbours, an older couple called Eileen and Harry, had been very happy to call round to do that once each day – another reason why hiding the key was a useful strategy. Angus was a favourite of theirs, and when, from time to time, Eileen and Harry spent a few days staying with their daughter and son-in-law who lived on the coast, Laura and James returned the favour by feeding their elderly cat.

When Laura unlocked the door, Angus shot out of it. He was sniffing round the garden, now, as Laura stood in the doorway and watched him. She was looking forward to the Harvest Festival, she realised. They had held a harvest assembly at school that morning. Parents had been invited, and those who were able to be there were clearly pleased to be part of it. The children each walked to the front of the small hall (which doubled as a lunch room and the indoor space for physical exercise) and placed an offering on the small raised platform. We all love our ceremonies and traditions, Laura had reflected. She had found herself singing the harvest hymns in her head all day. She hummed quietly to herself now, and then called Angus in, "Come on, boy!"

She was loving her job. The dozen children in her class ranged in age, temperament and ability, but she had enjoyed getting to know them all – as individuals, and in terms of the dynamic of the group. She was becoming more and more familiar with their families, too: their parents, their siblings, and the place of each family in the two village communities. At the start and end of the day, together with Hester Willoughby and Cynthia Johnson, she stood at the gate (clutching her umbrella if the rain fell) welcoming or saying goodbye to her charges and chatting to those who delivered or collected the youngest ones. Within the classroom she was calm and capable. From time to time, when she felt she could be spared from her own classroom next door, Hester Willoughby stood in the doorway and watched her.

"You are a gifted teacher," she had said simply, on one occasion. Laura had basked in a glow which lasted several days.

In preparation for the Harvest Service, Laura and other women from the village had worked hard to decorate the church and fill each nook and cranny with the abundant harvest produce to which all the villagers had contributed in some way. Laura herself had bought flowers and then collected greenery from the local hedgerows and put together some beautiful floral arrangements. She had used apples Eileen and Harry had shared from their own well-established garden and baked several pies. Next year, she said to James, they would be able to contribute some of the fresh vegetables they had grown. In time, she said, they would plant fruit trees and bushes, too.

Sadly, however, Maisie had not been among the group of women Laura had worked with on the harvest preparations. Maisie had withdrawn from the church flowers rota, claiming that, even with Clara's help in the shop, she was simply too busy to fit it in. Laura had seen relatively little of her friend since the start of September, over a month ago now. She herself had, of course, been occupied with her school commitments, planning and preparation. She had seen Maisie briefly and exchanged a few words from time to time but, now she thought about it, she could not remember their having a prolonged conversation since the day they had walked Angus together, following Laura's visit to the school two weeks before the new term started. She had missed her, she realised. But she was very much hoping that they would have the opportunity to catch up later this evening.

Laura had been told by her neighbours that when the service was over, all the flowers, fruit and vegetables which had been displayed in the church would be carried to the village hall where the wooden boxes would be packed before being distributed over the weekend to families across the parish. Refreshments would be served and the women would drink tea, eat cake and chat as they worked. The men of the village traditionally helped with the carrying of the produce and the subsequent distribution of the boxes, but they would retire to The Plough Inn while their wives, mothers and daughters prepared the harvest offerings. All the women helped with the task, Laura had learnt.

James arrived home in good time, having left work a little early on this occasion.

"How was your day?" Laura asked, when James had removed his overcoat and made a fuss of Angus, who always greeted him as if after a long voyage.

"Same old, same old, I'd say. Yours?"

"Good. We had a lovely harvest assembly this morning, which has got me into the right mood! I'm so pleased you agreed to come to the service with me, tonight."

"It's no hardship, especially as, you tell me, I'm allowed to go to the inn with the rest of the men afterwards – our reward, I expect?"

"I thought we'd just have a light tea and then perhaps some supper when we get home – unless I'm too full of tea and cake and you're too full of beer..."

"That sounds like a plan."

As the couple got ready upstairs later, Laura reflected on how much she would enjoy the service – the singing of harvest hymns, the prayers, the address from the neighbouring village minister, now their village did not have a minister of its own. She liked the man - his warmth, wit and wisdom - and had persuaded James to come along with her on this occasion. She hoped he would attend the Christmas services with her, too, and that this might encourage him to accompany her to church a little more often, especially when – and every time she thought of this she felt a rush of pleasure – at some point in the future they might have a child to take with them. Laura found herself smiling as she readied herself for the evening, choosing autumn colours for her outfit, and several layers for warmth against the chill of the church.

"Are you ready, James?" Laura turned to him.

"As I will ever be," and the couple descended the narrow staircase.

The couple stood in the kitchen and looked at each other.

"You look very handsome!"

"And you, my love, are simply the most beautiful woman I have ever seen!"

"We plough the fields and scatter…"

Laura sang well, and she loved how the music sounded in their little church. She was aware of Maisie sitting a few rows behind her, and turned to smile at her friend, who she saw looked preoccupied. She hoped nothing was wrong, and looked forward to catching up with Maisie's news when they worked alongside each other later in the evening.

Once the service was over, the minister and the men transported the harvest goods to the village hall, and then they headed for the inn while Laura and the other chattering women began the work of assembling the boxes. Laura turned several times to the door as more helpers entered, and eventually asked, "Where's Maisie?" A few neighbours shrugged or shook their heads. Eventually someone offered, "Perhaps she felt unwell and went home?" And Laura remembered that Maisie had looked out of sorts when she had turned to smile at her in the church.

"Perhaps she went to The Plough with the men instead!" volunteered another, which made some of the women laugh.

Laura was disappointed, and she determined to go to see Maisie the following morning.

She was tired when she returned home, at around ten o'clock. Not seeing Maisie had put a dampener on her spirits, she realised – she had been sure that this evening would give them the opportunity to refresh their friendship. Had she neglected the relationship since she had started her job?

"Perhaps all friendships need to be invested in. We can't assume that they are sustainable unless we put in the effort. I told James Maisie was my first ever best friend – I still think that's true. Am I such an amateur at friendship that I haven't done what's needed to keep the friendship strong? Or is this all fanciful, and whatever is wrong with Maisie is actually nothing to do with me, and it's egotistical of me to think it is?"

She badly wanted to talk this through with James, she realised. He would help her find her sense of perspective, and although he, inevitably, knew Maisie less well than Laura did, he was more adept than she was at forming positive relationships with a wide range of people and he might have advice to offer.

Angus whined at her feet, and she let him into the garden and stood looking up at the moon. She had expected James to be home by now. What time did the inn close? She hadn't expected it to be this late, though she realised she didn't actually know the opening and closing times – it wasn't a place she and James had frequented since their arrival in the village. It was too late for supper but, in fact, she wasn't hungry and didn't feel she could have eaten anything.

"Angus! Come on in now," and the young dog responded to her call.

Back in the kitchen, Laura sat at the table for a further half an hour, watching the clock. She could, she realised, put on her coat and walk across to the inn to find out what was happening. But she dismissed the thought quickly – surely James would be embarrassed, and might be teased by the other villagers, if his wife turned up there to bring him home. "To drag him home," some might say. Eventually, her eyes and her spirits drooping, she decided to retire to bed and read until James returned. She realised she felt a little uneasy about leaving the kitchen door unlocked and unbolted at this time of night – it was the first time since they had moved into the house in the spring that they had not secured the door by the time it grew dark.

"What if something has happened to him?" Laura found herself unable to dismiss the thought. Though if he had met with an accident of some description, someone in the village would have known about it, she thought, and would have come to the house to alert her. She desperately wanted the door to open and James to walk through it. She began to fear that there might be a knock on the door, instead.

She shook her head. "You're being alarmist and overly dramatic," she told herself, "and you have always prided yourself on being a sensible, practical woman. James is simply enjoying the company of our neighbours. He may have a sore head in the morning, but that is the worst that will happen to him."

Laura settled Angus in his basket with his well-chewed blanket. She fondled his ears and he looked up at her with his trusting eyes.

"Sleep well," she whispered to him, before climbing the stairs, undressing and washing and settling herself into bed with her book. It grew so late, however, that she found her head nodding and her eyes closing, so eventually she set aside her novel and was deeply asleep by the time James returned home.

Chapter Thirteen: *caught in the cross-fire*

Early the next morning Laura visited the Hamiltons' shop. She had a few purchases to make, but seeing Maisie was her main purpose. As she entered the shop and the bell sounded, Maisie was serving another customer at the counter; her eyes slid away from Laura's and she did not return Laura's smile. Eventually the customer left and Laura and Maisie were alone. Maisie began unpacking provisions, half turned away from Laura as the two spoke.

"You were missed at the village hall last night, Maisie. Is everything all right?"

"It's fine. I had a headache and just couldn't face the chattering so I came home for an early night." Maisie spoke in a low voice.

"I'm so sorry to hear that – how are you this morning?"

"Still a bit under the weather, but Saturdays are always busy in the shop so I just have to get on with it." The bell chimed to announce the arrival of the next customer, as if in vindication.

"Isn't Clara helping – "

"Not today," Maisie interrupted sharply, sounding uncharacteristically disgruntled. Her routinely cheerful temperament was one of the features which had attracted Laura to her from the first time they had met, which was, Laura reflected, the first time she had stepped into the shop, during the week she and James had moved into The Old Vicarage.

"Is there something I can get you, Laura? I'd love to chat, only you can see how I'm fixed." Laura shrank from the coldness in Maisie's tone, and her unsmiling countenance, as another customer entered. She asked for a loaf of bread, paid quickly and left the shop as soon as she could.

Outside, Laura stopped on the path, and realised she was clutching her stomach where she felt a dull ache. What had happened to upset her friend? She thought back over their last exchanges but could identify nothing which signalled a cooling of their relationship, and she found it difficult to think of anything she might have done or said which would provoke this sudden distance. There was no one else in the village to whom she felt so close, although she counted a good few of the neighbours as her friends, now. She had realised that Maisie might be busy in the shop this morning, but had hoped at least to arrange a time when they could share a walk, or a cup of tea, and catch up with each other's news, as they had done so often in the early months of their friendship.

"What has changed?" Laura kept asking herself, and, "What did I do wrong?"

Laura realised that her relationship with Maisie had been key to her developing confidence and building self-belief in the months since she and James had arrived in the village. "Maisie helped me to feel good about myself," she reflected. "She was such a good-natured, positive presence and she had chosen me to be her close friend. But now..." The sudden inexplicable coldness was hurtful, and it damaged Laura's self-esteem, which could be fragile, she knew.

"I was starting to feel so differently – James is wonderful, and when he asked me to be his wife.... And he's appreciative and loving. We're enjoying our home, and we've found a place in this community. My job is going well – I feel valued at the school, and I know I make a positive contribution. There's so much to feel good about – but a sharp response from Maisie, and a brusque dismissal, and everything seems to crumble."

She stopped and sat on the bench near the war memorial, breathed deeply for a few moments and tried to collect and calm herself. She looked out across the village green, and saw her neighbours going about their Saturday routines. Each person who passed nodded and smiled, or said hello. Laura returned their greetings in something of a daze.

"Could it be that something else is going wrong in Maisie's life?" she wondered. "Trouble in her marriage, perhaps? And although I have somehow been caught in the cross-fire, this isn't really anything to do with me at all?"

Laura wondered again, as she had the previous evening, whether it was selfish of her to assume that she was the cause of the change in Maisie's demeanour. She had wanted to talk to James about it last night, but had been asleep before he returned. This morning he had been subdued - Laura assumed he was nursing a hangover - and he had called to Angus and taken the dog out while Laura was dressing. Laura had decided to visit the shop first thing, and then make breakfast for the two of them when James came back.

"I need to talk to James when he is home. He will help me try to make sense of this," Laura decided, and immediately felt a little better at the prospect. She walked home slowly, thoughtfully, trying to decide on what exactly she should say to her husband, who would, she was sure, listen carefully, empathise and advise.

In fact, James seemed dismissive and uninterested.

"Friendships wax and wane," he said, with a shrug. "You said yourself that you found it difficult to form close friendships when you were a girl. I think that perhaps, if you had, you would realise that people – girls and women especially, in my experience - fall in and out of friendships all the time. You've admitted to me that you and Maisie are very different. Perhaps initially this was an attraction, but as time has passed, she has realised that the two of you have little in common and so little to talk about."

Laura found this painful to hear. If she had expected words of comfort from her husband, she was to be sorely disappointed.

"So is it my fault in some way?"

James shrugged again.

"It isn't about blame – just about compatibility. You thought you were compatible, but perhaps you aren't. You will make other friends."

"I did wonder whether there was something else going on in Maisie's life – perhaps trouble in her marriage? She often seems critical of Joe."

James paused for a moment, and became suddenly more attentive.

"What makes you think that?"

"Nothing specific, just that she sounds increasingly irritated by him – his reluctance to help her in the shop, for example."

"But you have no other evidence that there's a rift with Joe?" 'Evidence' seemed an odd word for James to use. Laura was unsure what she could say. She shook her head mutely. Then she looked up at James and realised he was already mentally moving on.

"As it's not raining, I'm going to spend a few hours in the garden," he said, going upstairs to change into his gardening clothes.

Laura felt even more hurt. James had not expressed any sympathy or even seemed particularly interested in how she was feeling. She had expected more from him.

The weeks passed. November came and went, and December arrived. Laura kept herself busy preparing for Christmas, at school and at home. She showed her class how to make Christmas tree decorations to give as gifts to their family on Christmas morning. She and James had invited both sets of parents, and James's sister and her husband, to join them for their first Christmas Day in their new home and the house would be full, but Laura relished the prospect. They could seat eight adults round the kitchen table, although it would be snug. Laura baked and iced her first Christmas cake, and it turned out well, she thought. She planned to gather winter greenery and use it to create garlands to decorate the walls of the house. She was looking forward to taking all their visitors to the Christmas Day service in the church. There was, she reminded herself, much to look forward to.

Laura saw little of Maisie during this time, and when they did happen to meet, for example at the school gate, the two were cordial but cool. Laura did not try again to engage Maisie in conversation; Maisie did not seem interested in what was happening in Laura's life.

"I just have to accept that," Laura realised, with a sense of sadness. She did not try to talk to James about it again.

In the first week of December, James arrived home from work one day, earlier than usual and clearly bursting with good news.

"I've been offered a promotion!" he announced, as he came through the door – before he had even removed his coat or greeted Angus, who was jumping up excitedly, as always thrilled to see him.

Laura was sitting at the kitchen table, looking over some of her pupils' work. She smiled up at him.

"That's brilliant news! Tell me."

"Calm down, boy – I'll take you out soon. Well, Charlie Middleton called me into his office this afternoon. He hardly ever speaks to me, and, to be honest, I wasn't even aware how familiar he was with my work. But he was positively effusive – told me I'd made a really good impression in what I'd done so far, and, with Peter Clarke moving on, there was a vacancy he thought might suit me." James grinned broadly at his wife. He looked youthful and energised – Laura felt she could see the excited schoolboy he had, no doubt, once been.

"Do you have to apply for it, or...?"

"No! That's what's so great about it. They've earmarked the position for me because they think I have just the skills needed to step up – those were Charlie Middleton's exact words, more or less. No one else is being considered, apparently. I'd start in January, and it will be more money – not a huge amount more, but that isn't the point, really. It just shows the confidence they have in me, and that they recognise my potential. Honestly, Laura, I'm so pleased..."

"I can see that," Laura smiled.

"I feel like I'm on my way. A couple of years in this role and then I'll be ready for the next step. I'll end up in Charlie Middleton's office in no time!" James laughed. "We should celebrate. I should have called to buy champagne..." James began to root through the pantry, "...but I didn't think of that. Too eager to rush home and share the news with my wonderful wife!" He laughed again. "But we have a bottle of red here that will serve the purpose. Now where's the corkscrew? Why can I never find it?"

"Because you're looking in the wrong drawer!" Laura laughed. "Try the one to the left."

When James had, finally, opened and poured the wine, he raised his glass in a toast.

"To moving onwards and upwards!" he grinned.

"To you, and your success – my clever, ambitious husband!"

"I *am* ambitious, I agree. That's a good thing – right?"

They drank and beamed at each other over the top of their wineglasses.

"I'll finish this and then I'll take Angus for his constitutional."

"I'll come with you today, James – I'd enjoy a breath of fresh air and a little exercise."

"No, you stay here. It's pretty dark by this time, and I don't want you to lose your footing on the paths. We'll have a walk together this weekend, during the daytime. You go back to your schoolwork. I won't be too long."

He went to fetch Angus's lead. Laura felt a little subdued that James didn't want her company, but, as she usually did, she hid her disappointment.

"Ah – one more thing I should mention." James paused in the doorway and turned back to her. "I need to go on a residential training course to prepare for the new role. It will be a week away in the middle of the month – in a couple of weeks' time. Will you be all right on your own for a week?"

"Of course I will, James. There's no need to worry. I will have plenty to occupy me at school as the end of term approaches, and all is in hand with respect to our Christmas preparations here. I hope you enjoy it."

"Not sure that's the purpose of it, but I'm keen to learn, and I'll take any opportunity to demonstrate my commitment."

"I know you will. I feel proud of you!"

And James kissed her cheek before he and Angus disappeared into the early evening twilight.

Chapter Fourteen: *it's odd, what's happened*

During James's absence, the rains came. December was one of the times in the year when, if high tides coincided with unusually heavy rainfall – and this year the region experienced a month's worth of rainfall over a 48-hour period - the river level rose alarmingly and then the water meadows quickly filled. Having never experienced flood - though she knew it was a possibility when they purchased the property, and had discussed historical flooding with Maisie during the period when they were close friends – Laura was understandably anxious, but she was reluctant to ask James to return, reasoning that his employers might take a dim view of this in the light of his new responsibilities. She felt she needed to inform him, however.

She telephoned the conference centre one lunchtime from school, and the helpful receptionist managed to track James down and bring him to the phone.

"I just wanted to let you know what's happening, James, but I don't want you to worry. It all seems to be happening very quickly. It's the high tides in combination with unusually heavy and prolonged rainfall, I'm told. The river tops its banks and the water meadows fill. In the past, if this has carried on, sometimes the water gets into the houses. I don't think there's anything we can do at this stage, really, so there isn't any point in you coming home early."

There was a brief silence at the other end of the line.

"I'm not sure that would be possible anyway," James said slowly. "They might think I'm not committed if I said I couldn't complete the training. I don't think they could withdraw the offer of the promotion at this stage, but I wouldn't like to give the impression that I'm half-hearted about this. I know you appreciate how serious I am about my career."

"I understand that, and I'm not asking you to come home. I'm sure I can cope, and it may not be that bad, anyway. If the rain stops and the levels start to go down, the houses will be safe. I have friends here who can support me. Hester has been reassuring and sensible, and Eileen and Harry have been helpful too. They've been in the village forever, as you know, so they've lived through several floods..."

As has Maisie, Laura couldn't help thinking. She had tried not to dwell on what had happened with Maisie in recent weeks, and to come to terms with their estrangement, but under the current challenging circumstances she wished desperately that she still had Maisie as a confidante. She remembered Maisie's positive outlook and sound good sense. She needed both right now, especially in James's absence. But she knew she was remembering the old Maisie, and their former relationship. For whatever reason, they were in a very different place, now. She said nothing about any of this to James.

"Hester's house is next to the school – I think I told you that? This village isn't as much at risk as ours is, and the school and her house are built on slightly higher ground in any case. She has said that if the worst comes to the worst and The Old Vicarage is under water..." Laura tried to quell the feeling of panic which rose up within her as she said the words, "I can come and stay with her. Then by the time the flood water goes down, you will be home and we can sort out what we need to do together."

"That's good," said James. "At least you know you have somewhere to go if you need it."

"Yes. And when I talked to Eileen and Harry, they recommended a local handyman, Ben Winters, who they said could come round and talk to me, and offer his advice. He's another person who's lived in the village forever and survived floods in the past. And as he's a handyman he's also something of an expert on the clean-up procedures. What do you think?"

"When is he coming round?"

"I haven't asked him yet – I thought I'd check what you thought first."

"I don't see any reason to delay," Laura detected a suggestion of impatience in James's tone, she thought. "Get in touch with him and see what he thinks. And now I really have to get back into the session, Laura. You'll be all right?"

That was a question to which there was only one acceptable answer, Laura realised.

"Of course I will. Please try not to worry. And I hope the rest of the training course goes well. I'm sorry I disturbed you."

She hoped James might tell her that there was no need to apologise. Secretly, she realised she had hoped that he would insist on coming home, and that he might say something along the lines of, "Nothing is more important to me than your safety and your peace of mind..." But she was being fanciful, overly dramatic and selfish again, she chided herself. She would manage this.

"Bye then," was all James said.

Laura sat by the phone for a few moments, gathering her thoughts. Her heart was fluttering and she realised that she could, quite easily, give in to the tears which were threatening to overwhelm her. But she was at work. When the bell rang she would need to teach her class and be the measured, calm presence that required of her. She breathed deeply and evenly and managed to get her emotions under control.

Hester stuck her head round the door.

"How did that go?"

"It was fine. I'm fine – thank you," and Laura gave a wan smile as she stood and prepared to welcome back her class after lunch.

After school, Laura stood, as usual, at the gate to bid farewell to the children, her umbrella raised against the steadily falling rain. Sally had been absent today – Laura assumed perhaps a winter cold – but Maisie sometimes came to meet the younger boys, Daniel and Robbie, and Laura thought that she might be particularly likely to do so today as their elder sister was not there to walk home with them.

She told herself that if she did see Maisie she would ask after Sally's health. Perhaps they might even exchange a few words about the flood. "I suppose I haven't really come to terms with our estrangement after all…" she reflected. In the event, Maisie didn't appear, and Laura didn't catch sight of Daniel or Robbie either.

As soon as she arrived home, Laura clipped on Angus's lead and went to call on Eileen and Harry to ask if they would send a message to Ben Winters, to see if he could call. She told them that James had agreed that this was a sensible step to take – the more information they had, the better prepared she would be for whatever lay ahead. She did not, of course, tell them that James appeared irritated that she had not already arranged to speak to Ben, but the thought played on her mind.

"I'll get in touch with him straightaway, never you worry," Harry said. "I shouldn't be surprised if he didn't call tonight, on his way home from work. I know where he's working today, so I'll step along and have a word with him," and Harry went to get his coat and cap.

"You are so kind," Laura's voice wavered. The tears were threatening again, she realised.

"It's no trouble, dear," Eileen reassured her, reaching out to pat her hand. "You remind me of my daughter. I hope someone would be there to support her if she was alone and anxious." Angus had curled up and was dozing on Laura's foot. Eileen looked down and smiled at him.

"And how is my best boy, today? Missing his master, I'll be bound."

Laura smiled. "I think we both are. Angus definitely seems out of sorts when James isn't around!"

"He's comforted by your presence, though. As he's settled, will you stay and have a cup of tea with us? It's always lovely to have your company."

"Thank you, I will." Laura recognised that she was seriously in danger of feeling extremely sorry for herself. Sitting with Eileen in her comfortable cottage by a blazing log fire seemed infinitely preferable to returning to the cold and empty Old

Vicarage. "I can't stay too long, though. I need to be home in case Ben does call. But a cup of tea with you first will be perfect."

Ben did, indeed, call on his way home after work that evening. When Laura opened the door to his knock, she realised that she had seen him around the village from time to time, but that they had not, to her knowledge, spoken to each other before. He was a serious, thoughtful man, and she was relieved that he was not in any way dismissive of her concerns. He spoke slowly, weighing his words carefully. They sat together at her kitchen table – he politely refused her offer of tea.

"I need to be getting home along shortly, missus, though thank you kindly for the offer."

But he did not rush her, and she definitely felt reassured by his solid, dependable presence.

"It's unlikely to be a big one, we reckon, though there's the possibility it might get into the gardens and lanes. That don't mean the house will flood – the buildings at this end of the village are raised up a bit higher, see?" Laura nodded, though this was something of which she hadn't been aware.

"I'll keep an eye on it and let you know if there's things you need to be doin', like. You try not to fret, missus, especially being on your own, and this being your first winter in the village."

Laura wondered what Eileen and Harry had told Ben about her circumstances.

"I'll just call in on my way home every day while your man's away, to check how you're doing."

"Thank you so much, Ben. You are very kind, and I really do appreciate it."

As Ben was getting ready to leave, he hesitated.

"You were friendly with Maisie Hamilton, I think? I've seen the two of you together on and off."

Laura felt a little uneasy.

"We were friendly for a time when James and I first arrived in the village, yes," she admitted carefully, "but haven't seen each other for a while, now. I'm busy at the school, and she's busy in the shop, so..." Laura trailed off, unsure what else she could, or should, say.

"I'm not one to gossip," said Ben, and Laura believed him, "but it's odd what's happened with the Hamiltons, isn't it?"

Laura was puzzled. She knew of nothing odd about Maisie and her family, excepting the sudden change in their own relationship.

"What about them, Ben? I don't know what's happened."

"They upped and left last night. Cleared out without a word to anybody. The shop's empty. No news about where they've gone or why. All of them – Joe and Maisie, his folks and the bairns. No one knows what's happened." He shook his head.

Laura was mystified. She had registered, of course, that Sally had not been in school today, but nothing had been said about her or her brothers. She had heard no rumour of anything unusual happening.

"Could it be connected to the flood, somehow?" she asked.

"Not likely. The waters come up every few years or so – no need to panic, and, as I say, this year don't look to be a big one. Can't see how that would drive them out. I just thought, you being her friend, like, you might know. As I say, I'm not one to gossip, and this isn't idle curiosity. We pull together in this village – I've known Joe all his life. We were lads at school together. People are just wondering if they're all right. Sorry if I've worried you. I need to be getting home myself or my wife will be the one who's worrying".

"Goodnight, Ben – and thank you. I appreciate you calling, and I do feel reassured. Do let me know if things change, and if there's anything you think I should be doing."

"I will. And if you need help, carrying stuff upstairs and such like, I'll be round with some others to do that with you. Like I said, we pull together in this village."

"And thanks for telling me about the Hamiltons, though I'm as confused as anyone about what might have gone on."

" 'Night then, missus."

And Ben left Laura to her bemused reflections.

Chapter Fifteen: *are these yours?*

Ben was right about the flood. The waters slowly rose over the next few days until the lanes, and most of the gardens, were inches deep in water, and stout boots or wellingtons were needed as the villagers moved from place to place, but the houses, on this occasion, turned out not to be in danger.

"This would have been one of the times when Old Jack said, 'Not this year,' " Laura mused, remembering her conversation with Maisie as they had walked back to the churchyard on the day she learnt more about the history of these early inhabitants of her home. It seemed much longer than three months before.

Laura walked slowly and carefully along the riverbank to and from the school each day, and, despite the children's excitement at the novelty of the depth and expanse of the water, lessons proceeded as normal. Laura continued to enjoy her teaching, and the structure it brought into her life. She wondered how she would have felt during James's absence if she had been at home with Angus all day, each day, as the waters rose around her.

"I am so grateful that you gave me this job!" she said to Hester one day, as they stood at the gate welcoming the early arrivals.

Hester turned to her with a smile. "You have repaid my faith in you many times over, Laura! I am the one who is grateful; you are an asset to the school. In fact – and I hope you don't feel embarrassed if I say this – I can imagine you stepping into the role of headmistress one day."

Laura blushed, but was deeply gratified by the compliment.

"Thank you. And thank you for offering me sanctuary should The Old Vicarage be flooded! I am so grateful, especially with James away from home. But Ben Winters assures me that the danger is past for the moment. I trust his experience and his judgement."

"He is a very good man. (Remember, I know everyone, Laura!) I'm pleased he has been keeping a watchful eye on you and your home."

Ben, as good as his word, had called in on Laura each evening to give her an update and offer further reassurance. James was due back at the weekend, and the indications were that the water would have begun to recede by that stage. The rain had already abated, and the village seemed to breathe a collective sigh of relief.

Angus had been deeply unimpressed with the arrival of the water. His regular evening walks had to be suspended, and when he was let out into the garden he skirted the flood water to find, and make use of, the dry patch at the higher, far end of their plot. Occasionally he would dip a paw in one of the flooded areas, and then look up at Laura with a disconcerted expression and a faint whimper.

It was interesting for Laura to observe how the villagers responded to the situation. She could see that navigating the challenge of the flood had brought the neighbourhood community even closer together. Knowing that she was currently on her own, several of the villagers whom she felt she did not yet know well made a point of checking on her wellbeing and offering support, and she was touched by that. In addition to Ben, and Eileen and Harry, and the group of women she had got to know during the decoration of the church for the Harvest Festival, Laura felt she was significantly extending the number of her acquaintances in both of the villages, and she looked forward to telling James all about this at the weekend. The parents of children in her class, and several of those who lived in the village where the school was located, sought her out to ask how she was, and she saw villagers helping each other and bolstering their neighbours' spirit. So, despite the unfortunate circumstances of the encroachment of the water, Laura realised that she was appreciating living in this community even more. She did not, for one moment, regret their decision to buy The Old Vicarage. She thought James would feel the same.

And something else was beginning to preoccupy Laura. It had not been confirmed, and she had not, as yet, had the opportunity to talk to James about this, but as each day passed, she became firmer in her conviction that she was carrying a child. It crossed her mind briefly to telephone James again, to let him know what she thought, but she dismissed the idea just as quickly.

"I felt uncomfortable in our last telephone conversation," she remembered, "and he didn't seem overly happy to hear from me. Even though this may be good news, rather than unwelcome information, disturbing him a second time might not meet with a positive response. And, of course, I may turn out to be wrong, which would make the interruption to his training course even less forgivable."

However, Laura found it impossible to put her potential condition out of her mind.

"If I'm right, the baby should be born in September," she reflected. She tried to stem the building sense of excitement. "Until I've seen the doctor, I can't be sure but – I feel differently. I know my body – I've lived with it for 25 years! And I feel pregnant."

She knew she would have wanted to talk to Maisie about it, had that been possible. Having had three children, Maisie would be a good source of information. Certainly in the early days of their relationship, she would have been thrilled that Laura had confided in her, and thrilled at the possibility of a baby in The Old Vicarage. Laura could not help herself: in her head she played out the potential conversation - what she might say and ask, and how she thought Maisie might have responded. But then she checked herself.

"I have to remember that, even if Maisie were still here, she might have had no interest in listening to me - and I couldn't have borne another rebuff."

There was no news as yet of where the Hamiltons had gone, or why they had left so suddenly. Speculation was rife. Laura was careful not to be drawn into any conversations on the subject. It made her deeply uncomfortable. She was not fond of gossip and rumour in any case – it was not in her nature to be so – and as it involved Maisie, she felt that speculating about her was somehow disloyal to the memory of their friendship.

But Laura badly wanted to talk to someone about her condition. She wondered about confiding in Eileen, who was maternal in her approach to Laura – much more maternal, Laura thought ruefully, than her own, rather cool and distant, mother. Eileen would be very pleased for her, she realised, but Laura knew the sense of not broadcasting news before it was positively confirmed, and, even after it was, the likelihood of miscarrying in the first few months was high enough for couples to be circumspect about transmitting the information far and wide. She needed to be patient, and she needed to wait.

She consoled herself with the thought that James would soon be home. Instead of playing out in her imagination what she might have said to Maisie, as she walked to and fro along the riverbank, and as she sat with Angus in the evening, she started to run through what she might say to James, and what he would say in response. This was far more satisfying. She even said, aloud, "James will be here, soon. James will be thrilled, as I am," and Angus cocked his ear and looked up at her expectantly.

Laura and James had talked often of starting a family. The timing was good, Laura thought, hoping that she would be able to complete the year of teaching. She and James would need to discuss whether, and if so when, she might return to the job. She had always assumed that she would want to give up work completely, following the arrival of her first child. But she had loved her first term of teaching, and she knew it was a profession to which she was very well-suited. She remembered how she had felt when Hester had said, "I can imagine you stepping into the role of headmistress one day." And, of course, her salary had been helpful.

"Could I cope with a baby and a job, without close family nearby to help me? There are others in the village who appear to manage it, and I know of at least one woman who minds children for others. And there I am again, anticipating and planning!" Laura smiled to herself. She would make an appointment to see the doctor in the town as soon as James returned.

On his final visit to Laura, the evening before James was due home, Ben sat at the kitchen table and drank tea with her, educating her about floods he had known, and those he had heard of, in the past.

"There were a bad one at the turn of the century, before I were born, but I've heard tell from my family..." He paused, looking at Laura, momentarily unsure whether this was something a woman currently living alone would want to hear, but, in the end, the desire to share dramatic news was too strong to resist. "A little girl what lived here in the vicarage was drownded in it."

"Molly, aged four," murmured Laura. "I've seen the gravestone in the churchyard, though didn't realise drowning was the cause. How tragic." And Maisie – unexpectedly vanishing Maisie – was the one who'd shown her that, she reflected.

"She had a baby brother, who was my partner until he died. After the war, he helped me get going, like. We worked together for a good few years – as he got older I took on more of the heavy stuff. I learnt a lot from Jack Jensen."

"Old Jack..." murmured Laura.

"That's what they called him – though he wasn't much older than I am now when he was demobbed from the army, and we started to work together. But he'd had a hard life, and that ages a body. That family's sadness all started when that little girl was lost."

Laura shivered.

"Well, Ben," she continued briskly, "I really appreciate your looking after me while James has been away this week, and all your advice and reassurance about the flood. I expect you think I'm silly, making such a fuss, but this is a new experience for us, and I didn't really know what to expect. I love my home, and we've worked to make it cosy and comfortable and

– James has just painted that dresser, for example, and I'd hate to think of water coming into the kitchen and spoiling his handiwork."

Ben turned to look at the dresser.

"He's done a good job," he said, and he moved over to inspect the work more closely. "It's a good solid piece of furniture – well-made, whoever made it – and that little fieldmouse is clever. I don't reckon the water would have done it much harm, though it might have needed another lick of paint after, if the water had come in."

Ben knelt and ran his hands appreciatively along the base of the dresser, touching the fieldmouse lightly, and murmuring about the quality of the carpentry. Then he stopped.

"This is odd, missus."

Ben examined the bottom right panel more closely.

"There's something different about this panel, it's – ah!" as his fingers found the catch and the drawer – Molly's secret drawer, Tom's gift to her – slid open. "There's a shallow drawer here and it's..." Ben pulled out a number of pieces of paper. He creaked to a standing position and placed the papers on the table.

"Do you use this drawer, then? Are these yours?"

"We had no idea it was there! It's a bit too low to be useful - why would someone put a drawer at ground level?"

"These might have been there some time, I suppose," Ben said, without looking closely at what he had retrieved. But the paper didn't look aged, and Laura was already examining what was written there.

"Perhaps so," she murmured.

"Well I'd better be off for my tea." Ben put on his cap and prepared to leave. "Just give us a shout if you need any help, though I know your man is back tomorrow."

"Thank you, Ben," said Laura, not looking up from the papers he had found. Ben tipped his cap as he let himself out of the door. Laura read for a short while longer, and then she laid her head on the broad, well-scrubbed kitchen table, and wept.

Chapter Sixteen: *a capacity for deception*

Reading this one-sided correspondence, and the hints it gave of the messages which had been returned in response, Laura pieced together when the relationship between James and Maisie must have begun, how it had progressed, and how it had ended. The final message, which Laura realised she was reading before James had seen it, explained how Joe had discovered what was happening and insisted that he, Maisie and the children left the village immediately with his parents. They were moving temporarily to live with relatives some distance away, while preparing to emigrate to the other side of the world. In this last note Maisie explained that Joe had, apparently, been investigating the possibility of emigration for some weeks. Why had Maisie not shared that with her? Laura wondered, before realising that the affair had already begun while Joe was exploring the possibility, and so her friendship with Maisie had already started to die. Joe's discovery, only a few days before Laura's own, had galvanised him into taking immediate action and acting on his provisional plans. Laura had never realised that Joe had so much energy and drive. Perhaps Maisie had also been taken aback by that.

Laura remembered when James had met Maisie for the first time. It had been on that lovely early summer day when they had sat in the garden of The Old Vicarage, listening to the sound of cricket being played on the village green. Before tea they had wandered over to catch the end of the cricket match. Laura remembered James had said, "Perhaps you'll have the chance to introduce me to the infamous Maisie, who I've heard so much about," as they were preparing to leave. When they reached the village green, the match was over, but all those involved – the village team, and their opponents from one of the neighbouring villages, with the supporters they had brought - were still there, enjoying the refreshments. Joe had been playing; Maisie had been helping with the cricket tea. Laura had spotted her immediately, her dark hair shining and her ready laugh reaching them across the grass, and she had taken James over to meet her.

"Maisie – this is James. James, Maisie." Laura felt an absurd sense of pride in introducing the man she loved to the woman she felt she could now call her closest friend.

The pair shook hands and smiled at each other.

"It's very good to meet you at last - I have heard a great deal about you, from this one here!" said James, warmly, his left arm encircling his wife's trim waist.

"And I could use those exact words to you!" laughed Maisie. "You do know, I hope, how fortunate you are in your adoring wife, who I have never known say anything remotely critical about her husband! And I can say with certainty that she wouldn't be able to say the same of me!" Maisie cast a baleful look in Joe's direction. He was guffawing with some of his fellow players, and the beer was flowing freely, Laura could see.

"How did the cricket match go?" asked James.

"It went well, I'd say – it was a close one, but we won. And, as we all know, it's the winning, not the taking part, that matters!"

"I wondered about asking to join the team. Do you think they'd welcome that?"

"I'm sure they would – they're always on the look out for fresh players, and you look younger and fitter than about half of them! Laura tells me you're naturally good at most sports, so I'd say they'll snatch your hand off if you make the offer."

Laura felt pleased that Maisie had remembered her words about James's facility for sport, and she knew James was gratified by the compliment. She looked at the cricket tea which Maisie had laid out and felt she should offer her support.

"Can I help with anything?" offered Laura, gesturing at the refreshment table.

"No – I think all is in hand. Let me pass you something – sandwiches? Cake? A cup of tea, perhaps? Or I could grab you a couple of cold beers?"

"Actually, cold beer on this warm day might just hit the spot. What do you think, Laura?"

"That would be perfect. I'll see if I can find us a couple of seats in the shade. Do you want to bring the drinks over?"

And Laura located an empty bench under one of the trees that edged the village green and settled to wait for James to come across. He took his time, chatting to Maisie for a while before he appeared with the beer. And Laura was pleased – pleased that the two seemed to get on, that Maisie appreciated her wonderful husband and that James appeared to approve of her choice of friend.

James and Maisie had met again at the summer fete a few weeks later. Laura had been busy on that occasion, running a cake stall to raise funds for the church. She had done a lot of the baking herself, but had also collected contributions from several of the women in the village, and was now selling slices of cake, scones and home-made biscuits, to accompany the tea that Maisie was providing at the stall next to her. Each of them was relieved by another villager at some point in the afternoon so that they could have a break, and Laura felt a twinge of disappointment that Maisie chose to take her break at a different time from her own rest period. She caught sight of Maisie laughing with James at the coconut shy on the far side of the green. Again, Laura felt a warm pleasure at the knowledge that her husband and her friend were getting on so well.

When Maisie returned to her stall she said, cheerfully, to Laura, "I really like James, Laura. You are lucky – a youthful, handsome husband who very clearly dotes on you."

Laura blushed and smiled. "I do appreciate him. I sometimes wonder why he picked a shy little thing like me; I feel positively mouse-like next to him – and next to you, in fact."

Maisie gave her an odd look.

"Why do you run yourself down, Laura? You are beautiful – don't you know that? You have bone structure to die for, blonde hair that doesn't come out of a bottle, and you're slender and graceful. You also have multiple talents – I certainly couldn't bake cakes like this, for a start, and Sally is always falling over herself to tell me that you are the BEST teacher, as she puts it. James is lucky to have you. Yes – thruppence a cup. Two cups, is it?" and Maisie turned to her next customer, leaving Laura thinking about her words.

All this came back to Laura with painful clarity as she spread out the notes on the kitchen table. She read them carefully, using the various cues to put them into some kind of chronological order. Remembering this afterwards she was unsure at what point she decided she needed to put them back into the drawer in the right places, with the last note, still to be read by James, on the top, for him to discover and read when he came home the following day.

Fitting it all together, Laura realised that James must have arranged to meet Maisie when he was, supposedly, walking Angus. Their affair had been brief, intense, passionate. It had started not long after the summer fete, she discovered. They had been together on the night of the Harvest Festival – James was not at The Plough, as Maisie was not in the village hall. Persuading Joe to appoint Clara to help in the shop was a strategy for buying Maisie a little extra time to be with James, Laura learnt.

"Stone House..." Laura murmured. That was their refuge, the deserted building where Old Jack Jensen had lived alone, the baby from The Vicarage in 1900 who became the recluse Maisie remembered from her childhood. Stone House offered a space where James and Maisie could be intimate and private, giving a degree of shelter from the elements, and from village eyes. They started to meet there shortly after James brought Angus into their home.

"How could I not know?" Laura asked herself. "When he came from her arms into our bed? Am I so stupid that I didn't suspect anything – didn't detect something? Why didn't I find his eagerness to take Angus out alone odd? And, now I think about it, why didn't it strike me how suddenly alert he was when I started to talk about possible trouble between Maisie and Joe? He must have been suddenly worried that Joe was suspicious. But I was blissfully unaware. So trusting. I made it easy for them."

James must have discovered the hidden drawer when he was painting the dresser but he had said nothing to Laura about it – the affair having already begun by this time, James must have seen this as a clever hiding place for their exchanged messages, Maisie letting herself into the house when Laura was at the school using their hidden key. The likelihood of Laura discovering the drawer must have been deemed remote – though perhaps this all added to the frisson. James kept all of Maisie's messages in there, rather than disposing of them once they had been read – revisiting them must have been thrilling, detailing, as they did, the depth of her feeling for him and the excitement of their meetings. Arrangements for the next meeting were made. James would leave a reply and Maisie would, Laura presumed, collect it. Maisie must, then, have had a corresponding stash of letters from him. Perhaps Joe had found them? Or did Maisie confess? Was she troubled by her conscience in a way that James, clearly, wasn't? Laura realised that she would probably never know how Joe had discovered what had been happening. What she did know is that exposing the couple, including telling Laura, wasn't an option for Joe. Fleeing the country with his family was the route he had chosen.

And what about her? What route would she now choose? Laura, sitting at the table after Ben had left, reading the messages, filling in the blanks and then considering her options, took far less time than she might have expected before she rose, and carefully returned all the pieces of paper to the drawer, with Maisie's last letter, explaining Joe's discovery and his insistence that they move out immediately, on top. In this letter Maisie explained that she had no choice. Joe was her husband, she had three children. James had his own responsibilities, and they had no future together. Presumably they had both known that this was a dalliance, thrilling and enjoyable, but not a prelude to divorce and a new life together. Would James grieve when he read that Maisie had left – not just him, but her life in the village, Laura wondered, or would he be in some way relieved? Might he confess to Laura, and admit the truth of what had happened?

Laura reflected that that was unlikely. "He has a greater capacity for deception than I ever realised," Laura thought. And she discovered that this was a capacity they shared.

If she were not pregnant – though Laura felt sure that she was – would she take the same steps? Laura didn't know. She was only sure that she would keep the secret. She would welcome James home the next day and share the dramatic news of the Hamiltons' sudden departure. When she was out of the house – she would call on Eileen and Harry, she decided, to give James the opportunity – he would read the last note from Maisie and piece together the puzzle. She expected he would say nothing to her when she returned. Normality would resume.

In due course Laura would bear their child, and perhaps further children in the years to come. She would be loving and dutiful, but, remembering James' exclamation when they sat in the garden in the summer: "This is idyllic!" Laura realised that she would never feel that depth of happiness again.

PART III: 1945:

Chapter Seventeen: *it's grand to see you safe and well*

When Jack Jensen and the rest of his battalion were demobbed, he was aware of how keen his army buddies were to return home. He felt differently. He had no family in the village where he lived - his two elder sisters had moved away as soon as they could, and Jack seldom saw them – and he had no close friends. But he realised he lacked the imagination to envisage any existence other than taking up residence once more in Stone House, and resuming his old life. The village was, at least, the place where his memories lived, and those memories had become increasingly precious to him over the years.

There was one living creature, he realised, who might be pleased to see him. His border collie, Tom, had been little more than a puppy when Jack enlisted. He had hesitantly approached a couple in the village, realising how much he hated to seek help from anyone, to ask if they would consider taking on the dog while he was overseas. He had no idea how long that would be, he explained. But Harry Jameson – who had always been friendly and made a fuss of the puppy when he met Jack out walking - had readily agreed, and Eileen and their daughter welcomed Tom into their home with warmth and enthusiasm.

As Jack remembered this on the long, uncomfortable and crowded train journey home, he thought, ruefully, "Perhaps Tom won't be pleased to see me. Perhaps he won't even remember me!" and he slumped into his seat and closed his eyes.

The army had given his life a structure and a purpose which, despite the privations and, at times, the fear, Jack had found comforting. He discovered in his dealings with his comrades an ease which recalled his relationship with his elder brothers during their childhood in The Vicarage – an ease which he had somehow lost in the dark years following the Great War. But he felt he knew all along that his time in the army was only an interlude and that, once the war was over, his life would settle back into a familiar groove. Jack was 46 years old. But he felt like an old man.

He hoped he could pick up his work as the local odd job and handyman. He would take Tom for long walks in the surrounding countryside, and along the river, each day – whatever the weather. He would smoke his pipe in the evenings, sitting by the fire, often reading, the dog resting at his feet. He needed little. His work brought him sufficient to meet his modest requirements. Often local farmers and villagers paid him in produce, home-cooked food and goods he could make use of, so he had little use for cash. The puppy had, in fact, been received in part payment from a farmer for whom he had done some labouring in harvest season. Jack's previous dog – an elderly border collie, also called Tom – had curled up at his feet by the fire one evening and never awoke.

So life would resume its natural rhythms. He would work, feed himself and his dog, walk, smoke, read, rest – and he would remember.

Jack called to collect Tom from Harry and Eileen's cottage as soon as he arrived in the village, his kit bag slung over his shoulder, his army greatcoat enveloping him, and still feeling grimy from the long journey. Harry was clearly pleased to see him, shaking his hand warmly and speaking heartily.

"Welcome home! It's grand to see you safe and well."

Eileen beamed at him, and their daughter, Susan, looked out shyly at him from behind her mother's skirts. Tom – no longer a puppy – watched him steadily, but when Jack crouched down, the dog approached him cautiously, sniffed and then licked his hand, and his tail began to wag slowly in recognition. Jack felt his spirits lift a little.

"Will you stay and have a bite to eat with us?" asked Eileen. "You'll have nothing in the house, and Hamiltons' shop will be closed at this time. You'll need to take your ration book if you call there tomorrow, but, tonight, I've baked a pie, and there's plenty. Stay."

Jack always found social situations uncomfortable, and had grown accustomed to avoiding them at every opportunity in recent years, but he was conscious of not seeming rude, especially to this family who had been so accommodating. The kitchen was warm, and he could smell the pie in the range. As if prompting him, his stomach chose that moment to rumble loudly, and the little girl laughed, which helped Jack to relax.

"That's kind of you, missus. If it won't be any trouble, it would be a comfort to me to accept your hospitality," and Jack gave a short nod. He removed his greatcoat and stored it by the door with his kitbag. Tom followed him, and Jack reached out to rub the dog's ears.

As they ate, the Jameson family chatted, and did not seem disconcerted that Jack himself had little to say. Harry – who was in a reserved occupation – knew that asking returning soldiers about their experiences was not a sensitive thing to do, though he was certainly curious and, when those who were now returning to the village were keen to talk about all they had seen and done, he was eager to encourage them, and he would listen, rapt. Now he watched Jack carefully while Eileen and Susan served the food, as they chatted about inconsequential things. "He will never talk about the war," Harry reflected. "He is a private person and will not readily share such information. How well will he adapt to village life again?" Harry looked forward to talking this through with Eileen later that evening. He trusted her insights and her judgement. She understood people.

Jack asked no questions at any stage of the evening, but the family recognised that he might be interested in what had happened in the village during his absence, and this fuelled the conversation.

"Reverend Bailey has been badly," Eileen told him, "and so he hasn't been able to take church services in recent weeks. Reverend Morris has been coming over from Anderling to take them. There's talk that when Reverend Bailey passes on..." Eileen paused, wondering whether this was a fitting thing to say to Jack, whose own father, Reverend Bailey's predecessor, had died when she was a girl, still performing his duties every Sunday until a stroke took him. Eileen caught Harry's eye, but he nodded shortly and she resumed, "When that happens, it may be that Reverend Morris takes over responsibility for both parishes, they say, so we won't have a minister of our own. I wonder whether The Vicarage would be left empty, then, or whether it might be sold as a private house. It was your home for some years, I think?"

Jack nodded. He hesitated, and then, faltering, volunteered something of his own, speaking softly. "It was. I have happy memories of living there with my brothers and sisters when my father was alive."

"Have you been into the house in recent years?" asked Harry.

"I have. I've done a few jobs for the Baileys from time to time, working in the garden and such. And…"

The family waited.

"..there's a dresser in the kitchen – a dresser that's as old as I am. It's fixed to the wall, or my mother would have wanted to take it with us when we moved out after my father's death. I have no memory of it being built – I was but a baby. It's just been there all my life. My mother loved that dresser, and whenever I have had call to visit The Vicarage I have liked to check up on it."

Jack smiled faintly, and then lapsed into silence. This was the longest speech he remembered making for some time.

The Jamesons knew Jack's family's sad history, something they would also talk through later, lying in their bed in the darkness, when Eileen would say, "I wish we could do more for him, Harry. He has had such a difficult life, and he seems a thoughtful, gentle man." And she was grateful that, at least, he had taken some warmth, sustenance and, perhaps, comfort from them that evening.

Jack had thanked them shyly when he came to take his leave, with Tom not hesitating to go with him, and trotting companionably by his side as they walked down the path and into the street. Harry, Eileen and Susan stood together, framed in the bright doorway.

"Please come back and visit soon!" Eileen called, and Jack raised his hand in acknowledgement.

The route to Stone House took them past The Old Vicarage, and Jack paused at the gate and looked at the house. He could see a faint light in an upstairs room – no doubt where Reverend Bailey lay, ailing. Jack remembered his interactions with Mrs Bailey – a waspish, pinched woman. He had worked in their kitchen garden over the years, tending the vegetables, building and burning bonfires, repairing the wall at the far end of the plot. He would stand in the kitchen doorway to receive his instructions, or his payment, but he never made it further than the threshold, and Mrs Bailey never invited him in, never offered him refreshment (even a drink of water on a baking hot day), or, in fact, a kind word. But from the doorway he could see the dresser.

Jack remembered it from his childhood, cared for and regularly polished by his mother and his sisters. As a small boy, he had been fascinated by the carved fieldmouse at its base. The dresser seemed to have a glow, he remembered. Pretty china graced the shelves – china which now lay in the cupboards of his own home, unused. The kitchen at Stone House was not large enough to have accommodated the dresser, even had it been possible to move it when they left The Vicarage back in 1920. But whenever Jack had had the opportunity, he would check that it was still there – battered and unloved, now, but still standing strong.

Jack recalled when the Baileys had arrived in the village, a few weeks after his father had died. His mother had thrown herself into cleaning their home thoroughly, leaving everything spic and span for the incoming family. Martha and Betsy, now married and living with their own families in other places, had both returned to help her. Jack had worked tidying up the garden, and he had given the gate a fresh coat of paint.

When the Baileys arrived, Revered Bailey meek and wordless, Mrs Bailey straight-backed and formal, and two young boys who looked cowed and terrified, Alice had tried to be helpful and welcoming. Mrs Bailey, Jack remembered, simply sniffed and looked sour. Jack knew the boys had left home as soon as they could, and he didn't remember seeing them ever visit. Now Reverend Bailey was in decline, and Mrs Bailey, he suspected, would be as cold and bitter as ever. Once her husband passed, she would have to leave The Vicarage, as Alice had done 25 years before. He wondered where she would go – perhaps to one of her long-suffering sons. He doubted either would be pleased to take her in. He remembered the discussion about where he and Alice might go, in 1920. Martha and Betsy had each offered them a home, in a spirit of affection, rather than duty, he thought. But Alice had always been independent, Stone House was empty, and affordable, and Jack and his mother settled there.

"I would find it hard to leave the village," Alice had told him, and Jack knew she was thinking of her husband's grave in the churchyard, and the small headstone nearby which was then 20 years old. Alice still regularly put fresh flowers on Molly's grave, and now she did the same with Edward's.

"I will join Edward there when my time comes," she had told Jack, taking his arm as they walked slowly away from the churchyard.

Neither of them knew how quickly Alice's health would deteriorate, and how she would join Edward within two years.

"Come, boy!" Jack called, and man and dog made their way through the village lanes to their home, which lay on the very edge of the village – dark, cold and empty.

Chapter Eighteen: *this is what I really want to do*

A week after Jack's return to the village, he sat reading by the fire, pulling on his pipe, with Tom stretched out on the rag rug at his feet, luxuriating in the heat. The curtains were drawn against the night and the lamp glowed. There was a sharp rap on the door.

Jack seldom had visitors, but if one of his neighbours had a job for him, this was where they knew they would find him each evening. He rose heavily to his feet, and opened the door to see a young man standing on the doorstep, rather nervously, it seemed, as he shifted from one foot to the other. Jack peered out into the gloom.

"I'm sorry to disturb you, Mr Jensen. It's Ben Winters – I'm Dora Winters' son."

Jack remembered the young man, who he recalled had joined the navy at the outbreak of the war. His mother Dora was Jack's age, and he had known her since they were children together, walking along the riverbank to the small school in the next village. He knew she had lost her husband some years back. Perhaps if Dora had work for him, she had sent her son to give him the message. He said nothing, but waited for Ben to explain.

"I wondered – do you think – could I come in?"

The young man *was* nervous, Jack realised. He remained silent, but he opened the door more widely and stepped back to allow Ben to enter. Ben removed his cap, and clutched it in both hands as he moved into the room.

There was only one chair by the fire, but Jack drew up one of the chairs from the table towards the hearth, and gestured for Ben to sit in it. Tom had raised himself up on his haunches and looked at the visitor with one ear cocked.

Jack settled himself, resumed drawing on his pipe, and looked steadily at Ben.

Ben's mother had warned him that Jack was a man of few words, when they had discussed this visit and what Ben might say. Ben was, himself, a reticent young man, who did not find conversation easy. But he had thought this through carefully, and determination fuelled him.

"Mr Jensen. I've not long been home after serving in the navy. I learnt a lot while I was away, and it gave me plenty of time to think about what I might do with the rest of my life. I'm 25 now, and I'm my mother's sole support. She won't ever want to leave this village, so this is where I'm bound to stay too. I've never been much of a one for book learning, but I'm good with my hands. I've always had a knack for fixing things, and the navy taught me some new skills. I'm keen to keep learning."

Ben paused briefly, and then continued.

"I've been doing some farm labouring since I left school, and I'm always willing to try my hand at outdoor work – gardening and such. But I'm not so keen on going back to labouring. What I really enjoy is work like yours – mending and fixing, like."

Ben fell silent and took a deep breath. Jack had not reacted in any way to anything he had said so far and, looking into Jack's dark eyes, Ben realised he had no idea what the older man might be thinking. He asked no questions, even as Ben paused to give him the opportunity to do so. He showed no particular interest, and the younger man's spirits sank a little.

"I know you've always worked on your own, and my mother was very clear that if I wanted to set myself up doing odd jobs in the village, I would need your blessing – I'm not trying to take any work from you. But – and this is my thinking, not hers – I'd like more than your blessing. I'd like your help – to teach me, so I can keep learning and getting better at what I do. What I'd really like is a kind of partnership where we can work together. You can give me any jobs you don't want to do, but I thought I could be, I suppose, sort of an apprentice..."

At this word, Jack looked up sharply, and his eyes seemed to grow even darker, Ben thought. Was that somehow the wrong thing to say? He rushed on.

"I know this might not be what you would have chosen – you like your own company, and I can respect that. But I promise I'm a good, steady worker. I wouldn't complain, or demand anything except to work alongside you and watch you and learn..." Ben realised that was a word he kept coming back to. It was what motivated him – to develop his skills, and to build his craft by close association with someone whose talents far exceeded his own at this stage.

Jack looked into the fire, as memories momentarily flooded him. Then he inhaled deeply. Ben decided it was his turn to wait, quietly. To give Jack time to think, and respond when he was ready. The younger man did not feel hopeful, but he felt he could say no more to put his case. He found himself gripping the arms of his chair tightly. Tom had edged towards him, and Ben put out one hand and gently touched the top of the dog's soft head. Jack watched the gesture, and thought. Finally he spoke.

"What about a trial? We work alongside each other for a month, and see how we get on?"

Ben exhaled – and only then did he realise he had been holding his breath.

"That would be – I'm so grateful, Mr Jensen. I promise you won't regret taking a punt on me. I'll work hard..."

"It's a trial, Ben. If either of us decide we're not happy with the arrangement, we can end it in a month. I'm working at Hamiltons' shop tomorrow, putting up some shelves for them. I'll see you there at 7am sharp." Jack rose to his feet, and Ben did the same. Ben thrust out his hand.

"Thank you - thank you. I'd like to shake your hand, sir. You won't regret it..." Ben's voice petered out, as he realised he'd already said that, and remembering his mother's advice: "Jack Jensen is a man of few words, my boy, and he's not so keen on others rattling on, so be sure you don't ramble, which you're apt to do when you're nervous."

Jack accepted the handshake and moved towards the door, a clear sign that the discussion was over.

"And one thing, Ben."

"Anything…"

"Mr Jensen will do – no need to call me sir."

"Yes, Mr Jensen. Thank you, Mr Jensen."

Ben stepped out into the night, put on his cap and turned back, but the door was already firmly closed. He smiled broadly as he walked home, turning over in his mind how he would describe the conversation to his mother.

Jack sat down again, but he did not pick up his pipe, or his book. He did not register that Tom was wagging his tail and hoping to be stroked. Jack looked into the flames, and thought back to two conversations – two of his most powerful memories – from the year before the start of the Great War.

The first was with Tom Weatherbury. Jack knew that Tom had built their dresser. He had admired Tom's craftsmanship throughout his childhood, and the local carpenter always had a friendly word for the lad when he saw him around the village. Like Ben, Jack had always been good with his hands, and far keener to make and mend things than to study, although he enjoyed stories – initially hearing them, usually from his mother, and later reading for himself. He was a bright boy, quick to learn, and eager to emulate whatever Matthew and Benjamin were interested in and experimenting with. It was hard to keep up with boys – now young men – five years his senior, but Jack never gave up trying. The twins had found employment – together, inevitably – with the local smith, where they worked with energy and enthusiasm.

As the time approached for Jack to leave school and to embark on some area of work of his own, he would look at the dresser and reflect on how much satisfaction he would gain from being able to construct such pieces himself. Whenever he managed to get hold of a small piece of wood, he would try to carve something – the penknife his parents had given him was his most treasured possession – and the fieldmouse on the dresser was the first model he attempted to replicate.

He knew Tom had an ailing wife and no children. He also knew that Tom had learnt his craft from his own father and that, had his life turned out differently, Tom would have prepared his own sons for the carpentry trade.

"Why should he not train me?" Jack wondered.

In the spring of 1913, shortly before Jack left the village school, he sought Tom out, with the intention of engaging him in conversation on the topic.

Tom was working at Home Farm, repairing a plough, when Jack tracked him down. The boy sat on a nearby wall, watching Tom work for some time, admiring his skill, confidence and patience. Tom was initially absorbed in his work and unaware of the boy, but eventually he looked up and caught his eye.

"Well, young man. And what are you up to?"

"Watching you."

"I have no objection to that, though I would have thought you had more entertaining options on a bright spring Saturday. Was there something you wanted?"

Jack took a deep breath.

"I want to learn from you. I want to be a carpenter, like you, and to make the kinds of things you make - like our dresser. I like to mend things, too. I thought, perhaps, when I leave school, I could be some sort of apprentice..."

Tom looked at the boy without speaking for several seconds.

"Have you talked to your mother – your parents about this?"

"Not yet. I wanted to ask you, first. I know – I think – that they have to give you some money to take me on and teach me. That's what happened with Matthew and Benjamin and the smith. But I have to do something, and this is what I really want to do."

It seemed, in fact, so simple.

Tom scratched his head.

"I want you to go home along, now, Jack. And I want you to talk to your mother and father, and see what they think."

"But are you saying yes?"

"I'm not saying no. But the Reverend and Mrs Jensen will have to give the plan their approval, and I'm not sure... well, ask them, and then, if they want to discuss it further, they can come and see me."

Jack leapt down from the wall, his spirits soaring. He could see no reason why his parents would not agree. He had just a few short weeks of school and then, come the summer, he could be with Tom – alongside him in his workshop, out and about doing carpentry work in this village and the neighbouring villages. Repairing, constructing, creating – and learning. He would have a skill, a respected craft, a purpose. One day, perhaps, when Tom was ready to step back – he was, of course, thirty years older than Jack – the apprentice might become the master carpenter, with his own workshop, his own business, even his own apprentice. Jack couldn't stop smiling as he ran back to The Vicarage.

But the second conversation Jack relived, as he sat by the fire, was very different.

When he arrived home his mother was out, and his father was on his regular parish visits. He sat in the kitchen, looking at the dresser: polished, fragrant, perfect, he thought, and waited for their return.

Alice came in first, placed her shopping on the table, and smiled at him.

"I thought you'd be out, Jack – it's unlike you to be indoors on a fine day."

"I have been out..." Jack knew that he should perhaps wait until his father was home and speak to his parents together, but he was too excited to wait. "I've been to find Mr Weatherbury and to ask him if he'd take me on as an apprentice when I finish school and teach me the carpentry trade. And he hasn't said no. He just told me to talk to you and father about it and, if you agree, you can meet him to talk it through. I know you have to reach an agreement with him, and I don't quite understand how that works, but it must be like the twins and the smith and..."

"Stop!"

Jack became aware that his mother was standing with her hands over her ears and a pained expression on her unusually pale face.

"Jack. It's out of the question. We will find you an apprenticeship if that is what you hope for, but not with – with Tom Weatherbury. There are things you don't know - things I can't talk about, but it concerns…"

Alice was unable to go on. Jack was mystified, and horrified. He saw his hopes and dreams for the future wither and die in his mother's expression and tone.

"It concerns Molly's death. A punishment…"

Alice turned to her son, and he saw her eyes were full of tears.

There's no hope. Jack realised. Alice never talked about Molly's death. Whatever the problem was - and he realised he might never know the detail – there was clearly no way forward from it. He rose slowly, and walked to where Alice stood, shaking and sobbing. The boy took his mother in his arms and held her until she quietened.

Neither of them spoke to his father about the idea, and Jack never again talked of it to Tom. Tom's silence on the subject reflected his understanding that this formal connection between him and the family at The Old Vicarage could never happen. Jack found work as a local handyman. After Tom's death, in the absence of a local carpenter, Jack realised he had, in fact, become the first person the villagers turned to for all kinds of repair work and odd jobs, but he never learnt how to create something as beautiful as the dresser.

Jack looked up. The collie whimpered and Jack reached out to stroke his soft fur.

"So now I have an apprentice of my own, boy. I never became a carpenter, but at least I have a skill I can pass on."

And he rose and stepped out into the night for one last walk, with the dog – another Tom, a name he had chosen for his border collie companions only after Alice's death - trotting at his heels.

Chapter Nineteen: *too much death*

Ben was already waiting outside Hamiltons' shop when Jack arrived shortly before 7am. He looked pinched with cold, and Jack wondered how long he'd been standing there.

"I can't fault his keenness," he mused. There was something about Ben's pent-up enthusiasm that reminded the older man of the puppy he had left with the Jamesons. He reached down and scratched Tom's ears. "You wait here, boy," he said in a low voice, and the collie, used to lying patiently outside wherever Jack happened to be working, settled down on his haunches near the shop doorway.

Jack and Ben spent the morning in the shop and its storeroom, Ben watching intently while Jack worked on the shelving; Jack giving him tasks to do whenever it was appropriate. Joe Hamilton, the shopkeepers' son, hovered in the doorway for the first half an hour, trying to engage Ben in conversation – Jack recognised that Joe and Ben were a similar age and had known each other since they were boys. But Ben was focussed on watching and learning, and eventually Joe retreated sulkily into the back room.

"They're very different characters," Jack reflected. Ben had enlisted in the navy as soon as he was able to; Joe had stayed at home with some unspecified medical condition, according to his parents. Joe always appeared ungracious and reluctant when the Hamiltons set him to work in the shop or making deliveries. Ben was clearly eager to work and to build his skills.

Ben was careful, this morning, to keep quiet as far as he could, to give Jack time to concentrate, and in recognition of the fact that Jack clearly valued silence. Occasionally Ben asked a question, and Jack gave a succinct and careful response.

"He asks the right things," Jack thought to himself, and by mid-morning, when the pair stopped for a short break and accepted the cups of tea Mrs Hamilton brought them, Jack was feeling cautiously positive about the chances of the arrangement with Ben being successful.

By midday the work there was done. Jack had brought a slice of cold meat pie, which he shared with Tom, and he was pleased to see Ben had also brought provisions with him. They sat on one of the benches by the village green and ate in a companionable silence. Jack had envisaged sending Ben home after the work at the shop, but he looked sidelong at the young man now and made a decision.

"I have work to do in the churchyard this afternoon – tidying the grave plots. Would you be minded to come with me, and help? This isn't paid work – just something I do for the village."

Ben's face brightened.

"It's as if I'd offered him a gift," Jack thought.

"Thank you, Mr Jensen. I'd be honoured to help. I wonder – should I call at home and pick up some gardening tools? Shears and such?"

"A good idea." Ben glowed at the praise. "We ought to be thinking about you putting together a tool bag," Jack nudged his own collection of tools which sat in a well-worn canvas bag at his feet. "You'll be needing your own gear."

The two lapsed again into silence, Ben mentally running through the tools he knew his father had left in the shed, and which he could clean up and make good use of.

"I'll meet you at the churchyard, will I?" Ben said after a pause, and Jack nodded.

The older man rose slowly to his feet, and whistled to Tom.

"We'll take a walk, first, and I'll see you there come one o'clock," and Jack and Tom turned away, Ben watching their steady progress and wondering whether he, too, might have a dog at some point.

As he walked along the country lanes, with Tom constantly tearing ahead and then running enthusiastically back towards him, Jack gathered greenery and berries from the hedgerows. It was his custom to leave an offering by his parents' graves, and Molly's – whatever he could find, according to the season. His mother had grown flowers, alongside vegetables, in the garden of The Vicarage, and in a small patch of land at the back of Stone House, so that she could do the same, every week, until she became too unwell, and in her final weeks she had become agitated that the graves might be neglected. Jack had reassured her that he would always tend them.

As Alice became less lucid as the end approached, she rambled increasingly, and Jack had sat by her bed, offering what comfort he could and listening to the scraps of remembered conversations and inner dialogue his mother unwittingly shared. Often her words made little sense, but occasionally a phrase struck him, and had remained with him still.

"Too much death," was one refrain. "This is my punishment," was another.

Jack's memories both comforted and troubled him. Living alone, working alone, with Tom's companionship but few opportunities for dialogue with other people, he recognised how much time he spent replaying the past in his head. Perhaps working with Ben would help him to live more in the present, he thought.

Ben was already in the churchyard when Jack and Tom approached, and had made a start on trimming the grass around some of the oldest gravestones with a pair of newly sharpened shears. He looked up, flushed, and a little hesitant.

"I hope it's all right to be doing this?"

Jack nodded, and then turned towards the section of the graveyard where his parents were laid to rest. He wondered whether Ben had deliberately chosen to start at the other side, leaving those family grave markers for his own attention.

'Reverend Edward Jensen, who served this parish faithfully from 1900 to 1920. Born 1850, departed this life October 1920, aged 70'

'Alice May Jensen, beloved wife of Edward, 1873 to 1922'

Jack cleaned up the stones and left his offerings of berries and greenery. Then he turned to the small headstone nearby, which marked the grave of Molly Elizabeth Jensen, aged 4.

Jack had no memory of Molly, which saddened him. Growing up, he had heard often from his mother about how well Molly had cared for him.

"She was such a little girl herself, but she tended you like a mother. She was the one who could settle you when you were fractious, and she never tired of playing with you, and chatting to you. She used to say she wanted to be a teacher – and she would have made a good one, I am absolutely sure. She was excited about starting school. She would quiz Martha and Betsy all the time about what they were learning, and she would say that as soon as she learnt to read she would read stories to you."

Talking of Molly always made Alice smile, and the boy Jack would ask questions to encourage her to keep talking, and smiling.

The family had one, faded family photograph – a little worn round the edges from so much handling. It showed the full family group, formally posed, and unsmiling, as was the custom. Edward and Alice were seated in the centre, baby Jack on Alice's knee. Molly was holding Edward's hand. Martha and Betsy stood together behind their father, and Matthew and Benjamin – indistinguishable in this photograph to Jack, which delighted the twins - behind their mother. Jack would gaze into Molly's eyes, and then he would close his own and will himself to remember her.

He tended the small gravestone now – 45 years old, and weathered, but still clearly legible, thanks to the ministrations of Alice, and then Jack, in his turn.

Jack knew that one day he would be laid to rest here, too. Who would tend the grave after his death, he wondered? Martha and Betsy were settled with their families at some distance away and never returned to visit the village now, although they both wrote to Jack from time to time, as Jack had written to tell them he was returning home. And then Jack looked up and caught sight of Ben labouring away at the far end of the churchyard and it suddenly struck him that Ben was the one who would continue his work, and care for these graves, after Jack's passing. Helping Ben to establish himself and to develop his craft was a kind of investment in the future – something Jack had never considered before.

"I live too much in the past," he told himself.

He remembered his conversation with Martha and Betsy as they had walked away from their mother's newly dug grave, and made their way slowly back to Stone House.

"This might sound fanciful," Martha began, carefully, "but I've given this some thought. I expect it's mother's passing that has made me realise it. I've told Jacob and the children that, when I die, I'd like to be brought back here and buried in the plot with our parents – close to Molly, and to the war memorial, which is all we have of Matthew and Benjamin."

Betsy turned to her with a watery smile. "Not fanciful at all. I should like the same thing when the time comes. The village, and especially the church, have a pull on me, somehow. Jack – can you arrange this for us?"

Jack rubbed his hand across his brow.

"Too much death..." he said, and the girls looked quizzically at him. "It's something mother used to say – often – in the last days. But of course I will see to it – unless I go before you..." and the sisters, each side of him, took his arms in theirs as they continued on their way.

Jack became aware of Ben hovering near him, unwilling to disturb him but eager to tell Jack what he had done and to ask for any further instructions. Jack levered himself to his feet.

"There's one more grave I like to give special attention to," he said, and made his way to another headstone, Ben following on his heels and Tom watching from under the yew where he had settled.

"In loving memory of a devoted wife, Mary Anne Weatherbury," Ben read aloud, "departed this life 23rd May 1914, aged 42."

Jack rubbed at the stone, and tidied around it. He waited for Ben to ask who she was, but Ben kept silent, respecting his privacy, perhaps.

"He will tell me if he wants me to know," Ben thought.

Jack said nothing, but he could still see Tom's drawn face as he stood at his wife's graveside. Mary had never been well, as far back as Jack could remember. She didn't appear to suffer from any particular illness, but she never left her cottage, and for the last year of her life he was told she hadn't left her bed. She faded away, it seemed. Tom was always mindful and solicitous where his wife was concerned, and a deep sadness appeared to settle on him after her death. Jack could still hear his father intoning the solemn words of the service, his mother standing, pale, at his side. He bowed his head for a moment – not a prayer, exactly. Jack had lost his faith a long time ago. A sign of respect, perhaps. Then he rose to his feet.

He turned to Ben. "You've done a good job today," he said, gruffly. "You go home along now. Come to the house tomorrow morning and show me your tools and we'll see what else you need."

"Thank you, Mr Jensen. I'll be there bright and early!" and Ben picked up his father's gardening tools and made for home, eager to tell his mother all about his day.

Jack looked over at the collie, who immediately ran to join him, his tail beating vigorously.

"One more stop, boy," said Jack, and the pair moved off.

They made their way home by way of the village green, and Jack spent the last part of his day giving attention to the war memorial, ensuring it was clear of moss.

He touched his brothers' names gently, before running his fingers down to the last name on the list.

The war had broken out not long after Mary Weatherbury's death, and Tom had been among the first to enlist, closing up his cottage and leaving several villages without a master carpenter, although Jack was, by this time, building his reputation as a young man who could turn his hand to any kind of repair work, and villagers would turn to him in Tom's absence. The twins had enlisted too, and The Vicarage rang with their excited chatter about the adventure that lay ahead.

Jack sought out Tom to say goodbye.

"Why are you going?" Jack blurted out. "Aren't you too old?"

Tom couldn't help giving a short laugh at Jack's candour – and, as he did so, he realised that it was the first laugh to escape him for a long time.

"I am old, young man. But I'm skilled. They're talking of constructing wooden trenches to fight from. I'm a master carpenter, remember?"

"I remember," Jack said sombrely, and both of them recalled, though did not mention, the conversation in which Jack had described his dream of one day being able to say the same.

"Matthew and Benjamin will be in France, too," Jack offered. "They have their blacksmith skills – will they be able to use them?"

"I expect they will - we're shipping out horses, so there will be a call for smiths, I'm sure. But they are also young and strong, I know."

Tom hesitated, but then continued, "I'm glad you won't be with them."

"I'm not glad!" Jack burst out, with an uncharacteristic show of temper. "I wish I were going! I wish I were older. They say the war may be over by Christmas. I hope not. I hope it lasts long enough for me to join up and fight – alongside my brothers and with you!" Jack was ashamed of the tears that had sprung to his eyes, tears of vexation, more than anything else.

Tom spoke calmly.

"I understand how you feel, son. But I'm sure that your mother will find having you at home a comfort. She will worry about Matthew and Benjamin."

Jack was quiet for a few moments, and then he looked up at Tom, his eyes still shining.

"Would you – would you perhaps write to me? The twins say they will, but I bet they don't. And if you tell me where you are, I'll write back and tell you about all that's happening in the village. Though I don't expect much *will* be happening with everyone gone."

Tom was thoughtful.

"I could write to you – I certainly don't have anyone else to write to. But your mother – your parents might not like it. I'm not family, after all…"

"But you're my friend, aren't you?"

Tom grinned suddenly.

"I am. I've known you since you were a baby, meeting you the first time I ever came to The Vicarage to build the dresser. I would have been proud to have had a son like you, Jack. I will write to you, and, if your parents give it their blessing, I would be very pleased to get letters in return. Now, I'd better be off. Look after yourself – and look after your mother. Remember she will need you to be especially loving while the twins are away."

And Tom shouldered his bag, and turned to walk towards the village hall, where the transportation was due to arrive shortly. Jack watched him go, feeling a hard knot in his stomach. He hoped Tom would return on leave at some stage, but he never did. True to his word, Tom wrote to Jack periodically throughout the war years, and Jack kept all his letters, treasuring each one, especially the final one, dated shortly before Tom's death in 1918.

He turned away from the war memorial.

"I need to read it again, boy," he muttered to the collie as they made their way back home.

When they returned to Stone House, Jack lit the kindling and coaxed the fire to life. He set down water for Tom, and set the kettle on the stove to make tea for himself. Then he retrieved from his bedroom the box in which he kept Tom's wartime letters.

Jack reread them periodically – it was a treat he savoured. Sometimes he read them all in the order in which he had received them; sometimes he pulled out letters at random and read them out of turn. They told him something of life in the trenches, although Tom was not lavish with the detail. Initially Tom had been mindful that Jack's brothers were experiencing some of the terror he himself was subject to, and he did not feel he wanted to share that with Jack and worry him further. Then, after the boys were killed at Passchendaele in 1917, he was even more careful not to fuel Jack's imagination with images that would surely trouble him.

In fact, in the last year of their correspondence, Tom said very little at all about what was happening in France. He talked instead of his boyhood and growing up in the village, of his life before Jack was born. This was what he wanted to share – the memories which were precious to him. He talked, too, of building the dresser – how Jack's mother had imagined it, and Tom had brought it to life. It was clear that the early autumn of 1900, when he was engaged in this work, was one of the happiest times of his life. The dresser, Jack felt, had benefited from the love Tom had poured into it. And Jack realised that reliving this experience was something from which Tom drew comfort. Jack was painfully aware of the fact that, although he talked much about the past, in none of his letters did Tom refer to the future, to what he might do after the war.

The last letter Tom had sent, dated in the early autumn of 1918, was the most worn and fragile of all the collection. It was the one Jack had taken to war with him, more than twenty years after it was written, and it had been unfolded and refolded many times. Jack handled it gingerly now, opening it up and sitting quietly with the letter on his knee.

He looked down at the dog lying stretched out at his feet, and he spoke softly.

"A letter from your namesake, boy. The last letter he wrote to me – which would have been the last letter he ever wrote in his life, as I know he wrote to no one else. Will I read it to you?"

The collie looked up at Jack, his eyes bright and his tail faintly moving on the rug, as it usually did when the man spoke to him.

Jack adjusted the lamp so that its light fell full on the delicate, discoloured paper. He began in a wavering voice, which grew stronger as he continued to read.

" 'France, 15th September 1918….' He never told me exactly where he was when he wrote – wasn't allowed, see?
'It's night time here, Jack, and quiet, for once. I have been thinking about you and your family for much of the day, and have set aside time to write this now, and saved a candle so that I can see to do it. Your last letter made me smile, as your writing always does – thank you. I enjoy reading about your life and your work in the village. Your letters show how you are making a name for yourself as a capable workman, and I know that will serve you well throughout your life. It was good to hear of Martha's visit, too, with her little one, and when you described the conversation at the kitchen table I could imagine you all there and hear your voices.

I feel in a melancholy mood tonight and want to try to explain how much your letters have meant to me over the years. I know you had to work to persuade your family to give their blessing to us exchanging letters, and I'm grateful you did. It may be hard for you to understand how precious these letters have been. What you write connects me to happier times, and people I think of warmly. And writing to you has helped me to remember, too. When the present is difficult, the past becomes more important.

But some of the things I remember cause me pain, and stir up feelings of guilt. I have thought long and hard about this –

there is plenty of time for thinking, here – and I've finally decided there is a confession I must make to you. It may help you to understand some of the things which have been difficult over the years.

I know I am unburdening myself here, but hope this does not mean that I am burdening you. I have the strong sense that time may be running out, and if I don't tell you this now, you may never know, and the secret will follow me to the grave. What I want to say involves the dresser, your sister Molly, and your mother...' "

Jack paused in his reading and passed his hand over his eyes. He looked into the flames for a few moments, then moved to add more wood to the fire. He bent down to touch the collie's head, and the dog lifted his muzzle to sniff and then lick Jack's hand.

"You know how to comfort me, boy," Jack said quietly, and then picked up the letter again and continued to read.

" 'I grew to know Molly well during the autumn of 1900 when I worked on the dresser. She was a sweet, friendly girl – as you know, a caring sister to you, and always cheerful and talkative when I called at the house. She also enjoyed her secrets, and I was honoured that she shared one of them with me. Since arriving in the village she had collected a number of things she called her treasures. She kept them in an old tin, but before I finished the dresser, as a parting gift to her, I constructed a hidden drawer at its base, and showed Molly how to open it. It became the place where she kept her precious things.

On the night of the flood, I believe Molly came downstairs to rescue these things from the drawer, that she slipped and fell into the water, hitting her head and losing consciousness. For the rest of my life, I will be tortured by the memory of her floating, drowned body, which I held in my arms knowing that if it had not been for my gift, she would have lived.' "

Jack paused again. He remembered the first time he had read these words, and what a torrent of different emotions they had stirred in him. He had read each of Tom's letters sitting on the churchyard wall. His mother had only grudgingly agreed to the correspondence – and Jack still felt guilty about how he had manipulated his parents into that agreement – and as a result he always wrote to Tom, and read Tom's replies, away from The Vicarage so as not to draw further attention to the letter exchange. On reading Tom's account of how Molly came to die, he had moved to sit by her small grave, his eyes misting with tears and blood pounding in his head. He felt angry, distraught, confused. Why was Tom telling him this, and why now? What was he supposed to do with the information?

Jack recalled the emotional turbulence coursing through the eighteen year old boy, and then thought of himself, now, only a few years younger than Tom had been when he had written these words. Over the years, as Jack had grown, suffered, and aged, he had come to a better understanding of why Tom needed to share this confession with him. Jack took a deep breath, and read aloud the last section of the letter.

" 'I will never forget the look of horror on your mother's face when she reached the bottom of the stairs and saw me holding Molly's body. I had to tell her. I had to explain that this was my fault – my responsibility. She couldn't take it in at first. But then she gave the most terrible cry – I still hear it in my dreams, and none of the terrible experiences I have known in France can compare with that. It woke the others and suddenly the kitchen was full of people in the water. Your father took the body from me and I edged to the door. The family closed around Molly, and I felt as if I would be shut out forever.

I think that your friendship towards me has been my salvation. Somehow the spirit of Molly lived on in you – she loved you so much – and because you befriended me I felt in some way forgiven. But brooding on this today I realise I am not forgiven. You did not know the truth and, now you know, I see that you may well want nothing more to do with me.

I don't believe your mother ever shared the truth about the secret drawer with your father and the rest of your family - their relationship with me did not change in the way I am sure it would have done if they'd known. Perhaps she wanted to spare them further pain. But when you asked to be my apprentice, Alice's anger and distress showed me that she would never forgive me.' "

This was the first, and only, time Jack had known Tom to use his mother's name.

" 'If you are also unable to forgive me, I will understand, Jack. But I wanted to be honest. I am surrounded by death, ugliness, pain and fear, here. If there is a time for truth, this is it.

So there is one more truth I must share. I loved your mother, Jack – a deep, life-long love. I never told her, and would never have acted on it. But I love her still. It was a sin, and I have been punished. At least I have found the courage to tell you – her remaining son, her pride – a son any parent would be blessed to have.

Thank you for your friendship. Thank you for hearing me. Tom.' "

Jack had never replied to this letter. Only a few weeks later, the news came through that Tom had been killed. The war ended soon afterwards.

"He's not the only guilty one," Jack muttered to the dog at his feet. "I feel guilty that I didn't write back before he died. That I didn't forgive him..." for Jack realised that forgiveness had come, in time. What had Tom done, after all? He had made a little girl a gift she loved. Fate had done the rest.

Remembering the argument which had taken place in The Vicarage when fourteen year old Jack had told his mother that he and Tom wished to write to each other when Tom was in France troubled him, too. He was already aggrieved that he was too young to enlist, as his brothers had done. He feared that the war would end before he reached the age at which he could do so. Unreasonably, he took out his frustration and anger about this on his mother. He even used it in the argument – the only argument, where angry words were exchanged in loud voices, that he could ever remember in that house.

"I don't understand why you won't allow the letters! What harm is there in that, mother? Tom is my friend and he has always been kind. He made our dresser – you were his friend, too, then. Why are you so upset about this? I can't join the fighting, and now I can't even swap letters with a friend who is out there. You tell Benjamin and Matthew they must write – why is this different? If - if you don't let me do this, I'll – I'll…" Jack had grown more angry and impassioned as the argument had progressed. "I'll run away, and lie about my age, and enlist anyway!"

And he had stormed out of the house, leaving his final words ringing in Alice's ears.

Jack discovered from Betsy, who had overheard the conversation, that his parents had discussed the argument that evening, and that his father was perplexed about why Alice felt so strongly. Edward understood that his wife found it difficult to untangle the family's relationship with Tom Weatherbury from the terrible memory of how Molly had died and Tom had found her, and he had accepted her reluctance where the apprenticeship was concerned. But her reaction with respect to the letter writing seemed disproportionate, and Alice could not find the words to explain and persuade him. So Jack got his way. He never quite got over his feeling of shame at his cruel threat, however.

"We all make mistakes," he murmured to the collie. "Well, perhaps you don't, boy, but I certainly have."

Jack had often wondered over the next few years whether Alice had known about Tom's passion, and whether she had held that against him, too – but not, of course, shared that with her husband. It was only when Alice lay dying, mumbling as a result of the pain and with her grip on reality slipping away, that Jack had listened to some of the things she had said and realised that, in fact, Alice had loved Tom, too. He had never known. Neither of them would ever have acted on their emotions. Like Tom, Jack's mother felt that she had sinned, and that losing Molly was, in some way, a reckoning. It was, he felt, a very sad state of affairs.

Now he folded the letter very carefully, and placed it with the others in the box. He did not fully understand his desire to keep revisiting the correspondence – it was in many ways a painful experience to reread Tom's words, certainly in this final letter. But at the same time, he knew, it was a comforting feeling to reconnect with the past. He loved Tom, too, Jack realised – one reason why, over the years, he had given his different border collies his friend's name.

He looked down at the current recipient.

"Time to sleep, now – we're up early tomorrow, Tom," and the dog followed him, as usual, up the narrow stairs, where it would sleep curled up on the floor at the foot of his bed.

Chapter Twenty-One: *I turn to my memories*

On his way to meet Ben, as they were working at Home Farm together that day, Jack paused at the gateway of The Vicarage. Reverend Bailey, he had heard, was hanging on, but unlikely to live through the winter. Mrs Bailey was seldom seen outside the house, now. Jack, as he had told Harry and Eileen, had kept an eye on the dresser over the years, though since he and his mother had moved out of The Vicarage he had never been able to get close enough to examine it properly.

After receiving Tom's final letter in the autumn of 1918, Jack had waited until he was alone in the kitchen and then knelt on the floor to examine the bottom panels – the one on the left with the running fieldmouse, which formed one of his earliest memories, and the one on the right that looked unexceptional, but when he carefully ran his fingers underneath it, he eventually found the small catch which opened the drawer. Jack remembered now how it had felt as the drawer slid out and its contents were revealed.

He had wondered whether once Tom told Alice about the drawer, she might have removed Molly's possessions herself. But he could see that, if his mother had done that, she had subsequently replaced them, as there his sister's treasures lay. He carefully took them from the drawer and laid them out gently on the floor. Being submerged in flood water had apparently not done much damage to the collection – water had been into the house on more than one occasion since the flood of 1900. Jack examined the objects before him. There was a feather, dusty and discoloured, a couple of buttons, an old farthing – Jack rubbed at it and could faintly make out the date: 1900. He found a glass marble, and cleaned that up, too, to expose a sharp blue centre. He picked up a shell, a few pebbles and a tarnished buckle. That seemed to be it – the things his four year old sister had collected and which were precious to her. Not much, he reflected, but perhaps the very fact that these things were kept secret – a secret she chose to share with

Tom, who became her friend that autumn - was what really gave them their value. And he could imagine how delighted she would have been to have this special hiding place created just for her.

Jack had handled the pieces gently, and then, thoughtfully, returned them to the drawer and closed it. There they should remain, in honour of this little girl of whom he had no recollection, but who he knew had always cared for him.

As Jack stood at the gate this crisp, autumn morning he wondered whether they were still there. Had the Baileys discovered the drawer? Had they emptied it, if so, casting out Molly's treasures without a second thought? He remembered the two meek boys – though he struggled to recall their names. Might this have become a hiding place for things they valued? He doubted it, somehow.

He walked slowly up to the farm, Tom at his heels. Ben was already there waiting for him, as ever, keen to begin the day's work. Ben smiled broadly at the older man, and they moved towards the farmhouse together to receive their instructions.

When they broke for their midday meal, moving to sit outside in the weak sunlight, Ben asked, "Will you be going to the harvest festival tonight?"

Jack chewed thoughtfully before he replied.

"I haven't crossed the threshold of the church since my mother's funeral, over twenty year ago, so I should say it's unlikely."

"You spend a lot of time in the churchyard, I know, so I wondered whether you might."

There was another pause, and Ben wondered whether this might be the end of the conversation. It was notable that he and Jack rarely exchanged words that were not related to the work they were doing.

But after a while Jack spoke again.

"I pay my respects at the gravestones, and I don't mind tidying up out there and making sure it all looks trim. But I parted company with religion many years ago now."

"I hear the minister isn't likely to recover. Reverend Morris will be coming over to take the service tonight, and word has it that he will take over all our services after Reverend Bailey has passed. We won't have a minister of our own."

Jack remembered the Jamesons telling him the same thing on his first evening back in the village.

"I wonder what will happen to The Vicarage, then?" Ben mused. "The church owns it, I hear."

Jack did not respond to this, and eventually he threw the last scraps of his dinner to the dog, folded the waxed paper and put it carefully into his pocket to use again, and he and Ben returned to the barn where they were working.

That evening, Jack took Tom out for his last walk of the day, and he paused at the church, from which he could hear the singing of the harvest hymns. He reflected on the loss of his faith, and how it was perhaps linked to other losses – the loss of his brothers, of Tom, his father and mother. Some sought comfort in worship in the light of the tragedies in their lives, he knew. But, for him, religion felt redundant. He had known army buddies who had spurned religion but who sometimes turned to prayer when they were fearful and under duress.

"I turn to my memories," he thought. "That's what sustains me."

But he hovered to listen to the music, which he liked.

"We plough the fields and scatter
The good seed on the land…"

Indeed we do, thought Jack.

"Come along, boy."

Three days later, a knock on the door in the evening roused Jack from his seat by the fire.

"Not work this time, Tom. I think I know what this will be."

He opened the door to the two church wardens, one of them, the taller of the two, clutching a wooden box.

"Good evening to you, Jack. The church thought you might be able to make use of this," and he thrust the harvest box forward.

Jack removed the pipe from his mouth and looked squarely at the two men.

"Delivering the boxes yourselves this year then?"

"Aye," replied the shorter man. "The minister is badly, so it's been left to us this time."

"Will you be wanting to accept it, then, Jack?" asked the other, with a note of exasperation in his tone. He was still holding the box out in front of him, and the weight was starting to tell. Jack had made no move to take it from him.

Jack tilted his head and a faint smile played on his lips.

"What do you think, Tom?" he said to the dog who stood by his side, looking curiously at the visitors. "Shall we be taking it off their hands?"

"There are others who will be grateful for the charity if you're not," the church warden with the box grumbled.

Jack bridled slightly at the word 'charity'.

But he did want the box. He reached out and lifted it easily from the tall church warden.

"I'm stronger than you are," he thought to himself, "though I have a good few years on you."

He nodded at the two men.

"Oh, I can make use of it," he said, breezily. "And I know to return the box to the church porch in a few days – I'm familiar with the drill." Jack turned to place the box on the table.

"And there's one more thing – a message from Mrs Bailey."

Jack raised an eyebrow. This certainly wasn't part of the drill.

"She'd like you to call at The Vicarage at your earliest convenience – her words. She didn't say why. I expect it's a job for you," the shorter church warden informed him, with the self-importance of someone with information to impart.

"I expect it is," said Jack. "Well, goodnight to you both." And Jack closed the door on the two men, who he could hear muttering, "No word of thanks, did you notice?" as they made their way down the path, which caused Jack to chuckle.

He turned to the box on the table, emptied its contents slowly – vegetables and fruit, potatoes and a pie, and a small pumpkin – and then he picked up the empty box and took it back to his chair by the fire, with Tom settling at his feet.

"See this now, boy," Jack said to him, turning the box slowly and lovingly. "This is a beautiful piece of craftsmanship. The first time I saw one of these harvest boxes, I was only a boy – and I knew. I knew without anybody telling me, that this was Tom Weatherbury's work. The same man who made our dresser, see? He chose the best wood, made it with great care, and added a faint design on one side - do you see that?" He tilted it down to the dog, who sniffed at it.

"I'm not so fussed about the produce – though we will eat it – but having this box in my home for a few days is the real treat." Jack stroked the wood as he spoke. "I'll have to take it back to the church next week – they store them to use each year. But these boxes are older than I am, Tom, and much more well-preserved!" Jack chuckled again. "A work of art."

Jack placed the box on the hearth, where he could see it from his chair, and he watched the light of the flames playing on the warm wood. He was quiet and thoughtful for a few minutes, pulling at his pipe again.

"What do you reckon the Reverend's wife wants with me, then, Tom? If her husband is on the edge of death, and she'll soon have to be moving out of The Vicarage, I wouldn't have thought she'd want work doing on the place. She isn't the type to want to leave everything ship-shape for whoever follows on, and if the Jamesons and Ben are right, then there may be no one to follow on, in any case."

Jack remembered anew his mother, Martha and Betsy working so hard to leave The Vicarage in the best possible order for the Baileys' arrival, and how unimpressed Mrs Bailey had seemed. And he thought about the dresser - perhaps standing in an empty, echoing kitchen after the Baileys' departure: unused, unloved.

"Well, we'll find out in due course. We'll call tomorrow – I think that's 'our earliest convenience', don't you agree?" and

Jack leant down to ruffle the dog's warm fur. Tom rolled over to expose his underbelly and Jack scratched him automatically, thinking of the beautiful harvest box, and the dresser, perhaps to be neglected in the abandoned house after yet another death. He had never warmed to Reverend Bailey, but he did pity the man, dying slowly in the company of a cold and bitter wife.

Tom knocked out his pipe on the hearth and straightened up, thinking it was time he readied himself for bed, and suddenly felt a sharp pain in his shoulder, which took his breath for a moment. He stilled, and waited for it to pass.

"That serves me right for showing off when I took the box… I may be stronger than that lanky church warden," he thought to himself, "but I'm ageing. It's as well that I have Ben to help with the heavy work, now, and I won't live forever." And he suddenly thought of Tom's letters in the box upstairs. Who would find them after Jack had passed on? Who might read them and learn of Tom's secrets? He realised he was pitying Reverend Bailey, with only a sharp-tongued wife as his companion at the end, but who would Jack have?

"Only you, Tom," he mused. And he rose slowly to make his way upstairs.

Chapter Twenty-Two: *I always hated it*

Jack had arranged to meet Ben at the church the next morning, so they could walk up to Home Farm together to complete the work they had begun there several days before.

" 'Morning, Mr Jensen," Ben greeted him with a grin.

" 'Morning, lad. Slight change of plan this morning. Can you go on up to the farm and make a start – you know what you're doing – while I call in at The Vicarage? Mrs Bailey wants to see me. I'll be up to join you shortly."

Ben drew himself up, Jack's 'you know what you're doing' ringing in his ears.

"Thank you. Yes – of course. I won't let you down."

"I know you won't. Come, boy," and Jack turned away, Tom trotting after him.

Jack paused at the gate of The Vicarage, remembering painting it over 25 years before. It hadn't received any attention since, he realised. The front garden was overgrown, too. Apart from the work he himself had done in the vegetable plot, and repairing the wall at the back of the house, before the war - Mrs Bailey, Jack remembered, being very keen on firm boundaries - it didn't appear as if the Baileys had invested any time or energy in maintaining, and certainly not on improving, the property. Perhaps they intended to rectify that before they left it, he said to himself, before immediately dismissing the thought. It seemed unlikely, from what he knew of the family.

He and Tom reached the door, and Jack knocked and waited patiently for some minutes. He thought he could hear footsteps coming down the staircase. Then the door creaked open, to reveal Mrs Bailey, looking considerably older, and a little more fraught, than when Jack had last seen her. Her sour expression was instantly recognisable, however. Without a word, she opened the door wide enough to admit Jack.

"Not you, though," she said sharply to the dog, who had not, in fact, made any move to cross the threshold but, rather, sat on his haunches and looked up at her, his head cocked.

"He knows not to come in," said Jack shortly. "He'll wait outside until I'm done."

Mrs Bailey closed the door and stood for a moment with her back to him before she gathered herself and turned towards Jack. She was thinner, too, he realised, and her bony shoulders more bowed. Jack remembered her upright stance the first time he had met her, in this kitchen, a short time after his father's death.

"She is to be pitied," he found himself thinking. "When I grew up in this house it was full of life, and there was joy, even in the wake of Molly's death. Five healthy children with parents who loved them – there was laughter and hope, at least until the war broke out, when everything changed. This woman seems to have had little joy of The Vicarage, and little hope remaining."

"I have a job for you," Mrs Bailey announced.

"Yes, missus." Jack had removed his cap, which he held in his hands, lowering his eyes so as not to meet hers.

"It's about that dresser."

Jack looked up quickly, and felt, for a moment, slightly light-headed. He waited.

"I always hated it," Mrs Bailey said, unexpectedly.

Jack turned to look at the piece of furniture he remembered so well. He knew from his earlier visits that it had not been cared for. Now he was closer to it he could see the stains and marks upon it – and one of the doors seemed not to be hanging true. Several chips had been taken out of it over the years. It even looked as if the fieldmouse had lost the tip of its tail, though he would have to crouch down and examine it more closely to be sure.

It occurred to him to ask the minister's wife what there was to hate about an inanimate piece of furniture, though asking questions of anyone was not something Jack routinely did. And then he remembered how his mother had loved it – and why should anyone love an inanimate piece of furniture, either? He was sure that Mrs Bailey would find that just as mystifying. Jack knew that his mother was proud of the dresser, because she had envisaged it and directed Tom to construct it. He realised that the autumn months in 1900 were a golden time in his mother's life, and that the undeclared affection between Alice and Tom had played its part in making that period so memorable to both of them. The building of the dresser was also somehow bound up with Molly, and Jack had heard often over the years about the sunny temperament of the little girl who was preserved in the collective memory of the family – frozen in time, almost. And the dresser had been regularly polished, cared for and treasured by the Jensens for all these reasons.

But Mrs Bailey examined it now, and her lip curled, Jack thought.

"It's too big. It's ugly – look at the marks on it. And that ridiculous mouse – how childish. I want you to paint it. Cover up all its imperfections."

Jack looked at the dresser and said nothing for a few moments, but then spoke up.

"It will need to be rubbed down and primed first. I can remove some of the stains, repair the cupboard door that looks to be askew, and deal with some of those blemishes – imperfections, as you call them."

"I don't care for it to be repaired and improved. I just want it covered up – with this," and Mrs Bailey reached into the space beneath the scullery sink and pulled out, and laboriously opened, a heavy tin containing thick, black, oily paint. It looked like tar, or pitch, Jack thought. He was immediately aware of a noxious smell.

"Black?" Not only was Jack unaccustomed to asking questions, but when he was given instructions for work he was required to do, he rarely expressed surprise, and never disapproval. However, he thought now of the effect of covering this substantial item of furniture in viscous black paint and the effect that would have on this dim, low-ceilinged room.

"Yes," said Mrs Bailey brusquely, replacing the lid on the paint tin. She clearly sensed Jack's reluctance – or at least his hesitation. "So will you do it, or must I ask someone else?"

If it's to be done, thought Jack, I have to be the one to do it. At least that will give me some control. And he realised he was keen to have the opportunity properly to examine Molly's drawer.

"I can do it, missus. It isn't just a case of slapping on that black paint, though. The paint won't take unless the wood is prepared first. It should take me a couple of days – one to rub down and one to apply the paint, I should think."

Mrs Bailey sniffed.

"I can't pay you much, mind. The minister is badly, and we don't have much to spare."

Jack nodded. "I'll leave that up to you and Reverend Bailey, missus." Money was the last thing Jack was thinking of at this point. He was wondering how much he would be able to do to restore and repair the dresser, and to limit any damage this black paint might do to it, without Mrs Bailey being aware of that. He assumed it could be helpful to him that the minister's wife might need to spend much of her time upstairs, by her husband's bedside, rather than scrutinising Jack's work.

As if on cue, a faint knocking could be heard from the room above them at this point, and Mrs Bailey looked upwards.

"Well, I dare say you need to be off. When can you come back to do the work?"

"Tomorrow and the next day, if that suits."

Mrs Bailey gave a short nod, and moved to open the door.

"Tomorrow, then," she said, dismissing him, and Jack felt he could breathe properly again when the door was closed behind him.

Jack was thoughtful as he and Tom made their way up to Home Farm.

The work at the farm was completed within the day, and evening was drawing in as the two men walked back towards the cottages. Jack had explained to Ben that he would be working at The Vicarage for the rest of the week, and that this was a simple painting job – though it's far from simple to me, Jack thought.

"There's nothing you can learn on a straightforward job like this, so I think you'd better take a couple of days for yourself." Jack knew Ben's face would fall at this, and he was right. But Jack needed to be alone in the kitchen of The Vicarage to do what he hoped to do.

"Is there nothing I can be doing by myself while you get on with that?" asked Ben. "I like to be useful."

Jack thought for a while.

"You could call in at The Plough and take all the details for the work John Brewster wants us to do next week." The publican had recently spoken to Jack about various odd jobs that needed doing around the place. "See if there's measuring up to do, and make a list of the materials we need to put together – you can start to get things ready."

Ben had brightened up considerably at this suggestion.

"I will. I won't…"

"…let you down!" Jack interrupted, wryly. "I know that. I trust your judgement, Ben. Our trial is going well, and I've every expectation that we'll be working together for some time to come. Get off home, now. Your mother will be wondering what I've done with you."

Jack started to turn away, and, as he did so, he felt again the sudden, piercing pain he had experienced the night before. He stopped, and breathed deeply, and then turned back to Ben.

"Just before you go, Ben… There's something - I wanted to ask you if…" Jack hesitated, and Ben looked instantly concerned.

"Is something wrong?"

"Not wrong, exactly – it's just… I'm a good few years older than you, you know. And that got me to thinking. If I was unwell, and unable to look after Tom – it may be visiting the minister's house that made me think of this – do you think you and your mother would be willing to give him a home?"

Ben was dumbfounded for a moment.

"Are you sick, Mr Jensen?"

"No! I'm only – looking ahead, like. I wouldn't want to think of this fella here not being properly cared for, if – you know."

"Of course we'd look after Tom – and be proud to do so. He's a grand dog, Mr Jensen. But I hope it wouldn't be needed for many years to come. You're not an old man – you're strong, still."

Jack gave a faint smile, and as he did so he thought of how much more frequent his smiles had become since he and Ben had started working together.

"Have you never heard that I'm known in the village as 'Old Jack', then, Ben?"

Ben looked momentarily uncomfortable. He and his mother had always referred to Jack Jensen by that name in the past, though since they had started to work together, it was 'Mr Jensen' in their household now.

"The name isn't something I mind," Jack continued, "And I am getting older, that's true. Thinking about who might care for Tom, if it came to it, just sets my mind at rest, that's all it is. Thank you, Ben. And goodnight. Call and let me know what John Brewster has to say in due course."

"I will. Goodnight," and the men parted company.

Jack looked down at the dog.

"You know when we're talking about you, don't you?"

The collie wagged his tail, panting up at him.

"Ben's a good man. You'd have a good home. That's all I want."

Chapter Twenty-Three: *what would Molly want?*

Jack was at The Vicarage early next morning, with his tools and painting equipment. Tom settled himself comfortably outside – he was a biddable and patient dog, Jack thought, now well-accustomed to waiting for his master for several hours at a time. Jack felt easier in his mind since his conversation with Ben the previous evening, though he had had no recurrence of the pain in his shoulder.

"Perhaps I wrenched it, working up at the farm, and it will ease in time," he thought.

Once again it took Mrs Bailey a few minutes to let him in. Jack assumed she was sitting upstairs with her husband when she could. He was hopeful that was the case, so that he could work as he wished on the dresser. When the minister's wife opened the door to him, her face looked grey, Jack saw. Once more, wordlessly, she opened the door to admit him, without any word of greeting.

Mrs Bailey had emptied the dresser, and the objects she had taken from it were ranged on the scrubbed table. They were few, and of poor quality, Jack saw, remembering again the delicate china which Alice had displayed on the dresser shelves.

"That china should go to Martha and Betsy, really," Jack suddenly thought. "It serves no purpose gathering dust in Stone House."

Jack would write to his sisters at Christmas time, as he usually did, and he would suggest it then. Both of them would ask him to visit them at Christmas, he knew, but he would decline and spend the short holiday at home with Tom. He had not seen his sisters since Alice's funeral – being a recluse had come easily to him, he realised. He knew the sisters saw each other frequently, and he was comforted by that thought. It occurred to him now that Dora and Ben Winters might invite him to share a Christmas meal with them this year, but he thought it unlikely that, if that were the case, he would accept.

Jack's train of thought was interrupted by Mrs Bailey saying, sharply, "Are you listening to me?"

"Sorry, missus."

"I was saying that in addition to supplying the paint, I have found out these brushes. This will all, of course, be taken into account when the payment is settled with Reverend Bailey."

Jack wondered whether her husband was, in fact, sufficiently robust to make such decisions, but he knew Mrs Bailey was the kind of wife who, even when she was herself pulling the strings, would give others to believe it was the master of the house who was doing so.

Jack examined the brushes she had indicated, his face impassive. They were no good to him, having never been properly cleaned and cared for after earlier use. He said nothing, but realised he had anticipated this when he had packed his own brushes and white spirit the previous evening.

"Thank you, missus," was all he said.

Jack started to lay down dust sheets at the base of the dresser, and to prepare the equipment he needed for the first stage of the work. He would not need the paint at this point, but he made a point of opening up the tin and stirring the contents. He knew that the unpleasant smell which immediately filled the room was likely to drive the minister's wife out of it.

"Well, I have to get back upstairs to see if the Reverend wants anything," she said, as she retreated towards the staircase, and Jack, his back turned to her, hid a small smile. "I'll be back down in an hour to check on your work."

Jack only nodded. Once she had left, he replaced the lid on the tin and opened the door to place it, and the stick he had used to stir it, outside. He rubbed Tom's ears and filled a bowl he always carried with him from the water butt. Tom started to lap noisily, and Jack returned to the kitchen.

Having arranged his tools, Jack stepped back and gave his full attention to the dresser, his hands on his hips. He would repair the cupboard door first, and he had brought his penknife to make good the fieldmouse's tail. He would do what he could to smooth the deeper scratches and chips in the wood, but the stains and marks would be covered with the paint, so he realised he needn't worry about them. Once he'd made the repairs he would rub down and prime the wood.

But before any of that...

Jack knelt carefully by the right hand panel. He remembered doing the same thing after he had received Tom's final letter in 1918, and reflected on how much easier it had been to get down on his knees, and to rise again afterwards, when he was more than a quarter of a century younger. His fingers found the catch, though he suspected it had rusted in the flood water which had encroached on the property in the intervening years, and it took a short while before he could operate it successfully and open the drawer.

And there they lay. If anyone in the Bailey household had discovered the drawer, they had not bothered to empty it. Molly's treasures were left undisturbed, though older and grubbier than when he had last seen them. The feather, by this time, was practically unidentifiable, but he recognised the rest of the collection. He removed it, carefully, piece by piece, wrapped it in the cloth he had brought for the purpose, and placed the loose package gently in a side pocket of his toolbag.

Then he started work.

It was, in fact, two hours before Mrs Bailey returned to check on his progress. She would not examine the dresser closely, he knew – he saw that she could barely bring herself to look at it, her strong aversion to it clearly evident. The door which was askew now hung true, and some of the chunks which had been taken out of it were planed smooth, and less noticeable. The carved fieldmouse was restored to his former glory. Jack felt reasonably confident that all these changes would not be recognised and commented on disapprovingly. By the time Mrs Bailey entered the kitchen Jack was absorbed in rubbing down the wood, and after his short lunch break he would apply the coat of primer.

Jack returned home as night fell. He fed Tom, and made himself a mug of tea. It has been a good day's work, he considered. The dresser looked considerably better than it had before he had started to work on it. He didn't like to think what it would look like, and how he would feel, the following day, when it was smothered in the viscous, black paint. But tonight he felt at peace with what he had done.

He sat at the table, his tea steaming by his elbow, and unwrapped the cloth containing Molly's treasures.

The feather, he felt, he could do little with, though he cleaned it up as best he could. It was on the verge of disintegrating, he could see.

He spent some time on the farthing, using a cloth and some spirit to bring up its shine, so he could clearly read the date: 1900.

He washed the handful of pebbles in a shallow saucer of water and their different shapes and patterns emerged.

The two buttons were made of wood, and had been dyed different colours. The colours were faded now, but he could see that the smaller one was a blue/green, and the slightly larger one a rose pink.

The glass marble, he was delighted to see, polished up as good as new. Its blue eye winked up at him.

The shell had fared well, too, and he was able to restore some of its pearly hue.

Lastly, he picked up the brass buckle, which he thought may have come from a horse's harness - a plough horse, perhaps. He spent some time on that, and it was satisfyingly transformed from its tarnished original state to a soft gold-coloured glow.

Then he arranged the collection on the table in front of him, and looked carefully at each piece, muttering to the collie as he did so.

"What do I do with it all, Tom, do you reckon? Do I put it back, or do I keep it safe here? What would Molly want, do you think? And is this something I should share with her sisters?"

Tom had given more thought to the family china, and his conviction that he should perhaps pass the pieces on to Martha and Betsy had strengthened. He would invite them here to collect them. He would see them again – for the first time in over twenty years. Should he show them Molly's collection? Should he tell them about the drawer?

But if he did that, he realised, he would need to explain Tom's letters, and he was unsure that he wanted to share those and expose to the light the secrets of 1900.

"I think she'd want them put back, boy. I think she would want the secret to stay a secret, and the drawer Tom made for her to be the safe place she thought it was. I could fix the catch so that the drawer doesn't open again – but I'm not sure that feels quite right. Maybe one day someone will find the drawer, but what's in it won't mean anything to them, and so Molly's secret won't be known."

Tom whimpered slightly, and Jack smoothed his soft ears.

"I find that now I've started to think about what might happen when I'm no longer here, those letters are on my mind. I shan't give them to my sisters, but I don't want anyone else to find them either. I do find comfort in reading them, but..."

Did he live too much in the past? Jack asked himself. Was it time to let the past go? The letters, the treasures, the secrets – the dresser?

"And tomorrow, it'll be like I'm covering the dresser in a black veil – its mourning dress. Mrs Bailey looks at it like something sinful she wants hiding..." He remembered her use of the word 'imperfections' the previous day. "But I see it as protecting, guarding, not hiding. Is that what Tom would want? And Alice? And Molly?"

He shook his head.

"It's too much for my simple brain, boy. I'll sleep on it and give it some more thought tomorrow."

The next day Jack applied the black paint, a cloth covering his face to mitigate the effect of the fumes. Mrs Bailey kept her distance, as he had expected she would. One coat was sufficient to achieve a good coverage, as Jack had hoped it would be, so it only took him part of the morning. The dresser certainly looked sombre when he had finished, and the room, as he had anticipated, was considerably gloomier. He stepped back and regarded his handiwork.

The fieldmouse was definitely less noticeable now under the black pall. The hidden drawer, Jack suspected, was also less likely to be detected. Although he would never have selected this particular paint, had the choice been his, the dresser was better, Jack felt, for the rehanging of the cupboard door, the tightening of all the other hinges, and the smoothing away of the worst of the ravages wrought by time and neglect. He had cleaned it out thoroughly, and it stood tall and strong. Whatever Mrs Bailey's intention in engaging him to do this work, the dresser had benefited from his attention, Jack saw.

He moved to the bottom of the stairs and called up to Mrs Bailey, though he kept his voice quite low out of respect for the minister's ill health. She came to the top of the stairs and looked down at him.

"You can't have finished already?"

"I have, missus. One coat of paint did the job. It may take a couple of days to dry properly, the paint being so thick, like."

Mrs Bailey looked down at him.

"Reverend Bailey has decided on suitable payment. I'll come down and get that for you, but..." she hesitated. "As you're here, will you come up and pay your respects?"

Jack shifted uncomfortably. But he didn't see how he could refuse the request. He stood aside while the minister's wife descended and then he slowly climbed the narrow staircase, recalling, as he did so, the many times he had torn up and down those stairs as a boy.

The bedroom smelt stale, and the atmosphere was airless and cloying. Jack stood by the doorway and closed his eyes for a moment, remembering. This had been his parents' room, and he knew he had slept by their bed in his crib until he was old enough to join his siblings in the room next door. In Alice's day it had been an attractive room, with the lightly patterned curtains she had sewn stirring in the breeze as the window was invariably ajar. A rocking chair with cushions in the same fabric had been placed in one corner, and a jug of wild flowers usually sat on the small chest. A brightly coloured patchwork quilt, to which Alice and her sisters had all contributed at the time of her marriage to Edward, had covered the bed.

Jack opened his eyes and looked at the figure now lying there. Reverend Bailey appeared skeletal – Jack would have feared that the minister had already passed, were it not for the faint sound of his rattling breaths. He was, clearly, close to death. His eyes were closed, and Jack didn't know whether he was awake and able to hear him, but he said softly.

"It's Jack Jensen, Reverend. I'm sorry you're badly and just wanted to pay my respects..." and then he could think of no more to say. He stood there for another minute, while the minister's eyes remained closed, and his breath continued to rattle. This was death, Jack thought, closing his eyes again. It can take different forms – he thought of Molly in the floodwater, of Matthew, Benjamin and Tom in the trenches, of his father, collapsing in the church, of his mother, by whose bedside Jack had sat until her final breath. And it will come to me, too – I don't know when and I don't know how, but it will come.

He looked up at the minister again, and was suddenly minded to express his gratitude.

"Thank you," he said softly, "for giving me the chance to visit The Vicarage again and work on the dresser. And God be with you."

I'm not a believer, but he is, Jack thought, as he backed out of the room.

In the kitchen, Mrs Bailey thrust the coins into Jack's hand – a meagre payment, as he had expected, but it mattered little.

"Thank you, missus."

Jack could think of nothing more to say, but Mrs Bailey had already turned away from him. He picked up his bag and let himself out, pleased to see Tom and to breathe in fresh air.

"We'll go home so that I can leave my tools," Jack told the collie, "and then we'll go for a long walk along the river, my boy."

And man and dog left The Vicarage behind them.

Chapter Twenty-Four: *a memento*

November brought Reverend Bailey's death, Mrs Bailey's immediate departure from the village (and no one knew exactly where she had gone), and heavy rainfall. The Vicarage was shut up, for the reverend was, as anticipated, not to be replaced. Future services were to be taken by the minister from a nearby village, in response to the dwindling congregations in both places. Jack would look up at the windows of the house as he passed – curtains drawn, and no lights or life within – it seemed that the house was blind. He thought about the dresser inside. The Vicarage would remain abandoned until the church decided what it intended to do with the property.

By the third week of the month the river had overflowed its banks once again, and the water meadows filled as a consequence, but Jack, accustomed to living through so many floods where the water reached different levels, could see that this was not one of the times when the water would encroach into the cottages and make the lanes impassable: "Not this year," he said, when the publican John Brewster asked Jack if he thought the villagers should start to move their furniture upstairs. Jack's judgement was respected. The word was passed on.

As November passed into December, the rain eased off, the water, very slowly, began to drain away, and then the temperature plummeted. The icy cold, the heavy frost each morning and, in due course, snow, did not deter Jack and Tom from their daily walks. Winter brought plenty of work for Ben and Jack, their professional arrangement now permanent, and a source of satisfaction to both parties. Ben continued to be quick to learn and eager to please. He was especially keen to take on the heavier work. Ever since their conversation about Ben and his mother giving a home to Tom, "if it came to it," as Jack had expressed it, Ben had been especially mindful of Jack's health, strength, and capacity, which he realised would inevitably deteriorate as the years passed.

Occasionally Jack felt breathless, but this was not something he would ever discuss with Ben, or, in fact, spend much time thinking about.

"What will be, they say, will be..." he said to Tom one evening, following one particular episode where he had found it difficult to "get to the top of his breath", as he thought of it. Tom whimpered softly, sensing that all was not well with his master, and then he nuzzled Jack's hand, the best way he knew to comfort him.

On their early walk the next morning, Jack and Tom could hear excited chatter and laughter in the distance, as they approached the local pond. As had been eagerly anticipated by the villagers for the last few days, the ice was now sufficiently thick to bear the weight of the children who were enthusiastically donning their battered skates – footwear which had usually been passed down through several generations. Jack saw that Ben was there, and he stopped to watch with him.

"I remember skating on the pond as a lad - the best part of twenty years ago," Ben smiled up at him. Jack gave a short laugh.

"And I remember doing the same the best part of *forty* years ago!"

Jack was aware of the fact that he laughed, and smiled, more often these days. It was one of the positive effects of his working relationship with Ben, he realised. The two men, although a generation apart, were becoming friends, and friendship was something that had eluded Jack for much of his life. He had been close to Matthew and Benjamin when they were children growing up in The Vicarage, and they had played together, often on the river bank. They had explored, gone fishing, and even repaired (with Tom Weatherbury's help) an abandoned rowing boat, which they took out onto the water – much to Alice's consternation. Perhaps because of his relationship with the twins, Jack had cultivated fewer friendships among his contemporaries at school. When the Great War started, Jack recalled his brothers saying,

"Our country…."

"…needs us!"

with their typical energy and enthusiasm. Jack had felt bereft when the twins left, hugely excited at the prospect of joining the fighting. It was one of the reasons why he was so keen to get to France – a determination which only increased when Tom joined up, too. Everyone seemed to be abandoning him. When conscription was brought in, Jack was two years too young, and he often expressed the hope that the war wouldn't end before he was old enough.

One of his most difficult memories was of the morning at The Vicarage when the telegram arrived to announce that Matthew and Benjamin had perished at The Battle of Passchendaele. Jack could vividly recall his mother's agonised crying, and the pall that seemed to settle over their home. He never talked of enlisting again, and he remembered with regret all the times he had talked of his hope that the war wouldn't end too soon. A year later, it did end, but not before Tom Weatherbury had also been killed.

Jack became aware that Ben, beside him and still watching the children on the ice, was speaking to him. "I see the world is changing, but some things don't – especially in a village like ours," Ben mused.

Jack saw young Susan Jameson, Harry and Eileen's daughter, venturing out onto the ice arm in arm with her friend. Both girls laughed nervously but, holding onto each other, they began to build their confidence and managed a circuit of the pond without falling. Then Susan's friend turned suddenly and both lost their balance, clutching on to one another as Susan shrieked, "Maisie - stop!"

"Ma wanted me to ask you something," Ben said, a little awkwardly. "Don't feel obliged, of course, but – we'd be very pleased if you'd join us on Christmas Day. Tom too, naturally!" and Ben smiled down at the dog.

Jack turned towards him and looked into the fresh face of this earnest young man who he liked and respected.

"It's not that I'm ungrateful, Ben – and you must thank your mother for the offer. But I've grown so used to my own company that I'm easier in my own home, with Tom as my sole companion. You know me well enough to see conversation doesn't come easily to me. Though I do chatter away to Tom, sometimes, I grant."

Ben nodded, unsurprised at Jack's refusal, though he found the thought of the older man sitting alone in Stone House all through Christmas a sad prospect.

"Would you never think of visiting your sisters at Christmas?" Ben asked. He was reluctant to ask personal questions and to seem to pry into Jack's life, but sometimes his concern and growing affection for the man gave him the courage to do so.

Jack shook his head. "We exchange letters, and they may come over to the village in the spring to collect some things of our mother's I want them to have, but I'm content staying here. My wartime travels were enough for me – I don't see myself leaving the village again, now."

"Well, if you change your mind about Christmas Day, you're always welcome."

"I know – and I thank you. And..." Jack was unaccustomed to talking about his feelings, but he had the sudden urge to do so, "I've appreciated your company in these past weeks, Ben. Thank you for that, too."

Ben blushed, Jack saw, and he said, more gruffly, "Time we were getting on. Come on, boy!" and Jack settled his cap more firmly on his head, grasped his walking stick and set off towards the river bank with Tom at his side.

Ben watched after him for a while.

On Christmas Eve, Jack took Tom out late, and they sat on a bench by the village green listening to the singing of the carols from the church service. It was a cold, clear night, the moon bright in the sky, and Jack found he was enjoying the peace.

His hands were in his pockets, clenched for warmth, his muffler was wound tightly about his neck, and Tom pressed close to him, for mutual comfort. Jack was mulling over in his mind something which he had been deliberating in recent weeks. It was time to make a decision, he realised.

He withdrew his left hand from his jacket pocket, and slowly opened his fingers to reveal an object which reflected the light of the moon. It was something he carried with him always, now, stroking it with his thumb as he walked along. He looked down at the collie and then spoke softly.

"I don't think she'd mind, Tom. I put all her other treasures back safely, but I wanted to keep one thing as a memento. I think about her every time I put my hand in my pocket."

Jack turned the brass buckle over in his fingers.

"I reckon she'd like that."

Jack rose stiffly, put his left hand back into his pocket and clutched his walking stick with his right. Man and dog made their way carefully along the icy lanes towards Stone House, the sound of the singing dwindling as they walked on.

"Christmas Day tomorrow, boy. And there's something I think I need to do tonight." The decision had been made.

Back at home, Jack banked up the fire in the grate. The collie curled up on the rug. Jack pulled his chair closer to the warmth and settled into it. The box containing the wartime letters sat at his feet.

"I'll read them again, my boy. But I don't want anyone else ever to have the chance to read them. I'm glad Tom trusted me enough to share the truth with me – about how Molly died, and about his feelings for my mother. This isn't for anyone else's eyes, though."

And one by one, after he had read each letter in the order in which he had received it, Jack fed each sheet to the flames.

He held the last letter in his hand for a long time after he had finished reading it, but then, gently, he placed it into the fire and watched it catch light.

"I have lived too much in the past, Tom," and Jack felt he was talking to his current companion, and perhaps also to the writer of the letters. "The present may be a solitary one, and the future may be short, but it's time to move on. And to protect the secrets I've been entrusted with." He took out the buckle, which gleamed in the firelight.

"But I won't cast you on the fire," Jack murmured. "I'll keep you with me, in my pocket, every day, and think of Molly. Even though I *don't* remember Molly, which saddens me, Tom. I know *of* her – and how loving and caring she was when I was a baby. The rest of her treasures will, I hope, be safe in her secret place. But this one will stay with me until I die…"

And so it did. When Jack's weakening heart finally gave out, ten years later, and he was found by villagers who were alerted by Tom's howling, his left hand was in his pocket, clasping the brass buckle, which was polished to a deep shine.

Epilogue: Afterwards

Alice lived in the village for 22 years. Jack lived there for 55.

And Laura remains in The Old Vicarage for 60 years. She bears James three children, and is a faithful and loving – if never entirely trusting – wife to him. She continues to teach in the same school in the next village along the riverbank, and does, as Hester Willoughby predicted, eventually become its headteacher, a job she loves, for the final ten years before her retirement in 1994. She looks forward to rest and relaxation, time with her family and friends, the opportunity to do a little travelling, in the years that remain to them. Their plans are shattered when James dies of a sudden heart attack, two years later, at the age of 62, collapsing in one of the village lanes when walking one of Angus's many descendants – just as Old Jack Jensen had died, Laura remembers. Initially grieving and rudderless, but ultimately comforted by the village community and her secure and well-respected place in it, Laura lives in The Old Vicarage alone until 2020, when she leaves to join John, her first born, and his family on the other side of the world.

During Laura's time in the village, patterns change. Unlike Tom and his contemporaries, those born into the village are unlikely to take over their family homes and remain there all their lives. Young people leave school, and are eager to move to study or work elsewhere, and they return only to visit their families from time to time. Those who move into the village are those who seek a quiet, rural location for their retirement, rather than families with young children. As a result, the village population becomes elderly. Few babies, now, are born to those who inhabit the cottages. The small village school, where Laura taught and where her children, and Alice's, were educated, is eventually deemed unsustainable, the diminishing number of children in the village taken by bus to be educated elsewhere. The village shop becomes commercially unviable, and is closed. Eventually the pub shares the same fate. Church services become less frequent and then stop; those who wish to worship locally travel to other villages. or the nearby town, to do so. The village hall falls into disrepair, as does the war memorial, the creeping moss eventually covering the names of Edward and Alice's twins, and Tom Weatherbury.

And the weather patterns change, too. Over the decades following Laura's departure in 2020, as sea levels rise, the climate alters and extremes of weather become more commonplace, the flooding of the village happens more and more frequently. After each significant flood, when water invades the houses, some families move out and eventually an increasing number of the homes are left empty, and, over time, they become derelict.

The village dies.

The Old Vicarage has been uninhabited for many years, now. The dresser is still there, the keeper of secrets: a tribute to Tom's craftsmanship. But it is warped from standing in water several times each year. It is no longer possible to open Molly's secret drawer, and no one is there to admire the carved fieldmouse, forever scampering to an unknown destination.

#ONEWORD

CONTENTS:

Gabrielle was always the first to arrive. She was a planner, who looked ahead, and this morning, as usual, she had set off in plenty of time. As she settled herself at their reserved table with a coffee and her Kindle, she breathed deeply and relaxed in these moments of quiet before the others joined her.

Kay and Sam arrived together ten minutes later, and they were laughing and shaking the rain out of their umbrellas as they moved through the pub. The three friends hugged and kissed, and the new arrivals removed coats, scarves, hats and gloves – "It's *miserable* out there!" – before Sam went to the bar, returning with a bottle of red and four glasses.

"I've asked them to bring the menus over when we're all here."

"No sign of Lily?" asked Kay.

"Not yet, but I spoke to her on the phone last night – she'll be on her way," Gabrielle replied.

"Do I need this…" murmured Sam, pouring glasses of wine for the three of them.

"Tough morning?"

"Not tough, exactly, but frenetic. The children all seemed to need to be in different places, so Adam and I have been running the usual taxi service. Then I called to see if mum and dad needed anything, and mum was in a particularly tricky mood…"

"I do wonder if public holidays bring out the worst in us rather than the best," mused Kay. "Do you think we're all more likely to get tired and irritable at this time of year?"

"So much for the season of goodwill and peace to all men, then!" laughed Gabrielle.

Lily burst through the door breathlessly.

"I am SO sorry – why do I always seem to be late? I was just about to leave and Johnnie… well, you really don't want the details!" She laughed and settled herself at the table.

A young man brought their menus and, once they had ordered, there was a collective exhalation of breath, and the women looked at each other and laughed.

"How have we all been?" began Gabrielle, as she invariably did.

It was a month since the four of them had met for a meal – the usual interval between their gatherings - and Christmas had happened in the interim. The conversation moved smoothly from one subject to another.

"How was Thailand, Gabrielle? I can't imagine Christmas Day on a beach. My God, the idea of sunshine and heat at this time of year is so appealing..." said Lily.

"So cooking Christmas dinner for eight is something I now have off pat..." offered Kay.

"Were all the children with you, this year, Lily?" asked Gabrielle.

Sam initially sat quietly and watched as the others exchanged their news. These New Year's Eve lunches always made her reflective. The group of friends, who had met thirty years earlier as 11 year olds at their girls' grammar school, had honoured the tradition of lunch together in this same pub for the last ten years. In September 1989, on their first day at secondary school, they had all been initially solitary, friendless and hesitant. Each of them was the only girl from their respective primary school to be placed into this particular form group. As if by homing device they had identified and gravitated towards each other, and the friendships formed on that day had sustained them throughout the previous three decades – through their education, their jobs, marriages (and divorce), children, successes and disappointments. They had instituted the New Year's Eve lunch idea when they gathered to celebrate their thirtieth birthdays. This year they had all turned forty.

Sam searched the faces of her three companions to find the round-faced, freckled 11-year olds within. How well had each of them aged, she wondered? She herself had kept in shape, and invested in products and treatments to keep bags and wrinkles at bay. Her bobbed hair was still a glossy dark brown. She thought that it was Gabrielle, however, the only one not to have children, who looked marginally younger than the rest of them – fewer sleepless nights, Sam thought ruefully. Gabrielle's hair was freshly coloured, too, and copper highlights shone in the winter sunshine now coming through the pub windows, the rain having finally abated. She was slender and smartly dressed. She smiled often as she listened to the others.

Lily was the most voluble, as she regaled them with stories of her family Christmas. Her fair hair was caught up in a loose knot on the top of her head and she pushed back occasional escaping tendrils with her expressive hands, which she waved around as she talked, her long legs stretched out beneath the table.

Kay looked tired, Sam thought. Her hair was gently greying, and her figure was fuller. Kay was the only one among them to have a grandchild, and, thrilled as she had been when Robbie arrived, Sam knew that caring for him, in addition to her part-time job in the shop, looking after the rest of the family, including her parents and a needy sister, was draining Kay. Sam's own parents were in decline, something that caused her considerable anxiety, and she recognised that, for so many women, the increasing independence of their own children segued seamlessly into the time when the older generation required greater time, attention and care.

"What about you, Sam? How was Christmas?" Gabrielle drew her into the conversation.

"Frenetic – as always!" Sam smiled, realising it was the second time she had used that word since she had arrived.

"I can't believe how difficult teenagers are to please when it comes to Christmas!" groaned Lily. "Johnnie is a doddle, but Molly and Fay seemed to argue and complain about *everything*. God, it's wearing!" and they exchanged stories of adolescent responses to successful and unsuccessful gifts.

Gabrielle smiled as the others talked about their children, and, in Kay's case, her grandson. She asked questions and listened with interest to their replies, but could contribute little to this part of the conversation. She and Harry had few family members between them; neither had siblings and so there were no nephews and nieces, and the only children she came into contact with were her friends' offspring – and of course, the 900 girls and young women at her school, though that was, inevitably, a quite different relationship. Gabrielle realised that the pattern of talking about children would continue as the oldest of her friends' offspring began to have children of their own; Kay's daughter Susanna, now in her early twenties, had been the first. Gabrielle and Harry had gone away for Christmas itself, and had enjoyed the warmth of a different climate and the opportunity to relax which it had offered them. They had had a lovely Christmas, she reflected, which was simply very different from the experiences her friends were recounting.

"And how is your dad, Sam?" asked Kay.

"Struggling, I'm afraid – and mum is finding it hard to cope." Sam paused, and thought for a moment. "I'm not sure which is the toughest to deal with – dad is physically OK, but mentally, well, he isn't really my dad any more. Mum is alert and as sharp as she ever was, but she's increasingly physically frail. The combination of the two – "

"Two ham hock?" They were interrupted as serving staff delivered the first of their starters and they sat back and suspended their conversation until they had begun to eat.

"It's so sad, Sam – I can sympathise but I suppose it's hard to understand what it's really like until you're dealing with that – but we will all have to face it at some stage in the not-too-distant future, I suppose." Lily looked around and thought for a moment about the parents of her friends – how old, how well, how independent they all were.

"Well, that's a cheery proposition..." offered Kay, and the friends smiled briefly.

"I have to say that facing your parents' ageing seems harder when you don't have children, though." They all looked at Gabrielle, understanding her suggestion that the arrival of the next generation can in some ways make the decline of the older generation a little easier to bear.

Sam was often the one to change the subject and take their discussions in a new direction.

"How much time off work do we all have, and have you got work you need to do while you're at home, Gabrielle?"

Gabrielle had moved to a school leadership role in a local girls' school in September, the culmination of a successful career as a teacher, Head of Department, deputy head and now head. She had shared with her friends how much she loved it. She worked hard, including at weekends and in the holidays, though she did try to find, and model to other staff, a sustainable balance in her life so that work didn't dominate everything.

"I worked out how much I needed to do before we went away – just catching up from last term and planning ahead for January, and I spent a couple of days clearing the decks before the holiday," she told her friends. "It's all about balance, isn't it? I'll go into school the day before term starts to sort out my office. But I do feel rested and refreshed and ready for the spring term, I'd say. How much work have you been doing, Sam?"

"I worked for a few days in between Christmas and New Year, as I usually have to do – Friday was my last day, and I'm not back until 7th January, now. It's obviously busy in holiday periods, but there are enough of us in the team to pull together so that we cover all we need to, so everyone gets a bit of a break."

Sam worked as an executive within a high-end spa hotel chain, which her friends knew was quite a demanding job. With four children, and a husband who worked away much of the time, Sam's life was a constant balancing act – made even more challenging by the current state of her parents' health. Sam's only brother lived overseas, so the responsibility for looking after their parents fell squarely on her shoulders. Sam rarely complained, though, and her friends always felt that she had things under control.

"At least you both enjoy your jobs," Lily chimed in. "I am *so* fed up at the bank! It's...you know...always the same and the days move so slowly. I was counting them off before Christmas..."

Lily recognised how unfulfilling she found her work. She very much 'worked to live', and had never been professionally motivated, but when she listened to Gabrielle talk about teaching, or Sam discuss the leadership challenges she faced in her high-powered role, Lily was aware that she felt disgruntled. At 18, Lily had chosen a job in the bank rather than taking up the university place she had been offered. Always the feistiest of them all, she remembered declaring that she was "sick of learning and ready to start earning". In those early years she had very much enjoyed spending what she earnt, especially when others were eking out their student grants. However, twenty years on, she could see that this had been a short-sighted decision. She had said on more than one occasion to Kay, "You and I have jobs, while Sam and Gabrielle have careers – don't you think?"

Kay accepted that she had never been driven by career, either. She was the only one of them who had left school at 16 with no interest in studying for A levels, although she had been bright enough to do so, had she wanted. No one in her family had gone on to Further Education, and the expectation was that all the children would begin work as soon as possible, and contribute to the family income until they left home and started their own families. So Kay had started work in a shop, and had worked in a number of different stores over the last 25 years, part-time now, so that she could help Susanna look after Robbie. Unlike Lily, however, she did not feel the lack of stimulating employment. For Kay, work was just a way of earning a living to support what really mattered: her family and her home.

"Well I've been working in the shop most of the time!" she exclaimed now, "And I'll be back there tomorrow for the start of the New Year's sales. But, to be honest, I don't mind. I like the people I work with, and, apart from the fact that customers always seem more fraught round Christmas time, I like the holiday spirit."

"So do *you* think public holidays bring out the worst in us, then, Kay?" Gabrielle smiled, repeating Kay's earlier question back to her.

Kay was thoughtful for a moment.

"I see some people have money worries at this time of year – it comes out when they're shopping, of course. And often they're trailing children who are tired and fractious. It can be an exhausting time for some of us. But I do think the lights and the decorations and the Christmas music can lift people, too – don't you think?"

Kay did realise that, recently, she had been feeling more tired than usual. It wasn't work, exactly, but the combination of work and everything else she was juggling. She was, she thought, to some extent taken for granted by her family. Her husband, William, was a quiet man, who enjoyed running a painting and decorating business with a friend, fishing at the weekend, a few pints in the pub with his mates. Their marriage had been a steady one, with few arguments, but little passion either. The house, the children and now Robbie were very much seen as Kay's responsibility. Susanna did not seem overly appreciative of the support her mother gave her. "She just expects it," Kay thought, although that wasn't a phrase she would necessarily share with her friends, out of some sense of family loyalty. Their son, Michael, now 18 and an electrician, still lived at home, and definitely seemed to view his mother as a carer and provider. He paid rent as he was working, but as she picked up his dirty clothes from the bedroom floor to add them to the laundry basket, Kay often found herself thinking, "Am I a servant in this house?"

Sam turned to Lily. "So it must have been good to have the girls with you all over Christmas. Was Tony OK about that?"

Lily pulled a face. "He and I argued, as usual, about who was having them when. They play us off against each other no end – it's as if they work out how they can possibly get the best deal in terms of having their own way! But I do think they like to spend time with Johnnie, who's great fun at Christmas - he's still so excited by it all..." Lily smiled at the memory of her six year old son, the product of her second marriage, and his enthusiasm on Christmas Day, "...and they really don't much like Tony's new girlfriend, which doesn't surprise me."

Lily decided not to share with her closest friends the current tensions in her marriage. Peter was cooling, she felt – he had been besotted with her in the early days – and she had found him increasingly distant and distracted in recent months. There had been a time when she felt strongly that they brought out the best in each other, which had been refreshing after her increasingly venomous relationship with Tony. But now she was no longer convinced that this was the case. He was nothing like as solicitous and attentive as he had been in the early years of their relationship. "Perhaps he knows me too well, and so likes me less," she thought. And although she was close to these women, with their shared history and strong mutual affection, she was always mindful of the fact that she was the only one of the four who already had a failed marriage behind her. She was reluctant to admit that there might be a second.

So the four women discussed Christmas, families, work, their various interests, and enjoyed their meal. And then, just before they went their separate ways, they made their ritual choice.

"So #oneword2019. What are we going for?" It was usually Gabrielle who asked this question.

There was a pause, while each of them considered the words they had been deciding between. For the last few years, at their traditional New Year's Eve lunch, they had abandoned any discussion of New Year's Resolutions and, instead, chosen one word each which they determined would characterise the year ahead for them. They selected, shared, and sometimes discussed the reasons for their choice, and the resonance of the word at this point in their lives. But on this occasion, it had taken them a little longer than usual to reach this point in the afternoon, and they all had other commitments drawing them away from each other this New Year's Eve. They simply announced their words without explaining the rationale behind their choices, smiled, hugged and wished each other Happy New Year and then collected their belongings and made their way out into the gathering gloom.

JANUARY 2019

Chapter One:

Kay : #oneword 'control'

"Can't you sort it out for me?" pleaded Rachel, in a tone Kay could only describe as whining. Kay was three years younger than her sister, but she reflected on how many times, as they grew up, Rachel had used these, or similar, words, trying to pass on responsibility for whatever it was she herself didn't have the energy to deal with.

Kay took a steady breath.

"Rachel, it isn't that complicated, and you're not daft. We can read it together and I can talk it through with you, but I'm sure you're capable of sorting it yourself. I'm pushed for time today..." and Robbie, in his buggy, started to grizzle.

Rachel flapped the paperwork as if in weak protest, and looked cross. "You never have time for me these days."

"I have even less time for myself!" Kay tried not to snap, but she could hear the edge in her voice. "I'm calling to pick up mum and dad's shopping list, then after I've dropped off their groceries I need to take Robbie round to Susanna's, and I'm working this afternoon." Kay plucked Robbie from his buggy and nuzzled him, inhaling his baby smell and trying to coax a toothy smile. "But first I need to change you, don't I?" and she picked up the changing bag and headed out of the room as Rachel said, as she always did, "Well do it in the spare bedroom. I can't stand..."

"The smell!" Kay completed the sentence in a low voice as the door closed behind her.

As she cleaned and changed the baby, Kay reflected that when she had chosen 'control' as her #oneword2019, not one of her closest friends had registered surprise. Of the four of them, she thought, she had the least control over her life. They all had responsibilities and pressures; they all had others who relied on them, professional and personal duties, but Kay considered that she was the one who had the least time for herself, and the others knew that and sympathised. She was unsure whether anyone else really understood, though. She had no hobbies or interests outside her family. She had never seemed to have time to develop them. She had left school and started work at 16, met William at 17 and married him at 18, and Susanna had arrived when she was 19. Michael came along three years later.

Kay picked Robbie up and cuddled him back into good humour as her thoughts continued to drift. She remembered a slightly awkward meeting with Sam and Gabrielle when they were in their final year as undergraduates. They had both been home for the weekend, preparing for their finals and so had arranged to meet at the library. They were leaving the building, laughing together with their arms full of books and files, when they rounded a corner and met Kay, pregnant and clutching toddler Susanna's hand. The friends stopped to chat, but Kay was fundamentally aware of the differences in their lives. Sam and Gabrielle were in sweatshirts and jeans, flicking back their long hair, and looking like teenagers still. Kay, in her floral maternity dress and with her hair serviceably cropped short, felt she was of a different generation. She mused at the time, as she slowly mounted the steps of her bus, how little they now had in common. And yet the friendships had survived, and, two decades later, the four of them still enjoyed each other's company and conversation. They were the same generation again, Kay thought, despite her new grandparent status.

Back in Rachel's front room, Kay felt contrite.

"I'll call in tomorrow and go through it with you. We'll work it out together." Rachel still looked disgruntled. Kay held a now dozing Robbie out to her and Rachel kissed him perfunctorily. "I'll give your love to mum and dad, shall I?" asked Kay, and Rachel nodded mutely.

As she left the house, Kay thought about her sister – unmarried, currently unemployed and managing on benefits, with few interests and friends. She had time, which was the resource Kay felt was in short supply in her own life, but that certainly didn't bring Rachel joy.

"She's worse off than I am. I should be grateful. But still..." Could 2019 be the year when Kay took a little more control of her life?

Kay called goodbye to her fellow workers and left the shop, pulling on her coat. As she walked home she thought about what vegetables she had which she could serve with the pie she had taken from the freezer that morning. Michael would be home, and Susanna and Robbie would join them, before Susanna left Robbie with them overnight and went out with her friends. Robbie's father was no longer in her life, and Susanna, who worked part-time in a hair and beauty place, lived for her nights out, making the most of the fact that Kay and William would always look after Robbie whenever she needed a babysitter. Kay worried about her – and she worried about the boyfriends who came and went and their possible impact on Robbie's life. She loved Robbie deeply and felt that she and William could give him stability and security, and this might well be something he needed, especially if, at some stage, one of the boyfriends became the father of a second child. Robbie's father had no contact with him, though he paid maintenance. Kay sometimes felt the need to compensate for the lack of a father figure in Robbie's life.

William was heading up the stairs as Kay let herself into the house, needing a bath at the end of a day's work, and he called back over his shoulder: "Hello, love."

"Good day?"

"Not bad. We made good progress with that old detached on Somerville Street so might get it all done by the end of the week." William enjoyed his work as a painter and decorator and took considerable pride in doing a good job. He often came home physically exhausted, though, and Kay knew there was a strong likelihood that, after they had eaten, he would fall asleep in his armchair in front of the television.

Michael was in the kitchen, polishing his shoes, a clear sign that he had plans for the evening.

"Where are you off?"

"Just meeting a mate down The Oak Tree," Michael replied, bent over his task.

Kay smiled. Polishing his shoes meant that the 'mate' was a girl, but Michael was always cagey about his dates. He had never yet brought a girl home to meet his family, and cringed when Kay had once suggested it.

"Steak and kidney pie for tea."

"Great."

Susanna and Robbie arrived soon afterwards, Susanna looking glamorous, as ever – she made full use of the expertise of the friends she worked alongside. The five of them sat down to eat, William running his hands through his damp hair, Robbie chatting as he mashed his hands into his potato, Susanna and Michael good-humouredly bickering. Kay took a breath.

"I've been thinking…"

"Steady on, love."

"I'd like to take up a new interest this year – something that gets me out of the house and gives me a bit of time to myself."

The family stared blankly at her. Even Robbie, struck by the silence around the table, gave her a quizzical look.

"Something like voluntary work?" asked William. "There's a sign in the charity shop saying they're looking for…"

"Not voluntary work."

Kay was determined to be assertive, and not to be derailed.

"I realise that I spend a lot of time doing things for other people – looking after other people. Service."

"Like you serve in the shop?" said Michael with a grin.

"I do serve in the shop, and I serve all of you, and mum and dad, and Rachel. I want to do something that's just for me."

"Have you got time, though?" Susanna helped herself to more vegetables. "I was thinking of working more hours, as I could do with a bit more cash, and I'd need you to look after Robbie…"

Kay paused. "I need you to..." was one of the phrases she was aware Susanna made frequent use of. "Please" and "Thank you" and "I'm grateful..." featured less often.

"What kind of thing are you thinking of?" asked William, and he would, Kay knew, be the most supportive and understanding. He enjoyed his fishing, his pint with friends down at his local, and could see the attraction of interests that were outside home and work.

Kay took a breath. She had spent some time, since New Year's Eve, thinking about this, and considering the kind of interests her three friends managed to create time for. Gabrielle was a great reader and a keen member of two different Book Groups; she enjoyed film and theatre, and she and her husband Harry managed frequent short trips away and longer holidays. Kay and William hadn't managed to get away from home since before Susanna became pregnant. They didn't have a huge amount of money, but they were comfortable. It was time, rather than finances, that made it challenging.

Sam sang in a choir, and often said how therapeutic she found that: "It's something to do with the breathing, and the fact that you have to focus – really concentrate – which I find relaxing." Kay appreciated that she wasn't musical, and her family always smiled to each other if ever she sang to herself while she got on with jobs round the house.

Lily had joined a gym and she regularly exercised and swam. Of the four of them she was perhaps the most committed to looking good and to keeping fit. Kay was aware that she herself was the least interested in her physical appearance, and had never been sporty or someone who exercised. She had seen a local walking group, and a dance class, advertised the last time she took Robbie to the library, but neither had appealed.

"What do the rest of you think I might do?" Kay was interested to know.

There was a pause and the family shifted uncomfortably in their seats.

"Well, you like cooking," hazarded William. "Maybe a cooking course…"

"So that we can sample the results!" enthused Michael. He wasn't taking this seriously, Kay realised.

"As long as you have time, mum," offered Susanna, "And you don't take up something that…"

She didn't finish the sentence, but Kay knew she was thinking how mum having a new hobby might mean that others were inconvenienced, that she was less available to do all the things they 'needed' her to do. That they might have to pull their weight, help more – around the house, with Robbie. Maybe Rachel would have to show more energy and initiative and do more for herself, and also for their parents. Was it unreasonable to expect it? Kay wasn't deterred. "I deserve this," she thought. "I am 40 years old and I deserve to do something just for me, that won't necessarily benefit others, and that might actually mean others have to support me, for once."

"I've decided I'm going to refresh my French and Spanish at nightschool," she announced. "I passed GCSEs in those subjects a lifetime ago, so I'm hoping I can build my skills again quickly and I may even take A levels in those languages in due course, if that's the case. And when I've done that I'm going to do a bit of travelling and try out what I've learnt. Just on my own. I'm going for a bath, now. Will you clear the table and wash the dishes before you go out, you two?"

Even Robbie gaped as Kay left the table and headed up the stairs.

Later, after Susanna had left to join her friends at the club, Michael had met his date, and Robbie was asleep upstairs, Kay and William settled in front of the television to watch the news.

"Train fares up – that'll not please the commuters," observed William, and later, "Monarch Airlines – well. All those people losing their jobs, and people stuck at airports all round the world." And then, "Greggs bringing out a sausage roll with no meat in it. What's the point of that, then?"

When Kay did not comment, William looked sideways at her. "You all right, love?"

Kay looked levelly at him. When she had come downstairs in her dressing gown, Susanna and Michael had just been leaving the house. Neither they, nor William, had made any comment on her teatime announcement. Susanna had, as usual, left Kay to feed and settle Robbie in his cot. Her daughter could have done this before she left, and met her friends a little later, but this wouldn't have occurred to her, Kay knew. She said nothing now, and William looked uncomfortable. Then she relented.

"I'm fine."

There was another pause. If I don't fill it, perhaps he will.

"I think it's a good idea - the French and Spanish thing. I bet you'll enjoy it, and be good at it..."

William even picked up the remote and turned down the volume on the television.

"But I'd just say that if you do want to go abroad afterwards to use what you've learnt, maybe I could come with you sometimes. I do get that there are times you might want to be by yourself..."

"Yes," said Kay. "I realise that I'm hardly ever by myself. And I think I'd find it restful. It's not just now. Since Susanna was born, I've never really had much time alone. I'm not sure how you can miss something that you've never really had, but I think I do."

William nodded, and then hesitantly offered, "Are you unhappy?"

William was a good man, Kay reflected, and it had cost him something to ask that. He was not a man who readily talked about feelings - his own or anyone else's. But he had understood more than the children had about what she was saying at teatime. And he did want things to be better for her. She turned to him, then gently took the remote from him and turned the television off.

"It's not that I'm unhappy, exactly. I love you, William, and Susanna and Michael and Robbie, and Rachel and my parents.

I don't hate my job, though I have to say it doesn't exactly bring me joy. It's just something I have to do. Rachel frustrates me at times, but I do understand she isn't as strong as I am, and I don't resent helping her, or mum and dad, who are going to need more of our support in the next few years. I look at what Sam is facing with her parents and realise we're a fair way off that yet, but it's no doubt coming."

Kay swallowed, and looked up at him.

"It's just that I feel a bit taken for granted, I suppose. And I don't feel I have much control over my life. I react to things, and to what others want, and certainly with Susanna and Michael and Rachel, I don't even feel others appreciate what I do – not you, William," as he started to interrupt, "I'm not saying you don't value me. And I do see that this is a situation I've probably created for myself. If Susanna takes advantage, then I've let her do that and I haven't had the nerve to explain to her how it makes me feel. I could have said, tonight, that I'd have liked her to get Robbie to sleep before she met her friends, but I didn't. And if I have felt resentful that I'm the one who has always done all the childcare, and the housework, with very little support, then I should have said and done something about that a long time ago."

Kay smiled ruefully.

"You never, ever, changed a nappy when the children were babies – do you realise? I accepted that. I didn't have to, but I did. I saw it as my job. It was the same when the children were ill - I always felt it had to be me that cared for them, not you, not my parents. There's a kind of….I don't know - what's the right word? - maybe arrogance there somewhere? Feeling that it could only be me and that no one else was up to the job. And now I feel trapped, and that making a change, even carving out a little time to learn something new, to travel a bit, isn't going to be easy because of everyone who needs me. But it isn't impossible."

A soft gurgle from the baby monitor grew into a low grumble and then rose to a wail. Kay turned and spoke to the monitor as if it could hear her. "Shush, now."

Kay got to her feet.

"And it isn't too late."

She pulled William from his chair.

"I'm going to teach you how to change a baby's nappy."

And Kay led William from the room.

Chapter Two:

Lily : #oneword 'courage'

"Oh, mum!" The second word, as usual, had three syllables, and communicated exasperation.

"Fay. It isn't unreasonable to say you need to be home by 9pm on a school night, so we're not going to make a drama out of this."

Lily kept her voice level, and Peter raised his eyebrows at her from the other side of the table.

Fay left the room with what could only be described as a flounce.

"I do ask myself whether I was such hard work when I was 14. Everything seems to be a battle."

"I expect you were worse," said Peter.

"Gabrielle gave me a book for Christmas: 'Untangled' - something about guiding teenage girls into adulthood. She said it would help – that it had helped her in her job. It's around here somewhere…"

"But I don't think it works unless you read it, Lil."

"You may well be right. I wondered whether I could persuade YOU to read it, and just give me a quick summary?"

"Nice try," Peter muttered.

Lily looked thoughtfully at her husband. She had been starting to think that, as had happened with Tony, they no longer saw the best in each other – though she wasn't sure that she and Tony ever had. Something Sam had said to her three friends a few months ago had struck a chord.

"Do you like who you are when you're with your husband?"

The others had looked at her for a moment.

"Do you mean do we like our husbands? I didn't much like Tony in the end – or, in fact, probably for most of the time we were together. I do wonder whether I ever loved him. I think I was in lust with him…"

"Not what I meant," interrupted Sam. "The question is: do you like the person *you are* when you're with someone? I often think about this. I like who I am when I'm with the three of you. I don't always like the person I am when I'm with my mother."

"So, do you like who you are when you're with Adam, Sam?" asked Gabrielle.

"Well, we're so rarely together," Sam mused. "He's working away, or I'm working away, or one of us is taking some child or other somewhere or other...."

It was only afterwards that Lily reflected on the fact that Sam had evaded the question.

Lily had definitely not liked the person she was when she was with Tony. After the girls were born, the relationship deteriorated rapidly. He said something hurtful to Lily, so she found something to hurt him back. They ended up scoring points against each other, trying to find and exploit each other's weak spots. With some sense of shame she remembered how they even used the girls against each other – certainly during the protracted and acrimonious divorce proceedings.

Lily gave a shrug, as if to fend off difficult memories. Then she thought about Peter.

When they got together ten years ago, she had been bruised and battered by the divorce and its aftermath, and was exhausted bringing up two young children without the support of a partner. She had met Peter through a mutual friend, and he had quickly shown an interest in her. He had been gentle, solicitous, clearly enamoured by her, and this was so good for her sense of self-worth. She wondered whether she had fallen in love with him because he clearly loved her and she was grateful.

In recent months, however, Lily had been aware of tensions that hadn't been there before, and had started to wonder whether the marriage was working. Johnnie was a joy – certainly much easier than the teenage girls, and far less likely to cause friction in the household. Peter clearly adored him, and she appreciated the fact that he was a far more solicitous and caring father than Tony had been when the girls were little. But increasingly, it seemed, there were times when Peter seemed distracted, and it did cross her mind that he might have met someone else. She became aware that she was constantly looking for any indication of a possible romantic interest elsewhere; knowing Peter, it would be a romance rather than just a physical thing. At the same time, she felt disgruntled with herself: jealousy and suspicion are such unattractive qualities, she recognised.

And then she met Jim at the health club she visited regularly: 'Gym Jim' as she thought of him. Nothing specific had happened between them, but there was obviously a mutual attraction. Without ever discussing it, they had started to time their visits so they usually saw each other, and quite often had a coffee afterwards. He knew about her family, and she knew about his - he was married with children too. She enjoyed his company and felt flattered by his attention. They had gone no further than this, and she felt he was perhaps waiting for her to make the next move. She realised that she was also waiting, to see what happened with Peter. If it transpired that he did have someone else, and certainly if he wanted to leave the marriage, then she would, she thought, suggest she and Jim met for a drink one evening, and see what happened from that point. Lily could see that there was an element of insurance, or revenge, or – she wasn't sure what, exactly, and she didn't feel happy with the situation. She risked destabilising her own family, and perhaps Jim's, in order not to be alone. But she remembered vividly the early years with the girls after Tony had left, and how difficult she had found it.

"I'm not good at being on my own," she reflected. "And I need someone to make me feel attractive." But she didn't like this about herself. It seemed selfish and shallow.

Peter headed to the study, where he sometimes worked in the evening on various projects he was managing for the building firm which employed him. "Are you going to the gym?" he asked as he left the kitchen.

"Not tonight, I don't think." Lily knew Jim wouldn't be there this evening. "There's a programme I want to watch, and I might ring Sam later for a chat."

Lily had said nothing to her friends about Jim. They had been completely supportive when her marriage to Tony had broken down, rallying round to do all they could in the difficult months which followed. But she didn't think there would be so much sympathy this time. They all liked Peter, and adored Johnnie. Although the four friends tried not be judgmental about the different choices others had made, beginning a relationship with a married man with children of his own might be something they would find hard to accept, although their friendship was strong enough to survive it she felt – or at least hoped.

Lily settled down in front of the television with a coffee, catching the end of the news, "I am SO bored of Brexit already...." she muttered to herself, before one of the reality programmes she loved came on. Fay would normally have watched this with her, but she was still sulking in her room. She would be glued to her phone and sharing with her friends how unreasonable her mother was, Lily thought. Johnnie was having tea and playing with a friend, whose father would be dropping him off later. Molly was doing her homework upstairs; she had found a new energy for schoolwork since she had started her final year of GCSEs and chosen her A level subjects, and Lily felt this was at least one reason to be cheerful. Molly was unlike her mother and would, Lily knew, want to go on to university and to find something professionally fulfilling in the future – she was a bright girl and was talking about Law at the moment. If she could live her life again, Lily reflected, she would make a number of different choices.

She had chosen 'courage' as her #oneword on New Year's Eve, because she realised she needed to make some decisions and take action this year. Should she really commit to her marriage and try hard to make a success of it, or should she accept it hadn't worked out and step away from it? Could she build a new life for herself and the children on her own, rather than clinging to, and relying on, the next man? Whichever path she chose, she would need courage.

And her job. She felt profoundly bored at the bank. Time dragged; the routine was stultifying; the colleagues she worked with increasingly irritated her – and she suspected she irritated them. She had been offered the opportunity a number of years ago to complete a management training scheme and to take examinations which could prepare her for taking on some supervisory responsibility in the future. She was bright, quick to learn and had the strength of character to manage others, but she lacked the motivation.

"Why would I want to take on more responsibility for not much more money?" she said at the time, "and exams? No, thank you!" Not long after that, Tony had walked out, and just managing work and the girls had been challenging enough, without considering professional advancement. The chance to prepare for possible promotion in the future had not been suggested again, and she had never felt sufficiently interested to ask about it.

"I ought to resign, and look for something I'd enjoy more," Lily thought. Sam and Gabrielle had both said in the past that work was too big a part of their lives not to feel engaged and satisfied with it. Gabrielle loved teaching, and now headship. Sam regularly faced challenging leadership decisions which stretched her and made her think, and learn. The focus of Kay's life was different, Lily knew, and any frustrations Kay felt weren't work-related.

"If I'm so disgruntled, I really need to find the courage to do something about it," and then the theme tune was playing and Lily realised she hadn't really registered what was happening and hadn't enjoyed the programme as she usually did. Talking about it with Fay, she recognised, was part of the pleasure. Suddenly the whole thing seemed pointless, even ridiculous.

The doorbell rang and Lily levered herself upright. Johnnie stood on the threshold and launched himself at her, talking ten to the dozen, when she opened the door.

Lily laughed, "Johnnie – take a breath and say thank you to Edward's dad," and she turned to exchange smiles with the man who was backing off down the path towards his car.

"Thank you! 'Night!" called Johnnie, and then resumed his monologue – the games they had played, Edward's puppy, what they had had for tea. Johnnie needed little conversational input, and Lily smoothed back his hair and realised how overwhelming her love for him was. "I can't turn my back on this marriage!" she thought suddenly. "Johnnie needs us both – together and as happy as we can possibly be." She needed to invest in making that happen.

Peter was reading to Johnnie in bed. Molly and Fay were upstairs – she knew they would be listening to music, chatting to each other and completely enmeshed in conversations on their phones at the same time. Lily curled up on the settee with her phone and rang Sam.

"Is now a good time, or do you want me to call back?"

"Now is good. The children are settled and I've just poured myself a glass of red."

"Good plan," Lily moved towards the kitchen. "I think I'll join you. Cheers. How were your mum and dad today?"

"The same, really," said Sam. "Mum seems less and less stable on her legs, so I'm trying to talk her into buying a walking frame – I could take her to that mobility place at the weekend – but she's so independent and stubborn, and – vain, I think! She's really trying to resist the ageing process. It's so hard – it's just like with the kids. You want your children to make good decisions, not to fall into making the mistakes you made when you were younger. You want to control the choices your parents make at this stage of their lives, too - to do what you think is best for them - but you can't control that, really. I know that to some extent they have the right to make their own decisions, because it's their life, not mine, but it's difficult when they make what you think are the wrong ones."

"And your dad? Did he know who you were today?"

"He did – and that's one of the tricky things about dementia. He seems better and your heart lifts, and then the next time I visit he's just blank and you realise there's no real recovery from this. Anyway – enough. How are things in your world?"

Lily took a breath. "I'm wondering whether I should change my job."

"After all this time? What brought that on? I know you haven't much enjoyed it, but what are you thinking of doing instead?"

"I don't know! What am I fit for? Is 40 too late to do some kind of retraining? Peter's earning a reasonable wage so, if necessary, we could manage without me earning a salary for a while. Would I be able to get into a job that's more demanding and fulfilling, do you think? I always feel Kay and I have jobs, and Gabrielle and you...."

"..have careers," broke in Sam, with, perhaps, a touch of irritation in her voice. "I know – you've said that before. But how do you explain the difference?"

Lily stopped to think.

"Well, Kay and I don't earn much, and don't have much – any? – real responsibility. When we leave the building, that's it until the next time we're there. We don't even think about it. There's not much challenge, or anything to really stretch us, to make us think, or to learn. I've watched Gabrielle grow from a young teacher, to be a Head of Department who's led a team, then a deputy head and now a head. She's learnt so much, and she's had an impact in all her jobs. She loves it. It's part of her identity."

Lily paused again and thought how she could describe Sam's professional role.

"You have a great salary, perks, interesting people to work with, the opportunity to travel. What you do at work makes a difference to the people in the teams you lead, and to the business. You make the hotels better!"

Sam gave a hollow laugh. "We provide a service for wealthy, bored people who are looking for luxury, and businessmen and women who want a plush location for their latest dalliance.

Most of those I work with are shallow, self-interested, ruthlessly ambitious and perfectly prepared to stab others in the back to get on."

Lily had never before heard Sam talk about her work in these terms and there was a shocked silence while she processed what Sam was saying.

"Sam! I'd no idea you felt - "

"Sorry - sorry," Sam sounded contrite. "Bad day. Forget it. Let's talk about you and what you might like to do."

"No. If you're unhappy at work we ought to have a proper conversation about this - not on the phone. Let's meet for lunch, just the two of us, and talk about what's going on here. I don't know what I want to do. I need to do some thinking and some research and then I'll ask your advice about the next steps. I need to talk to Peter, too, and make sure he supports me. I'm pretty sure he will. I know you'll help me, but maybe talking through your frustrations will help you, too."

"Thanks - but will you...not say anything to the others about me, and this? I just..." Sam was uncharacteristically lost for words, and Lily was quick to reassure her.

"Of course I won't. Look, let's leave this now. You sound tired. I'll text you a few possible dates and we'll find a time when we can get together over lunch and talk about it all face to face."

"Yes, thanks. OK. Sleep well."

"And you."

In bed that night, Lily turned to Peter and murmured, "Are we OK?"

There was a pause before he replied, which was, in itself, revealing, Lily thought.

"Do you mean, as in, me and you?"

"Yes. Are we strong?"

"I think so. I hope so."

They moved closer together and held each other in the darkness.

"I know sometimes I must be hard to live with – selfish and irritable and short-tempered..."

"And those are your best features!" Lily could hear the smile in his voice.

"But I do love you, Peter, and our children, and our life."

Peter was quiet for a while. This is where I need my courage, thought Lily, and she began, hesitantly, "You just seem quiet, distracted sometimes, and I've started to wonder – is there someone or something else in your life that's taking you away from us?"

Peter turned on the bedside lamp, and sat up and faced her.

"Are you thinking another woman? Really?"

Lily felt uncomfortable.

"I don't know – I'm just asking because, recently, you've seemed distant, and it seems like we maybe haven't connected as well as we used to. You take yourself off into the study in the evening more often, and you're not always listening when I..."

Peter gave a mirthless laugh.

"You think it's because I've found someone else. God, no..."

Lily realised she should feel relieved, but there was something in his tone which gave her pause.

"Something else then?"

Peter took a breath.

"I think I'm about to lose my job."

Chapter Three:

Sam : #oneword 'purpose'

Sam knew that the others thought she was the one who had it all. She had been the brightest of them at school, one of those students who was actually strong in every subject on the timetable, so she could have followed any academic path she chose. She had an attractive, ambitious husband who earned a high salary; four healthy, amenable children who adored her and who didn't cause her the stress her friends' offspring seemed to generate; a beautiful home and regular, expensive holidays and mini-breaks, several of which were connected to her job, working at management level within a luxury hotel chain. She got on well with the CEO of the company, and he had recently had a tentative discussion with Sam about her applying for the Deputy CEO role when the current incumbent stepped down later in the year. Sam was calm and capable, always looked stunning, and never seemed worn down by life.

So her outburst to Lily was unusual, suggesting as it did dissatisfactions and tensions of which her close friends were unaware. When she put the phone down, Sam quietly cursed herself for her lack of control. She would meet Lily for lunch and play it down, try to laugh it off. She would explain that she had had an altercation at work that day and had then called to see her parents on the way home, which was always difficult. Her mother struggled physically; her father mentally. He had been a GP, a much-loved member of their local community, and Sam had quietly idolised him for as long as she could remember. A few years after his retirement, the early signs of dementia had become evident, and the condition had tightened its grip on him ever since. Today he had smiled and seemed pleased to see her, as he sat in his armchair drinking tea.

"But dad's been a lifelong coffee drinker! He hates tea – I don't remember him ever drinking it!" she had exclaimed, and her mother shrugged.

"He doesn't know that now – he drinks it without complaining." Sam found this profoundly depressing.

Sam's mother had gone on to talk about the news that Prince Philip had been involved in a car crash while driving near Sandringham.

"The man is 97 years old, for God's sake! Why in hell is he still allowed to drive? He could have killed someone. I hope I'm dead before I get to that age..." Sam found, increasingly, she had to tune out when her mother launched into one of her diatribes.

So when Sam and Lily met she would reassure her friend that she had been tired and irritable at the end of a challenging day and had spoken rashly. Of course her job was fulfilling – and it was certainly well-remunerated, with a range of attractive benefits. She could confide that she was being primed for the Deputy CEO role, something she hadn't yet shared with anyone. Together with Adam's salary, her job allowed the family a lifestyle they cherished – their beautiful home, a second house in France, skiing holidays and new cars and whatever the children wanted, which still hadn't led to them becoming selfish and spoilt. They were loving and appreciative. Sam had so much to feel grateful for. She certainly didn't hate her job, she would declare.

And yet she did.

"So tell me why you were feeling so disgruntled about your job when we spoke on the phone," started Lily, when they took their seats opposite each other in the bistro they had chosen for lunch.

Sam took a breath.

"Honestly, Lily, you just caught me at a bad moment. Everything is fine. It had been a frenetic day, and I was just feeling tired, I think. There's been a disagreement with one of my team which left a bit of a sour taste, and then when I called to see mum and dad, mum was in a particularly acerbic frame of mind. There's really nothing wrong at work. Anyway – much more importantly, tell me about Peter's situation."

Sam found it even easier than she had anticipated to convince Lily that all was well. Lily accepted her explanation and was relieved to hear that the woman whom they all quietly envied did, in fact, have a life that was enviable, despite the worry of her parents' deteriorating health. But that was, sadly, something they would all face, and part of a natural, inevitable cycle. Lily was, in any case, keen to move on to share her own news; after they had spoken, Peter had admitted that his job was at risk. They might even need to sell the house and relocate if he lost his job and had only limited prospects of quickly securing another on a comparable salary. There was no more talk of Lily changing her job at this point in the light of this new situation. Sam listened and sympathised. Lily just needed to pour it all out.

Driving home, Sam thought about her lack of honesty with one of her closest friends and wondered what made her so cautious about admitting the truth. Was she so used to being considered successful that she wished to preserve the illusion? Did she believe her dissatisfaction with her professional life, and her unhappiness with some of her earlier educational and career choices, reflected badly on her, and did she expect her friends might think less of her because of it? Was she wedded to the image of herself as the controlled and competent one, and protective of that identity?

Sam suddenly felt the ache of loneliness. She didn't feel this was something she could easily share with her friends. Adam was abroad on business but, even had he been home, she feared he wouldn't understand; she could hear him saying, "Count your blessings..." which was his stock response to any grumbles – he used it with the children all the time. And Sam wasn't the kind of mother who offloaded to her children – the twin girls, Emily and Annabelle, the eldest at 15, were mature and empathetic, and would have been a receptive audience, but Sam didn't believe in burdening the young: she should nurture and protect them, not make them anxious. Sam had always had an uneasy relationship with her own mother, and, though she had been close to her father, he was no longer the same person. Sam had an amenable relationship with her younger brother, but he lived abroad, and she reflected that she didn't even know him that well now – she could never remember having a conversation with him that had gone beyond the relatively superficial. She kept him informed about their parents' deteriorating health, and he periodically offered to come back to the UK for an extended period to help her and to support them, but Sam invariably reassured him that she was coping perfectly well and that he didn't need to do that.

"But I do need to talk to someone. Otherwise this is just going round in my head and it will drive me mad eventually."

And suddenly the answer was clear.

The first session took place two weeks later. Sam felt uncharacteristically nervous. Adam was away again, though he was expected home at the weekend. The children were all in school. The day had started like any other with an animated family breakfast before the children left together for the school bus, the girls chivvying Charlie, the youngest, who, at 11, needed considerable support to get organised; 13 year old Joshua was glued to his phone. Sam dressed as if for work, picked up her work case and locked the door and got into the car as the children disappeared round the bend in the road, and there was no reason any of them would suspect that this was not an ordinary working day for her.

But Sam drove into the city, an hour away, to meet her counsellor for the first time.

"Just tell me about yourself."

Why was this such a difficult question?

Sam talked of her family – Adam, the children, her parents, her work situation. The circumstances of her life. The facts. The counsellor listened, smiled, nodded from time to time. And Sam suddenly stopped.

"But I'm not telling you about myself, am I? I'm telling you about all those around me, and my interactions with them. I'm not talking about me."

Jane waited.

"I have three close friends, and every New Year's Eve we meet for lunch and at the end of the meal we all decide on one word which we hope is going to be key for us in the year ahead. I think we all give this careful thought, and when we meet during the course of the year – we usually meet and have a meal together about once a month, either lunch, or in the evening - we talk about how the word is proving to be relevant, and, sometimes, what we've achieved..."

Jane let the silence do the lifting, and after a pause, Sam continued.

"This year I chose 'purpose'." And she stopped.

Jane waited for several seconds, and then prompted, "Can you tell me what you were thinking when you chose that word, and do you think there's a connection between your choice of word and why you decided to see me?"

There was another silence and then, without directly answering the question, Sam began, "When I was at school, I was good at everything – sorry that sounds immodest, but it's true, and it's relevant. My friends all said how lucky I was that I could have chosen any subject at GCSE, any subject at A level, or degree level, and probably made a success of it. But actually, it can make things difficult. If you could do anything, where do you start, when you have a decision to make? And I loved all my subjects too – I just loved learning. So the sciences, drama, languages, art – I soaked it all up."

Sam stopped and took a sip of water.

"But my father was a doctor, and I'd grown up seeing how much that meant to him – and how he made an impact on other people's lives. He was admired, and respected and – loved. There were challenges and sadnesses too. He obviously couldn't save everyone, and I saw him tired and drawn sometimes. And exhausted. Mum found that difficult. I think she was protective of him, and I remember sometimes hearing her on the phone being sharp with patients, or their relatives probably, who wanted him to come out to them at night, when he'd just got in and was completely worn out. I used to cringe listening to what she said and how she said it. If dad heard he'd just gently take the phone from her and the next thing we knew he'd be putting his coat back on." Sam smiled, wanly, at the memory. "But being a doctor was who he was, not just what he did. And his life had purpose. He had a purpose within the family, too, of course. He was a good husband, a provider, a great dad to my brother and me, a dutiful son while my grandparents were alive – and he was a strong and supportive friend. But his professional identity was his significant contribution to the world. I just knew, growing up, that I wanted to have that, too."

There was a long break in Sam's monologue while she gathered her thoughts and decided how to frame the next part of the narrative.

"In the end… I decided I'd take sciences and maths at A level. I wanted to study Biomedical Sciences at university and become a doctor – maybe a hospital doctor, or go into medical research, rather than being a GP – I wasn't sure, but I knew it was medicine in some capacity that I wanted to devote my time to. And then mum fought me. She was angry. She said that it was no life - especially for a woman, a woman who would probably want to have children one day. She said it would be a selfish choice – selfish!" Sam laughed, but there was bitterness in the laughter, and her eyes briefly filled with tears. She drew a long breath and composed herself.

"But the thing that was hardest of all was that dad didn't stand up for me. I think he was so used to bending to her will that he didn't have the strength to stand against her. I felt so disappointed in him. I'd been a very biddable daughter up to this point – always keen to please, so I wasn't cut out for rebellion. Some of my friends were natural rebels..." Lily sprang to mind, with her secret tattoos and piercings and the vibrant hair colour which had caused consternation at school and at home, "but not me. So I gave in. I gave up. I did take a science degree – Chemistry – but I never used any of what I'd learnt. I had a job working for a hotel in the university holidays, and when I graduated they offered me a place on a graduate training scheme to become a hotel manager. Now I'm part of a team which manages a chain of hotels. The CEO even talked to me a few weeks ago about applying for the Deputy CEO role when it comes up in a few months, and the implication was that, although it isn't a done deal, I'd be a strong candidate. It's a significant promotion so that's flattering and seductive of course – to feel you're highly valued for doing a good job. The money and the perks are great. My closest friends think I've got it made. And there's no sense of purpose in my professional life at all. I compare it to the role my father had and I think – what difference do I make to anyone, really? What's the point? My children are wonderful, but they're growing up fast – it doesn't seem two minutes since Charlie was born, and he's at secondary school now. Josh is a typical teenager – he's a sweet boy, and he doesn't cause us any trouble, but he looks at me and I think I'm an irrelevance in his life, really. The girls are talking about A level choices and what they might do next. I realise it won't be long before they're leaving home. I love them all fiercely but every day they seem more independent and to need me less. And I know that will be increasingly the case. And my parents…"

Sam knew she would cry through this bit, so she took another deep breath and more water.

"Mum is still mentally sharp – and 'sharp' is the right word for her - but she has various health issues. Her mobility is deteriorating and she has problems with blood pressure and her breathing. Dad seems physically OK, though he's a few years older than she is, but he has dementia and he's – not my dad anymore. They still live in their own home but I know that's not something that we can sustain much longer. I've talked to them about social services support but mum won't consider it yet. I think they need to be in residential care so the support available is tailored to their needs, as things change….

get worse. Living with us isn't really an option, but mum wouldn't stand for that anyway.

"Dad doesn't even remember he was a doctor. Sometimes he doesn't know who we are – thinks mum is HIS mum, and he says the most surreal things. Mum gets quite cross with him sometimes, which upsets me because he can't help it, of course, but at the same time I can understand how hard it is for her..."

Sam's tears were flowing freely by this point and she helped herself to the tissues on the table. She resisted the impulse to apologise – Jane must be used to this and, in a way, this outpouring was the whole point, wasn't it?

"So I will care for them as best I can for as long as it takes. And I will carry on, I suppose, in my purposeless job where what I do – and I do work long hours and sometimes it's difficult – has little real impact on people's lives in any meaningful way. And when I have to go to the GP surgery or the hospital – my sporty son Joshua is especially fond of A & E..." Sam managed a faint smile, "I look at the medical professionals and I think, 'How did I get here, when I was so bright, hardworking, capable of so much – and I've achieved so little in my working life?' "

Jane gave time for Sam to calm herself, and then spoke quietly.

"So let's talk about how you can find your sense of purpose."

Chapter Four:

Gabrielle: #oneword 'hope'

Harry looked up from his biography and let his gaze rest on Gabrielle who was reading her novel on the other side of the log fire. He peered over his glasses and considered for a moment.

"The worst thing about your Kindle is that I can't just glance at you and know what you're reading. It could be lurid porn..."

Gabrielle smiled, removed her own glasses and smiled at him.

"Why would you want to know? And what's wrong with lurid porn anyway?"

"I'm just interested. I used to look at the cover, read the title and the author and ask you about it. Didn't we have more conversations about our reading in your pre-Kindle days?"

"Perhaps we did – not sure, really. Anyway, this is a fairly new Douglas Kennedy, 'The Great Wide Open'. I've read a few of his, you may remember."

"I remember."

It was one of the things she loved about her husband, Gabrielle reflected. He remembered.

"Is it a Book Club book?"

"No – just one of my own choices."

"What's it about?"

"It's about teaching, among other things. In actual fact, I read a sentence in it the other day and bookmarked it to share with you – I thought you might find it interesting."

Gabrielle flicked to the 'view notes and marks' option and located the passage:

"Here it is. 'If history teaches us anything, it is that only after the proverbial dust settles do we see the true shape of life's immensely difficult and frequently contradictory narrative.' What do you think?"

Harry was quiet for a moment, and Gabrielle found herself thinking, "That's something else I love about him – he's thoughtful."

"It *is* interesting. I might just take that to my A level lot tomorrow and ask them to consider it. Maybe there's hope that Brexit will make sense one day..." Harry turned back to his book, and Gabrielle picked up her glasses.

For a while she didn't carry on reading, however. She thought about the question Sam had asked them: 'Do you like the person you are when you're with your husband?' and how it had caused her to reflect, not only on her own marriage, but on her friends' relationships – though she conceded that we never fully understand anyone else's relationships, much as we might believe we do. She and Harry had a strong marriage, she felt. In fact, of the four friends she suspected her marriage was the strongest. Was it smug of her to think that? she wondered. She didn't like to think of herself as a smug person.

One of the novels she had read over the Christmas break – a long novel, but in holiday times, especially in a warm climate, Gabrielle would read all day as she sat in the sun – had included a phrase which she had also bookmarked, and she flicked through and found it again.

'He now viewed a successful relationship as one in which both people had recognized the best of what the other person had to offer and had chosen to value it.'

At the time, she had considered sharing it with her friends as a follow-up to the conversation they had had in response to Sam's question, but now she thought that might not be such a good idea. She felt strongly that it applied to her relationship with Harry, but wasn't convinced that it would resonate in such a positive way with respect to Kay and William, Lily and Peter, or Sam and Adam. She didn't, she realised, want her friends to consider her smug, either.

Gabrielle's thoughts then drifted into an accustomed groove. At some point, she needed to talk to Harry about what was on her mind. She wanted to find the right time, but they were already several weeks into the new year, term had resumed and they were both occupied with thoughts of work. This conversation needed time, and care. Although she felt she knew Harry incredibly well – they had been together for twenty years now and had been married for fifteen – she had to admit she was unsure about how he would react. They needed to have the conversation in private, and when they had time fully to explore the ramifications of what she wanted to suggest. So the conversations they had most days in the pub on their way home from the Health Club they had joined a year ago really didn't fill the bill. Talking it through on a long car journey – they were visiting friends in Norfolk the following weekend – might seem somehow claustrophobic.

"Am I just putting it off?" Gabrielle mused. "How committed to this am I?"

But she knew she was committed, and in a moment of clarity, realised a long walk in the open air would be the best option. Not looking at each other while they were talking was sometimes helpful – she had learnt this in her professional life, when both students and staff would occasionally open up and talk much more frankly if, at the same time, she and they were engaged in an activity which occupied their hands and eyes.

"I know we're at Marie and Simon's this weekend, but next weekend, if the weather is fine, shall we drive out into Derbyshire and have a good walk – blow the cobwebs away?"

Harry looked up and raised his eyebrows.

"If that would bring you joy, we certainly shall."

Once the idea had been proposed and Gabrielle had decided this was when she would broach the subject, she felt herself relax. As an inveterate list-maker, literal and metaphorical, she could clear her mind once she had a date and a plan.

On her way back from assembly, Gabrielle saw Juliet hovering, and realised the signs.

"Did you want to see me, Juliet?"

"Yes please - if you've a minute…"

"Come on in," Gabrielle gestured for her Assistant Head of Sixth Form to go through the office door ahead of her, and they relaxed in the easy chairs under the window – or, at least, Gabrielle relaxed. Juliet perched on the edge of her seat, looking uneasy. Gabrielle smiled at her and waited.

Juliet spoke in a rush, "I just wanted you to know that I'm – I'm pregnant. Just passed the twelve week mark so I felt I could start to tell people." Juliet blushed and paused. "We're really pleased – but I know it's inconvenient – you've only just given me the Assistant Head of Sixth role, and I fell pregnant much more quickly than we… It wasn't planned that way – we thought it might take a while before it happened. But we're really pleased…Sorry. I already said that…"

Gabrielle felt her young colleague needed rescuing here. She leant forward and took Juliet's trembling hand in her own warm one.

"That's tremendous news, Juliet! Many congratulations to you and your husband. You must be thrilled."

"We are – Gary, my husband, and me. All our family will be. It's just that I felt a bit worried about the job and.."

"Please don't. We will work it out. We can look at dates and detail nearer the time but, for now, enjoy your news. Are you feeling well?"

"Fine so far, Mrs… Gabrielle…"

Unlike her predecessor, Gabrielle had asked the staff from the outset to use her first name, and she recognised that some struggled with it. Her predecessor, though an impressive, capable head in many ways, was considerably more formal, and had been known as "Mrs Jenkins", even by her senior team.

Gabrielle also suspected that the previous head had not necessarily welcomed such news as Juliet's, and this was partly what led to her colleagues' anxiety if they had such news to share. As if she had read Gabrielle's thoughts, Juliet continued, "It's just that I know from what others have said that Mrs Jenkins wasn't always pleased at the disruption when staff needed time off – for any reason. And maternity leave was something she always sighed about, apparently. Odd, really – she had five children of her own…"

Gabrielle smiled again.

"Well, I'm certainly not sighing. I'm pleased for you. And when the time comes I'm happy to talk about flexible working if that's what you decide you'd like to do. We have to find ways of making that work. In the meantime, look after yourself and do let me know if you feel especially tired or unwell – if you need any particular kind of support, in fact."

Gabrielle stood, and Juliet took the cue and stood too, backing towards the door – and still looking nervous, Gabrielle thought, despite her best efforts. Perhaps it was the enormity of what lay ahead – Juliet was relatively young, and this was her first pregnancy, Gabrielle knew.

"Look after yourself, Juliet, and keep me posted."

Juliet smiled wanly and let herself out of the office. Gabrielle sank back into the chair and leant her head back against the cushions.

During her time as a Head of Department, then a deputy head and now as a head, Gabrielle had had several of these conversations. She always made sure she smiled, congratulated, reassured. Occasionally she had said, "Schools are all about children! If women didn't have babies, we'd be out of business!" Sometimes it struck her how ironic it was that some senior staff who had, themselves, had children and so had managed the personal and professional balancing act, were grudging and ungenerous when it came to supporting the next generation of mothers. Mrs Jenkins had, presumably, fallen into this camp. And Gabrielle remembered one tight-lipped deputy in an earlier school saying, "Well I managed with very little help or understanding at school when I had my children and I just got on with it. Why should she be any different?" At the time, Gabrielle had kept her counsel. Now, she realised, as head, if anyone voiced such a view in her school she would be very firm and clear in her response. That wasn't going to be the culture here.

In the last few years Gabrielle had become involved with #WomenEd, a grass-roots initiative across the education profession which had developed in response to a need for exactly the kind of support women like Juliet needed, and which her deputy head former colleague had been unwilling to provide. It was a network of men and women who were committed to helping, encouraging and mentoring women in education, particularly aspiring leaders at all levels, and often those who were juggling responsibilities at school and at home. Gabrielle was firmly of the belief that it was possible to have a fulfilling career and a rewarding and manageable life beyond work, but support was crucial, and networks such as #WomenEd certainly helped. It was also necessary for women to resist the impulse to be overly self-critical, to guard against a perfectionist streak and the guilt which often accompanied it, and to recognise that 'good enough' could be good enough – in a professional and personal context. Her own life, she recognised, had been simpler in some ways – she had worked hard, and although she had responsibilities and interests beyond work, raising a family hadn't been one of them. She still felt it was important to model to those who were potential future school leaders that it was possible to strike a healthy balance, and to resist the impulse to work to the exclusion of all else.

Gabrielle rose slowly from her chair and went to her desk to consult her diary: she was teaching Year 7 History before break, then had a meeting with a prospective parent, lunch with her team of Sixth Form prefects, a phone call booked with her Chair of Governors and an appraisal discussion with her Head of Science. At the end of the day she was meeting her Senior Leadership Team for their weekly catch-up, and she would tell them about Juliet, if they hadn't already heard it on the grapevine. They would talk about possible options for supporting the Head of Sixth Form in Juliet's absence.

The weekend with Marie and Simon in Norfolk was relaxing and enjoyable. The four had been friends since university days, and, as with Kay, Lily and Sam, Gabrielle always appreciated the richness of relationships where there was a shared history – where they had grown up together and now, she recognised, were growing older together. The pair had three teenage children, but all were away for the weekend, and, much as they loved their sons and daughter, Marie admitted there was a giddy sense of freedom about being teenager-free for two days. The two couples ate and drank, chatted and laughed, had a substantial breakfast on Sunday and then went for a long stroll 'to walk it off', as Simon said. They reminisced, and planned ahead, and felt comfortable in each other's company. Gabrielle and Harry left late morning to drive home, and there was a companionable silence in the car as they were each absorbed in their own thoughts.

Gabrielle had a little planning to do for the week ahead, and she closeted herself in the study and worked on the laptop while Harry went to the Health Club and swam his usual twenty lengths. He was back a little earlier than usual - "Didn't fancy the pub without you" – and the pair ate the late, light supper Gabrielle had prepared.

"Did you get your work done?"

"Pretty much," but Gabrielle realised that she had actually spent most of the time staring at a flickering curser and thinking, instead, about how she would feel this time the following week, when they had been on their long country walk and, she hoped, talked through what had been preoccupying her since before Christmas.

Harry pulled the car into the car park and stepped out and opened the boot to reach for their walking shoes and waterproofs, although the weather looked fine and they thought they would stay dry. Gabrielle realised she felt nervous, which was ludicrous, she thought, given her closeness to Harry. But she just wasn't sure how he was going to react to what she had to say.

They had walked for half an hour, chatting a little, enjoying the crisp, fresh air and the early signs that, although winter was still with them, spring wasn't too far behind. Then Gabrielle took a deep breath.

"I want to talk to you about something important. I'm not quite sure what you're going to think."

Harry slowed to a halt, and turned and looked at her quizzically. "This sounds ominous – is something wrong?"

He's thinking about my health, Gabrielle realised and was quick to reassure him. "No, not wrong, exactly – I'm fine, we're fine. It's only that…" She struggled with her thoughts for a moment, and Harry teased her gently. "Hey! It's not like you to be lost for words, especially with me!"

Gabrielle stood and looked at him, and her eyes suddenly filled with tears.

"I want a baby, Harry. I want your baby – I want to have a baby with you. You'd be a fantastic father, and I feel I've – I've let you down by not getting pregnant when we were younger. Is it too late? I hope it's not too late…" and Harry enclosed his sobbing wife in his arms.

On the journey home, Gabrielle reflected that they had probably talked themselves out. She had, in fact, done most of the talking, and it had been difficult because she had cried throughout. Harry had listened, holding her hand when the tears left her gasping. Her plan that they would talk as they walked and so not have to look at each other during this conversation hadn't worked at all. They had sat together on a fallen tree trunk and stayed there until Gabrielle finally ran out of steam, and then they had walked slowly back to the car.

Harry had simply said, at the end of Gabrielle's monologue, that if this was something she felt so strongly about, they should, of course, act on it. Over the years they had talked about having children at several stages of their marriage. In the early days they had simply assumed it would happen, and then, when time passed and it hadn't, sought medical advice. They had both undergone tests, but the results were inconclusive. Harry's tests confirmed that there was no problem on his side, so Gabrielle concluded the difficulty must lie with her. But no doctor had ever definitively established why Gabrielle shouldn't conceive. They had discussed IVF briefly, but Harry had been unenthusiastic about Gabrielle undergoing what seemed such an invasive and uncertain procedure. They had discussed adoption, and later fostering, even more briefly. The point was that Gabrielle has always wanted Harry's baby, not just *a* baby. The medical professionals they consulted just advised them to keep trying, and "trying for a baby" became Gabrielle's all-time least favourite expression. And then her career had taken off and she had found great satisfaction and reward in the different roles she had taken on. They had resumed using contraception, and hadn't talked about becoming parents in recent years.

When in January 2018 Gabrielle had been successful in the headship appointment process, they had both been thrilled. Harry enjoyed teaching history and he was a capable Head of Department, but he had no aspirations to senior leadership. Gabrielle had loved deputy headship, and when, having been internally promoted to a senior deputy post, she had occasionally represented the head, she found she felt increasingly comfortable in this role. "I need to go for a headship of my own", she had told Harry. "If I don't, I'll regret it. I want to challenge myself and see if I can do this." Harry had been fully supportive, practically and emotionally. Gabrielle had succeeded in her second headship interview, and had stepped into the role in September.

And it was all she hoped it would be. There were challenging decisions to make and sometimes difficult days, but she found joy in headship. "You can make a difference on a scale unlike any other you have ever known," she had told a group of aspiring heads at a conference a few weeks before Christmas. "Yes – it's not easy, but it's worth it. It's a privilege to lead a school." She had especially enjoyed talking about the rewards of leadership to groups of women at #WomenEd events.

And yet. Inevitably at these #WomenEd events, a common topic of conversation was how to combine leadership responsibility with motherhood and family life. Gabrielle was understanding and supportive, but a small voice within her whispered, "but they're *lucky*..." Just as she had felt, about headship, "If I don't, I'll regret it," over the course of the last term this feeling had taken hold with respect to becoming a parent. She was 40. It wasn't too late. True, she had failed to conceive when she was younger, but she wanted to try again.

She turned to Harry as he turned into their drive.

"Did I tell you my #oneword2019 was 'hope'?"

He shook his head.

"This is what I'm hoping for."

APRIL 2019

Chapter Five

Lily

"It's not fair!"
  "You cannot expect me to share a bedroom with *her*!"
  "That's all you ever say: 'We can't afford it'!"
  "Fine! I want to live with dad."
  In recent weeks, every exchange between Lily and her daughters seemed to contain variants of the same phrases, delivered at high volume and often followed by noisy fits of crying and then Ed Sheeran and Justin Bieber's 'I don't care' blasting out loudly from the bedroom. Lily did her best to soothe, rather than argue. She could understand the teenage girls' response to their current predicament, and tried hard not to lose her temper. As far as she could, she shielded Peter from the worst of it. He, she knew, was feeling guilty enough. She tried to protect Johnnie too, who was bemused but aware that some upheaval was imminent.
  Peter had lost his job at the end of January, and had not yet been able to find anything suitable in his field. The difficulty arose from the fact that something had gone badly awry with the last building project in which he was involved, and, although he swore to her that he was not to blame, it seemed that he was being made the scapegoat. Reputational damage was quick to follow, despite the agreed reference his previous employer had committed to supplying. Peter had come to terms with the fact that he would have to find alternative employment in a different professional sphere which was unlikely to bring with it anything like the salary he had been able to command in the last ten years. One consequence of this was that they had had to put the house on the market.
  Explaining this to the girls had been a challenge. Lily had initially talked about "finding somewhere smaller", by which she meant, of course, 'cheaper'. The girls quickly realised this would mean going back to sharing a bedroom, which they had

been happy to do when they were younger, and living with Lily and Tony in a much smaller place. But at 16 and 14 – and their relationship was fiery at the best of times – this filled them both with horror. Their current house wasn't huge, but it had four bedrooms and two 'reception rooms' (as the estate agents termed them – Lily was becoming wearily familiar with estate agent-speak) which enabled the teenagers and their friends to gather and socialise separately from the rest of the family. The new house – and it was proving very difficult to find something suitable for the family within the budget they had decided upon – was unlikely to boast such luxury.

One of the difficulties was that Lily was trying to find an appropriate, affordable house in the same area. Taking the children out of school was too drastic to consider: Molly was about to sit her GCSEs, and Fay to start hers in the autumn. Johnnie was happily settled at the primary school the girls had attended. Whatever else happened, avoiding disruption to their education, on top of everything else, was a priority.

The threat to go and live with Tony was, Lily knew, an empty one. Tony lived in a small flat with his current partner, Kelly, whose relationship with the girls was tense. When the girls stayed over, as they did from time to time, it wasn't a great success – they squeezed into the tiny second bedroom together, and argued and fought for much of the time they were there. Lily resisted the urge to remind them of this, however, determined to try to restore peace rather than to ramp up the conflict.

On this particular Sunday, the girls had retreated to sulk in their rooms, Peter was desultorily watching television, and Johnnie was at a party – Edward's mum Jennifer had promised to collect both boys at the end and walk Johnnie back home. Lily felt the need to get out of the house.

"I'm going to go for a walk – I might call in on Kay for a coffee and a chat. OK?"

Peter looked up and gave a half-hearted smile. Lily was torn between sympathy for him, and irritation – at him, and at their situation – but she was trying to be supportive. Once he had confided to her that the reason for his distraction was professional, and not romantic, she had determined to work hard on their relationship. He did still love her, she knew, and he was devastated at the position in which they found themselves. But they had not made love in recent weeks, and Lily was drained by the effort to appear positive – about his job prospects, the house, their finances, the children.

"I need a break," she thought. "And a walk and a coffee with Kay aren't really going to cut it. But it's the best I can do right now."

The conversation with Kay was, in fact, restorative. In the weeks since their New Year's Eve lunch, Kay had seemed increasingly positive, Lily realised. She had started a French refresher class, met a new friend there called Abiola, and this new interest was something separate from her work and her family and "just for me", she said. She planned to add in a Spanish class after Easter, and was talking about studying for A levels from the autumn, if all went well. In addition, she was being more assertive at home, ensuring William and Michael pulled their weight around the house and that Susanna did not take her so much for granted.

"It's a long, slow process," she told Lily. "It's easy to slip back into the old habits – that's me as well as the others. My #oneword was 'control', and it's been more telling than I realised. I thought this was about me taking more control, but in some ways it's about letting go of it. So the other day I asked Michael to peg out the washing, and he just didn't do it as I would have done. I always feel the socks might be happier if they were pegged in their pairs! It would have been so easy to go out and redo it all once he'd gone to the pub with his mates!" Kay laughed. "But I resisted. At the end of last year I was starting to feel ground down and knew I had to do something different. And I think William and I are getting on better, because I've been stronger…"

Lily caught the faint blush on Kay's face and smiled. "Are you saying you've rekindled the passion in your marriage by whispering sweet nothings to him, in French, when you're in bed?"

"I don't think my conversational French will run to that just yet!"

And the pair laughed.

Lily cut through the park on the way home, reflecting on her conversation with Kay, and her own predicament. She was absorbed in her thoughts and at first didn't hear someone calling her name, but then became aware that Jim was standing on a parallel path, his gym bag slung over one shoulder, watching her and smiling.

"Well – and I thought you'd disappeared from my life completely!"

Lily smiled back, and took the fork in the path towards where he stood.

"On your way back from a workout, I see," Lily looked up at him.

"Yes – and I can't say the same for you."

Lily felt momentarily uncomfortable.

"I've let my gym membership lapse. I didn't think I was going often enough for it to be worthwhile. There are other forms of exercise."

Jim laughed. "I was watching you walking at your leisurely pace for a while before you saw me. You won't burn off many calories that way!"

He paused, his head on one side, considering this attractive woman with whom, he knew, he had had a sustained flirtation. "Are you in a rush to get back, or…"

"No rush. What about you?"

"Same. There's a café at the entrance to the park."

"I know it."

"Let's have a coffee – maybe even a cake."

"Scandalous, Jim. You'll undo all the good work you've just done."

And they walked together towards the park gates.

When they had found a table, Lily offered to buy the drinks. As she walked to the counter she could sense Jim appraising her long legs in her slim-fitting jeans. She remembered the thrill of knowing he found her desirable. Their time together in the gym had always been characterised by a frisson of mutual attraction. As she waited for their coffees, she caught sight of herself in the mirror behind the counter. Her blond hair was swept up and she was suddenly pleased that, although she had had to forfeit her six-weekly visits to the hairdresser, she had recently coloured her hair at home in a determined attempt to keep the grey at bay. She turned back to Jim with a smile.

He was a good-looking, physically fit and easy-going man – the kind of man she had always been attracted to in her youth. He reminded her more of Tony than of Peter, which she found briefly troubling, but she pushed that thought aside. Life was tough at the moment, and was likely to continue to be so, through the trauma of a house move, making savings and, perhaps, borrowing from her parents (something she and Peter had already discussed) to tide them over until Peter found work. Might a casual fling with someone like Jim be just what she needed to add some life and colour to her days? Prior to her marriage to Tony, Lily had enjoyed a number of such relationships. But, of course, that was also before she'd had children, she reflected, as she carried the coffee back to the table and relaxed into her seat.

"So tell me what's been happening in your world," started Jim.

She remembered that in their conversations in the past she and Jim had always been able to move beyond the small talk to explore interesting topics – their thoughts and hopes and dreams rather than just chatter about the superficial elements of their lives. She had appreciated that – it was something that characterised her relationship with Kay, Sam and Gabrielle, too. But she realised that with Jim, now, she couldn't be so honest. She couldn't share with him her current anxieties – she had talked to him about Peter and the children before, and he had talked about his own family, but suddenly that seemed difficult. She had shared with him in the past her frustrations about work and her desire for something better, more stimulating, more rewarding. That seemed such an irrelevance now.

Suddenly there was a hammering at the plate glass window, and Lily turned at the sound to see Johnnie's face pressed against it. "Mummy!" Jennifer and Edward stood with him, and Lily realised immediately that they had been walking home from the party and Johnnie had caught sight of her through the café window. Unnerved for a few seconds, she quickly regained her composure and said to Jim, "Let me introduce you to my son." She met Johnnie at the door, thanked Jennifer, who turned for home with Edward, and led Johnnie through the tables to meet Jim.

Jim and Johnnie chatted while Lily bought her son a milk shake – "Choclate!" requested Johnnie, as if Lily didn't know that was what he always chose. By the time she returned to the table, they were clearly friends. A father to boys of Johnnie's age, Jim knew exactly what to ask, and what would engage and interest him. He made Johnnie laugh, and that made Lily smile.

Eventually, Lily started to gather her things together and said, "Well, young man, it's time we started for home." Johnnie looked briefly crestfallen – he was enjoying himself – but, "Pizza for tea," was all it took for Lily to distract him and to give him something else to look forward to.

As he rose from his chair Johnnie stuck out his hand to shake Jim's and said, "Pleased to meet you!" which was something he'd recently observed adults do, and started imitating.

Jim was amused, but graciously returned the handshake and said, "You too, Johnnie. Mind how you go!" and with a last smile at Lily, he too rose to his feet.

Lily and Johnnie left first, and Johnnie turned and shouted back to Jim, "Mind how YOU go!" before the door closed.

Over their pizza tea, Johnnie had chattered happily about meeting "mummy's friend" in the café, and, "Mind how you go!" was clearly to become a new favourite expression.

Peter looked quizzically at Lily and she said, "Just someone I used to see at the gym from time to time. He wondered why I'd stopped going and we went for a coffee and a chat." And then she added in an undertone, as Peter raised one eyebrow, "I didn't tell him the real reason."

The girls were subdued, and left the table as soon as the meal was over. Lily bathed Johnnie, read him a story and settled him in bed, and then joined Peter downstairs.

Peter had his laptop open and moved so she could sit beside him and see the screen.

"I've found this. It's hardly ideal – the pay isn't brilliant – but looking at the details, I'd say I have the skills they're looking for, and it's only half an hour's drive."

Lily read over the information and nodded. "If you think it's something you think you'd like to do," before realising that wasn't the right thing to say. Fulfilling his professional ambitions wasn't at the top of Peter's priority list at this point.

"Money is still going to be tight. If we could ask your parents for a loan - "

"Yes. I've already said I'll do that." Lily could hear the sharpness in her tone and she took a breath. "I'll go over and see them at the weekend. Shall we take the clan and make a family trip of it?"

"Can we face the rebellion?" Peter asked. They both knew the girls would resist. Lily reflected on how much they had loved their grandparents' company when they were younger. Filtered through their teenage perception such visits were now the epitome of boredom.

"You're right," Lily replied. "Can you bear holding the fort here and keeping an eye on the girls while I take Johnnie? He'd love to see them and they are always so happy when I take him over there."

Lily curled up next to Peter and rested her head on his shoulder. Considering for a moment that she and Jim might actually get together seemed pure madness. She remembered Johnnie in the café. How could she possibly consider taking a course of action that might cause pain to those she loved the most? She was by nature – or she had been in the past - careless and selfish, she thought. She compared herself with Kay, who had always put herself last, and invariably did so much (too much?) for other people at the expense of her own comfort and well-being ("ground down" was the phrase she had used today, Lily remembered). Lily knew she was so different. She was always tempted to put herself, her own happiness and satisfaction, first. Finding some excitement in an affair with a man who was clearly attracted to her was just symptomatic of that. Lily shook her slightly head as if to rid herself of her uncomfortable thoughts.

She considered the words she would use with her parents. They already knew, of course, about Peter's unemployed status and the reason the house was now on the market. She would explain that they had examined their financial position carefully and were hoping for a loan to help them through this period – they would pay it back, with interest, as soon as they could. Her parents had had well-paid jobs throughout their lives, with generous pensions. They had investments and savings - though she knew that current interest rates had significantly eroded the returns they had enjoyed in the past. They had helped her younger sister when Tara had wanted to get into the housing market in London. "My turn now," thought Lily. She felt confident that they wouldn't refuse.

But one thing troubled her. When, at 18, she had taken the decision to leave school to start working, and earning, as soon as she could, her parents had been dismayed, and they had tried hard to dissuade her. There hadn't been rows – that wasn't her parents' style – but they were both graduates, and professional people, and they were committed to the view that if you had the capacity to move on to Higher Education, that was a privilege you didn't turn your back on. Yes, it would give you greater earning power across your professional life, but it was also about fulfilment, and making the best of yourself.

Lily had a place to study Finance at Newcastle – she could see the appeal of a career in the finance industry, and she liked the idea of living for three years in a vibrant, northern city. At the eleventh hour, having secured the A level grades she needed, she withdrew because... Why was it? She knew she was capable, and she knew that taking a degree and moving into a professional field was what her parents had always hoped for and expected from her. However she rationalised it, was it basically a rebellion against what seemed to be the course plotted for her? She went to work in the bank and, despite finding the work routine and generally uninteresting, she had resisted the suggestion that she pursue professional advancement there. She had relied on Tony, and then Peter, to give her financial security and, certainly with Peter and his higher earning capacity, a degree of luxury in her life. What troubled her was the thought that her parents might be thinking, and might discuss privately, how Lily's current economic situation would not be so perilous if she had fulfilled her potential and embraced a career which could have given her both satisfaction and reward. She could perhaps have earnt a salary closer to Sam's, and found her work as interesting and challenging as Gabrielle did, had she made different choices at 18.

When Lily chose 'courage' as her #oneword on New Year's Eve, she had been thinking about the possibility of making some bold changes in her life – professionally and perhaps also personally, if it transpired that her marriage to Peter had run its course. Since then, the need for courage had come to mean something more to her. She needed the courage to confront her own failings and her own mistakes. To stand by Peter and support him practically and emotionally. To guide her children through the challenging times that might lie ahead. To resist the temptation to put herself first and to distract herself with something as pointless, and potentially damaging, as a relationship with someone like Jim.

She needed to talk to her parents - not only about securing their help but also, perhaps, about the past decisions she had made, which she now regretted, the consequences and her future options. She needed, perhaps, to tell them that they had been right and her naïve, self-absorbed and rebellious 18 year old self had been wrong - and it had taken her until her fifth decade fully to realise that.

She would show courage. And she would take greater care. "Mind how you go," she whispered to herself.

Chapter Six

Sam

"If only I had your energy!" her mother said, bitterly.

Sam leant across and took her mother's hand in hers, and said, softly, "Mum. You have. Anything you need me to do for you, I will. My energy is at your disposal," and she smiled.

"But you're so busy – the job, Adam, the children, your friends, holidays - your life!"

"I'm not too busy to help, though. And I can arrange other help. We can contact social services…"

Her mother made the dismissive sound she always uttered when the term was mentioned, and Sam resisted the urge to sigh. Kay's parents were younger than her own, but they had agreed to a number of measures such as an emergency call button which connected to a helpline should one of them fall and need assistance. Sam's mother, though physically considerably frailer, wouldn't yet consider it. And the proposal that they arrange visits from professional carers was anathema to her. Some people, Sam realised, are much more difficult to help than others.

"Where's that woman gone?" broke in Sam's father, querulously. Sam and her mother turned to him.

"Which woman?" they asked in concert.

"That woman who was here this morning – you know – where did she go?"

Sam and her mother exchanged glances and then her mother said, "There wasn't anyone here this morning. We haven't had any visitors except Sam - your daughter," she added, which always caused Sam a pang.

"I tell you, there was! She sat right there!"

Sam's father was becoming increasingly agitated. He had been such an even-tempered, genial man all his life, she thought, until the dementia took hold, and now he could become irritated, even aggressive, quite quickly. She understood this was a symptom of his condition, but it made him more of a stranger – even less recognisable as the father she had loved deeply ever since she could remember.

"Oh, THAT woman..." said her mother unexpectedly. "She went out to buy some fish and chips."

Her father paused for a moment as if in thought, then, "Ah," he said, and grew calm again. Sam closed her eyes for a moment.

"It was lovely when Robin was here," her mother mused. This was to be a reprise of a conversation they had held several times since February, Sam realised. She and Adam had taken the children for a few days' skiing in their half-term break, to Morzine in France, a favoured destination over the years. Robin, her younger brother, had flown back from Hong Kong to stay in their house, use their car and call in to see their parents each day.

"He was such a tonic! He took us out into the countryside and we had a very nice lunch in that pub we used to go to when you were children – you remember the one, near the river. Different owners now, of course, but still very nice. Not warm enough to sit in the garden, of course, but we had a nice table by the fire. Robin did make us laugh."

Sam knew what was coming next.

"We do miss him. I always hope, when he comes home, he might meet a nice girl and decide to settle down and come back here for good."

Sam wondered, as she often had over the years, whether, at some level, her mother actually realised that Robin was gay, and that meeting a nice girl and settling down near their parents was most certainly not on the cards. Was this a question of simple, deeply-rooted denial, or did she really know her younger child so little? It was Robin's business, and if he did not elect to share the truth of his life with his aged parents, that was his decision to make. Sam was pleased that Robin had a long-standing, loving partner in Hong Kong, where he was happy and settled – professionally and personally fulfilled. Which is more than I can say for myself, she thought, ruefully.

"Is there anything else I can do for you, mum? I have a meeting at work so I need to leave in about half an hour. And is there any shopping you want me to get you before I call on Tuesday?"

"I'll have a think and perhaps give you a ring later on."

"That's fine. I should be home by six. And, you know, if you want me to run you out into the country for a pub lunch at the weekend, we could always do that."

"Oh no, Sam, we couldn't trouble you. You're much too busy."

"Samantha! Come in. Coffee?" Lawrence reached for the intercom as he looked expectantly at her, but his hand hovered as she shook her head.

"I've just come from my parents where I drank enough tea to sink a battleship – or is to float a battleship? Whichever – I'm fine, thanks."

"Have a seat, then." And as Lawrence moved towards the comfortable settees beyond the huge, polished boardroom table, she realised this was to be an informal conversation.

"How are things with your parents?"

Sam realised this was a polite enquiry and that her CEO really didn't want a detailed report.

"Pretty much the same. We're coping."

"That's good to hear. Well, I wanted to have a chat today because Duncan has finally bitten the bullet and written to inform me that he intends to retire in the summer. I know we've talked briefly about this before, but I wanted to see whether you'd had any further thoughts about putting yourself forward for the Deputy's position. The board think very highly of you, Sam – you know that. You're very capable, not afraid of hard work, well-respected across the organisation. You're attractive…"

Sam blinked at him.

"Oh, don't look at me in that 'Me too' kind of way, Samantha! You understand what I mean. In this business, being attractive, whether you're a man or a woman, is always going to be an asset. You look the part, that's what I'm saying – you're smart and always very presentable."

Sam found herself tugging her skirt down a little.

She wondered how long the flattery might last if she didn't, at some stage, show she wished to speak. Privately, she considered that the reference to the importance of being 'attractive' was just one indication of how shallow and superficial this business was. The company certainly wasn't renowned for being a diverse employer. It probably considered, in fact, that it was ground-breaking because it was now considering a woman as a potential Deputy CEO. Throughout her time working here, since she graduated at 22, Sam had not known a more senior female executive. She forced herself to focus and tune in to what Lawrence was now saying.

"Of course, I won't be around forever, and a highly competent Deputy CEO would be in an extremely strong position to consider applying to step up to the CEO role in due course."

Lawrence paused. He was, Sam realised, trying to work out the reason for her lack of response so far.

"There would have to be an external advertisement and a proper, rigorous application and selection process, of course. It would have to be seen to be transparent and fair. However, if I could tell the board that you were definitely interested in throwing your hat in the ring, I think I could persuade them to save the expense of going through one of the professional search firms…"

Ah. So that was the reason for this conversation.

Lawrence paused again, but only briefly. He wasn't skilled, as her counsellor Jane was, at leaving silences to encourage the other person to speak, Sam found herself thinking.

"So what do you say, Samantha? What are you thinking? I know the board would like to know."

Sam took a breath.

"What's the time frame, Lawrence?   When would they advertise?"

"Well, Duncan will leave us in August. I think we would like to have the appointment of his successor finalised by the beginning of July. If it is an internal appointment – and there's no one other than you who has the calibre and the seniority to step up within the company, I should say – that would give a good block of time for a proper induction and solid handover. Of course, if you decide you aren't up to this…" – an interesting turn of phrase, Sam thought – "..and they will have to appoint externally, I think they will want to engage a firm of headhunters – and it make take a while to organise a beauty parade so that they can select the firm they favour – I suspect they will want to move on that by the beginning of May – so the start of next month."

Sam rose from her seat, smiled and held out her hand to shake Lawrence's.   He stood, too, a little bemused, and dutifully took it.

"Thank you for letting me know the situation, Lawrence. Obviously, I need some time to think it through. I'll let you, and the board, know what I decide before the end of April."

And she turned and left the room, quietly proud of her composure.

A short while later, relating all this to Jane, Sam found herself alternately amused and irritated.

"So much of all this is so typical of the business I'm in, and the particular company I work for," she explained.   "I'm expected to be flattered, even seduced into applying – grateful that they would even consider me. If I don't apply, they assume it will be because I don't believe I'm 'up to it', as Lawrence graciously put it – not that I might decide it isn't what I want to do, even though I know I'm capable."

"And do you feel flattered, seduced and grateful?" asked Jane with a slight smile.

"I feel a number of things - but, no, those adjectives don't hit the mark!"

"I suppose the key question is: do you want to do this job? Could it be that simple?"

Sam was thoughtful for several minutes.

"I certainly wouldn't do the job as Duncan has done it. One thing I need to think through is the extent to which I might be able to mould the role so that I can make a more significant impact in that position, and whether the status of the title would give me the opportunity to have a positive influence on the company. Or is it so much of a juggernaut that my sphere of professional influence would be limited? It would probably mean more travel, so more time away from the family – and I can't say that appeals. It would mean a considerably higher salary, but that has never been a motivator for me. If I ask Adam and the children - well, the twins, at least. I can't see the boys being that interested! – I suspect they would feel proud of me for being considered and keen that I should accept it and go for a fresh challenge, but…"

"Are we back to the idea of purpose, perhaps?" Jane asked, after a silence.

Sam grinned. "I suspect we might be!"

Sam's phone buzzed in her bag.

"I'm so sorry! I thought I'd turned it off completely." Sam knew that having her phone switched off was one of the 'rules' of the session. Embarrassed, she quickly turned it off – she thought – and returned it to her bag. She would pick up her messages later.

"Anyway," she turned back to Jane and continued. "I do need to think, and to talk to the family. And perhaps my friends - they know me well, and I'll be interested to know what their reaction is, although…"

Sam reflected on her lack of honesty with her closest friends concerning her recent professional dissatisfaction, which she knew to be somehow bound up with her father's decline and the examination of her life's choices that had been triggered by that. Even after she blurted out some of her frustrations to Lily on the phone a few months ago, she had then been quick to back-pedal and reassure her friend that all was, in fact, well. So was it fair to expect her friends to give a considered response to the news about the potential change of role at work when they were, in reality, in the dark about how Sam was feeling about it all?

"I'll make a decision, as I promised, by the end of this month and let Lawrence know."

Jane sensed that the discussion about work was over for this session.

Sam had shared with Jane the fact that her lack of honesty with her closest friends troubled her. It was something she found difficult to explain, and certainly to justify.

"Have you thought any more about what motivated you to keep your dissatisfaction at work from your friends?" Jane recognised these were important women in Sam's life. She did not add that Sam had also not told them – or her family - about the counselling sessions. Sam thought that perhaps a number of Jane's clients met her without sharing the information with those who knew them best.

"I think part of it is that they have their own issues, and I don't want to burden them with mine – though I have to say that, of the three of them, Kay seems happier than she did when we chose our words on New Year's Eve. She's found a new interest, and that seems to be going well – she's learning again, and I think she's finding that refreshing. She's also been more assertive with her family, encouraging them to be more independent and not so reliant on her – even her sister, who seems to have 'learned helplessness' off to a fine art - and that's been positive for them all, I think. So I feel less concerned about Kay. I'm pleased for her, and I know she'd be supportive if I shared this. But I don't feel I can tell one and not the others. And I'm worried about both Gabrielle and Lily. Gabrielle seems unusually preoccupied – I'm not quite sure what's happening there. She says she loves her job – and she's clearly very good at it. She invited us all to a school event a couple of weeks ago – a cabaret evening, a PTA fundraiser, where the students played in a band and sang nightclub numbers. It was superb, and when she stood up to say her thanks at the end we could all see how comfortable she is in her own skin, how composed and poised she is in her role. But there's something – perhaps in her marriage, that's unsettling her, I think. Or it did cross my mind that there might be an issue with her health, or with Harry's. I've noticed that the last couple of times we've been out she hasn't drunk any alcohol at all, which is unlike her – although she's usually driving, so I suppose that might be why she's decided to abstain completely. I have asked the 'How is everything?' type of question when we've met, but she invariably says, 'Fine!' – as people do, I know. I'm sure she realises she can talk to any of us when she's ready, but we try hard not to pry into the most sensitive parts of each other's lives. It's a delicate balance in friendship sometimes."

Sam thought about this for a while – and how it related to her own unwillingness to share with her friends some of the things that mattered most to her. She should, she decided, be more forthcoming with them. She knew without a shadow of doubt that she could trust them and that they would support and bolster her.

"And Lily – Lily is really struggling, I'm afraid. I know I told you about blurting out something to her on the phone, and immediately regretting it, and back-pedalling like mad. Since then she's been taken up with her own problems, and Lily can be quite..."

Sam hesitated to say 'self-absorbed', which seemed disloyal.

"Focussed on herself and her own difficulties, I'd say. I know she's standing by Peter and being as supportive as she can, and she's trying to protect him from the wrath of her girls, who are just so unsettled by the changes in their lives. Her parents are going to help them financially, and Peter is applying for jobs now. I talked to Adam about suggesting the family came with us for a fortnight in France in late July, after the schools have broken up. I've told you we have a house near Bergerac, haven't I? I thought it might give them something to look forward to. Adam thought it was a good idea so I talked to Lily about it – I was a bit bowled over by how grateful she was. She actually cried - which isn't like Lily. So then I asked Adam how he'd feel about inviting Gabrielle and Kay, too – not for the full fortnight, but just to come and stay for a few days so, at one point, we'd all be there together. It could be lovely, I think. It will be a tight squeeze when we're all there, but manageable."

"You're thoughtful and generous." Jane smiled.

"Hmmm – not sure about that! But Lily just needed a treat to anticipate, and her girls always get on well with my twins, Johnnie is delicious and Josh and Charlie will look after him, so it should all work, I think."

"You've talked to me before about your concerns that your children are becoming increasingly independent. How are you feeling about that?"

"Well, the fact that they seem to be growing up so quickly is unnerving, I think, and there's somehow a sense that, from being indispensable to them when they're younger, you suddenly become irrelevant. Oh, I know they do still need me in many ways, but sometimes I look at them all when they're at home and feel I'm slowly becoming invisible. I'm just not the focus of their lives any more. Charlie, the baby of the family, has grown up so much since he started at secondary school last September – he's almost unrecognisable compared with a year ago. But he has good friends, seems to be coping with the work – though neither of my boys do half the homework the girls do, I have to say! So he's settled and happy, which I'm grateful for, of course. It's just that…he used to be so demonstrative with me, so loving, but now he's embarrassed if I accidentally touch him! Joshua has, I think, found a girlfriend. The twins know something but they're being wonderfully loyal to him and not teasing him or gossiping, so I'm not going to pump them for information. He's still really into his sport, but suddenly he's taken this bizarre interest in his appearance, and is generating much more washing! I look at him and I can see the man he's going to be – and that's not far off. It's a real mix of emotions –

pride, definitely, but combined with regret that his childhood is over. And Emily and Annabelle are, as ever, fine human beings. I really *like* them, you know? And I do appreciate that because I know a fair few parents who wouldn't say they much like their teenage offspring – even though they still love them! I am so lucky in my children. I should feel appreciative of that, I know..."

Sam's phone started to buzz again - she glanced at her bag as it continued.

"Oh my goodness – I am SO sorry, Jane. I really thought I'd turned it off completely! It's a new phone, and I clearly haven't mastered how it works yet." Sam fumbled in her bag. "It's probably Lawrence calling to butter me up some more!" she laughed uneasily, embarrassed at her failure to turn the phone off. She looked at it and tried to work out how to do so.

"Sorry, Jane - I'll just... Oh, it's Adam. He never normally rings me at work - or when he thinks I'm at work. I suppose it might be something to do with one of the children..."

"Sam – please answer it if it's making you feel unsettled."

Sam stood and walked over to the window, still muttering her apologies, and then she answered the phone.

"Adam, sorry, I'm in an important meeting..." – Sam knew this was an evasion, but as she had not yet shared with Adam the fact that she was regularly visiting a counsellor, this clearly wasn't the time to say exactly where she was. She listened while Adam spoke, and Jane saw she went very still. Then Sam said, quietly, "I'll be right over."

When she turned to Jane, her eyes were full of tears.

"It's my mother. She's had a stroke."

Sam's voice wavered. She swallowed and took a deep breath. "She's died."

Chapter Seven

Gabrielle

"So – it looks like a non-starter, you think?" Harry's brow was furrowed with concern as he looked at his wife.

Gabrielle nodded, mutely.

The conversation Gabrielle and Harry had about IVF, following their walk in Derbyshire in January, had been short; they had both examined the statistics relating to the likelihood of success once women had reached the age of 40, and had decided that fertility treatment was not an option they would choose. Gabrielle looked, too, at the success rate for women at age 30, and reflected on their discussions on the subject ten years before. At that time, Gabrielle knew that Harry had had reservations about IVF treatment. She would have been willing to undergo it had he been more positive, but she did not, at that time, feel desperate to have children. Then around her thirtieth birthday she had started to apply for Heads of Department posts, and had secured a position quickly – it was a school she loved and a job she found enjoyable and fulfilling. They had resumed using contraception and set the question of parenthood aside for a few years.

Five years later, they had tried once more to conceive, and after several months with no success, Gabrielle started again to look at job advertisements. She moved to another school to become deputy head, they bought a larger house, and Harry found a new role as Head of History and Politics. This would be, he said, his last career move. He was good at his job and found it sufficiently rewarding. However, Gabrielle found she was increasingly energised by fresh leadership challenges. After another four years, when the head alongside whom Gabrielle had worked as deputy (latterly the senior deputy), and for whom she had great admiration and respect, decided to take early retirement, Gabrielle had no hesitation in applying for the role. She was unsuccessful this time, and the school appointed externally, but, within a year, Gabrielle had secured a headship in a girls' school nearby. Much as she had enjoyed being a deputy head, Gabrielle recognised that she loved headship even more.

It wasn't a question of choosing between a family and a career. Gabrielle simply realised that now she wanted both, and she felt confident that, with Harry's support and paid childcare when they needed it, she could navigate the roles of headteacher and mother. They had sought medical advice about their failure to conceive a decade before, and received no conclusive explanation of what the difficulty might be. Gabrielle remembered vividly that on her medical notes, the doctor they consulted labelled 'cause of infertility' simply 'unexplained'. Ten years on, she and Harry now decided that they would just stop using contraception again, enjoy the healthy sex life which had characterised their relationship from the very beginning, and – Gabrielle's #oneword again – hope.

Gabrielle charted her monthly cycle, calculating her most probable fertile period so that they could concentrate their 'efforts' accordingly ("but if you ever use the phrase 'trying for a baby', Harry, I will definitely plead a headache..."). Gabrielle had been concerned that this might make their physical intimacy seem overly regulated and mechanical. In fact, they were enjoying each other even more than usual, and the added possibility that it might lead to pregnancy actually led to feelings of particular closeness and warmth.

"Have you talked to the girls about this?" Harry asked one evening, propped up on one elbow and looking at his wife as she lay, holding herself very still, next to him. Sam, Lily and Kay had been "the girls" in their conversation since they had, in fact, been 'girls'.

"No. And I'm not sure why. We've shared so much over the years, and they're my very closest friends. But this is so personal and sensitive, and I certainly don't want them asking, or wondering – or for them to share the disappointment when another month passes, and..."

"I know." Harry lightly brushed back a strand of hair that had fallen over Gabrielle's cheek as she turned to look at him.

"I do wonder whether we all have some things we don't share with each other – even though we're such good friends and we've known each other a very long time. Perhaps we all need our private spaces."

There was a short interlude where Gabrielle thought of what these 'private spaces' might involve, for each of the women.

"How is Sam coping?" Harry asked after this period of silence.

"She's amazing. I think we all felt her mum was indestructible, despite the way her body was weakening. We expected Sam's dad would die first, I think, and it was a shock. She wasn't quite 80. I imagined her grumbling her way well into her 90s... Sorry – does that sound mean?"

Harry smiled. "She wasn't an easy woman. I always thought Sam showed great patience."

"Well, she managed to be very composed at the funeral. Her poor dad seemed completely bemused."

"Is he settled in the care home, did Sam say? He must be confused."

"Apparently he seems quite calm. Sam thinks he likes to have so many people around him. He can't hold a coherent conversation any more, sadly, but she says he doesn't seem agitated or distressed."

Gabrielle looked at the clock.

"Have I rested for long enough, do you think? Shall we get up now?"

"I think we should." Harry swung himself out of bed. "Shall I pour you a glass of red?"

"I'm trying to steer away from alcohol just at the moment – for obvious reasons. I think what I'd really like is a nice cup of tea...."

On the morning of the final day of the spring term, Gabrielle had arranged a meeting with Jo, the Head of Personal, Social and Health Education, who wanted to discuss with her the planning of the following year's programme, which Jo hoped to do some work on over the Easter break.

"I have to say, I'm really impressed with what you cover here," Gabrielle began, as they settled with their coffee into the easy chairs. "It's a really thorough, interesting, relevant course."

Jo blushed slightly and smiled. "I'm proud of it – I've got a really good team to work with, and we evaluate it and develop it each year so that it's current, and we improve it in any way we can. That's why I wanted to see you – just to check with you that you were happy with what we're thinking. There's inevitably some sensitive stuff we'd like to include."

Gabrielle suspected that Mrs Jenkins had not always been accommodating. But her own response was to respect the expertise and to trust the judgement of capable staff such as Jo and her team.

"So what are you thinking?"

"Well," Jo took a breath. "Looking at the activity around climate change protests at the moment, and this girl Greta Thunberg and what she's been saying, I thought we should spend some time on environmental awareness and the role young people can play in raising the profile of the issues, and so on."

Gabrielle laughed. "That should definitely strike a chord. I saw the debating team organisers at break and they want to choose as their next motion: 'This House would strike to support global action on climate change'! I'm looking forward to hearing what they have to say on both sides of the argument."

"They really appreciate that you go to those debates, by the way – Friday nights, not all heads would…" and then Jo looked a little embarrassed at what she had just said.

"But I really enjoy them – and the girls speak so well – on the panel and from the floor – I feel really proud of them. It's honestly a joy rather than a chore. So, anyway, yes to adding something on environmental awareness. I think the girls will enjoy it and I'm sure they'll have plenty to say. I expect one of your challenges is what you can possibly leave out when you add new content."

"Definitely. And we're aware that there is a new curriculum coming in with respect to Relationships and Sex Education, so we need to think about how we want to develop that part of the course, too. We've already had a discussion about gender fluidity..." Jo paused to gauge her head's reaction. Gabrielle simply nodded and waited. "Are you happy if we look at how we can integrate learning about that into the programme? I know it's a sensitive subject..."

"But it's an important one, and considering the size of the school, there must be some here who struggle with gender identity. To avoid it because it's sensitive would seem cowardly, don't you think?"

Jo considered the new head for a moment, who waited, her head slightly tilted, to hear what she thought. "This is going better than I thought it might..." she reflected.

Later in the meeting, as they were starting to wrap up their discussion, Gabrielle ventured, carefully, "There is something within Relationships and Sex Education that I wanted to ask about."

Jo waited.

"I remember when I was at school – several centuries ago, naturally – sex education was very much about the mechanics of it all. The expectation was that pregnancy could happen very easily and might well happen too early – in fact the main focus of the lessons seemed to be how to avoid pregnancy until the time was right."

Jo nodded, and Gabrielle paused for a few seconds.

"The implication was that whenever we wanted to have children, it would be straightforward – it would just happen. But given how many couples actually struggle to conceive, and the emotional repercussions of that – in fact the emotional repercussions of becoming sexually aware generally, which seem to me something our girls really need to reflect on - I just wondered what you thought about including more on the subject of fertility, by which I suppose I mean the possibility of infertility…"

Gabrielle stopped, and Jo thought that, for the first time, she seemed to lose some of her composure. Jo knew Gabrielle did not have children, just as Gabrielle knew that Jo had an eight-year old boy, Jack. Jo thought for a moment, and then said, "Yes – I agree that this is important. We do include sessions on the emotional side of RSE – expectations, pressures, and so on, for example what can happen to friendships when girls start to be attracted to boys – or to girls, of course. We've asked the girls about the kinds of things that concern them during adolescence, and that was one of the things that came up. We haven't done anything specifically on fertility issues, but, as you say, they aren't uncommon, and it would be a worthwhile addition to the programme, I think. Are you happy for me to talk it through with the team and put together a proposal to discuss with you?"

Gabrielle looked a little more relaxed. "That would be perfect – thank you. Even though I know it may give you another headache in terms of how you create the space for it."

"Maybe at some stage we could revisit the curriculum time that's always been allocated to PSHE," Jo smiled, "but I see that this isn't the moment!"

"Thanks for your time, Jo," as Gabrielle walked her colleague to the door.

Jo hesitated when she reached it, and turned back.

"Gabrielle – I just want to say that… It took us three rounds of IVF before we managed to conceive and have Jack. I would be prepared to talk about my experience if you think that would be a helpful part of the programme."

Gabrielle was surprised – this was something she hadn't known.

"This is personal and sensitive, Jo. I think it would be wonderful if this were something you felt you could share with the students, but do, please, give it some careful thought. You really mustn't feel pressured to do this. I would never expect it."

"I actually think it might be good for me to talk about it," Jo mused. "And – I need to talk to her first, but one member of the team actually went through five cycles, and never managed to conceive. I don't know whether she might also be prepared to talk to the girls, but I can certainly speak to her about it."

Gabrielle smiled. "I appreciate that you're prepared to do that, Jo. But, again, there's no pressure and no expectation on my part. I know how hard this must be for both of you. We'll talk again. In the meantime, have a wonderful Easter holiday. Make sure you take plenty of time to relax and re-energise."

Jo nodded and thanked her as she stepped out into the corridor.

Gabrielle, thoughtful, returned to her desk where she sat for a few moments, deep in thought.

"Would I have been prepared to talk openly about my own experiences and disappointments? I would like the pupils here to consider potential challenges around fertility so that, if it does happen to them at some stage in the future, they're better prepared. I'd like them also to see that if they don't choose to have children at all, that is perfectly fine, and a decision which should be respected. And if, like me, they decide they really want a family, and it just doesn't happen, then that doesn't mean their lives won't be rich and full. Could I talk to them about this, or is it just too sensitive and might it make them, and the staff, uncomfortable?"

Then she thought about #WomenEd. Would that be an appropriate forum for discussing some of these issues with the women who supported these events? Could she, in fact, speak publicly about possible childlessness and its relationship to professionalism without becoming overcome with emotion? She didn't know.

Her phone rang, and Susie, her PA, let her know that her next appointment was waiting in the sitting room, so Gabrielle made her way downstairs.

That evening, Gabrielle and Harry talked about their respective days, and Gabrielle shared what had been discussed in the meeting with Jo.

"Could you stand up in front of staff and pupils and share something so personal, do you think?" Harry asked.

"If it helped them, yes, I think I could. But that's a discussion for the future, perhaps. I'll see what Jo comes back with when she's talked to the team and fleshed out a few ideas about this part of the PSHE programme. I think I might like to have some input into PSHE next year, in some way. I'm loving the Year 7 History, and it's a great way to get to know the girls, year by year, but if I taught some of the PSHE lessons I could build my relationship with some of the older girls too. We'll see."

The couple relaxed on the settee, relishing the moment where the Easter break stretched out before them. They had the weekend to relax and then they had booked a city break in Tallinn for the first week of the holiday. Harry poured a glass of wine for himself and sparkling water, with ice and lemon, for Gabrielle. He'd asked her whether he, too, should give up alcohol for the moment but Gabrielle had smiled and said that, considering he was a moderate drinker who just really enjoyed a glass of wine from time to time, she didn't think that was really necessary.

"But I do appreciate the support!" she had said.

Now Harry picked up his laptop and scrolled through his Rough Guide. They enjoyed European short city breaks in their holidays, and found it helped them both to unwind to explore a new destination. In the last few years they had visited Prague, Krakow, Budapest, Berlin, but this was their first visit to Estonia.

"Listen to this.." Harry read, " 'The heart of Tallinn is the Old Town, still largely enclosed by the city's medieval walls. At its centre is the Raekoja plats..' – not sure about my pronunciation there! – '...the historic marketplace, above which looms Toompea, the hilltop stronghold of the German knights who controlled the city during the Middle Ages. East of the city centre there are several places worth a visit, such as Kadriorg

Park, a peaceful wooded area with a cluster of historic buildings, and the forested island of Aegna.' Sounds good, don't you think?"

"Yes – I'm really looking forward to it. I'll sort out the packing tomorrow. What time did you say you wanted to leave for the airport on Sunday?" They had arranged to stay in an airport hotel the night before their early morning flight.

"Not too early. We can eat here and then just arrive at the hotel and go down to the bar for a drink – non-alcoholic for you, I appreciate - before an early night." Harry smiled at her, as 'early night' had become a particularly meaningful phrase in the last few months.

Gabrielle smiled back and leant forward to pick up the remote.

"Do you want to watch the news?"

Harry set aside the laptop as Gabrielle rose and went into the kitchen to replenish their glasses. As she returned, he said, "So another big High Street name goes into administration. It's amazing, isn't it – companies that we thought were large enough to be around forever closing down with huge job losses."

"Oh no…" groaned Gabrielle, as she looked at the screen and saw which retailer he was referring to.

He looked quizzically at her.

"Is it a shop you're particularly keen on?"

"It isn't that, Harry. It's the shop where Kay works."

Chapter Eight

Kay

"Hello, dead woodlouse..." Kay muttered, "Haven't we met before? Yes... I think I sucked you up in the downstairs loo a few minutes ago."

Kay looked at the ancient vacuum cleaner her parents owned. It appeared incapable of picking up anything that was large enough to be visible, or, if it did, Kay thought, it then spat it out, as if in a bad temper, a few minutes later.

As she thought of the 'bad temper' of the machine, she reflected on her tendency to anthropomorphise. Abiola, whom she had met at her French refresher class at the College, had pointed this out in their conversation in the pub after a recent conversation class. Kay hadn't heard the word before, but as Abiola explained, "You treat inanimate objects like they were living things, girl..." Kay recognised that this was definitely something she frequently did. She wondered why.

Kay abandoned the machine in the hall and went into the living kitchen where her parents sat, half watching the television while entertaining, or being entertained by, Robbie, who sat in his high chair enthusiastically and good-naturedly banging plastic things together and occasionally launching them across the room.

"There's another condition."

Her father raised his eyebrows.

"You invest in a new vacuum cleaner. This one is useless, I'm afraid. Was it pre-war?"

"Depends which war you're referring to," quipped her father.

Her mother furrowed her brow. "How much do they cost?"

"Mum," said Kay patiently. "You can afford it, and I'm confident we'll get years of use out of it." Kay's mother was inclined to refer to possessions as things which would 'last them out'.

Rachel came in from cleaning the bathroom. "All done!" She sounded positively upbeat, thought Kay. "Are you finished?"

"Well, the vacuum cleaner certainly is," announced Kay. "I'll bring mine round tomorrow to finish off, and then we'll have a trip to Curry's to buy a new one. Is that a plan?"

"Let's have lunch out and make a trip of it," suggested her father. Kay knew which pub he would choose and, in fact, which meals each of her parents would order. She smiled.

"I'll come straight here after my morning shift at work. Ready, Rachel? I can drop you off."

"I think I'll stay and have a cup of tea first and then walk home. It's a nice day."

Kay wiped down the high chair and returned it to the hall cupboard, before fastening Robbie into his carrier and shoving the plastic missiles into her bag.

"See you tomorrow." She kissed her parents and sister, picked up Robbie in his carrier and left the house.

This was working out well, she decided. A few weeks earlier, she had arrived at her parents' house to find her mother breathless and her father anxious.

"We were doing the cleaning," he explained, "and I think it's getting to be a bit much for your mum."

"That's understandable," said Kay, dropping into an armchair and taking her mother's hand in her own. "Is it time we talked again about social services support? A home help?"

"We've been discussing that," said her father. "We wonder if we might just be able to employ a cleaner – we only need a couple of hours a week. There will come a time when we need more than that, I know, but at the moment, we think that might be enough. How much do you reckon that might cost?"

Kay was thoughtful for a few minutes.

"How would you feel about paying, say, £20 for two hours each week?"

"Well. That sounds all right," replied her mother. "We thought it would be more."

"It probably would be, but what about this idea? You pay me to do it. Under one condition."

"What's that?"

"That Rachel comes and does it with me."

Kay's plan was that they would initially start by working alongside each other, but that she would gradually do less and Rachel would do more, until Rachel took full responsibility and full payment. It wasn't very much money, and she knew her parents, who tried to be as self-sufficient as they could possibly manage, despite their modest means, would feel better if they were paying rather than expecting their daughters to do the work for nothing. But it had been some time since Rachel had received payment for work and Kay thought it might perhaps have a positive impact on her sister's general state of mind.

Today had been their third visit. They had varied how they allocated the work, so Rachel had already tried the dusting, vacuuming, cleaning the kitchen and bathroom, and she seemed reasonably content with each job. Kay smiled as she heard Rachel humming while she worked. Helping their parents, doing a good job and receiving a payment for it was something Rachel seemed to find satisfying. If they worked together they could get through the small bungalow in an hour. Kay's plan was to say she could only manage half an hour in a week or two, so that Rachel would take an hour and a half (and three quarters of the payment), and shortly after that Kay was hoping to bow out completely and leave Rachel to get on with the job on her own. Kay knew her sister well enough to recognise that if she had suggested Rachel took responsibility for the cleaning by herself from the outset, she would have felt overwhelmed by the prospect.

"You see, Robbie," she explained to the chattering boy, as she strapped his carrier into the back of the car, "There is such a thing as a win/win."

Tuesday was Kay's French class, which she always looked forward to. She had made good progress, she knew, and felt proud of her growing confidence. It seemed that the French she had learnt for GCSE almost 25 years before had been dormant, all along. Now she was using it again, it was coming back to her. She looked forward to adding a Spanish class after the College's Easter break.

Meeting Abiola at the class and making a new friend had been a bonus. The two of them usually called at the pub on the way home for one drink, initially for a debrief of the class and to share their observations about the teacher (a formidable woman) and their classmates. Kay had been struck from the outset by how easy it was to talk to Abiola, how well she listened and how, as a result, they moved from small-talk to a discussion of more significant things quite quickly. Abiola had come to England from Nigeria as a teenager. Kay found the opportunity to get to know someone whose background and culture were significantly different from her own very interesting.

This week, as they settled in a booth with their halves of lager, Abiola asked, "So tell me what's happening with the shop."

"Our branch is closing at the end of June."

"What will you do, do you reckon?"

Kay was quiet for a moment.

"I'd like to take a little time out. I've talked to William and he says we can manage financially if I don't earn anything for a couple of months. I thought I'd look for work again in the autumn. I want to see what's out there, and not just go for the first part-time shop work I see. Also..."

Abiola said nothing, just waited while Kay considered how to phrase what she wanted to say.

"I have this idea that William and I could spend a month in the summer touring round France. We've had relatively little holiday in our lives, and most of that has been in England. We've never been away just the two of us. We didn't have the money when we first met, and then the children came along. I'd like to try out my French," Kay smiled shyly and blushed a little, "and we could visit different parts of the country. William has talked to Tom about taking a month away from the painting and decorating business. It actually works out quite well because Tom's son Ed is home from university and he's going to work with his dad for the summer. I told you Sam has invited us all to her place out there at the end of the month, so we can make that one of our stops and spend time with the others, then make our way home after that. It's just that…"

Kay's words petered out, and after waiting a moment to see if she would continue, Abiola prompted her.

"You go, girl! Great chance to practise the lingo. So what's holding you back, then?"

"Well, we haven't mentioned it to Susanna yet, and I think she'll be thrown when she realises that she'll have to make other arrangements for Robbie for a month. I'm hoping she might be able to book some time off work, as she has a holiday entitlement, but it won't be a month. And mum and dad and Rachel can help with Robbie a bit, but I don't think any of them could manage him for an extended period. I realise I haven't gone more than two days without looking after Robbie since he was born."

"Paid childcare, maybe?"

Kay lifted her eyebrows. "Susanna works in a hair and beauty place, remember – pretty much minimum wage."

"Ah. Can your boy Michael help?"

"He'll be working, and he is definitely getting better at looking after himself, I think, but I'm not sure he'd be sufficiently confident to look after Robbie for long stretches. He'll have to shift for himself a bit more while we're away, but that will be no bad thing. I'm just trying to decide when might be the right time to bring it up with the two of them."

After a pause, in which Kay looked glum, Abiola changed the subject.

"So, what about these A level courses, come September?"

"Definitely. I've loved learning again. I thought I'd had enough of it when I left school but, in fact, it's been enjoyable."

Kay had investigated the possibility of taking further qualifications in French, Spanish and English at night classes from the autumn. Abiola, who worked as an administrator at the College, had promised practical help with the application process. William was supportive, and Sam, Lily and Gabrielle had all been loyally enthusiastic and encouraging when she had told them her plan.

"What about your summer, Abiola? Any holiday plans?"

"Oh, I usually hang out with friends in Scotland. It's a kind of commune – yeah, a cliche, I know!" as Kay smiled at the word. "It's just women together – very relaxing. A few take their children. I just love it. I come back at the end of the holiday feeling chilled. Then we go straight back into College admissions and it's manic again, of course!"

"It sounds perfect. Do you meet the same people there each year?"

"Some of them – yes. There are always some who are new. There's one woman, Annaliese, I really hope to see."

Kay caught the gleam in Abiola's eye.

"Do you keep in touch with her throughout the year?"

"No – it's not that kind of relationship. But whenever we have been there at the same time, we've been together. It's cool."

Abiola was unlike any other close friend Kay had ever had, and she found the occasional references to the different women she had been involved with to be both fascinating and mystifying. It was so different from Kay's long-standing, stable relationship with the predictable, steady William. Like the French class, Kay's friendship with Abiola had proved exhilarating. "I think I'm waking up," she sometimes thought.

"So how are plans going for your big shindig?"

Kay's parents' golden wedding anniversary fell on Easter Monday, and a family party had been planned, to be held in Kay's garden, as the weather was forecast to be hot and sunny. They had borrowed from Sam a small marquee, so that there would be shade and shelter. Kay and Rachel were preparing the food - salmon with salads, and strawberries. Michael was picking up the Prosecco and soft drinks. Susanna was sourcing bunting and balloons. Kay was looking forward to it, she thought.

"Under control, I think. There will only be the eight of us – including Robbie. We thought we'd keep it to the immediate family as the garden is small, and mum and dad aren't so comfortable in larger gatherings these days. 50 years married – imagine..." though she and William had been together for almost half of that, now.

"I'm kinda hoping there's a huge cake..."

"Oh yes – bought, I have to admit, not baked by any of us. I think they will love it."

The pub clock showed it was 10pm so Kay started to gather her things.

"I'd better be getting back. See you in a fortnight?"

"You certainly will. I'll miss not having a class next week. Let me know if you're up for meeting for a drink anyway?"

"I will. Au revoir!"

Abiola said, "A bientot!" at the same time, and the two of them laughed as they parted.

The party was due to start at midday. The marquee had been set up by William with Adam's help, Susanna adding the bunting and balloons, and the garden looked lovely. The Prosecco was cooling in ice buckets; the cake waited in the pantry; the best china was laid out alongside the linen serviettes. Kay had poached the salmon the day before and she and Rachel had prepared a range of salads while Susanna had hulled the strawberries. This had been an impressive family team effort, thought Kay, satisfied that everyone had played their part. She knew her parents would appreciate it.

William had offered – actually *offered*, thought Kay - to look after Robbie all afternoon so that Kay and Susanna could focus on looking after their parents and serving the food. Kay had asked Michael to take responsibility for ensuring everyone's glasses were refreshed throughout the party, and he had agreed with equanimity. He had seemed so much steadier and, well, more adult, in the last few months, Kay reflected. Taking control hadn't always been plain sailing since her New Year's Eve #oneword commitment, but there had certainly been progress in the past four months, she reflected. A month touring France with William in July, starting A levels in

September and finding a new job would be additional steps forward. She realised that had her current employer not hit financial difficulties she probably wouldn't have been motivated to look for employment elsewhere, but, now that had happened, she hoped she might be able to turn a challenge into an opportunity. She wondered what different professional avenues she might be fit for.

Kay's parents arrived and she hugged them at the door and led them through the kitchen to settle them into the most comfortable garden chairs. The family gathered to offer their gifts, including a huge bouquet of 50 golden roses, which made her mother particularly emotional, "50 years! And I remember our wedding day like it was yesterday." The family had unearthed as many photographs (black and white, of course) from the day as they could find, and Susanna had copied them, together with many other snaps of her grandparents from over the last five decades, and these were pegged among the bunting. The guests of honour kept catching sight of different ones and exclaiming over the memories they evoked.

The sun beat down – it was very hot - but under the marquee and in the shade of the one tree the garden boasted, they were comfortable. "It's the hottest Easter Monday on record!" Kay's father had informed them – several times, now. Kay and Rachel served the food at 1pm, Michael plied everyone with drinks, and there was much chatter and frequent laughter. Robbie was on form, tottering around the garden and trying out his newly acquired walking skills, with William keeping a careful eye on him. He was a child with a sunny temperament and today, perhaps affected by the general cheerful atmosphere, he was in particularly good humour. Kay knew he would flag later, and that William would take him upstairs for a nap. This could, in fact, turn out to be a perfect day, thought Kay.

Later, Susanna and Michael helped the two sisters clear away the food remnants and stack the plates and bowls in the kitchen. Kay had always resisted William's attempts to persuade her to buy a dishwasher, saying that she found the rhythm of washing and drying by hand quite soothing – though in recent months she had insisted it was a shared task. They would wash up after her parents had left, but they tidied up and restored order.   Rachel and Michael returned to the party but Susanna was, Kay realised, hovering. Kay waited.

"I wanted to ask you something, mum."

"Go ahead." Kay felt she was in such a positive frame of mind, nothing could cloud this wonderful day.

"Sally, Gina and the others have talked about going to Greece for a couple of weeks in the summer, and they want me to go with them. I've been saving up, and I think I can manage it, and I already have some time off booked. But I'd need you and dad to look after Robbie for the fortnight.... Please."

Kay went very still. Her first thought was that the 'Please' was an afterthought, but, in fact, a few months ago, it might not even have been added. Her second thought was the sinking feeling that the dates were not going to be what she wanted to hear.

Susanna said, in a rush, "I know you told us Sam had invited you to France with the others at the end of July, and that you hoped you and dad might go, but it's OK, because this is the two weeks before that, so it shouldn't clash. And I haven't had a holiday since before Robbie was born. I'm the only one in the group with a child, and the others go somewhere nice every year. I always feel a bit left out when they talk about it but, this time, I have the money and the time and I really hope..."

There was a pause, and Susanna was acutely aware that her mother was saying nothing. She had chosen to ask today as Kay seemed in such a good mood. Susanna hadn't really anticipated anything other than, "Of course we will."

Kay meanwhile was thinking ruefully that she should have told all the family about their plan to spend a month in France several weeks ago, when she and William first discussed it. She knew she had avoided raising the subject because of the awkwardness it might lead to, and now, of course, it was going to be even more difficult. Susanna had clearly set her heart on this holiday and Kay could see why it was important to her.

Susanna was a young woman, a single parent, and the friends with whom she socialised were still all fancy-free – Susanna had always resisted building her social circle around other young mums.

Kay took a breath.

"I need to talk to your father. We'll discuss it after the party."

Susanna's smooth features were distorted by a momentary frown: this wasn't the response she expected. "I even said please..." she thought to herself. Her mother's face was impassive, and Susanna started to speak and then thought better of it. She turned and left the room with, Kay thought, the suggestion of a flounce. Susanna, at 22, could revert to fractious teenager when things didn't go her way. Kay stood at the sink and closed her eyes. Is this where I cave in, we change our plans and I put others first – as I always seem to have done? Or does the new, more assertive, me insist that we look for some kind of compromise? I don't want to think about this today.

William came into the kitchen with a sleepy Robbie in his arms.

"He's done very well," he said brightly, "but I think he's ready for a rest now. I'll stay upstairs with him for a while," and probably drop off to sleep yourself, thought Kay, but she just smiled at William as he headed for the hall.

And then Michael was there, too.

"Hey, mum."

He looked uncomfortable.

"What's wrong? Are your grandparents...?"

"Oh, they're fine – they're having a good time. Aunt Rachel is a bit drunk but it's making her the life and soul of the party. Susanna seems moody, but no change there."

Kay looked at this young man, fruit of her loins, now grown and soon, no doubt, to fly the nest. Although she always respected his privacy, it was evident that in recent months he had been seeing someone. Taking greater care of his appearance, liberally sprinkling aftershave lotion every time he went out, returning less drunk and raucous than had been the case a year ago. She hoped he would settle with a girl Kay liked and she looked forward to the possibility of a family wedding. He was clearly waiting to tell her something – perhaps today was the day he would share his news.

"What is it, son?"

Michael shuffled uncomfortably.

"I've been wanting to talk to you about something important – and it's just….You're in such a good mood today, and I thought…"

"Just spill the beans, Michael!" Kay smiled. "Is this about your love life?" I could do with some good news just at this moment, she thought.

The question made Michael even more uncomfortable and he became very quiet.

"Is she someone I already know?"

The question propelled Michael into a burst of speech.

"You know Sarah, Alex's wife?"

Kay blinked at him. "Of course I do." Alex was Michael's boss at the engineering firm where he had been employed since leaving school at 16, two years earlier. Sarah was his pretty blonde wife, in her twenties, and expecting her first child. "She's having a baby, isn't she? Are you seeing a friend of hers?" Kay knew there were only a couple of women who worked in the offices at the firm, both around her own age.

"The baby – it isn't Alex's. It's mine. She's going to tell him, and then she's going to leave him so we can be together, before the baby is born. In July."

A burst of laughter came from the garden – Rachel, the 'life and soul', telling rather rude jokes to her parents. Kay looked through the window and saw them all basking in dappled sunlight. A perfect day, she thought.

JULY 2019

Chapter Nine

Gabrielle

Harry looked up at Gabrielle as she walked out of the conservatory and joined him in the garden. Her expression was pinched, and his face fell. He didn't need to ask. Gabrielle sighed as she sank into the garden chair.

Neither of them spoke for a while. Harry reached across and took her hand lightly in his.

In the end, "I love you," he said softly. "Could that be enough?"

Gabrielle closed her eyes and felt the tears prickling beneath her eyelids.

"I know it ought to be," she said in a low voice which she tried to keep steady. "I know there is so much we have to be thankful for. But... It still hurts. I remember.... When I learnt to drive, and it seemed initially, so complex – the pedals, the steering, using the mirror, checking the position in the road, changing gears smoothly. I thought I'd never be able to grasp it, never be able to see it all as one fluid process which came naturally to me. And I used to look at all the cars on the road and think, 'Well, *they* can all do it. Surely I'll be able to one day'. Eventually I could, of course. Now, wherever I go, I'm acutely aware of the families, the pregnant women, the couples with toddlers, and I think, 'Well, *they* can all do it'. I see parents struggling with crying children in supermarkets, losing their temper. I read stories of those who abuse their children. In my school, I can see some girls who are neglected – often by quite affluent families, who just seem uninterested in them. It's hard to make sense of it. We would be loving, caring parents – you'd be a fantastic father..." and this was the thought that Gabrielle found particularly distressing. "Why can't we, Harry?"

Harry shook his head.

"I don't know, Gay. We could try medical advice again..." He stopped when Gabrielle shook her head quickly. "The only other thing we can do is to continue, to see what happens, and find ways of handling the disappointment if it doesn't lead to the outcome we hope for."

'Hope', thought Gabrielle. That word again.

"I was talking to one of my governors the other day," she said. "She lives in a village that floods from time to time. She was telling me about their latest near miss, a few years ago."

Harry leaned forward, listening.

"She said that when the waters start to rise, and you know there's a possibility that the houses will flood, the hardest thing is just waiting. You can take a number of measures to try to minimise the damage, but you can't control it. You see the water edging closer, but you don't know how bad it will get, when it will stop. Apparently in 2012, I think it was, her house was standing in water, the garden was flooded, the drive was under water and they had to leave their cars on higher ground outside the village. The houses are raised slightly inside, so the floors are about a foot – I think she said four housebricks – higher than the ground outside. It was Christmas, and each day they watched the water slowly rising up the bricks. They'd moved everything they could upstairs, and the heavy things they'd raised up on milk crates hoping to keep them out of the water. They'd bought a sump pump so that if the water did come inside they could try to pump it out as quickly as possible. She says sandbags don't work, because the water comes up from underneath the house – you see the carpets slowly lifting in the middle of the room."

Gabrielle stopped speaking. Harry just waited.

"You plan for the worst but hope for the best, she said. You just don't know."

"And what happened?"

"At eight o'clock on the evening of Christmas Day the water reached three and a half bricks high. And then it stopped. And, very gradually, over the next few days, it receded. They brought the furniture downstairs, put the house back to rights, packed the sump pump away in the shed, and carried on with their normal lives. But then she said, 'It will happen at some stage. We know that. Our house was under water in 2000, and it will be again. We just don't know when. So we use the agency we have to control what we can, and what we can't control, we just have to accept.' "

Gabrielle gave Harry a faint smile.

"So that's what we have to do."

Gabrielle always enjoyed the last few weeks of term – the summer concert, sports day, charity events and various end of year celebrations. The Upper Sixth, now their exams were over, came into school to write, cast, rehearse and perform their 'Sixth Form entertainment' to the staff and the rest of the school. This was an affectionate tribute to (and gentle satire of) the school which the vast majority of them had attended since they were 11 years old. The Head Girl traditionally played the role of the headteacher, and Maya, this year's Head Girl, called in to Gabrielle's office to ask if she could borrow one of her favourite, and most distinctive, jackets, and a pair of shoes which, Maya said, the girls especially loved.

"Of course you can," Gabrielle laughed. "I'll bring them in tomorrow. How is it all going?"

"It's a challenge – but an enjoyable one." Maya conceded. "Everyone has their own ideas, and it's a bit of a tightrope trying to respect the views of everybody but actually making some decisions and coming up with something workable and manageable in the time we have. But when it all comes together, it's a great example of teamwork!"

Maya grinned at her.

"It's excellent leadership experience, too," Gabrielle suggested. "I look at you all and recognise that many of you will take on leadership roles in all kinds of careers, as well as balancing personal and professional responsibilities, and I hope school has prepared you for that. In fact, while you're here, if you've time, I'd love to hear your reflections on how you feel the school *has* readied you for what comes next."

Maya thought for a moment.

"Well, for me, being Head Girl has been the most amazing experience, and I feel very privileged to have had that opportunity. I've had to take on several leadership challenges, and I've loved it. My public speaking is definitely more confident than it was a year ago! That will serve me well in the future, I'm sure."

"What else?"

"I know that often girls say how the school has helped them to feel good about themselves, and to have faith in what they might go on to achieve. You remember when you saw us all individually in the autumn and read our references to us?"

Gabrielle smiled. It was something she had introduced in her first term at the school, an idea she had taken from her previous head. When the Upper Sixth applied through UCAS for their university places, or made alternative plans for their future education or employment, she met each one and read their school reference to them. It had been an affirming and energising experience for both her and the girls she saw.

"It made us all realise what we'd accomplished here, how we'd developed and what we should feel proud of. That's the kind of thing that boosts your confidence and helps you to see what you could maybe go on to do in the future."

"Thank you, Maya. That's useful to know."

"Thank you, Mrs Talbot. And – if I can just say – I know you've only been here for a year, but we think you've been a great head, and you've made our last year here special. I hope you enjoy the Entertainment – and that I can do justice to you!"

The Sixth Form Entertainment made her laugh, the younger girls loved it, and the staff commented on what a great year group this was.

"I remember Maya Mukherjee when she arrived in Year 7," the school nurse said. "Such a shy little thing. What a fine young woman she is developing into!"

Teaching has its challenges and pressures, thought Gabrielle, but it's still such a rewarding job. Seeing the product of your efforts in the shape of students you've supported during their time in the school, the progress they've made and the challenges they've overcome – what could be better? Gabrielle reflected on her career path, as she pulled onto the estate where Lily and her family were making their new home.

Lily answered the door, looking fraught.

"Thank God you're here – I need reinforcements!"

"Anything I can do to help."

"You could start by pouring us both a stiff gin," Lily gestured towards the kitchen while she headed upstairs, from where came the unmistakable sound of her girls fighting.

Gabrielle found the gin, some tonic and there was ice in the freezer compartment of the fridge and even a wizened lemon she could slice up. She poured gin and tonic for Lily, and straight tonic for herself, musing briefly on whether this was deception of a kind. Reckoning that Lily would return when she had reconciled the warring parties, she moved a box, sank onto the settee and kicked off her shoes.

Lily returned in a few minutes, and gratefully picked up, and swallowed half of, her drink.

"So, how is it going?"

"Well, complete chaos may not be putting it too strongly," Lily replied with a groan. "Peter is at work, but I've managed to take a few days off to do some unpacking and to try to restore some kind of order. Though I have to say that the more I unpack, the less order seems to result! Johnnie is with Pete's parents at the moment – he's very willing but not actually very helpful."

"What can I do?"

"To be honest, just having someone to talk to is great."

"How is Peter's new job?"

"Not brilliant. He knows he's overqualified, and he will quickly become bored, I think. But he will stick with it as long as he can because we need the money – God, I am so sick of using that phrase!"

"And the girls?"

"Interestingly, after all the fuss they made about sharing a room, on the night we moved in when I went up to the bathroom I could hear them giggling in bed, and I said to Pete, 'I think it's actually going to be OK'. But since then there's some kind of territorial dispute going on, which I seem powerless to mediate. I think just stopping them killing each other may be the limit of my influence."

Gabrielle smiled. "This too shall pass. At least we all have France to look forward to."

"Thank God! I will be forever grateful to Sam for that. A couple of weeks away from here, with guaranteed sun and free-flowing French wine, sounds like paradise just at the moment. Only two weeks to go to the end of the school year and then we'll be packing. How are things with you?"

"Good. We had our Sixth Form Entertainment today, which was clever and heartwarming. I do enjoy the end of the summer term, and it's even better now I'm the head. I feel this is becoming *my* school, finally, and I'm no longer an interloper in Mrs Jenkins's office!"

"You never felt like an interloper!"

"I did, initially. You know, with most women, I think Imposter Syndrome is never very far away. I have days when I think, 'I'm actually doing all right in this job', followed by days where I think, 'Who am I kidding? I'm barely getting away with it, and someone is going to find me out!' "

Gabrielle laughed, but she meant it.

"You are, I think, the most capable woman I know, Gabrielle. I think you could succeed at anything you put your mind to."

Gabrielle smiled wryly at that.

"Anyway, can I help to unpack anything, or do some cleaning, or tidying, or…" as the volume of the dispute upstairs reached a new level, "…help to pacify the feuding tribes?"

When Gabrielle reached home, Harry was still out – the last parents' evening of the year – and Gabrielle took her briefcase into the study and unpacked her laptop. She worked for about an hour, preparing for the rest of the week, and then made herself a coffee and settled in the conservatory, watching the sun set.

"I think you could succeed at anything you put your mind to..." Lily's words returned to her. If only determination, commitment and hard work were enough. Over the years, Gabrielle had counselled both staff and pupils who had faced failure and disappointment, and talked about building resilience and the importance of our capacity to cope when something we really wanted (a job, a place at Oxford, or at Medical School, perhaps), for which we had worked and to which we felt we were well-prepared and well-suited, didn't come to pass. She had talked to parents too, who, concerned because their sons or daughters had been unsuccessful in some enterprise, wanted to change the outcome and protect their offspring from pain and disappointment.

"You do realise, Mr Smith," she remembered once saying to an angry, complaining parent, "that not getting a place in the Sixth Form Prefect team is not the worst thing that will ever happen to your daughter in her life? You and we have to work together to help her develop the resources she needs to cope with such disappointments. You can't smooth her path so that she will never experience pain, much as you might want to shield her."

How easy it was to say, Gabrielle thought now. How hard it could be to find the resilience and the strength to cope with failure when it related to something you wanted very badly: something that you felt you had earned and, in fact, deserved. "If you're not prepared to risk failure, you'll never taste success," she had said glibly in a recent assembly. She knew the theory, but could she put it into practice? Could she cope with failure, accept that her 'hope' might never be fulfilled, without it derailing her?

She heard Harry's key in the door, and went into the kitchen.

"How was that?" she asked.

"Good. I have a great Year 10 group, and it was a pleasure to see them with their parents. A long day, though."

"What can I get you?"

"Actually, what I'd really like is a hot chocolate with a nip of brandy in it. And perhaps a piece of that cake you baked at the weekend, if there's any left."

"I'll join you – maybe without the brandy."

"How was Lily?"

"Fraught, and in need of gin and conversation, when I arrived. A little better by the time I left, I think."

"I'm sure she'll have appreciated your calling. Oh – what was the Sixth Form Entertainment like?"

"Brilliant. Maya had me off to a tee, I have to say – all my mannerisms and favourite phrases! And a wig, of course!"

"Excellent." As Gabrielle passed him, setting the cake on the low table, Harry reached for her and pulled her to him. "I'm trying to imagine you as an 18 year old Asian girl but, I have to say, I think I prefer the original."

"I should hope so!" Gabrielle kissed him, and then pulled away so that she could finish making their hot chocolate.

"Lily is looking forward to France. So am I, I have to say. It will be good for the four families to have some time together. It's some time since we've all been out, the eight of us – and we've never managed a holiday together."

"How did Kay resolve her difficulty with Susanna and Robbie, do you know?"

"Yes. They reached a compromise. Susanna is just going to Greece for a week, so she has a week at home with Robbie before she goes away, when she has the time off from work. With the money she will save by only going away for seven nights, plus some money Kay and William are lending her, she's paying for childcare for Robbie during the day when she's away, and Rachel, Michael and their parents will manage him between them in the evenings. So Kay and William set off for France in a few days, and we will meet them there towards the end of the month."

"So do you think Kay is, finally, taking more control of her life?"

Gabrielle had talked to Harry about the #oneword each of them had chosen back in December, and how she felt the year was going for them all.

"I suspect that, of the four of us, she's achieved the most success this year. Sam and Lily have both had difficult years so far, for different reasons."

"And as for us..." Harry looked up at her with a smile as he finished his hot chocolate, "Is it time for an early night, do you think?"

"That would be lovely."

Chapter Ten

Kay

"You're just being obstinate!" Kay muttered to the suitcase, as she struggled with the zip. Eventually she gave up, stood back and looked at it ruefully.

"Or perhaps, to be fair, it's me that's being unreasonable…" and she started to remove some of the contents she had been trying to cram in.

William came into the bedroom. "Are you talking to the luggage?" he asked, with a rueful smile.

"Abiola says I anthropomorphise – I treat inanimate things as though they were living. I do, don't I?"

"There are worse habits, I'm sure. Well, the tennis has finished. Just under five hours – the longest Wimbledon final ever, I think they said. It was a fantastic game. Felt a bit sorry for Federer, but Djokovic deserved it."

"Sorry I missed it, but I'd promised Abiola I'd meet her today to talk about the job and to thank her for all her help, and I needed to finish the last of the packing."

"How was she?"

"On good form! She's been brilliant. I am so grateful I met her through the French conversation class, you know? She is definitely good for me. I feel nervous about starting the new job, but she's been so reassuring and helpful through the whole process. I'm not sure how much I'll actually see of her once I'm there – the College is huge and the staff is a real cast of thousands, but it feels good just to know she's around, and she'll certainly be supportive if I need to ask or check anything. I feel I have a backstop."

Kay had finished at the department store at the end of June. She and William had planned that they would take their holiday and then she would start looking for work once they returned. But in May, Abiola had talked to Kay about the possibility of her applying for a job at the College, working as a part-time administrator and receptionist in the Admissions Office. She had supported Kay as she applied, boosting her confidence and her self-belief. Kay had positively enjoyed the interview process, and was thrilled to have been offered a post which started in late August. She knew the fact that she had just completed her courses in French and Spanish, and enrolled to take A levels in evening classes from the autumn, had gone in her favour, reflecting her commitment to building her skills, increasing her qualifications and investing in her own learning. Many of those she would meet through the Admissions administration would, she knew, be mature students like her. Kay had a good record of holding down jobs in retail, and Abiola had talked through with her the transferable skills she had to build on – she was presentable, articulate, well-organised and reliable. Kay was feeling good about herself, and it showed. There was a glow about her at the moment, William reflected.

William had said he was proud of her and her new departure. Kay's friends and family were enthusiastic and supportive. "You deserve this, mum," Susanna had said, which Kay found touching.

She and Susanna had found their compromise with respect to their summer plans. Susanna was looking forward to her week in the sun, and was appreciative of the financial support Kay and William had been able to offer her to help with the cost of Robbie's childcare while she was away. And Kay felt excited about the driving holiday in France, including the opportunity to spend a little time with Sam, Gabrielle and Lily and their families.

And then there was Michael.

Shortly after the Easter Monday party, when Michael had shared with Kay – and she had shared with William – the story of Sarah and the baby, Michael had returned from work one day looking ashen. Kay turned from the cooker where she had been preparing their meal, took one look at his face and she knew, she thought, what had happened. She sank down at the kitchen table and drew Michael down next to her.

"What is it, Michael? Is it the baby?"

At her question Michael emitted a sob, and buried his face in his arms to conceal his tears. Kay held him and waited.

"She says it isn't mine," Michael eventually whispered.

Kay went still. This wasn't what she was expecting; she had feared a late miscarriage. The news that the paternity of the baby might be in question hadn't occurred to her. She thought rapidly – what does this mean, and how can we support Michael through it?

"I met her after work, trying to get her to say exactly when she was going to talk to Alex, and my thoughts about where we might live..." Michael gasped out the story in between sobs. "I knew something was wrong. She wouldn't look at me, and kept pulling away when I tried to take her hand. And then she just said it – said she'd made a mistake, realised the baby was Alex's, she didn't love me..." Michael was unable to continue for some minutes. Kay's heart went out to him. Once you've had children, 'you're only as happy as your least happy child...' went through her head. Kay didn't remember who had first said that, and where she had heard it, but it had struck her at the time, and it seemed especially resonant now. She knew there was nothing she could say that, at this moment, would make Michael feel any better. All she could do was listen, hold him, love him through it. She felt a spark of anger towards Sarah, but then closed her eyes and took a breath.

Sarah was a young woman, Kay reflected, in a situation she presumably felt she couldn't control. Michael was a good looking boy, and he clearly cared for her. But he was 18 years old. Once Alex knew the truth Michael would lose his job, Sarah would lose her home, her security – her current life. Where would they live and what would they live on – the three of them? Kay could see that they might never know whose child this was, and she certainly wouldn't be encouraging Michael to insist on a paternity test. Was he ready to be a father at 18? Would he cope? Would Sarah, without the stability and structure of her comfortable home and respectability?

"She doesn't want to be with me anymore. She says Alex is thrilled he's going to be a dad – that he's been especially loving and kind in the last few months. When we first got together she told me they used to love each other, but that had changed. She said she loved me…"

Gradually, Michael quietened. He doesn't need my advice, thought Kay. He just needs to pour it all out. But she desperately wanted to ask him, "What are you going to do?" She resisted the impulse. "Someone else will love you, and deserve you, one day," she thought. "This feels like the end, but it isn't." She didn't say any of that, either.

William came in from the garden and stood hesitantly in the doorway. Kay gave the briefest shake of her head and he slowly backed out. Michael didn't even notice.

Kay sat with him as the light ebbed from the room.

Once the cases were, finally, packed, William loaded the car. He checked their passports and travel documents for, perhaps, the tenth time. They were leaving for the tunnel first thing the following morning. This was their first overseas trip together, just the two of them. Kay was simultaneously nervous and thrilled about having the opportunity to use her French, and William, who enjoyed driving, and navigating in unfamiliar territory, was, in his own quiet way, relishing the thought of the journey ahead.

Susanna called in with Robbie in the early evening to say goodbye and to wish them well. She brought them sunhats as a farewell gift. "Don't get sunstroke!" she warned. William tried his on and decided he looked quite dashing. Robbie laughed and tried to pull it from his head.

"I'm pleased we were able to work this out," Kay said carefully to her daughter. "I didn't want to leave you in the lurch, but at the same time, we'd really been looking forward to our trip, and I didn't want to truncate it dramatically."

"I know, mum," said Susanna. "I know this holiday is important to you and dad – and…" Susanna found it hard to look her mother in the eye, but she had thought carefully about this and had decided on the way over what she really felt she had to say. "I do appreciate how much you've done for me, especially since Robbie was born. I know I rely on you – too much, really. I need to take a bit more responsibility." Susanna looked up, and Kay could see that her eyes were misted with tears. "I will try to do better."

Kay reached across and took Robbie from her daughter and settled him in his grandfather's lap. Then she hugged Susanna, and the two of them sat quietly together, saying nothing for a while.

They heard the front door open and close, and Michael came into the room. Two months had passed since he had sobbed with Kay in the kitchen. Although Kay felt he was still to some extent subdued, he had, in many respects, started to make a good recovery. He had left his job at the firm where Alex was his manager and, with his developing skills, found alternative employment with another engineering company quite quickly – a better job in fact. As far as he was aware, Alex knew nothing about his relationship with Sarah and the possibility she was carrying his child; there had certainly been no repercussions. Michael was finding his new role interesting, and starting to make new friends. Susanna and the rest of the family knew nothing about Sarah and the baby – Michael had insisted his parents kept it to themselves, and they were prepared to do that if it saved him pain. The only person Kay had confided in, other than William, was Abiola, who was a good listener, and completely discreet. It had helped Kay to share the trouble with someone whose empathy she could rely on and whom she knew she could completely trust. "He's lucky to have you, girl…" Abiola had said.

"What's for tea, mum? I'm starving!" announced Michael as he walked in.

Kay rose to her feet with a sigh.

"You do know that when you move into the flat you won't be able to say that as soon as you walk through the door every night, don't you?" She cuffed him gently as she passed. "It might be a tough habit to get out of!"

Michael was staying in his parents' house to look after things while they were abroad, but from the beginning of August, he was moving into a shared flat with two friends from school, Tricia and Billy. He was behaving coolly about it, but Kay knew him well enough to appreciate how much he was looking forward to the independence and the thrill of no longer living with his parents. He would need to start taking responsibility for sharing the cooking and the household chores, but that would be good for him, she knew. Tricia and Billy had shared with another friend, Matthew, who was moving out to get married, so they already had systems and structures which Michael would fit into. Although she was sad to see him leave, in some ways, she felt it was the right thing for him to do at this stage of his life, and it would help him to get on with his life and to move on from the Sarah experience and the pain that had caused him.

Over their meal, which Susanna and Robbie stayed for, the family talked about the trip to France, Susanna's imminent holiday in Greece, and Michael's intention to take a winter break in the sun with a group of friends once he had worked for his new employer for a few months. They talked about Kay's new job, William and Tom's plans for expanding the painting and decorating business, and Robbie's rapid development.

"He seems to be changing by the day!" said Susanna. "I bet you'll really notice the changes when you get back from France."

"We will miss him!" said Kay, ruffling the boy's hair, and he rewarded her with a chuckle.

"Well, you could have taken him with you!...Only joking!" Susann leant backwards and raised her palms as her mother gave her a baleful look.

They finished their meal and then Kay rose to put on the kettle.

"No tea for me, thanks, mum. I'd better get this little monster home to bed." Susanna scooped up her son and he nuzzled into her as she got herself ready to leave. "Have the best time – don't forget to wear your hats!"

"I don't want a drink either, mum, thanks – I've said I'll meet Rich for a pint," and Michael was in motion, too. Eventually Kay and William were alone, she washing the dishes while William dried.

"What did you think about Susanna's little speech about appreciating us, and taking more responsibility, earlier?" Kay asked.

William thought for a moment.

"I think she means it, but I expect there will still be times when she takes us for granted. It isn't a smooth path, is it, the road to independence."

Kay, in her turn, was thoughtful.

"It will be different in the autumn won't it? My new job and nightschool, Michael not living here, you building up the business – will that mean you'll have more work on?"

"Maybe less – we'll take on someone new, an apprentice, and that should mean we can tackle more jobs without overstretching ourselves. The business is doing well, so now is the time, we think."

"I'm proud of us – as a family," Kay said as she stacked the last of the plates in the drainer. "You work hard and you're planning for the future. And I do appreciate how much more you've done to help me at home, and with Robbie, since the start of this year. Susanna is growing up a bit, I think, and Michael certainly is. The Sarah thing was really painful for him, but he has a new job, a new home, and he is getting himself together and moving on with his life. Rachel has been much better in recent months – a far stronger support for mum and dad, which has made her stronger, too, somehow. And Robbie is a grand little boy. There are lots of reasons to be cheerful, aren't there?"

"And we're going on holiday tomorrow!" said William, throwing aside the tea towel with a flourish and catching Kay round the waist, before planting a kiss on the top of her head.

Kay found it difficult to sleep that night. She lay still, listening to William's gentle snoring. Was it like the night before Christmas when she was a child, too excited to switch off her brain in her eager anticipation of the next morning? She smiled at herself. "You were 41 years old last month. What are you like?"

She found herself thinking about the passing of time. She was growing older – they all were, of course. All their lives were changing in different ways. Her parents, she knew, were struggling with their ageing process, and she would find that increasingly difficult, but it was, she accepted, part of the natural order, and in some way balanced by the growth and development of the next generation. She thought of Robbie, and the children still to come. She thought, briefly, of Sarah's baby, who might, in fact, be her grandchild – it was unlikely that she would ever know for sure. She thought of the choices they were all making, and how those choices would shape the future path that lay ahead of them.

And she thought of Sam, Gabrielle and Lily, their families and jobs and *their* choices. It took her a while to recall what #oneword each of them had chosen back in December, but she identified them all eventually. She thought of the idea of taking 'control' of her own life, and what had changed since the start of the year. Sam had chosen 'purpose', and they hadn't, in the last six months, had a proper conversation about what she had meant by that, and how a commitment to purpose had shaped her year so far. Lily had opted for 'courage', and she had certainly had to draw on that in recent months with the loss of Peter's job, the house move and the repercussions of that, for them and for the children. But didn't Lily make her choice of word *before* they knew about Peter's job, Kay wondered. And Gabrielle selected 'hope'. What was it she was hoping for?

Why had they not talked more about these choices of word when they met for their periodic lunches or dinners? She was sure they had done so in years gone by. Perhaps all meeting at the house in France at the end of the month would give them the opportunity to do that – though that might not be possible with the children and their husbands around all the time. It was always easier to have conversations when it was just the four of them, over a bottle or two of wine. Kay thought of her friendship with these women, and how it had evolved and strengthened, she felt, over the decades. She also thought of her new friendship with Abiola. Was it significant that she had told Abiola about what had happened to Michael, but had not shared this with the three friends she had known for thirty years? She felt momentarily uncomfortable about this, and stirred beneath the bedclothes, though she was careful not to wake William.

Think of something else, she told herself – something restful and relaxing which would send her off to sleep. They had an early start next morning and she didn't want to feel weary on the first, long stretch of the journey, from home, down to the south coast, through the tunnel and into France as far as Saint-Quentin, which was their first stop.

Kay had a mantra which she would recite to herself when she wanted to soothe herself to sleep. It was something she had used with her children when they were tiny, and which she used now with Robbie. Chanting it in her head helped her to regulate her breathing and, eventually, to drift off to sleep. It was the last verse of her favourite hymn, 'Dear Lord and Father of Mankind'. Kay repeated it to herself now:

"Breath through the heats of our desire
Thy coolness and they balm.
Let sense be dumb, let flesh retire,
Speak through the earthquake, wind and fire,
O still small voice of calm,
O still small voice of calm…"

And eventually Kay fell into a deep sleep, dreaming of driving through sunny, rural France, wearing her sunhat and a brightly coloured scarf which flew behind her from the passenger seat of a vibrant red convertible.

Chapter Eleven

Lily

Lily paused to catch her breath. She had been running for the best part of an hour, pounding the pavements of the estate where they lived, crossing the paths that ran through the nearby park, and then, on this last stretch, jogging along the canal towpath. She sank onto one of the benches which punctuated the canal walk and plied her water bottle. She brushed the hair out of her eyes and allowed the sweat on her body to cool.

"I must look a sight," she thought, "I really hope I don't see anyone I know," before reflecting on her vanity and wondering how old she would need to be before she stopped worrying about such things.

It had been good to get out of the house, which seemed so small and noisy. Molly and Fay had settled down to some extent, after what felt like open warfare in the first few days. Molly had taken to spending stretches of time in the library, reading in preparation for her Year 12 courses. She felt her GCSEs had gone well, and was quietly confident about the results day in August. Having decided that she definitely wanted to apply for Law in due course, she knew she would need the highest possible grades at A level, too, and she wanted to make the most positive beginning. She was focussed and enthusiastic, and, perhaps as a result, was spending less time fighting with her sister. Fay found she couldn't sustain the arguments without Molly's contribution.

Johnnie remained a good-tempered child, but he took up so much *space*, thought Lily – something which was definitely in short supply. They all seemed to be constantly falling over each other. Peter had had a study of his own in their last home, but now he opened up his laptop on the dining table, at the far end of the open-plan lounge, as soon as they had cleared away after their evening meal, and if Lily and the girls were watching the television programmes they enjoyed, they needed to regulate the volume so as not to disturb him. On the positive side, his job had turned out to be considerably more interesting than he had originally anticipated; Peter was bright and capable, and that had been recognised. There was the possibility of promotion in the autumn, and that had helped significantly with respect to his sense of self-worth. Lily remembered the shy pride he had shown when he had explained this to her one evening after the children had gone up to their rooms.

And Lily had bitten the bullet herself and talked to her line-manager about her own prospects. She remembered the conversation they had had, and how uncomfortable she had initially felt. At least, she reflected ruefully, she had summoned up the 'courage' to go through with it.

"Come in, Lily, take a seat," Daniel had said as she arrived for the appointment she had made with him. "What can I do for you?"

Daniel was fifteen years her junior, and Lily had found it difficult to warm to him from the time of his arrival at the bank from another branch, freshly appointed to a promoted post. He is, in fact, young enough to be my son, she thought now, remembering what a precocious fifteen year old she had been. In his sharp suit, with his gelled hair and his self-satisfied (Lily thought) smile, he leaned back in his chair and appraised her as she settled herself across the desk from him.

"I wonder whether he finds me attractive?" Lily found herself thinking. Not that she was in any way drawn to him, but this was a question that she realised often went through her mind when in the company of men of her acquaintance. Then, "Focus, girl", she told herself.

"I've been giving some thought, recently, to my career progression," she began. She had given careful consideration to the words she would use, had talked this through with Gabrielle, who had even suggested they try out the dialogue together. "Not role-play!" Lily had exclaimed, when Gabrielle had made this suggestion, and Gabrielle had smiled. "That isn't a phrase I tend to use, because I know it brings some people out in a nervous rash. But I do think practice is a good thing, and if ever I need to have a conversation I suspect may be difficult, I always plan it and practise it beforehand – usually with Harry. Not that I'm suggesting this will necessarily be a difficult conversation, exactly," Gabrielle continued, noticing the expression on Lily's face. "Though I still think practising what you might say, and considering how you could respond to what he might say, would be worthwhile."

Lily now realised she was grateful for this practice, and said a silent prayer of thanks to her friend. Daniel said nothing yet, waiting for her to continue.

"I've been with the bank for... some years now, and I think I might be at the point in my career, and in my life, when I'm ready to take on additional responsibility. I know that we offer management training courses to those who are considering further promotion, and I wanted to talk to you about the possibility of enrolling on one of the residential courses later this summer, and seeing where that might take me."

Daniel nodded, but then turned to his laptop screen. He had, she realised, pulled up her personnel record.

"I thought you'd decided some time ago that taking on further responsibility at the bank wasn't something you were interested in, Lily," he said, arching his eyebrows.

"It wasn't," she had responded, "but my circumstances have changed. My children are older and less reliant on me, and I think I have the time and the capacity to take on a fresh challenge."

She had decided that she wouldn't specifically mention the desirability of an uplift in her salary, but Daniel was aware of the recent changes in her personal life and would know that this was one of the motivating factors in her decision. He was keen to find out, she realised, whether this was her only driver.

"Tell me more about that then, Lily..." Why does he keep using my name all the time, she wondered, biting back the feeling of irritation she could feel building within her. "Why do you feel you might now be suited to a management role, and what do you think you have to offer?"

Lily took a breath. "I've brought up a family and managed a household – not always in the easiest of circumstances" – I might as well get that out there, she thought – "and I think I've built a range of useful skills along the way. I'm resilient, calm, and able to solve problems and to work with others to find a way forward. I'm good at my job and I think that gives me credibility with my colleagues. I think I can earn respect and build trust. I know I still have much to learn about managing people, and I may not yet know all that I'm capable of, but the training course should help me to clarify my thinking and test out my commitment. I hope the bank would be prepared to invest in me, given the years of service I've put in, and the loyalty I've shown. I'm reliable, and keen, now, to stretch myself."

Lily raised her chin and looked Daniel in the eye. He paused, and then gave a slow smile.

"You are a valued employee, Lily, and, if this is something you are now eager to pursue, I would be prepared to recommend you for a management training course once you return from your annual leave. Then we can see how that goes."

"Thank you. I appreciate that." Lily had been relieved to get to the end of the conversation, and she gathered herself, rose from the chair and walked towards the door. She wondered whether Daniel knew how much she had disliked having this conversation, and how patronising she often found him. If she had management responsibility, she thought she would make a better job of it than several of those who had, over the years, managed her – Daniel included. She remembered Gabrielle once saying this, earlier in her career. "I think I knew I wanted to be a leader when I looked at other leaders and thought, 'I think I could do that job. And, actually, I think I could do it better!' " The friends had all laughed at this, as Gabrielle was usually modest to the point of being self-effacing, but she showed here a quiet ambition and a confidence in herself which they all admired.

I can do this, thought Lily. And if I go down this route I will work hard and make a success of it. She remembered that a few short months ago she had talked to Sam about the possibility of leaving the bank and retraining completely, in order to look for a job she would find more fulfilling. I probably would never have taken the plunge, she reflected. But at least this way I'm doing something to make a change, rather than drifting along feeling bored and disgruntled.

"One thing occurs to me, Lily," Daniel had said, as she was about to leave the room. "It's over ten years since you were approached about competing further training. I was still at school then!" he grinned, in what Lily thought he considered an endearing way. "Perhaps if you'd followed that path then, you might have been *my* manager by now, and we'd be sitting on the opposite sides of this desk!"

Lily gave him a level look, and then let herself out. For the rest of her life she would be half thankful for, and half regret, her restraint in not articulating the expletive that was going through her mind at that moment. She wondered whether it took more courage to speak her mind, or to refrain from doing so.

By the canal, reflecting on this episode, Lily realised how determined she now was to make a success of the course and whatever opportunities might come in its wake. She wondered whether Daniel knew how much his words had increased her commitment to professional advancement.

After a few more minutes Lily levered herself up, gave herself a good stretch, and then carried on running along the towpath and back through the streets which led her home.

That evening, Lily, Sam and Gabrielle received a WhatsApp message from Kay, who had now reached Poitiers and was really enjoying their cross-France roadtrip.

'Have managed to make myself understood in most places, and William is enjoying the driving. We've seen some beautiful towns and countryside. The weather has been glorious and I'm hoping you will be impressed by my tan! Have a safe journey. Looking forward to seeing you all soon.'

Lily, Peter and the children were flying out with Sam and her family at the end of the week, hiring cars to get them from the airport to the house, which was in the countryside outside Bergerac. Gabrielle and Harry were flying out later and joining them for a long weekend, and Kay and William had arranged to arrive by car at the same time. For two days they would all be together, and then Kay and William were dropping Gabrielle and Harry off at the airport as they started to make their way back home.

Lily considered that, although all the families had met from time to time, at parties and barbecues, birthday and Christmas celebrations, they had never arranged to meet on holiday like this. She had no concerns about them all getting on – the four men enjoyed each other's company and when the children were all together they seemed to bring out the best in one another. She was hoping there would be the opportunity for the women to have a little time together without everyone else around, although she wasn't sure how that might work in practical terms. Since their New Year's Eve lunch, they had met for dinner or lunch every six weeks or so, caught up with news and given each other support and encouragement. She remembered Sam's mother's funeral in May – the four of them gathered in the conservatory at Sam's house, just listening and being a quiet presence while Sam poured out her complex range of feelings about her relationship with her mother and her reaction to this sudden death. They had met once since then, a leisurely lunch where they had discussed their plans for France and laughed a lot, she remembered. She loved these women, and she knew they felt the same about her. The fact that they had known each other such a long time and had so many powerful shared memories had fortified their friendship, she thought.

She sat with her daughters at the table and made a list of what they needed to take on the holiday. The mood was genial and Lily closed her eyes briefly and basked in these moments when she and Fay and Molly were a harmonious unit who actually seemed all to like each other. Peter was playing football with Johnnie in their scrap of a back garden – she could hear Johnnie's giggles and Peter's enthusiastic encouragement. Life can be good, Lily thought. It's different here, but we can still fiercely protect the things that matter.

"What I'd really like…" mused Fay, turning to Molly, "would be if we and Emily and Annabelle could just share all our clothes – and every morning we just got up and looked at everything we had all taken and chose what we most wanted to wear – whoever it belonged to." The four girls were sharing a room in the villa, and they were all similar ages and sizes. Fay knew that Emily and Annabelle, as twins, pooled their wardrobes, and, inexplicably, this never seemed to cause arguments. Lily fervently hoped that some of Sam's daughters' equable temperament and the balance in their relationship might rub off on her own girls.

"Hmmm – not sure," Molly said. "I'm expecting to wear my new orange bikini with shorts every day, and I don't think I'd want to share it. Emily and Annabelle do have some beautiful things, though."

"I need to talk to Johnnie about his toys," Lily mused. "Space will be tight in the suitcases, but I don't think he can get to sleep without Mr Flump, can he?"

The three of them smiled as they remembered Johnnie's first solo trip to stay with his grandparents during the last Christmas holidays. He had been so excited about staying with them on his own and having their undivided attention for once, and Lily's parents were thrilled to have him there. The whole family had made the one and a half hour trip together, enjoyed a family meal at lunchtime, and then Lily, Peter and the girls had left and driven home, leaving Johnnie beaming at them and waving from the front gate, his grandparents standing, smiling, behind him, as their car pulled out of sight. At 8pm,

Lily had received an anxious call from her mother to say that they had tried to settle Johnnie in bed, but he was inconsolable because his stuffed elephant, Mr Flump, hadn't been in his overnight bag, and he couldn't get to sleep without it. Lily had tried to calm and reassure him over the phone, but with no success, and finally she and Peter had got into the car and made the three hour round trip to deliver the toy. Johnnie had settled as soon as they arrived and placed Mr Flump in his arms. Lily's parents later reported that he was sound asleep before their car pulled out of their road at the start of the return journey.

Lily suddenly felt a frisson of joy pass through her. "I am SO looking forward to this holiday!" she exclaimed suddenly, and she stretched out her arms around the girls, who grinned at her in response.

Shortly afterwards, Johnnie and his father came in from the garden, breathless and grubby.

"Bath-time for you, young man!" Lily announced, and then smiled. "You too, Johnnie…."

Peter reached out and tugged at her hair. It was so good to see Lily relaxed and happy, he reflected. This was going to be a good holiday.

As Lily followed Johnnie up the stairs to the bathroom, she said, "We must remember to pack Mr Flump for his holiday in France. You'll be wanting to snuggle up to him in bed."

"Nah…" replied Johnnie dismissively. "I'm not a baby."

Lily could hear the laughter from the kitchen.

Chapter Twelve

Sam

Sam had risen early and driven into Duras to buy fresh bread and croissants for breakfast. By the time she got back to the house, the table on the terrace had been set – it was a squeeze accommodating the 15 of them, but they could just about manage it – and Harry and Gabrielle were finishing packing the picnic baskets in the kitchen. This morning, the men were taking the children to the Saint Michel sports park in Bordeaux, and the four women were planning a leisurely day by the pool and a long late lunch. The teenagers had been slow to rise for most of the holiday, but on account of the day trip they were all at breakfast this morning. Johnnie was beside himself with excitement. The older children were behaving more coolly but Sam knew them all well enough to recognise that they were really looking forward to the trip, too. There would be the opportunity for some shopping in Bordeaux, a picnic lunch and a range of outdoor pursuits. The park was on the bank of the Garrone river, with extensive green space for relaxation and different activities. All three boys were keen on sport, and the four girls could sunbathe professionally, Sam reflected, if ever anyone offered them payment to do so.

The holiday had worked out extremely well, she thought, as she poured herself fresh orange juice and smiled at Lily, who was coming out of the kitchen with two cafetieres. The weather had been perfect, and they were all content to lounge outside, either in the bright sun or in the shade, depending on their preference, and dip in the pool when they needed to cool off. The children played a variety of games when they needed to burn off energy. Conversation among the adults had ranged over a wide number of subjects, reflecting the different interests of the group, although the four women had not yet had chance to talk without partners and children around, and Sam was looking forward to that today.

They had all got on well – she remembered one lively exchange about the appointment of Boris Johnson to the Tory party leadership, about which there had been a range of opinions, but it was a good-humoured debate. They *did* resist talking about Brexit, by common consent, though Sam thought they were probably all aligned in their views there in any case. We are lucky, she reflected, that we ended up with partners we all like (though Peter was definitely easier to warm to than Tony, who had always seemed in some way predatory, to Sam), and the four men, though quite different from each other - as were the women, Sam realised - always seemed able to communicate and to laugh together. They, too, were looking forward to their day out. As breakfast was finishing, Adam and William started loading the two cars.

Kay was tanned and relaxed – more relaxed, Sam thought, than she had ever known her. Although she sent the occasional WhatsApp message home, she seemed not to be fretting about what Susanna and Robbie, Michael, her parents and Rachel were up to. She had spent so much of her life looking after others, Sam knew. This was now Kay's time, and she was relishing the opportunities it brought.

Lily had certainly been ready for a break, and had expressed her gratitude for Sam's invitation so many times in the last week that Sam had eventually said, "Lily, stop!" and they had both laughed. She, too, looked rested and refreshed, and slim and beautiful, Sam reflected, as she watched Lily lay out her beach towel, don her sunglasses and stretch out her long limbs on her lounger.

Gabrielle and Harry seemed especially close, Sam had noticed, mindful of how often they touched each other naturally, casually, whenever they were in close proximity. She remembered talking to Jane back in the spring and saying that Gabrielle seemed unsettled, and Sam wondered whether all was well in her marriage, given that Gabrielle was clearly so positive and enthusiastic about her work. But now, Sam realised she had misread the situation. If something was troubling Gabrielle, it certainly wasn't her relationship with Harry, which seemed as strong and loving as ever.

And what about my marriage, Sam thought. Whenever she and Adam spent time together, such as on holiday, they were easy and comfortable with each other. They both enjoyed the company of their children, and family life was invariably busy, but fulfilling. However, Sam was very much mindful of all she had not shared with Adam. He was still unaware of the counselling, and she had not yet talked to him about what had happened at work, and what she had finally decided about her future. In fact, she had talked to no one about this other than Jane. She would need to do so before the summer was over.

But not today, she thought, closing her eyes against the sun. Today she wanted to relax, to soak up the warmth, swim a few lengths, enjoy her book. She and Gabrielle had spent some time exchanging reading recommendations prior to the holiday, and she was making her way through a satisfying selection of good novels and loving every minute of it.

Eventually Kay and Lily offered to prepare their late lunch, and they set out the cold roast chicken, salads and chilled wine on the terrace. The four friends slipped summer dresses over their swimming costumes – bikini in Lily's case – and settled in the shade to eat.

Sam poured the wine, and iced water for those who wanted it.

"I love my husband – and your husbands too, in fact - and I love all our children, but I have to say this quiet is blissful!" she smiled.

"It's so good to have time just the four of us," Kay agreed. "For one thing, I don't think we've had a proper conversation about our choice of #oneword this year, have we? We're half way through the year now – over half way, in fact – and we usually share a six month update, don't we?" She looked round at the others, and was aware that none of them actually caught her eye.

There was a brief pause. Lily passed round a basket of bread, and they sipped their wine and water and ate.

"Well, I'm happy to start," went on Kay. "Because I think you all know this anyway. I chose 'control' because I was concerned my life was dominated by what others wanted and needed and, somehow, what I might want or need seemed to be at the end of a very long list. It was making me feel disgruntled, I realised, and I needed to do something to take more control of my life. I don't want to sound self-congratulatory, but if I could have looked ahead six months, when we made our choices in December, I think I would have been amazed at how much has changed in that time. The redundancy obviously played a part, because I expect I would never have taken the initiative and changed my job if that hadn't happened. But I am really looking forward to a change of direction in my working life. And I'm proud of the fact that I stuck to the commitment to my own learning," Kay blushed a little here and looked down, but then raised her head again, "and I've been more assertive with my family and they've all rallied round to support me, rather than just taking me for granted. Rachel, especially, has been a revelation – she's really tried to stand on her own two feet, for the first time in - forever! I don't think all that would have happened if I hadn't spoken up and explained to them all how I was feeling. So, yes, I definitely feel more in control and happier with the balance in my life. And this holiday with William has just been the icing on the cake!"

Kay looked round at her friends, who were all smiling at her by this stage. Sam raised her glass.

"To you, Kay! I think of the four of us you've probably achieved the most in the last six months," and Kay blushed again as the three women toasted her.

"But what about the three of you? Remind us all – I think I know, because I spent some time thinking about this just before we came away, but perhaps not everyone will remember - what were your words?"

Lily topped up her glass and took a sizeable gulp of wine before she replied.

"So, I chose 'courage'. Like Kay, I felt I needed to make a change in my life. I was feeling dissatisfied too, and realised I needed to do something about it rather than just trundling along in the same groove. And like Kay, events outside my control had a bearing on my choices. Peter's losing his job, and the fall-out from that in terms of the dip in our income and having to move house – with the tension that all caused – meant I did have to show some courage, in ways I hadn't expected. Dealing with the girls' anxiety and, yes, anger, I'd say, and protecting and supporting Peter in the face of that, while making sure Johnnie didn't feel too unsettled by the instability – it hasn't been easy. I really needed this holiday!"

The others murmured words of support and comfort at this point, and Lily felt a little uneasy as she reflected on the part of the story she hadn't shared, and how she had been tempted – a vision of Jim in his swimming trunks came unbidden into her mind, but she pushed the thought away and carried on.

"I probably wouldn't have asked about doing further training at work, with a view to taking on more responsibility, if we hadn't needed the money, but I'm pleased that's happened – despite the excruciating conversation I had to have with Daniel! I may be out of my comfort zone when I do the training, but, as Gabrielle always tells us, that isn't necessarily a bad thing!"

"Absolutely!" Gabrielle chipped in.

"So I think I'm looking forward to the challenge. And Peter's new job has turned out to be better than he expected. He'll move into a different role there this autumn, and that has done wonders for his self-confidence. And there are other reasons to be cheerful – Molly thinks her exams went well and she's really looking forward to starting A levels. She and Fay seem less antagonistic towards each other at the moment, and Johnnie is – just Johnnie! I guess it hasn't been such a terrible year for us, looking back and looking forward." And Lily took another long drink and reached for a fresh bottle.

"Well done to you, too, Lily," said Gabrielle quietly. "You've stepped up for your family, and you should feel good about that. And you're stepping up at work, too. Sam - what about you?"

Sam spoke slowly and carefully. Suddenly, it seemed to be the right time to tell them. "I chose 'purpose', because, although I know the rest of you tend to think I have something of a charmed life, I was increasingly feeling my life lacked purpose – especially my working life. I know my job is well paid, that I have responsibility, and interesting professional challenges, and perks, but…"

Sam's words petered out, and the friends waited. When she didn't continue, Lily intercepted.

"Is this why you had that outburst on the phone at the start of the year? When you talked about people stabbing each other in the back, and the rest of it?"

Sam didn't reply, and Gabrielle asked, "What outburst? When was this?"

"It was in January," Sam said in a low voice. "And it isn't Lily's fault that you and Kay don't know about it. I asked her not to tell you."

Gabrielle and Kay exchanged glances.

Sam emptied her wine glass and sat back with a sigh.

"In fact – there's quite a bit I haven't told you about this year. I haven't told Adam either – or the children. In fact the only person I have talked to about all of this is my counsellor."

"Your *counsellor*?"

There was a silence while they all processed this information, and then Gabrielle took a deep breath.

"Sam – there is absolutely nothing at all wrong with seeing a counsellor if you felt it would help you. But I think we're just stunned you didn't share any of this with us. If we'd known we might have been able to support you better. We would obviously have kept it to ourselves if you hadn't wanted it to be broadcast more widely, but we've always been close, and yet…" Gabrielle stopped as she suddenly thought about her own secrecy. "I suppose there are things we all of us might keep to ourselves. We are such good friends, but…"

"We need more wine." Lily went into the kitchen to fetch another bottle from the refrigerator. After pausing to think for a few seconds, she returned with two.

"I'm sorry," said Sam. "It wasn't that I didn't trust you, but I just think I've always felt that the three of you saw me as such a success, and it was hard to admit that perhaps my life wasn't quite so rosy. It was somehow all mixed up with my dad's decline. He had such a strong sense of purpose as a doctor, and that was something I always wanted for myself. Compared with that, my professional life seemed so shallow and pointless."

"I remember you talked about applying for Medicine when we were in the Sixth Form," said Gabrielle. "I thought you changed your mind?"

Sam gave a hollow laugh. "My mother opposed it - vehemently - and my father didn't stand up for me, which I found really difficult. Looking back, I can see I didn't share all that with you, either. I didn't fight hard enough for what I wanted. I wasn't like you, Lily."

Lily smiled ruefully as she remembered how strongly she has resisted her own parents' plans for her at that age. "Ironically, I think I regret that fight now!" she admitted.

"So how did that lead to the counsellor, Sam?" from Gabrielle.

"I felt miserable about it - unable to talk to Adam, unwilling to burden the girls, reluctant to talk to you, and needing to talk to someone. I started seeing Jane early this year, and she has been excellent. It has helped me - including at the time of mum's death, and dad moving into residential care. But Adam and the children still don't know I see her. Talking to her also helped me to work out my feelings about what I should do about my job. I was offered the chance to apply for the Deputy CEO role - I know I have mentioned that to you all. But I haven't told you - or Adam and the children - that at the end of April I told Lawrence that not only would I NOT be putting myself forward for that position, but that from this autumn, when the new Deputy CEO starts, I wanted to reduce to three days a week and use the other two days to do some voluntary work."

There was a pause while the three friends digested this information.

"What did he say?" asked Kay.

"He wasn't happy, but he took it to the board and eventually they agreed. Apparently I'm too valuable to be let go completely," Sam gave a weak smile, "especially with a new Deputy CEO coming in, and the recognition that Lawrence himself is likely only to do another year or two at the most before he retires."

"Well, that's good," said Gabrielle after a moment, "isn't it? Is this how you recover a sense of purpose?"

"I hope so. I'm thinking of volunteering to do work with the elderly. Visiting the care home where dad is has been a bit of a revelation. So many of the residents are lonely and isolated. The home organises treats and events but what many of them need is just someone who will listen and take an interest in what they have to say. I actually find I'm quite good at that," and Sam smiled again, a little more brightly.

Lily topped up all their glasses and sat back.

"Well," she said, "this lunch has turned out to be even more interesting than I expected. I wonder whether we all keep secrets from each other. Gabrielle?"

Gabrielle blushed deeply, and the others all turned to her.

"Yes," she said, simply. "And, like Sam, I'm not sure exactly why I didn't share this with you. It's private and sensitive. But you are my best friends and I love you all. This has been a year of anticipation followed by disappointment – in fact a cycle of anticipation and disappointment – for Harry and me. Since January we have been trying to get pregnant. And with no success. My #oneword was 'hope', and that's what I was hoping for. But it seems increasingly unlikely." Gabrielle's eyes filled, and when she looked up at her friends, they all looked stricken.

"Perhaps I didn't want you all to feel the anticipation and disappointment, too. I know what strong powers of empathy we all have!" and Gabrielle gave a faint laugh, as the three women moved closer to her, until Lily and Kay were touching her arm and her shoulder, and Sam enclosed her in a hug.

They sat like that quietly for a short while, each enmeshed in her own thoughts – what they had told, what they had heard, and how they felt about it all. Eventually, they detached themselves, and as they returned to their chairs, they all four looked at the remains of their meal, little of which they had actually eaten. Kay rose to clear the plates, Lily once more filled glasses, and then they all settled again into their seats.

"I wasn't completely honest with you all earlier, either," Lily conceded. "I thought my marriage to Peter might be in trouble at the turn of the year, and I'd met someone at the gym that I was considering having a fling with. And he was married. With kids. Yes, I know!" as she looked round at their faces. "I probably wouldn't even be telling you this now had I not drunk a vat of fine French wine, but as this seems to be a day for confessions, I might as well get it off my chest. Nothing happened in the end – and it might not have done anyway, but then Peter lost his job and the world shifted a bit on its axis. Suddenly it was trivial and there were other things which were so much more important. And I did look at Johnnie and think, "How could I even consider it?" So, Kay, it looks like you're the only one who hasn't been keeping things from the rest of us."

There was a moment of silence after Lily finished, and then the others realised that Kay had, slowly, put her head in her hands.

"Kay?"

"It wasn't my secret to tell. But there is something I haven't shared. And in the light of all you've just offered up, that makes me feel uncomfortable."

"I'm not sure I can bear any more revelations, but I have to say that I am feeling lighter for pouring out my sins. God – this *is* the confessional, isn't it?" Lily looked round at the others.

"I can't tell you all about it, I'm afraid. It's actually Michael's secret, not mine, and no one in the family except William is aware of it. Sorry."

"There's no need to apologise, Kay," Gabrielle assured her. "I think we've all had too much wine, and this has been an emotional outpouring for all of us! I haven't really been drinking since New Year's Eve, but today I thought: sod it, and the wine I've drunk has gone straight to my head. But I can still see that, if it's Michael's secret, it's perfectly understandable that you haven't been free to tell anyone else. We all respect that, of course."

Kay shifted uncomfortably, and Lily, despite the wine she had consumed, saw in an instant what had happened.

"But you told Abiola..." she said evenly.

"I did! And I don't know why I would tell Abiola and not the three of you, but I felt the need to talk to someone and she was there, and..."

Suddenly, Lily started to laugh, and then Gabrielle and Sam joined in, and Kay, looking round, started to giggle herself.

"What are we like?" gasped Sam, as uncontrollable laughter took hold of them all, and at this point the two cars pulled into the drive and the children spilled out, followed by the men.

"Mummy!" Johnnie yelled, as he hurtled into his mother's arms. "We had the BEST time! We had a game of football with these French boys and I kicked our ball into the river! Mummy – are you listening? Why are you laughing?"

"Why are you *all* laughing?" asked Adam as he came up onto the terrace. "I take it this has been a good lunch?"

That night in bed, Sam lay in Adam's arms and he talked about their day.

"I was so proud of our children," he told her. "When Johnnie accidentally kicked the ball into the river, he was devastated, but Charlie and Josh immediately scooped him up and made a big fuss of him – said what a brilliant tactic it had been, as the French boys were winning – and what a great story it would make. Within five minutes he was a hero and he was over the moon!"

"They are wonderful kids," Sam admitted. "We are lucky."

"But we played our part in that," Adam suggested. "You especially – you've done a great parenting job while I've been travelling all over the place, and you've got demanding work, and you've looked after your parents - and you're still doing the best for your dad without much support."

They were quiet for a few moments.

"I think I might tell them at work that I want to travel less in the future. Spend more time at home, with you and the kids – I don't want to be one of those dads who turns round and finds his children have grown up and he's missed it. Being here just confirms that for me. It's what I want at this point in my life. What do you think?"

Sam kissed him.

"I think they would love to see more of you, and so would I. We might need to navigate a lifestyle change. There are things I need to tell you…"

OCTOBER 2019

Chapter Thirteen

Sam

Sam said goodbye to the Director of HR, shaking her hand and smiling, and then turned to the Receptionist to return her visitor's badge.

"Mrs Talbot wonders whether you're in a rush, or whether you might have half an hour to have a cup of tea with her?" the Receptionist asked, her head tilted.

"I'd love to! I thought she might be too busy."

The Receptionist smiled. " 'Busy but never too busy' is one of her favourite phrases! I'll show you round to the sitting room," and Sam waited as she made her way out of the office and round to the foyer where Sam stood.

Sam knew that Gabrielle had a working office upstairs next to the staffroom, but that when she saw visitors she used a small sitting room near the main reception, and the Receptionist led her there and then disappeared to make tea. The room was comfortable and welcoming – Sam looked round as she waited, and Gabrielle joined her a few minutes later.

"How did you get on?" Gabrielle asked, as they hugged.

"All good. She was lovely, and it seems straightforward."

"Yes – it's a process we're used to now. Anyone from outside the school community who has access to students needs to go through the system – all part of safeguarding in education, these days."

The friends settled themselves in the easy chairs and waited as the Receptionist brought in the tray, and Gabrielle poured the tea.

"It's lovely to see you – I thought you might not have time for this."

"I can usually find half an hour, and it's good for me to have regular breaks, too. Headship can be all-consuming if you're not careful, but I know the best leaders aren't the ones who work to the exclusion of all else."

"You're good at taking time for yourself, I know - and making space for you and Harry to do things together. Do you have plans for this weekend?"

"Actually I'm speaking at a conference in Sheffield tomorrow – it's the Women in Education one. I'm talking about balancing the personal and the professional, and, for the first time, I'm going to address the subject of fertility and share my experiences."

"That's going to be hard…"

"I think it is. I'm not phased by public speaking at all, usually, these days. And I've spoken at the last four #WomenEd annual conferences, on various issues to do with women in leadership. But I've never focussed on something this personal and emotional, so I feel a bit nervous, if I'm honest. I'm determined to do it, though, and I know if I do feel a bit wobbly, it will be fine. There's nothing wrong with showing emotion in this kind of situation, and it's a very supportive and empathetic audience."

"I assume it's all women?"

"Not exclusively, but predominantly. There are a fair few #HeForShe allies who attend, but most of the audience are women who are committed to supporting other women in education. These are always really positive and energising events. So that's Saturday and then on Sunday Harry and I are going out for the day – long walk, pub lunch – great for decompression! What about you?"

"It's our choral concert on Saturday night so I'll be rehearsing during the afternoon. All the family are around so they're all coming in the evening, and then we're going out for a curry afterwards. I'm hoping for a restful family day at home on Sunday."

"Remind me what you're singing?"

"Verdi Requiem this time. I just love it. And singing is so good for me - I always feel calm after a good sing!"

There was a pause while each of them reflected that Sam was, in fact, generally at peace with herself at the moment. The changes she had made in her life, including her openness with

Adam, were starting to bear fruit. She had had her last counselling session with Jane in September and had decided to see how things went without that support for a while, though she didn't discount the possibility that she might feel the need to resume these meetings at some stage in the future.

"So we can arrange a date for you to come in to meet the girls and start their preparation, probably in a couple of weeks or so, and then after October half term we'll begin the visits. Does that sound like a plan?"

"It sounds perfect, Gabrielle – and I am so grateful that you were keen to do this."

"Of course! The girls will get a lot out of it, and I hope the residents will, too. We shall try it and see. It's always good to have fresh options to add to the Community Service programme, and I'm really pleased you suggested this. How is your dad doing?"

"He seems better, I think – settled and quite content there. He enjoys seeing me, and the children when they visit, though occasionally he looks at them and I can tell he's trying to work out who they are. But they seem less phased by that than I am. It was watching how brilliant they are with him, and when they talk to the other residents, that made me realise this might be something your Sixth Form girls might be interested in. I'm so pleased they – and you – are prepared to give it a go."

"We'll start with a group of half a dozen, as we discussed, and see how we get on. But if it works well, and all those involved – on both sides - get something from it, then we can talk about expanding it, bringing in more students and contacting other care homes. We can use the school minibus and I can supply a driver when we need to, but it's good that your dad's home is within walking distance for our first foray into this. We'll see how this pilot group gets on and then discuss next steps. I'm happy to talk to other local heads, too, if at some stage in the future you decide you want to roll it out to other schools.

And now, I probably have to get ready for my next appointment. But it's so good to see you, and I'm really pleased we're working together on this. I'll see you in a couple of weeks' time, won't I?"

"Yes – looking forward to meeting the others at the Italian on the 15th."

The friends hugged again, and Sam gathered up her bag and her jacket.

"Love to Harry – and the very best of luck, tomorrow. Tell us all about it on the 15th, won't you?"

"I will. Give my love to Adam and the children, too. I'll see you round to the front door."

As she drove home, listening to the Verdi Requiem played through the car's sound system, Sam thought through how she might prepare Gabrielle's Sixth Form girls for the first care home visit. The main purpose of the exercise was to build relationships, to communicate, and to explore appropriate activities such as board games, which the residents might enjoy. Perhaps next summer she might invest in a few croquet sets and see whether that was something that they would like to try. She expected the girls she was to work with and accompany would have ideas of their own, too. Sam had watched her own children, the twins especially, during the visits to their grandfather in recent months and had seen how easy and comfortable they had seemed with the other residents, chatting in a warm and friendly way, and how some of the elderly had brightened in the light of this contact. Sam remembered Gabrielle telling them all about an annual party for the local Visually Impaired held at her school - many of the guests also elderly - which her Sixth Form girls had organised, and how natural and confident the teenagers were as they welcomed, hosted and entertained those who attended.

"They seem even easier with them than I and the other adults are, I think." Gabrielle had told her friends. "I find it quite humbling. One girl told me afterwards that it reminded her of the conversations she had had with her gran, who had sadly passed away last year, and that she missed her and that contact."

Sam had reflected on this conversation, and during her next visit to her father had asked if she could talk to the care home manager, Louise, about an idea she had. Louise had been receptive. When Sam outlined her idea to Gabrielle she found her enthusiastic, and the scheme was gong to be tried out in the coming months. If it worked, Sam would contact other care homes, with Louise's help, and consider how it might be expanded. With Gabrielle's support she might be able to involve a number of different schools.

Sam was determined to use the two days each week when she was not now working for the hotel chain to best effect. She had started her new schedule at the start of September, and so far felt pleased with how it was going. But she didn't want the two days to be subsumed by home and family tasks – she wanted her voluntary work to be structured and purposeful, and working with teenagers and the elderly together was something she felt could have so many benefits, including for her. She knew there were no guarantees, and she could only try to make it work, learn from the process and adapt, if necessary, in the light of experience. But she felt confident and optimistic about the plan.

As she pulled into the drive, she was pleased to see Adam's car was already there. Since France, he had been true to his word and had negotiated with the firm he worked for to travel less and to reduce his hours.

"One of the advantages of being high up in the company is that you do have bargaining power," he had mused. "If one of my junior colleagues wanted to do this, it would be seen as a damaging lack of commitment which could harm their career prospects. I've earned my stripes, they know my value, and they don't want to lose me. If at fifty years old I want a different balance in my life, they're prepared to respect that.
It's the same with you, too, Sam – if you hadn't been brilliant at your job, they would never have gone for the three days a week plan."

Sam had been relieved and heartened by Adam's reaction to her decision about work. He was totally supportive. He had been disappointed that she hadn't felt able to tell him earlier in the year – about her counselling appointments, too – but they had worked through that and he had accepted that, if she had been reluctant to tell him what she was thinking and feeling, he had to take responsibility for being distant (physically and emotionally), and he was committed to making a change.

Sam recognised that she was enjoying the work she did for the hotel chain more – or certainly feeling frustrated less often – now she had reduced her hours. She got on well with the incoming Deputy CEO, Dan, and could see that he would be more than ready to step up to the CEO role when Lawrence retired. She and Dan were working very well together, and she realised that they were aligned in terms of their vision and values, and their conviction with respect to how the chain might need to evolve in the future. Dan had already sounded Sam out about whether she might wish to consider the Deputy role in due course, and she had said that she would only be willing to discuss it if the company were prepared to accommodate flexible working and perhaps a job-share arrangement. Dan was very receptive to the idea, and Sam tried not to show that this had surprised her. She had had a conversation with Dan within which he had said, "Would *you* rather work with someone stunningly good three days a week, Sam, or have someone less good for five?" Sam realised that she had learnt a lot from talking to Gabrielle about flexible professional arrangements, and how they could be made to work successfully, including at the highest levels of leadership, in the world of education. She was also learning how to be more assertive, she thought.

But that was a discussion and a decision for the future. For now, she was content to see how her new life panned out, and to ensure she was happy with the balance she had found. And, of course, to enjoy a sense of purpose.

"Hello you," she leaned in to kiss Adam's cheek as he rose from the kitchen table. "Are we pouring wine already?"

"The sun is shining. There's chilled rose in the fridge. It's Friday evening – well, almost – and I thought we could take these out into the garden and enjoy an hour's peace before the children get home. Come and tell me how you got on at the school."

"That sounds like an excellent idea."

They settled onto the comfortable chairs on the patio, and Sam closed her eyes against the low sun.

"Today was good. Gabrielle is so positive and supportive. We're sorting out the DBS check – I think that's what it's called – and then I'm going to go in and do a kind of training session with the girls – just six of them in the first instance. We'll start the visits to the home after the half term break. I'm really looking forward to it."

"Great stuff. And is Gabrielle on form?"

"She is. She's going to a women in education conference tomorrow where she's talking about the relationship between the personal and the professional, including the tension around the issue of fertility. She knows it will be difficult and she will feel emotional, but she thinks it's such an important thing for women at an earlier stage of their career to be aware of. She's right, of course. I do admire her."

"Do I assume there's no good news on that front?"

"Since she told us about this when we were in France, I think we all have a tacit understanding not to ask. If the situation changes, she will tell us, of course. For now we just need to offer quiet support."

"And you're all good at that. A thirty year, unbroken, friendship. That's impressive. Not sure I know many – any? – men who have those kinds of bonds. I'm certainly not in touch with anyone I went to school with. Or university, either, come to think of it. My oldest friend must be..." Adam groped for a name.

"John, I should think," Sam supplied, naming their best man. "But you don't see him very often, and you rarely get in touch with each other."

"Maybe I should. Do you think women 'do' friendship better than men?"

"That reminds me – I listened to a podcast the other day – it was something Gabrielle recommended. Jane Garvie – from Woman's Hour? - was being interviewed, and she said something that really struck me. I wrote it down to share with the others. Now where did I put it?"

Sam rose and went into the kitchen to locate the notepad she'd found nearby when she was listening to the podcast. She returned with the pad and the bottle of rose, and flicked through the pages while Adam poured the last of the wine into their glasses.

"Here it is: 'I think there's a lot to be said for women who seek out the company of other women, want to help other women, and hugely appreciate the support they get from their female friendships.' I suppose this is what's fundamentally behind the women in educational leadership initiative Gabrielle is so invested in – and it's behind our long-lasting friendship too."

They were quiet for a few moments, and then Adam said, "I think I'll give John a ring tonight."

Sam closed her eyes against the sun again, leaned back in her chair and smiled to herself.

Chapter Fourteen

Gabrielle

As Gabrielle drove to Sheffield early on the Saturday morning, she thought about her godchildren. Over the years, she had been asked to act as godparent several times: to Kay's Susanna first; to the twins, Emily and Annabelle; and most recently when Johnnie was born six years before. Although none of the four friends were regular church attenders, all the children, and now Robbie, had been through christening ceremonies, and Gabrielle recognised she had a slightly different relationship with her godchildren, although she was affectionate and generous with all her friends' children. She had recently given the twins a copy of a book she had read which was written to support teenage girls coping with the complexity of adolescence – 'Girl Up', by Laura Bates. She had bought another copy for Molly and Fay, explaining to both Sam and Lily that, although she felt the content might be a little too direct for younger girls, it contained just the level of information and frankness that girls of their age needed and could benefit from. But she had then gone in search of good fiction books for Josh, Charlie and Johnnie, too, and a new picture book for Robbie. She enjoyed choosing and offering gifts to all the children.

Gabrielle felt that she and Harry would have been great parents – that was, she supposed, the main thing which had driven her commitment to try again this year. But if it didn't happen, and as each month passed she felt she was beginning to come to terms with the fact that it might not, she realised she was fortunate that, in the absence of nieces and nephews, the relationship they had with their friends' children was warm and loving. Gabrielle also found the company of the girls at school enjoyable and energising, and she knew Harry felt the same about the students in his classes and those he interacted with across the school. They were both well suited to teaching, she reflected.

She turned her mind to the workshop she was leading at the conference and felt, again, a twinge of nervousness. As she had explained to Sam the previous day, it wasn't public speaking, as such, which made her anxious – she had done so much of it over her career, especially in her current and previous roles, that she felt comfortable addressing audiences of all sizes, and found it an appealing and satisfying challenge to make a connection and to encourage others to think. But today she had chosen a topic which was so personal and sensitive, and about which she felt naturally emotional, and she was unsure whether she would be able to master and sustain the control and calmness she would need to get through it. However, she had a strong conviction that talking openly about this was the right thing to do, and that the issue of potential childlessness and how that could be navigated alongside a demanding career was important enough to deserve a platform.

Gabrielle pulled into the multi-storey carpark opposite the university and rose through the levels until she found a space. She collected her slim briefcase, handbag and coat and took the lift to street level, recognising a number of teachers and leaders she knew as she crossed the road and made her way into the building.

Gabrielle's session was taking place in the afternoon, but at these #WomenEd conferences every delegate was offered the opportunity to speak, and every speaker was expected to attend for the full day and to support other speakers' sessions, so it was different from education conferences Gabrielle had attended where usually well-known speakers arrived to fill their slot and then shot off straight afterwards. There was a strong sense of community, here, and Gabrielle met up with many contacts whom she now considered to be friends, and made some fresh connections, too. She was an advocate for the power of social media for networking and professional learning in education, especially Twitter and the word of online blogs, and this had led to some interesting opportunities, conversations and positive relationships over the previous five years. It was always fascinating to be able to identify and introduce herself to some of her Twitter contacts whom she had not yet met face-to-face, and she spent some time considering the delegate list and tracking them down to say hello.

She was also mindful that at every event of this kind there would be some individuals, or small groups, who had never attended one of these conferences before, and she was alert to those who stood slightly apart and appeared hesitant. She would make a point of going over to speak to them, aware that at a conference where many people were greeting established contacts and friends, first-time attenders could feel marginalised.

The presentations were run as workshops and all were interactive, encouraging discussion and response and the opportunity to relate the message of the facilitator to the experience of the participants. Gabrielle's focus would be on choice – where we have choice and how we can make the most of it; where we don't have the same degree of choice, and how we process and manage that. She would use the story of her own inability – so far – to conceive a child as an example.

The day began with an inspiring keynote from a headteacher Gabrielle knew well, who had just stepped down from headship and had recently been presented with a Lifetime Achievement Award. When she had been appointed as the head of her current school almost twenty years earlier, she had been its first female headteacher since the school was founded in 1579. She spoke warmly about her own career and the lessons it had taught her, but also about the changing role of women in educational leadership over the years.

Following the opening keynote, Gabrielle attended a workshop on intersectionality, looking particularly at race, gender and age, and then moved to a session which explored how best we can educate young people about what 'feminism' really is. She chatted to people she knew and met others for the first time. She shared coffee and later lunch with friends she was pleased to catch up with, and then in the early afternoon she chose a quick-fire #LeadMeet session in which five speakers shared their stories on a range of subjects, before making her way up to the room she had been allocated for her own session while the delegates had another short break.

She arrived first, set up her PowerPoint presentation and then sat in the empty room and breathed deeply for a few moments. Now the time had arrived she realised she felt composed and ready. Preparing what she planned to say had, she knew, helped her to clarify her thinking about her current situation. She was calm, now, and felt able to share her thoughts with others and to encourage them to reflect on their own lives and their hopes, and aspirations, for the future. She wanted them to consider what we can do when we don't get what we dream of; where, despite our best efforts, we realise it may not happen.

People began to arrive, and Gabrielle smiled and welcomed them. Some faces were familiar, and there were a few she felt she already knew well. Others were new to her, and she chatted to them while everyone settled into their seats. And then she moved back to the front of the room and began. "Good afternoon everyone, and thank you for being here. I want to talk to you today, and to encourage you to think about, choices..."

After this fourth session, everyone made their way back to the lecture theatre for the final plenary discussion. As the room filled, Gabrielle looked across the rows and recognised the extent to which her involvement in #WomenEd had given her the opportunity to connect with such a diverse group of people – all were involved in education but these men and women came from different ethnic groups and different social backgrounds. There were examples of physical difference, differences in sexuality and gender identity. These were educators working in a wide range of contexts. They came together at these events because of a shared commitment to supporting women to fulfil their professional potential. In this final session there was a focus on "what now?" where all the conference delegates were exhorted to examine what they might do differently as a result of their reflections across the course of the day. Could they make a pledge, a commitment which would move them forward in some way and which might help them better to encourage and galvanise others? Gabrielle thought carefully about her pledge, before entering it into her phone and seeing it displayed alongside all the others on the rolling screen at the front of the room. She sat quietly, absorbed in her own thoughts for a few moments, and then became aware that the steering group members who stood at the front were concluding the proceedings and the applause was starting.

As Gabrielle made her way to the exit she saw Jen smiling at her. "Gabrielle – are you in a rush to get home? A few of us are going for a drink in the pub across the way, if you're interested. Do you have time for a catch-up?"

Gabrielle smiled back. "That would be lovely."

Harry was putting the finishing touches to tea as Gabrielle arrived home.

"Good day?"

"A great day, thanks."

"Tea in fifteen minutes if you're ready?"

"Perfect."

"G & T or a glass of wine first? Or are you sticking with water?"

Gabrielle gave him a level look.

"A glass of wine, I think. Chilled white will hit the spot," and Gabrielle opened the fridge.

"Good call. Pour me a glass too?"

Gabrielle passed Harry the glass of wine and perched at the breakfast bar sipping hers while he cooked.

"Seafood with pasta and salad, madam. I assume it was sandwiches for lunch."

"It was, and I'm hungry. We shared some crisps in the pub." Gabrielle had phoned Harry from the pub to let him know what time she expected to be home.

"How were Jen and the others?"

"All good. Fired up at the end of a day of really good conversations."

"And your session? You said it was 'fine' on the phone, but do you want to talk more about it while we eat?" Harry moved to set the table.

"I actually enjoyed it. It felt liberating, in fact. As soon as I started I felt quite calm and in control. We talked about a range of issues – where we felt we had choice, and how we coped when we felt we didn't. We discussed how you cope with disappointment and failure, and how we need not to let it derail us and, especially, stop us from appreciating and enjoying other things in our lives."

Harry set down the warmed plates of food and the bowls of salad, brought the bottle of wine and a basket of French bread over to the table, and they settled to eat.

"It's helped me to think this through. Now I've been open and talked about it publicly for the first time, my pledge is to be prepared to do more of that if it might be helpful. I'm going to start by emailing Jo to let her know that, if she'd like me to contribute to the PSHE programme next year, I'd be willing to do that. And I think I might write a blog or an article about it, too. There are so many couples who struggle to conceive, for a range of reasons. It might help to share and hear different stories rather than just being silent about it. I know it's a sensitive subject, but it's hardly something to be ashamed of. And I know there are bound to be a fair number of girls in my school who will experience difficulties around conception at some point in the future. I don't want them to be worried and anxious, but I do want them to be aware and informed. It might help them to be better prepared if it did happen to them. We're going to include information about things like IVF. I thought I could provide a perspective from someone who didn't choose to go down that route. What do you think?"

"I think you're amazing – but you know that, already."

Gabrielle smiled.

"As are you. Actually my pledge at the end of the day was two-fold. Being prepared to talk and write more openly about possible infertility was part of it. But the other part was about fully appreciating the things I have, rather than allowing sadness over what I don't have to dominate my thinking. Our life is wonderful in so many ways – we are lucky, and I don't want just to see myself as a victim who is unlucky because of this one thing. And this spaghetti is delicious."

"Thank you. And as I had time on my own today, I unearthed the ice-cream maker and made up a batch of your favourite ice cream, so make sure to leave space for dessert."

"See? How lucky am I?"

Harry topped up their glasses.

"We both are. We won't let each other forget it."

Later that evening, Gabrielle opened up her laptop and scrolled through Twitter. She read the many comments which had been made about the conference, and what the participants felt they had gained from the day. She shared with Harry some of the tweets relating to her own session, which she found reassuring and heartening. Other tweets gave her an insight into the learning from the sessions she hadn't been able to attend, including workshops on the unique challenges of leading in different contexts; insights into a successful model of co-headship; and advice on how to negotiate pay unapologetically and effectively.

It occurred to her that there was something of 'the Sermon on the Mount' effect about tweets from a conference, enabling others who weren't able to be there to benefit from the key messages and the stimulating discussion. Certainly when there was a range of workshop options it was helpful to find out what had been covered in those sessions she would have liked to have attended, but wasn't able to fit in. She closed her laptop and leant back, closing her eyes.

Harry looked up from his book. "Tired?"

"Yes, but happily so. It's been a really good day."

"I'm pleased. Oh, and I meant to say - I've booked the table for lunch at the pub tomorrow, and we should manage a nice, long walk in the morning. The weather forecast is good."

They held each other's gaze for a moment, and Gabrielle knew that each of them was thinking, 'Lucky…'

Chapter Fifteen

Kay

The pace was painfully slow. Kay had collected Robbie from Susanna's flat and they were walking round to see her parents. Kay wheeled the pushchair along in case Robbie flagged, but ever since he had started to walk, he had resisted using it, and it had become a battle to strap him in. He held one hand as she manoeuvred the pushchair with the other. And he stopped frequently – to examine something on the pavement, to point to and comment on a bird in the hedge, and to chatter to other passers-by. He was a sociable individual.

Kay was patient, and there was no rush, she reflected. She did want to catch Rachel before she left – this was one of the days on which Rachel cleaned their parents' house. Rachel had assumed full responsibility for this since the summer, as Kay had hoped she would, and seemed quite happy with the arrangement. Rachel had mentioned on the phone the last time they spoke that she wanted to buy some new clothes, and would appreciate Kay's support and advice. This was a relatively new phenomenon, Kay recognised. It had been years since Rachel had appeared to care much about her appearance. Definitely another positive development in terms of Rachel's growing confidence and building self-esteem.

Kay saw a young mum approaching with a baby in a buggy, before she recognised who it was. She saw the mother hesitate, perhaps even consider crossing the road, but then seem to decide not to. Did Kay imagine it, or did the young woman raise her chin a little, as they approached each other?

"Good morning, Sarah. How are you?"

Sarah smiled faintly, and stopped. She hadn't been sure what reaction to expect from Michael's mother. This was the first time they had met since her baby was born.

"I'm exhausted!" she laughed, lightly. "But otherwise OK."

"May I?" and as Sarah nodded, Kay leaned over and looked into the buggy, where Sarah's three-month old daughter lay sleeping. "She's beautiful."

"We called her Sophie," announced Sarah quietly. "She's a good baby – and healthy, I'm pleased to say. Though she hasn't settled into any sort of routine at night yet, so I seem to be managing on very little sleep. But I'm not complaining. I know that's just how it is. And Alex is very good at doing his share, though I'm feeding her, so..."

Sarah realised she was starting to gabble, and she stopped. Kay gazed at the sleeping child, inevitably thinking of Michael at that age, and knowing that she would probably never be able to establish whether this was another of her grandchildren. She straightened up and smiled at the young mother.

"It will get better – you know that. In the meantime, look after yourself as well as her. Give my best wishes to Alex, too. I wish you all every happiness."

Kay looked at Robbie, who was peering into the buggy with great fascination.

"Come on, young man. Bye, Sarah."

"Bye. And thank you."

As they moved apart, each woman wondered exactly what the thanks were for.

A few minutes later, Kay turned into her parents' street and Robbie became even more animated. "Gammy!" he shouted, and as Kay let him through the gate and collapsed the pushchair, he broke into a wobbly run down the path. Kay's mother – Gammy – had been watching through the window and she opened the door. Kay lifted the pushchair into the porch and kissed her on the cheek while Robbie wound himself round his great-grandmother's body.

"I thought you'd be here half an hour ago – Robbie, let go, love!"

"Walking anywhere with Robbie always takes longer than you think it will. Is Rachel still here?"

"Yes – she's finished in the house, but she's chatting to Ben in the garden. Come in, come in – if Robbie will let go of my legs I'll put the kettle on."

"Morning, dad. Is all well?" Kay bent to kiss her father as she entered the lounge.

Kay's father reached for the remote and turned off the television.

"Hello, love. General election called for 12th December – did you hear? I think your mum and me might go for a postal vote this time. What do you reckon?"

"Sounds sensible to me – I'll have a look at the forms you need to fill in. I'm just going to have a word with Rachel before I settle down with my cup of tea." And Kay saw her parents exchange a look which she couldn't quite interpret as she prepared to slide open the patio doors.

Ben was her parents' window cleaner – a quiet widower in his fifties who had been coming to the house for years. If his visits had ever coincided with Kay's, she had met him at the door once he had finished and passed on his payment, and he was, Kay realised, painfully shy, dipping his head and blushing as he muttered his thanks. A few months ago, Kay's father had told her that, in addition to the window cleaning, Ben had agreed to come round once a week to tidy the garden – doing the weeding, or cutting the grass, tasks which had become increasingly unmanageable for either of Kay's parents. It had actually been Rachel's suggestion. This morning, he and Rachel sat on the garden bench by the tiny fishpond, and they were laughing – in fact, Kay noticed with a start as she reached for the handle of the patio door, they seemed to be holding hands…

Kay opened the door and stepped out, and Rachel and Ben dropped hands as they looked up, startled and, it appeared, a little guilty. What was happening, here?

"Hello there! Morning, Ben. Sorry to disturb you…"

Ben rose to his feet and, true to form, blushed and looked down at his feet.

"Morning," he mumbled. "I was just off," and he moved, with some speed, Kay felt, towards the fence where he collected his gardening bag and let himself out through the side gate.

Kay settled beside her sister, and looked at her. Rachel looked down at her hands, but she had the ghost of a smile on her face. Kay waited for her to speak, but after a moment's silence, realised that Rachel was waiting, too.

"Rachel?"

When Rachel raised her head, Kay was surprised to see her eyes were glistening.

"Rachel, what is it? Are you all right?"

Rachel nodded, and then took a deep breath.

"Better than all right, I'd say. We're going to be married, Kay."

"So, apparently, mum and dad knew, but Rachel had sworn them to secrecy – I'm not sure quite why. Did she think I'd disapprove, do you reckon? I'm actually thrilled for her. She seems happy, and excited, and – somehow - purposeful. I think she's been lonely for a long time, and so has he, it seems."

"When was she going to tell you?" Sam sipped her coffee.

"She'd asked me about taking her clothes shopping. I think she was planning to talk to me about it then – at least, that she had been meeting him regularly at mum and dad's and that they'd struck up a friendship which had developed into a romance. Maybe the element of secrecy made it even more romantic, somehow. Anyway, his proposal had come out of the blue a couple of days ago, but she was so happy to accept. They seem to bring out the best in each other. They want to marry at Christmas, and she will give up her flat and live with him in a nice little semi on the Highfields estate."

"Remind me how old she is, Kay?"

"She's three years older than us, and Ben is in his fifties – he's been a widower for over twenty years I think. His wife died of cancer, sadly, leaving him with two teenagers who are now both married themselves, with children, so Rachel becomes a grandparent too. A ready-made family! And financial security, and support."

Sam looked at her friend for a moment.

"Rachel has relied on you for years – forever, I think. So how do you feel now she has someone else to lean on? Relieved, or....?"

Kay was thoughtful.

"You know – it's all bound up with the 'control' thing. In January I felt others relied on me too much, and there wasn't space for me. As this year has gone on, that's changed, and it's given me the opportunity to do much more just for myself. I am pleased about that, of course, and grateful, but the loss of control has taken some getting used to, too. It does make me think of the 'Be careful what you wish for, because you may get it' idea!" Kay laughed, and Sam smiled back at her.

"And how is the job?"

"I'm enjoying it. The enrolment period was hectic, as Abiola warned me it would be, and I was new and having to learn so much, even people's names, and the College routines and processes. But I feel more confident and comfortable now we're a few months in. The A level studies are a joy – I even love doing homework, which wasn't the case when we were at school, I remember! And I'm such a glutton for punishment that I've opted to do an online IT course to boost my computer skills, too. Learning is liberating, I've found, this year. What about you?"

"All good, thanks. We start the care home visits with the girls from Gabrielle's school next week. I've done the training sessions at school – the girls are amazing, so positive and enthusiastic. I'm looking forward to seeing how their relationships with the residents develop. Work is OK – better. I get on well with the new Deputy CEO, Dan, and as Lawrence edges towards retirement, he is leaving us to it most of the time. I'm definitely feeling less frustrated and more fulfilled."

"And Adam?"

"He still has busy weeks, and probably a little more travel than he would ideally like, but he is home more than he was, and we're managing to spend more family time together – though it's perhaps ironic that just as we're at the point where we want to see more of the children, they all seem keen to see less of us!"

"I remember that stage! I think I'm still getting used to not having Michael in the house – even picking up his dirty washing from the floor of his bedroom! - but he's thriving on his independence, I can see. He's a man, not a boy, all of a sudden. Oh – and I haven't told you this. Susanna has a beau!"

"What a word! Who is it?"

"Someone she met at a friend's wedding. Neil – he seems nice, and very good with Robbie. It's early days, but I think he's lasted longer than anyone else she's met since Robbie was born, so we'll see how things develop. She certainly seems keen, and steadier. Less self-involved, maybe."

"This has been quite a year, Kay, hasn't it? For all of us, I think. There's certainly been more change than we might have expected when we met last New Year's Eve. Some of it self-generated, and some beyond our own agency. But, on balance, it's not been a bad year for any of us, I think – even given mum's death, and Peter's job and Lily's move, and then there's Gabrielle's situation. Actually, on reflection, this year has had its challenges…"

"And Michael's pain – and my not knowing whether I have a grandchild I will never have the chance to love…" thought Kay, but she kept this to herself.

"Well, I should go, Sam. I'm working at 2. It's been lovely to see you, as always." The two friends embraced, left the coffee shop and went their separate ways, each of them reflecting on the year that was drawing to its conclusion, and what the four of them had experienced. And each of them remembered the words they had all chosen ten months ago, and how those words had resonated in their experiences and the decisions they had taken since that time.

As they sat down to eat that night, Kay told William about meeting Sarah the day before, and seeing the baby for the first time. She had said nothing to Michael, and did not intend to. He was getting on with his life, enjoying living with Tricia and Billy – in fact, getting on so well with former schoolfriend Tricia that Kay suspected the relationship was heading in a fresh direction. His job was going well, and he had booked a holiday in Tenerife with friends in early November, which he was clearly excited about, though he was trying to be cool and casual.

"What did you feel, when you looked at the baby?" William asked, and Kay thought for a moment – both about the question, but also about the fact that William had asked that. She wasn't sure he would have asked her to talk about how she was feeling, in quite that way, a year ago.

"A little sad, if I'm honest. I would love other grandchildren, and I know it will probably happen at some stage. The thought that we might have a grandchild that we will never get to know, or be able to cherish, is hard. And thinking about how awkward and nervous Sarah seemed initially – it might just be because I'm Michael's mum, and she realises how much she hurt him. But she will know we know he thought the baby was his. Whether it really was his…"

"You don't wish we'd encouraged him to ask for a paternity test?"

"No. We needed to support him to move on and to live his life – and he is. And Sarah and Alex are doing the same. The baby will be loved and well cared for, I have no doubt of that. I think now I've seen her for the first time – seen both of them – it will be easier next time we bump into each other. This is a small town."

"I'm sure you're right." William finished his meal and collected their plates. "Cup of tea?"

"Please. I have some reading to do to prepare for next week's Spanish class, and a cup of tea will help me along nicely."

Kay gathered her A level work together while William was in the kitchen. As she had said to Sam, she enjoyed the homework she was set, and felt pleased with the progress she was making so far. She was already wondering about whether she might like to embark on a part-time degree course at some point in the future. She would talk to Abiola about it.

She settled at the dining room table with her work and her tea and had just started the reading when the phone rang. William answered it, and Kay paused while she listened to his side of the conversation – although there was very little of it – and worked out whether it was a call for him or for her. He turned and looked in her direction.

"That's OK, Peter. She's right here. I'm sure she won't mind. Sorry to hear Lily's so upset. I'll tell her. You all take care, now. Bye."

William replaced the receiver and gave Kay a baleful glance. "Sorry, love – I know you were just settling down to your work. Peter asks if you could possibly go round there. Lily needs your help."

"What on earth is it? Didn't she just want to talk to me?"

"I think it's more serious. Sam's on her way there, too. Gabrielle's away with Harry. It's some problem with the girls. I could hear crying in the background. It sounds like Lily is distressed and that doesn't sound like the Lily I know. Do you mind going over there?"

"Of course I don't – she wouldn't ask Peter to ring us if it wasn't important. This is what friends are for, I suppose."

Kay kissed him as she moved to the door.

"I'll ring you when I can to let you know what's happening and when I'll be back. Unless it gets late – you go to bed when you need to. I know you're up early tomorrow."

"She's lucky to have you."

Kay smiled as she collected her bag, coat and keys. The four of them were lucky to have each other, she reflected. The possibilities of what might have happened were running through her head. "I'll know soon enough," she thought. And she hoped that she and Sam, between them, would be able to give Lily whatever support she needed.

Chapter Sixteen

Lily

The day had started positively. The children were on their half term break, and so Lily and Peter had had a quiet breakfast together without the need to chivvy and nag in order to get everyone out of the door at the right time.

"It's so much easier now Molly is 17 and I can leave Johnnie with the girls while we're at work," Lily reflected. Peter left first, and she heard him whistling as he located his phone and car keys. His job had worked out so much better than he had initially anticipated. He had already been promoted within the firm and was relishing the challenge and opportunity it presented. He was planning for the future again, rather than just thinking about how to survive in the present.

And Lily felt happier at the bank, too. The training she had completed after they returned from France had been so much more interesting than she had expected, and had helped to clarify her own thinking about possible next steps. There was a written assessment at the end of the course, and she had achieved one of the highest marks, which was very good for her self-belief. She did now feel ready to take on more responsibility, and she was also considering whether she might be able to take the skills she was developing – Gabrielle was always talking about the importance of 'transferable skills' – and look for a fresh professional challenge in a new area. Banking was changing, she knew, with the advent of so many online transactions. She recognised that she was still only half way through her professional life – if she were working until she were well into her sixties, she did have time to explore new avenues. She saw how Kay had embraced a new direction, and was starting to believe this was something that might appeal to her, too.

She cleared the breakfast dishes and called upstairs before she left.

"I'm off. Are you stirring, girls?"

Johnnie was playing in his room, and she wanted to make sure the girls were awake and fully functioning before she left him in their care. Fay appeared on the landing, yawning and rubbing the sleep from her eyes.

"We're up, mum."

"What are you doing today?"

"It's half term – so nothing, of course!"

"Well, look after Johnnie, and don't go out, unless you take him with you. I'm trusting you to take good care of him."

"Do you have to say that *every* morning, mum?" whined Fay. "We know. We do. We will." She headed for the bathroom, still stretching.

"I'll be back by 5. Ring me if there are any issues?"

She paused in case there was any reply, although she wasn't really expecting one. She locked the front door behind her and headed for the bus stop.

Work was relatively uneventful. At lunchtime Lily went for a walk, and ate her sandwiches in the park – it was a fine, mild autumn day, and she watched the breeze dislodging the autumn leaves and realised she felt at peace with herself. She and Peter were getting on well again; the family had grown used to the new house, and the girls appeared to have settled to sharing a bedroom again – there had been far less angst and drama since the family had returned from the holiday, which had been a success all round. Lily sent Molly a brief text - All well there? x - and after a few moments received a thumbs up emoji in response. She breathed deeply and relaxed against the bench, closing her eyes against the weak sun.

It was Peter's birthday at the weekend. They were still being cautious with money, and he had suggested he didn't need a present from her this year, but Lily had booked a table for the five of them at Peter's favourite Chinese restaurant for the Saturday night, as a surprise. She knew Johnnie had made his father some kind of gift, which the girls had helped him with, and he was enjoying being mysterious about. Peter and Lily had attended the parents' meeting at Johnnie's school in the week before half term, and it had been wonderful to hear so many positive things about him – he was doing well: enthusiastic about his learning and making good progress as a result; had a strong group of friends who all enjoyed Johnnie's sunny temperament and sense of humour; and he was keen to throw himself into any new activity. He was a happy and well-balanced little boy. Lily counted her blessings.

She thought about the girls. Molly was now in Year 12, relishing her A level subjects and continuing to spend a significant amount of time in the local library, even during half term, packing her bag and going along there in the evenings when Lily got home from work. Fay was in Year 10 and had embarked on her GCSEs this term. She was less enthusiastic about school, worked less hard than her sister and, Lily realised, was less likely than Molly to be a high academic achiever, but she was capable and happy enough, and strong at sport, which she found a good way of building friendships and giving her kudos. Lily had watched her on the hockey pitch and had thought ruefully that if the determination and motivation Fay displayed there had been replicated in the classroom, she could rival Molly's achievements. Her children were all quite different from one another, and they were, without doubt, their own people. Her love for each of them was strong.

When Lily returned to the bank, Sue sidled up to her. "Interesting news about Daniel," she muttered.

"What is it?"

"Haven't you heard? He's off to pastures new. Transferred to another branch, and heading for the dizzy heights. So there'll be a reshuffle. Interested?"

"Me?"

"You never know!" and Sue moved on.

Was she interested? Might this present an opportunity? She didn't know, but it was something she would think about.

An hour before Lily was due to leave work, her mobile phone buzzed and, at the first opportunity, she checked it. There was a missed call from Fay's mobile. Lily rang her back. It took several rings before Fay answered and, when she did, she was hysterical.

"Fay. Take a breath and try to calm yourself. I can't understand what you're saying. Are you all right? Are the others all right?"

Lily listened, and grew pale. Although it was difficult to make out any coherent message from Fay's broken, sobbing, phrases, one thing was coming through. Johnnie had been hurt.

Lily swept through the bank, gathering her belongings and stopping only long enough to say to Sue, "I have to go. Something's happened to Johnnie. Tell Daniel for me?" She made her way to the nearby taxi rank and was relieved to see one cab sitting there – not always the case in the middle of the afternoon. As the taxi sped through the streets she rang Peter, but was only able to leave a message. She tried to control her breathing in order to feel calmer, counting the breaths in and out, but was aware that her heart was still racing. When they reached her home, she overpaid the driver and launched herself out of the car.

Fay and Johnnie sat at the bottom of the stairs, Johnnie in Fay's arms, looking a little dazed, but conscious, and there was no sign of any blood. Fay was hiccupping in the aftermath of crying, but was quieter than she had been on the phone. Lily took a deep breath and sat down beside them.

"Tell me."

As Fay started to talk, her tears started again, but now she was at least intelligible and Lily was able to piece together what had happened. Fay had been listening to music in her room, and Johnnie had been playing alone in his. He had decided he wanted a drink, and had hurtled, in Johnnie fashion, down the stairs. He had lost his footing, banged his head on the banister, and lost consciousness. Fay had heard the noise and raced to find him at the bottom of the stairs. "I thought he was dead at first! I couldn't make him open his eyes. It was just awful. I didn't know what to do. I rang you and then I thought I'd go round next door and ask whether we should call for an ambulance, but then he came round."

Johnnie looked bemused.

"Johnnie – look at me." He gave Lily a crooked smile. "How many fingers am I holding up?"

Johnnie was perplexed for a moment, and then replied, "Three of course – silly!"

Lily hugged him. She gently felt the bump on his head, and he flinched.

"That hurts, mummy."

"I know, and I can find something to put on it that will make it feel better. Fay, how long would you say he was unconscious for?"

"Only a minute or two. Not long, but I panicked. I didn't know what to do," Fay repeated. "I'm sorry, mum."

"I don't think you need to apologise, Fay. You did the right thing. You looked after your brother, you rang me, and you were going to go next door for help if he hadn't opened his eyes. You were sensible. And given how Johnnie does tear around the house sometimes..." Lily gave him a steady look, "This could have happened when any of us were home. But it was Molly I left in charge. She's the oldest. Where is she?"

Fay looked uncomfortable, and didn't reply.

"Fay?"

At that moment, the door opened, and Molly, looking wan, came through it.

It was several hours later, when Lily poured Sam and Kay sizeable glasses of wine, and, with a sigh, sank into the couch. Johnnie was asleep at last. Peter had been reassured by the GP that he didn't have concussion and that a trip to A & E wasn't necessary. The girls were in their room, where Peter was talking quietly to them.

"So, it took a while," Lily continued, "before we got to the bottom of it all. I feel so stupid – so many trips to the library. I took it all in. For God's sake, I was 17 once myself, and I was certainly no angel, as you both know. Why didn't I see it coming?"

Sam and Kay just listened and waited for her to continue.

"It started in the summer. I think Molly had perhaps had a crush on him for some time, and, ironically, it did start with a visit to the library, when she met him by accident, and they went for a coffee, and it developed from there. She's been meeting him secretly ever since. Fay knew, but, amazingly, none of Molly's friends, or I'm sure it would have leaked out. Fay says she wanted to tell me, but Molly put pressure on her to keep quiet. I'm cross about that, too. When it all came out this afternoon I was furious and both girls grew quite hysterical. Peter walked in in the middle of it. Johnnie doesn't quite understand what's happening but he always gets upset if anyone else is upset. In the end we decided Peter should take him to the local doctor's just to get her opinion about whether we needed to have him checked at the hospital. The girls and I thrashed it out. The question is, what do we do next?"

"Gabrielle is the one who would know best, I think," offered Sam, and Kay agreed. "Where are they, again?"

"A mini-break in Belfast this time. I know I could try her mobile and she would help, but I really didn't want to interrupt their break. I thought maybe the two of you could help me work it out. I'm sorry to drag you round here.."

"Not at all!" "Don't say that!" the two friends interrupted at the same time.

"You know we're happy to help if we can," Kay continued. "Tell us more about him."

"Thank you, both. Well, he's the Spanish Assistant, and he's mid-twenties, I think. He's called Miguel. He's been teaching Molly in Spanish conversation classes since he arrived from Madrid last year - for GCSE and now for A level. He's due to go back to university in Spain at some stage next summer. I haven't met him – the Languages Assistants don't go to parents' evening. She says he's wonderful – she's quite besotted with him, it seems. She's threatening all kinds of things if we stop her seeing him, or if we go to the school –

leaving the Sixth Form and moving in with him, and then going back to Spain with him next year." Lily's voice wavered and she closed her eyes. When she reopened them, they were filled with tears.

"So all these trips to the library – she's been going to his flat regularly since July. She says they love each other, of course. They've been sleeping together for some time, though she swears they use protection. For God's sake, how could I not know? She's my daughter…"

Sam and Kay leaned forwards, and Kay took her hand.

"Whatever you do, beating yourself up isn't going to help. Did your parents know everything you got up to at 17?"

Lily gave a rueful smile. "Can you remember the conversation we had when we were in the fifth form, sitting on the school field one lunchtime, and I said something along the lines of, 'We have a responsibility to protect our parents from the truth. They couldn't handle it!' "

The three friends laughed softly, and the tension was defused a little.

"I do feel torn, though," Lily continued. "My instinct is to go to the school and tell them, but I worry what she will do – or what they will do - if we take that step. She's above the age of consent so he isn't exactly committing a crime. What do you think?"

"It may not be a crime, but he's her teacher, Lily – or as good as. He's certainly in a position of trust." Sam offered. "I'm pretty sure Gabrielle would say that this is some sort of professional misconduct – it's like an abuse of power, I think."

"I agree. I think you have to go into school, but there's no need to say that to Molly at this stage. Just don't make any promises about what you will or won't do," said Kay. "It's half term, isn't it, so the school won't be open. I think you need to be able to keep Molly away from him for the next few days. And do you have her phone and laptop?"

"Yes – Peter thought of that, so at the moment we have both, and Fay's, too, in case Molly puts pressure on her again. We're sure he'll be trying to ring or text her to find out what has happened, so we've turned the phone off. Neither of them can easily enlist the support of her friends, who I suspect may be cross that she hasn't trusted them and told them. At least it wasn't actually Fay who shared her secret, so Molly can't blame her for that. I was angry with Fay, too, initially, but I do see she was in a really tricky position. After Fay rang me at work, she rang Molly, who left straight away, hoping to get home before I did. It's fortunate that she didn't manage it, or I suspect I'd be none the wiser."

"Wouldn't Johnnie have told you Molly was out today?"

"He may not even have registered that she was – he can get so caught up in his own games that he's oblivious. And, in fact, she hasn't been out during the day this week. She's stayed at home while I've been at work and gone to meet Miguel – the library ruse again – in the evenings after I've got home. But apparently this morning he rang her, said he couldn't wait to see her, and off she trotted. Her plan was to get back before I got in, and that's what would have happened, if Johnnie hadn't had his fall."

"Is he definitely all right?"

"He's fine – really. He has an impressive lump on his forehead which he'll be proud of tomorrow. But I'm hoping this has given him a bit of a scare, too, so he won't keep tearing down the stairs as he tends to do. He just throws himself at life, does our Johnnie!"

"So, this sounds like a plan," Sam offered. "Molly has no contact with Miguel for the rest of the week. Then you and Peter go into school on Monday morning and explain what has happened to the head and see what he has to say. I suspect Miguel's days here are numbered – I'm not sure whether there will be further professional repercussions for him. And Gabrielle is back on Sunday, so you can ring her when she's home and see whether she has anything more to offer, without disturbing their break."

"In the meantime," added Kay, "Your main challenge is trying to get Molly to see that she has to accept this isn't a suitable relationship. However they feel about each other, he has, in effect, taken advantage of her – she's a schoolgirl and he's quite a bit older and in a position of trust. She won't appreciate it yet, but she will get past this..." Kay thought momentarily about Michael. "And you will love her through the pain."

Lily was quiet for a few moments, and then she looked up at her friends and her eyes swam again.

"I can't tell you how much this means to me that you came over and listened, and helped me to work it out."

"You would do the same for any of us," Sam was quick to reassure her. "It's what friends do. And we have known each other a long time. We've all faced different challenges over the years, and I can think of times when we've all needed the support of the others, and it's been there. What was your #oneword, Lily - 'courage'? That will get you through this."

"I feel much calmer already. Thank you both. At lunchtime today I sat in the park and I felt good. Then this all blew up this afternoon and I felt worried, frightened, angry, frustrated, confused, and guilty – guilty because I hadn't protected and prepared her. That was the stage when I asked Peter if he'd ring you both and ask if you'd come round. I've been through the whole range of emotions today, I think! But now I feel much better – calm and relieved, and grateful. I know we'll find our way through this."

Kay and Sam rose to leave, and Lily hugged them both at the door.

"It's the beginning of November, tomorrow," Kay mused, as she put on her coat, looking out into the chilly night. "And then it will be December, and New Year's Eve before we know it."

The four friends would all be busy in the run up to Christmas, so they had arranged that their New Year's Eve lunch would be their next meal out together, although they were all due to meet, with their husbands, at Rachel and Ben's evening reception in early December.

"I'm looking forward to our lunch and our debrief of the year already," said Lily. "It's certainly been an interesting one."

"It has," Sam agreed. "It's been full of a lot of things we didn't necessarily anticipate. And I somehow think that's brought us closer. Does anyone else feel we know each other even better, now, than we did last New Year's Eve, despite the fact that we have been friends for over thirty years? Anyway, good night – and I'll see you soon."

Lily closed the door quietly, and thought about Sam's words as she walked back through the house. She remembered their lunch in July, and their revelations then. She agreed that they had, perhaps, been particularly open and honest with each other this year – in the end, at least - and it had strengthened their friendship.

Peter joined her on the couch, and she snuggled into him.

"What did they have to say?" he asked.

"They were brilliant, and it really helped. I think, in fact, what they said just clarified my thinking about what I know we have to do. They are such good friends. I'm going to ring Gabrielle, too, when she gets back on Sunday, but I'm sure she'll agree. We need to go into school on Monday morning. I think we have to take Molly into the meeting with us. She will hate it, but we will get her through it."

"I was thinking the same. It will be hard for her, but she has us, and we love her. I know there have been angry words today, but we need to get past the anger and just help her, now."

"I love you – have I said that recently?"

"Pardon?"

"You heard!"

"I can't hear it enough."

"Courage…"

"Why do you say that?"

"It's my #oneword 2019. We're going to need it."

"What will your #oneword 2020 be, do you think?"

"You'll need to wait and see. Time for bed, said Zebedee."

"Who's Zebedee?"

"Do you know, I have no idea? It's something my dad used to say when we were children. So I used to say it to the girls when they were little. I haven't thought of it for years."

"Let's Google it tomorrow. Now there's a phrase that sums up the times we live in," and Peter followed Lily up the stairs.

Gabrielle and Sam arrived together. Sam stopped at the bar to buy the (first) bottle of red, while Gabrielle found their reserved table, and the young barman followed Sam carrying the four glasses. By the time he'd brought the menus, Kay and Lily had joined them, and the four friends settled into their places, laughing and chatting, while Sam poured the wine.

"Happy New Year to us all!" Sam said, as they clinked glasses, took a sip and a collective breath.

"So how have we all been? How was Christmas?" asked Gabrielle.

"We had to buy a new table this year," smiled Kay.

They paused to consult the menus and to order their food, before Sam picked up the conversation again.

"How many for Christmas lunch, then, Kay?"

"Eleven of us, including Robbie. It was great, I have to say. Michael brought Tricia, and Susanna was there with Neil. Mum and dad, and Rachel and Ben, had met them both at the wedding, of course, but this was the first time we'd all been able to have a proper conversation, and it seemed to go well."

"And Rachel is happy?"

"Blissfully so, it seems. Ben is shy, but he's clearly devoted to her, and his daughters seem to have welcomed her into the family. I think they're relieved their dad has found someone to share his life with."

"I loved the photos of the wedding," Lily said. "It made me wonder why so many go for summer weddings. You could see it was a crisp, frosty day, and Rachel looked lovely in that fur wrap."

"Yes – we were lucky. It was cold but the sky was blue, and the sun shone on them. And I'm so pleased you could all come to the party in the evening."

"We really enjoyed it," said Gabrielle, "And it was so lovely to meet Abiola, after hearing so much about her."

"She said the same about all of you! Though, in fact, I think her exact words were, 'That's a group of kick-ass women…'!"

"Are you still enjoying your work and your studies?" asked Sam.

"Very much. And I will definitely look into the possibility of starting an OU degree when I get to the end of the A level courses. Not sure in what subject yet, but there's plenty of time to think about that."

"I think, of the four of us, your life has changed the most dramatically in the last twelve months, Kay, and in terms of your #oneword, you've taken control brilliantly," mused Lily.

"Thank you. I am pleased with how my life is now, and the fact that I have a clearer sense of direction for the future. But we've all had challenges and some sadness, haven't we?" Kay thought of Michael, but she had never shared his story with the others, so said nothing more.

Gabrielle looked up.

"We're sad that we haven't conceived, of course, and we're beginning to come to terms with the fact that it isn't going to happen. But we're also aware of how much is positive in our lives, and I'm determined to focus on that in the year ahead," she offered. "Talking about my situation, and writing about it, has helped me, I think."

"How did the session at school go?"

"The Year 10 PSHE lesson in the school hall? Positively, I would say. Several of us talked about our different stories, about choices and, sometimes, lack of choice. The girls listened really well, and asked some great questions. The other staff who were there said it had made them thoughtful, too, and perhaps more aware and able to understand other perspectives. We decided we will do this with the whole of Year 10 each year. I was grateful for the courage of the speakers – it's personal and sensitive but it's important."

"And I loved your blog. What was that bit you quoted from the podcast…?"

"Yes – the 'How to Fail' podcast with Elizabeth Day where she interviewed Phoebe Waller-Bridge. I'd listened to it because I admire Fleabag – I know we all do – and I'd enjoyed the first series of Killing Eve. Did you know she wrote that too? Anyway, Elizabeth and Phoebe end up talking about the "Do you have children?" and "Do you want babies?" questions women are usually asked, and how you respond if you don't or can't."

"I was struck by what you said in your blog about how this can be perceived as failure," Sam offered.

"That was what Elizabeth Day said in the podcast – how, beyond a certain age, women who haven't had children can be judged as having failed. But she felt that, without children, her life had simply turned out differently, and she'd had some opportunities and successes that she might not have had, otherwise. She said she feels life is opening up for women who don't have children – for whatever reason - but who can own it and not be seen as half a woman." Gabrielle smiled. "That's very much how I feel now. I think that's what I hope for – my one word turning out to resonate differently from how I perhaps saw it a year ago. Anyway, enough of me. How is Molly getting on, Lily?"

"Better all the time, I think. You were all right about how we needed to respond to the Miguel situation – as you said at the time, Gabrielle, it was a safeguarding issue. It was all really difficult, and Molly took a while before she could forgive us, but it was only the school's investigation that led to the discovery that Molly wasn't the first pupil he'd been involved with. And as soon as that came out, the narrative changed quite a bit – she at least stopped talking about running off to Spain to be with him. So she's recovering, even if it's slow. Her friends have been supportive, in the main, and although there was gossip and she had to cope with people at school looking at her and talking about her at the beginning, as time has passed that has eased off. Interestingly, Fay has been amazing in her defence and support of her sister, and the two of them are getting on better than they have for years, which is definitely something to be grateful for! Johnnie, of course, doesn't really have any idea what's happened, but he is his usual loving self, which is always good for us all."

"I can empathise with Molly, I think. I know people worry about ageing, but I wouldn't be 17 again for any money!" mused Sam. "Would you?"

"No!" chorused the others, and they all laughed.

"In other news," went on Lily, "we've managed to pay off the loan my parents gave us, and I've re-joined the gym! I am really enjoying exercising and swimming again."

"And do you see the man you told us about when we were in France?" asked Kay, raising an eyebrow.

"I do, but don't worry! We're definitely just good friends, as they say…"

"Did you make a decision about work, Lily?"

"Yes. I'm going to do further training and see where that takes me. I do need a change, I recognise – whether that's at the bank or elsewhere. Banking is changing anyway, as we can all see. Standing still isn't an option, I realise. Speaking of which, what's happened with your work situation, Sam?"

"Quite a lot! The care home visits with the Sixth Form girls from Gabrielle's school have gone exceptionally well," she and Gabrielle exchanged smiles, "It's been so good to see how positively some of the residents have responded, and how much the students have got out of it, so we're involving larger numbers of students from Gabrielle's school and I'm in discussion with another school and another care home about how we might roll it out more widely. I'm also volunteering to do some work with Age Concern, which should fit in well and, I hope, lead to other initiatives. And at work, Lawrence has finally announced his intention to retire next year, and the Deputy CEO Dan will definitely apply for the role. He's only been in his current role a short time, but he's very good, so I wouldn't be surprised if he's appointed. And he and I work well together – it's made me think that moving into the Deputy role, under his leadership, might be an opportunity for us to take the organisation in a new direction – a direction we're both happier with. If the company will consider my doing that on a part-time/job share basis, I will put myself forward for that. I know Dan will support me, so we will just have to see. There will be further changes at home, in any case. Adam has decided to take early retirement from his firm and move into some consultancy work. He's enjoyed the better balance in his life in the last few months and has decided he's ready to take the next step. We think this should be good for the family. We have to see how the finances work out. I suppose there's a chance we might need to sell the Bergerac house…"

"No!" chorused the others, and they all laughed.

"Well, maybe that wouldn't be the first economy we would make! Adam seems to think, from his research into what some of his peers have done, that the consultancy angle could be lucrative. Time will tell, I suppose."

"Did your brother come over for Christmas, did you say?"

"He did – with his partner, Jon, for the first time – they're staying until after New Year. Robin wanted to see dad, who is doing OK, just gradually getting vaguer, but he still recognised his son, which was a bit of a relief. Jon is great and they seem well-suited. They go back to Hong Kong next week, but it's been good to spend some time with them. The kids have loved it – it's cool to have a gay uncle, apparently."

"So our #oneword2019 has been interesting this year, don't you think?" asked Gabrielle. "You definitely have a clearer sense of purpose, Sam, don't you? Kay has certainly taken more control, and Lily has shown courage. Have we all given some thought to next year's choice of word?"

Their meals arrived, and the friends continued to chat as they ate and drank, but they only resumed the consideration of #oneword2020 when they were finally relaxing over their coffees.

"So who's going first?" asked Gabrielle.

"I will," offered Kay. "I've been thinking quite a lot about this, and I'm going to go for 'develop'. I feel I'm just starting to develop in a number of ways, and I want to carry on learning and growing. I want to build on all I've experienced and been open to this year. I think I'm still at an early stage of the journey. Forty, or forty-one as we are now, definitely isn't too late – I wonder who it was that first said that's when life begins?"

"Good choice, Kay," said Lily. "I've decided on 'invest' – no banking pun intended, but I'm at the point in my life where I want to invest in myself, and in my family. They deserve investing in. I was reflecting earlier in the year that I have tended to be selfish, and I don't like that about myself. I agree with Kay - forty isn't too late to change."

"I think my choice is similar to Lily's," Gabrielle picked up the thread of the conversation. "I've opted for 'appreciate'. I thought about 'acceptance', but that seems somehow a bit feeble. I want to actively embrace the good in our lives – I've talked this through with Harry, and he agrees. I know there will always be a nugget of sadness there that we don't have children, and we won't have grandchildren. But it isn't our fault – it isn't a failing, it's just a difference. I can't imagine living life as if I'm defined by what I'm not, and what I don't have. What do you think?"

The others all murmured their agreement. Lily touched Gabrielle's arm and Kay's eyes were glistening, Gabrielle realised.

"I think that's a brilliant way of looking at life, Gabrielle," said Sam. "I feel the same. We could make ourselves miserable wishing things were different. I'd much rather focus on where we have agency and how we can use it, and on ensuring we fully recognise what's positive. I've chosen 'rebalance'. I know this has started already, but I am going to give time to thinking how I strike the best possible balance in my life between my family, my voluntary work and paid work. I need to find the balance that works for me and for the people I love. And that includes my friends. Could we all meet in France again next summer, do you think? It worked so well this year, and I think the conversation we had then strengthened our friendship, despite the fact that this friendship is already thirty years old. What do you reckon?"

"Let's drink to it!" Lily had replenished their glasses and she now raised her own.

"To #oneword!"

And the others joined her in a series of toasts.

"To investing, appreciating, rebalancing and developing!"

"To friendship!"

"And here's to 2020 – whatever it may bring!"

THE BUTTON BOX

CONTENTS:

Prologue

"How is she doing?"

"She seems OK. I think she's better now the visitors have gone – she looks calmer and more settled."

The two nurses' voices were hushed as they observed the frail patient, her leg in plaster, from the vantage point of their station.

"Who were they anyway?"

"People from her church. Apparently she's been a stalwart attender for years. She's hardly missed a service, one of them told me, until she broke her leg. One of the parishioners has been picking her up and running her down there since her sight got so bad she couldn't make her own way. I have the impression that she's quite shy – the vicar said something about her 'always keeping her own counsel', but he said it with a smile and some affection, I think. And I suppose church congregations are so thin these days, they're grateful for anyone who's willing to turn up."

"So has she no family at all?"

"None. No children, so no grandchildren. No siblings, so no nieces and nephews. A husband once, I heard, but he's long gone."

"How sad, to spend your 100th birthday alone, except for those who might consider it a duty to call and see you."

"Yes. They didn't seem to be friends, exactly - just fellow churchgoers, and the vicar. They talked to one another, but not really to her very much, all the time they were here. Or, at least, if they said something to her she didn't respond."

"Can she hear, and understand?"

"We think so. She can hardly see, but she seems to know what's going on around her. She does speak, if you ask her a direct question. She says she isn't in too much pain, so that's something. She isn't one to chat, though, that's for sure. One of the visitors today told me that she was in church the Sunday before her fall, and apparently she could follow the service, and she knew the words to the hymns, so she can't have full-blown dementia. But at her age, a broken bone can be the beginning of the end. We see it all the time. They get confused, they're in discomfort, and sometimes they just give up."

"What is it she's clutching?"

"It's a box – a beautiful wooden box. She always has it on her lap. She insisted on bringing it with her when she was admitted, I was told. She slides it onto her bedside table before she sleeps. I thought about having a peek inside, but it seemed a bit disrespectful. I think tomorrow I'll ask her about it when I get chance and see what she says."

"Have you noticed she's been worrying away at one of the buttons on her nightie for the past half an hour?"

"Yes. Don't know what that's all about. She isn't much of a fidgeter, as a rule. Anyway, I'd better get on. Will you dim all the lights now? At least half the ward look as if they're sleeping, or on the verge of it."

And the nurses moved away.

After they'd gone, her crabbed arthritic fingers finally succeeded in detaching the small, pearl button from the nightdress. She rolled it in her fingers for some time, leaning back against the pillows with her eyes closed and the ghost of a smile hovering about her thin lips. Then she carefully opened the lid of the box, and popped it inside.

Chapter One: 1957

I am the only child of an only child.

My maternal grandmother was born in 1898. It's strange to think of her as a product of the Victorian era, but that's what she would always say, "I'm a Victorian," with a touch of pride. Her relationship with her own daughter was strained, though she was warm and loving towards me. She used to hug me and say, "You are my *favourite* grandchild!" and I would invariably reply, "But nana, I'm your *only* grandchild!" and we would both chuckle while my mother looked on.

When I was old enough to sense the tension that existed between them, I asked my mother what she thought was the reason for it. She was quiet for a while, and then said, "She had a very difficult time of it when I was born. She says she almost died, but I don't know whether she was being over dramatic about that. She certainly suffered and, somehow, she never quite forgave me."

"But that's daft, mum. It wasn't your fault." I was probably about twelve when we first had this conversation, though it was a topic we returned to periodically over the years.

"I know that, and I'm sure she knows it too, really. But all through my childhood she used to complain about her 'nerves'. Dad and I used to have to tiptoe around her when she was feeling particularly fractious. It was almost like her 'nerves' were a fourth person living in the house with us – unpredictable and in need of special treatment. And then she'd say something along the lines of, 'And it all started when *you* were born'. She was certainly adamant that there would be no more children after me. Her 'nerves' wouldn't stand it, she said."

Later, in my teens, I found myself wondering whether sexual relations between my grandparents had ceased completely after the arrival of their only daughter. Grandad was a small, delicate, exceptionally quiet man. He'd been invalided out of the First World War in 1918, when he lost half his foot at Ypres.

I remember being told that the army surgeon who operated on him gave him the shrapnel he had extracted from the wound to keep as a memento – and as proof that it was shrapnel, and not a bullet from grandad's own gun, that had caused the injury, the surgeon said.

My grandfather appeared to defer to his wife in all things. Nana – as I called her - was often sharp with him, but I never knew him to retaliate, or to raise his voice, even in defence of his daughter. My mum loved him fiercely, though.

"I don't ever remember my mother saying she loved me – not once, all the time I was growing up," mum mused. "My dad did, though never in her hearing, I don't think. And I loved him – I think we were united in the face of her unreasonable behaviour. I remember taking refuge with him in his potting shed – his favourite bolthole – on especially difficult days."

"She does say she loves me sometimes…"

"I know she does, and I'm glad of it. Maybe she's compensating in some way – I don't know. Anyway, what would you like for tea?"

It occurred to me later that mum was compensating, too, by lavishing on me the affection she had missed from her own mother. She told me she loved me all the time, and she was demonstrative, too, frequently hugging and kissing me – something that never changed, as the years passed. She would have dearly loved to have borne other children, I know, but it took my parents ten years before I was conceived, and she never fell pregnant again. I suppose this made me especially precious, although I don't think I was spoilt. My parents were firm with me when they needed to be, and I was a well-behaved child. But I always felt I was the centre of their world, and I was constantly aware of how much I was loved.

One of my earliest memories was visiting my grandparents' house one afternoon when I was, I think, three or four years old. It must have been in about 1957. They had a rag rug in front of the coal fire in the living room of their little cottage, and I can vividly recall sitting on it, looking up at nana in her rocking chair. I have no image of my grandfather in this memory, but he may well have been sitting quietly in his chair on the other side of the fireplace. Nana was looking after me for the afternoon – I can't remember why. It could perhaps have been the first time this had happened, though my grandparents visited our home every other Sunday, so I already knew them well.

On this occasion I'd been driven to their cottage in our Morris Minor – dad at the wheel, and mum, who never learnt to drive, by his side - and left there for several hours. It was a frosty day, I remember. I'd taken no toys or books with me so had nothing to occupy myself with, which in retrospect seems short-sighted of my parents. But I was a biddable, even-tempered child, and I rarely made a fuss. Nana watched me for a few moments, her head on one side, as I sat on the rug, looking back at her. She seemed to make a decision, and she suddenly got up and went to the sideboard – a heavy piece of Victorian furniture - and she took from one of its cupboards a tin, which rattled as she brought it back to the fire.

She sat with the tin in her lap, and she spoke slowly and precisely. I can't remember her exact words, so many years later, but I know they were along these lines.

"These are special, and precious. You must handle them carefully. You must certainly NOT put any of them in your mouth. When you've finished playing with them, you will put them back into the tin. Do you understand? Do you promise to be careful?"

I nodded, and I can still see myself reaching up with my pudgy arms. Instead of giving the tin to me – I suspect it was heavy – she placed it gently on the rug in front of me, removed the lid, and sat back. I looked up at her face, and she smiled. Then I looked down.

I can still see the glow of the buttons in the firelight. I remember the rich colours, the range of sizes and shapes – we think of buttons as completely round but they so often aren't – and textures, as I dipped in my hands and started to handle them. The word 'careful' had clearly made an impression, and I began to remove the buttons slowly, one by one, and place them on the rug, and on the hearth, and then on the square of carpet which covered the flagstones. In my memory there were hundreds of them – it took me a long time – but I imagine there were far fewer than it seemed to me then.

I played with those buttons for hours – on that occasion, and on many other visits over the years. I never tired of them. I would examine each button minutely. I would place them carefully, grouping them and regrouping them – according to colour, or size, or just as the whim took me. I made shapes and patterns and pictures out of them – pictures which became increasingly sophisticated as the years passed. Even as a teenager, the tin of buttons fascinated me, though by that stage I would arrange them on the table, rather than on the rug. It was a tin which had originally contained biscuits, and the picture on the top was of two young girls petting a small dog. When I asked who they were, the first time I saw it, nana smiled and said, "Princesses Elizabeth and Margaret Rose."

I had various favourite buttons at different times, and nana added new acquisitions to the tin periodically. She hunted in the shops for second-hand clothes, I know, just to find striking and attractive buttons which she would carefully remove from the garments and then add to her collection.

"Can you find what's new?" was one of my favourite games in later years.

But this chill afternoon when I was three or four years old was my first experience of the tin of buttons, and it was magical. I was mesmerised by them, by the variety and the beauty. I played quietly, and intently, and nana plied her crochet hook and peered at me from time to time over the top of her glasses. Eventually she put down the piece she was working on and said quietly, "Time to put them back now, Eve," and, without demur, I began to place each of the buttons gently back into the tin. I searched the rug – even underneath it – to check I hadn't missed any. The buttons I'd placed on the hearth were warm to my touch. Nana watched me with a faint smile on her lips, and said, "You're a good girl," when I'd finished. I followed her with my eyes as she picked up the tin and returned it to the sideboard.

"Can I next time?" I asked.

"Of course you can."

The afternoon had been a great success.

My memory of what happened after my parents arrived to pick me up that day has been bolstered by the conversations I subsequently had with my mother. We talked several times, over the years, about the significance of this visit. That afternoon my mum hugged me tightly as soon as she walked into the room, and she spoke to my grandmother over the top of my curly head.

"How has she been, mum?"

"Good as gold," Nana said briskly. "Will you take a cup of tea before you set off home?"

"We'd better not, I think," mum exchanged a look with my father, who stood in the doorway, car key in his hand. "But thanks for having her. Eve – say thank you to your nana."

I ran to the rocker and hugged her. Where was Grandad? Certainly not there when we left, and probably not in the potting shed, as it was such a cold day. Have I somehow airbrushed him out of my memory? My mum couldn't remember, either, when we talked about it in later years.

"Thank you. I loved them. Bye!" I remember my mother looked bemused, and nana looked – what was it? – triumphant, in some way? She nodded shortly to my mother as I was bundled into my coat and then scooped up in my father's arms.

My parents were quiet on the way home – a journey of about an hour. It was growing dark, and there was a touch of fog, which I remember swirling in the headlights. My father was a man of few words – like grandad, in that respect, though in all other ways they were quite different. Dad was a strong man, physically and mentally. He was decisive and firm in his opinions. He may have said little, but what he said held weight and, in our home, his word was law. But he was devoted to my mother and to me, I knew.

We were only a few moments away from the house, when mum turned to me and said, "What did you love, Eve?"

"Buttons," I said, peering out of the window into the gloom.

"She gave you the button tin?" I heard the gasp in my mother's voice.

"I played with them."

Dad had picked up the note of incredulity in his wife's words and turned to look at her for a second.

"What's the button tin?"

"Ever since I can remember, mum has had a tin where she kept buttons – lots of them. It was a battered affair when I was a small child. I remember she transferred them to a new tin when I was a teenager – a royal family souvenir she was very proud of, though that must be quite old, too, now. She always loved collecting buttons..." she trailed off, and after a moment my dad prompted her.

"And?"

"I was never allowed to touch the dratted thing – certainly not when I was a child, and even as a young woman. It was most definitely out of bounds. She treasured her button collection and left dad and me in no doubt that we were neither of us to handle it. Not that I wanted to, particularly, certainly not as I grew older. Though when I was little.... It was an object of fascination, I suppose. And she gave it to Eve to play with today." Mum shook her head.

"And next time..." I said, in a small voice, and my mum understood.

"There's no accounting for your mother," dad said, and that was the last word on the subject that day.

Chapter Two: 1959

I was a methodical, organised child who liked to put things in order. I remember that I found this especially therapeutic if I was feeling upset about anything, or unwell. Somehow, if everything around me was tidy, I felt better – physically, mentally. But even when nothing was wrong, organising things gave me a profound sense of peace.

I can see that this was true of me as an adult, too. I wonder now whether my early fascination with putting the buttons into different formations reflected that side of my character, or whether it actually encouraged its development. Did I enjoy playing with nana's button tin because of my innate desire to rationalise and order the world around me, or did I become increasingly obsessed with organising material possessions because of this early 'training'?

I remember tidying my bedroom on a regular basis – I must have been only five or so when I started this ritual. I reflect now that this was thirty years before Marie Condo was born... I would fold and straighten and neaten all my possessions. I would turn out every drawer, tipping my clothes onto the bed, and then replace everything, item by item, as carefully as possible, so that it all looked very neat and even.

We lived in several different houses as I grew up, moving areas as dad's job dictated – he had worked for the same insurance firm since he left the Air Force at the end of the war - but they were all small semis, and I always had the 'box room', which invariably had a 'box', created by the sloping ceiling of the staircase, eating into the space available. Above the box there was usually a built-in cupboard, part-wardrobe and part-shelving, on the highest level of which I kept my dolls (in height order) – the tallest, Mary, with curly blond hair (as I had) and blue eyes which closed when she was tilted backwards, revealing her beautiful long lashes. She was my favourite doll - though I always hoped the other dolls weren't aware of that. I liked to think she looked like me, and that this was the little girl I would one day have. On the shelves below were games, books and other toys. I would empty out the cupboard and put everything back – arranging things slightly differently each time, so sometimes organising according to size, shape or function; sometimes according to colour, frequency of use or my current favourites. Making the decisions about the organisational principles I would use was fundamental to the sense of joy I felt when all was accomplished.

When it was over, I would stand at the top of the stairs and call mum. She would leave whatever she was doing and come upstairs to join me.

"Yes, Eve?" she would routinely say.

"I've tidied my bedroom," I would smile at her.

"Have you now? Let me see," and she would follow me into the room.

The ritual involved my mother opening every drawer, peering into every corner of the small room, and, as a climax, my throwing open the cupboard doors so that she could exclaim, "Oh my goodness – this is wonderfully tidy, Eve!" while I beamed with pride and delight. (I hesitate to admit that a similar ritual continued into my teenage years and then into adulthood, although in later years the exchange was at least delivered in a spirit of irony…)

I didn't mind that my bedroom was the smallest room in the house. It encouraged me to use space well, and that was part of the challenge and the satisfaction. My parents had the largest bedroom, at the back of the house overlooking the garden, and so always quiet. The second bedroom, at the front and next to my own, served as a spare room (though, in truth, we seldom had visitors who stayed overnight), a storage room and a workroom where mum used her sewing machine. This was the arrangement in each house we lived in, and I have no memory of ever challenging it, even as a teenager, and asking why I couldn't move into the larger, middle bedroom.

Thinking about my life over the past seven decades, as I prepare to enter my eighth, I can see that this disposition towards order has extended to my relationships, too – and my general approach to so many aspects of my life. I wonder sometimes whether I have valued order above joy? Or is it fairer to say that order *brings me* joy?

Following my introduction to the button tin at around age four, my mother could see that my love of playing with nana's button collection contributed to my eagerness to visit my grandparents' cottage. Whatever else I did when I was there – baking with nana, or helping grandad in the garden, for example – the time when I was allowed to retrieve the tin from the sideboard and spread out its contents was always a highlight of the day, for me. My good manners and my even temper were always in evidence; I could be patient and wait. But I would have been sorely disappointed if the button tin had not been offered to me at some stage of the visit, and nana well knew that.

Whenever I was at my grandparents' cottage with my mother, or with both my parents, mum would watch me carefully as I played with the collection, but she never, I know, broached the subject of why something she was never allowed to touch as a child was provided to her own young daughter as a regular treat. It was just part of the anomaly that nana treated me very differently from how she had always treated - and, in fact, still treated - her own child.

Just before I turned six, my mother made a decision which meant that this birthday was one of the most memorable of my life.

The day before my birthday, mum took me shopping. It was mid-December, and a crisp, but bright and sunny morning. I was not a great fan of shopping, as a young child – are young children, ever, keen on it? – but, being the biddable little girl that I was, I didn't complain. Mum had a list of things she wanted to buy, and we visited the shops she needed in a methodical order and she ticked the items off on her list. I watched that with interest – later in my life, list making and crossing off what had been bought/done would be something else which brought me a deep sense of satisfaction. One of the things my mother enjoyed was making curtains – for our own home, but also for others. She had never worked outside the home; my father had been the breadwinner ever since they married, at which point mum quit her job in a shop, became a housewife and waited for the children to arrive. Sadly, there was only one, and I was dilatory in putting in an appearance.

Making curtains, and sometimes matching cushion covers, was something mum discovered at some stage was a skill she had, and a task she found soothing and satisfying. I suspect that contributing to the family income was also a bonus; dad's salary was modest, especially in those early days. Over the years mum's reputation as a seamstress grew and, without doing anything as proactive as advertising her services, word of mouth led to a steady stream of orders, which mum was more than happy to fulfil. Curtains were her speciality. During the shopping expedition on the day before my sixth birthday, we spent some time in a haberdasher's store where mum examined suitable material for the sewing she had already agreed to do.

Before she chose her fabric, however, she led me over to the 'fastenings' section, and left me to look over the vast collection of buttons on display. Mum crouched down beside me, and spoke softly.

"Now, Eve. You know it's your birthday tomorrow. What I'd like you to do is to spend time looking carefully at all the different buttons for sale here, and to choose one set of buttons that you think is especially lovely, and I'm going to buy them for you as one of your birthday presents. Would you like that?"

She looked at me steadily, and I nodded mutely. I had loved the look and feel of nana's button collection, but had never thought of owning any buttons of my own.

I must have stood before that display of buttons and other fastenings for twenty minutes. I became engrossed, and it was some time before I looked across the shop to find mum, who was standing, smiling at me, her chosen fabric in her hands, ready to take to the cash register. She had clearly been ready for some time, but had waited for me to take as long as I needed. I reached up and pointed, and she came over to see what I had chosen.

"They're beautiful, Eve," mum murmured, reaching up to take the card containing four buttons from its place. "And so unusual. I don't think I've ever seen a button like that before. Have you?"

I shook my head. It's now so many years later, but I can still remember the frisson of excitement that coursed through me at the prospect of owning such beautiful buttons. They were a vibrant red, semi-translucent and shiny on one side (I discovered when I examined them carefully later) and, best of all, each was in the shape of a lopsided heart. I knew from handling nana's button collection that I had a particular fondness for buttons which weren't round. Was it odd that I valued order, but was drawn to anything which defied the usual and expected pattern, I wonder now?

"It's a very good, thoughtful, choice. Let's take them over to the assistant and we'll pay for them, and the material I want to buy," and we did.

As this was the day before my birthday, my mother took possession of the buttons – I assumed to wrap them for the following morning. We told my father that evening what we had done, and he smiled and nodded, understanding my five-year-old enthusiasm for something so small.

I stretched up to kiss him, as he sat in his armchair listening to the radio (the "wireless", as my parents called it) when it got to my bedtime.

"Goodnight, princess. Sleep tight, and when you wake up you will be six!"

Mum followed me upstairs, supervised my washing and teeth brushing and climbing into my pyjamas, and then she tucked me in and kissed me.

"Such beautiful buttons..." she murmured, as I closed my eyes.

I woke at one point in the night, and could hear the soft droning sound of her sewing machine in the next room. It soothed me back to sleep.

The next morning, as I opened my eyes I knew immediately that it was a special day.

My parents were both early risers, even on a Saturday, which this was, and I could hear mum clattering pots and pans in the kitchen, and dad whistling in the porch, as I came downstairs, still in my pyjamas.

"Good morning, Birthday Girl!" mum turned from the sink and beamed at me when I entered the kitchen. Dad came in from the porch and they both burst into song, ".....Happy Birthday, Dear Evie. Happy Birthday to you!" while I stood, hopping from foot to foot and wriggling in my excitement.

"Breakfast first, I think, then presents, and then we'll plan our day," and mum turned back to finish making our porridge.

When the breakfast things were cleared away, I was washed and dressed and mum had pulled a comb through my unruly curls, we sat round the kitchen table and mum made another pot of tea for the two of them while dad went to the outhouse to bring in my gifts.

There weren't many – as a small family with very few relatives and a modest number of close friends, we had none of us been used to lavish present giving and receiving, but as I knew nothing different, this had never been a disappointment to me. My godparents (dad's sister, and a couple my parents had known since their schooldays) always gave me something, and my grandparents on both sides of the family – though dad's parents now lived in Scotland, and we saw them only infrequently. They didn't know me as mum's parents did, and consequently the gifts they sent were quite often too young, or too old, for me. But my parents always chose their presents very carefully, and I was invariably thrilled with what I received.

I have to say I can't remember any of the gifts I received for my sixth birthday – and neither could mum when we talked about this memory subsequently – except for those from my parents. The first thing mum did was to bring in my favourite doll, Mary. Mary was dressed in a smart new outfit, which mum had clearly sat up sewing as I slept. The narrow skirt with a matching short, fitted jacket was made from a pale pink, lightly patterned fabric, against which the red heart-shaped buttons on the jacket stood out perfectly. I loved it, and hugged the doll tightly, before running my fingers over the buttons and admiring their shine on one side. Three buttons.

"Three...." I said, and mum smiled, handing me the next gift. It was solid and square and quite heavy – a book, perhaps? Mum sat and watched me, her elbows on the table and her chin on her hands, while I removed the tape and opened up the thick paper.

Inside was a box: a beautiful box, in light wood, polished to a high shine, and with delicate, abstract carving on the lid and the sides. I ran my small fingers all over it, enjoying the texture, and examining it closely, perhaps seeking meaning in the abstract shapes. My eyes were glistening when I looked up at my parents, who glanced at each other, smiling, before turning back to me.

"Turn it over," suggested dad.

Very carefully, I turned the box upside down and rested it on the kitchen table so I could examine the base. There, to my delight, the craftsman who had made it had etched, clearly, the words 'Eve's box' in a beautiful script.

My parents both looked expectantly at me, but I was momentarily speechless before remembering my manners and whispering, "Thank you!" – the hushed tone somehow reverent. They both laughed. Then mum reached into her pinafore pocket and took out a single, red, misshaped-heart of a button.

"Four!" she smiled, and I realised the single button was to be the start of my very own button collection - although not quite the start, it turned out. Mum explained her idea that, on every one of my birthdays in the years to come, I should choose, or perhaps in some cases be given by someone who loved me, a single button to add to my box, so the growing collection would always be as old as I was.

"But you're six today. So that means we're five buttons behind. This is our final present, Eve," and she produced a small package which I slowly unwrapped. Inside were a dozen different buttons, a range of designs, shapes, sizes and colours.

"I've been visiting charity shops over the last few weeks," she explained, while dad looked on. "I've found that they often have a button box, or a tin, which you can sort through to find what you want. I think sometimes customers are trying to match buttons to replace missing ones, or they're hoping to find a complete set of buttons in the tin, or, like me, they're just looking for odd buttons which they like and want to keep. So I've got a selection here and I'd like you to choose five – one for each birthday so far – to go into the box alongside your red heart. I wanted it to be your choice and not mine, so decide which ones you like best?"

We went out for a walk together later that day, the three of us. Flakes of snow felt softly from the sky, which felt magical. We called at the park and I played on the swings. We visited the sweet shop and I made my choice from the row of tall, lidded jars on the top shelf. And we had a special birthday tea, with my favourite sandwiches, a strawberry jelly and, of course, a birthday cake, which mum had decorated with buttons made from icing.

But the best thing about the whole day was the time I spent choosing five special buttons to go into my button box. It took some time. I remember whispering to the buttons as I handled them and made up my mind. I was conscious of possibly hurting the feelings of the buttons that didn't make the cut. Having finally made my choice, I looked at the buttons remaining and said, "Do you think nana would let me put these spare ones in *her* button tin?"

Mum hugged me. "You can ask her when they visit tomorrow, can't you? I expect she will say yes, to you."

It was one of the best birthdays of my life.

Chapter Three: 1963

I remember vividly another birthday tea, a few years later – but this time the 'Birthday Girl' was my mother, rather than me. She was born in 1922, on the 22nd of November, and she was strangely proud of her palindromic birthdate.

When I was nine, mum decided that, in addition to the modest income generated by her curtain-making, she would supplement the family finances further by running a mail-order catalogue account. She had a number of 'customers', neighbours and friends in the village where we lived, who would choose items from the catalogue, and mum would issue them with a payment card, a record on which to log the payments they made each week. She kept careful accounts, and earned a small commission from the orders generated. She enjoyed the whole process, but I remember when she mentioned it to my grandmother on one of our visits there, nana had sniffed disapprovingly and said, "You'd not catch me buying something on the 'never never...' " She, clearly, would not be one of mum's customers.

I used to love looking through the catalogue. It was the size of a telephone directory, but with glossy, colourful pages. It began with a section on clothing and shoes – for ladies, then gentlemen, then children. Next came the home section, then items for the garden, and for hobbies, after that gifts and jewellery, and toys and games at the back, before the lengthy index.

We bought relatively little from the catalogue ourselves, but, for me the joy came from looking at what it contained and imagining what we might be able to possess. This may well have been the start of my list-making compulsion.

"Can I look at the catalogue?" became a constant refrain that year.

"Well, you could," said my mother hesitantly, one afternoon in the school summer holidays, "but it's a beautiful day, Eve. Why don't you go out and play?"

The weather was, indeed, perfect. 'Go out and play' meant to call for Jackie, the little girl my age who lived in the adjoining house, and set off across the fields. We would stay out for hours, only returning for our next meal. It felt safe, and our parents never seemed to fret about us as long as we were together, and came home as soon as we were hungry.

I stood by the kitchen counter and gently kicked one heel with the other foot.

"I'd rather look at the catalogue…" I said quietly, and mum observed me thoughtfully.

"What about this?" she said eventually. "You and Jackie go out and play for an hour or so – get some fresh air and make the most of the sunshine - and then you can spend an hour with the catalogue before tea. Does that sound fair?"

I nodded up at her – arguing or sulking wasn't my style, and I had the time with the catalogue to anticipate. Sometimes anticipation of a pleasure was almost as good as the actual treat, I found. I pulled my thin summer jacket from the hook and went to knock on Jackie's door.

I didn't possess a watch at that age – neither did Jackie - but we were good at estimating time. After an hour of walking the fields, wading the stream, sitting on the small stone bridge and dangling our legs over the water, chatting about nothing in particular, I jumped down and turned to Jackie.

"I have to go home now. There's something my mum wants me to do…" – not *quite* a lie – and Jackie, as biddable as I was, jumped down too and we made our way back.

When I walked into the kitchen, my mother poured me a glass of orange squash without asking, and set it down on the table with the heavy catalogue alongside, while I went up to my room to fetch pencil and paper. This is a routine I settled into – and enjoyed for several years. It's almost seventy years ago, but when I recall it now I can still feel the profound sense of satisfaction and pleasure that swept over me as I opened the first pages of the catalogue.

As I was nine years old when I started this, it might be expected that it would be the toys and games section which attracted me the most. But, in fact, it was the home section that held the greatest appeal. On the paper, I would map out a floor plan of the house I one day wanted to own. Without realising it at the time, the house always followed the design of our current home – the back door opening into the kitchen, which led into the small dining room and then the slightly larger 'front room', as we always called it. From this room a door opened into the hallway, with the (rarely used) front door, an under-stairs storage cupboard, and built in pegs for hats and coats at the foot of the stairs. From there a narrow staircase led to a small bathroom, the back bedroom, front bedroom and box room.

I always started with a blank piece of paper and carefully drew the floor plan, downstairs and upstairs, afresh. And then I opened the catalogue.

From the catalogue, I selected everything the house would contain. I chose colours and fabrics carefully first - carpets, rugs and floor covering for the kitchen and bathroom; curtains and blinds, cushions and bedding, towels and teatowels. I made a careful note of the colour schemes and patterns. And then I populated my dream house with everything it needed to make it a home: the furniture, kitchen equipment, electrical goods, crockery, ornaments - everything. Sometimes I added a garden shed and filled that with gardening equipment. Occasionally I gave the house's putative inhabitants hobbies and interests, and furnished those activities, too.

Every time I filled my house I chose different colour schemes, and different styles, but the whole thing had to cohere. Things had to match, and the combination of carefully chosen, well-ordered possessions gave me a great sense of peace.

If I had time I would design my family, too – almost always mother (me), father (very like my own), daughter (Mary – I still saw my imaginary future daughter as an animated version of my favourite doll) and younger son (John). John, as the youngest, would sleep in the box room, of course, and Mary in the room next door. I would choose the children's toys and games. Sometimes I opted to make John a baby, in which case I would pore over the pages of babywear and accessories. At other times I decided John was older, and I gave him hobbies which were very well resourced, "You are such *lucky* children!" I said to myself. I was reluctant to introduce more children into the family – where would they sleep? (It never seemed to occur to me to design a house with more bedrooms.) However, I do remember experimenting with twin girls on occasion, Mary and Ellen, and enjoyed choosing bunk beds for their bedroom, and deciding whether I would dress them identically, or distinctively. I suspect I favoured the latter approach as I could then spend twice as long selecting their outfits.

I could spend hours engrossed in this game. And at the end of it, I would gather together the paper I'd used, the room plan on which I had sketched an aerial view of all the items I had chosen (down to the smallest ornament) and listed what the cupboards contained, including the clothing I'd selected, and the jewellery in my jewellery box. I made a note of which hats and coats (gloves, scarves and umbrellas) were hanging up at the bottom of the stairs. Alongside each room I recorded carefully on the plan the colour and pattern combinations I had opted for. Everything matched. Everything was in harmony. And then I tipped all the pieces of paper into the bin (long before anyone thought of recycling) ready to start the whole process again on another day.

The first time I played this game, mum watched me for a while, then she sat quietly opposite me and waited until I reached a natural break (one room finished, and I was ready to move on to the next) and looked up.

"Tell me," she said, simply.

"This is my house," I explained carefully, "and I'm choosing everything I want to go inside it. I decide what I want and show it on the plan. I want nice things that go together." I smiled up at her. "It makes me happy."

She reached over and lightly brushed the curls out of my eyes.

"But isn't it the people in the house that will make you happy, not the things, Evie?"

"I might choose the people, too – and their clothes, and everything they want, to make them happy, too."

"Are you the little girl in this family?" she asked. I shook my head.

"I'm the mummy. I'm grown up. There's a daddy, and a girl and a boy."

"How old are the children?"

"Mary's nine, like me. I might change it when I do it next time. I can play it again, mum, can't I? I'm very careful with the catalogue," and I was, turning the pages gently so as not to tear them, taking my time.

"I know you are, love. And yes, of course you can. And they will send me a new catalogue after a few months – there's a winter one and a summer one – and when they do that you can keep the old one, if you like."

I beamed at her. She always seemed to understand.

"I wonder…" mum started, "Is this a bit like the buttons game? It's putting things in order, making choices, deciding on sequences and patterns. That's something you seem to find satisfying and enjoyable. What do you think?"

I'd turned back to make a start on the dining toom, and I gave a little shrug.

"Don't know," I said quietly. "I just like it."

Mum stroked my cheek gently, and then went back to her baking.

So I enjoyed looking through the catalogue and making my choices. Mum enjoyed the contact with her customers, and managing the mail-order account. She rarely bought things for herself, or for our home – there was little money to spare in our household, still – but sometimes when I saw her leafing through the glossy pages, I thought that perhaps, like me, she was imagining what *could* be.

But then it was 22nd November, and on the morning of her birthday mum came downstairs, a little shyly, in a new dress she had ordered from the catalogue.

During the war, and in the years that followed, mum had made almost all her own clothes, and mine. She had knitted dad's jumpers, sometimes unravelling old wool from garments that were past their best and refashioning it into new items. We bought what we had to, but we were a frugal household. 'Shop-bought', factory-made goods were a rarity and a luxury. But for this birthday, after careful discussion with dad, mum had treated herself.

It was beautiful. When she walked into the kitchen at breakfast time, I gasped and dad broke into quiet applause. If I close my eyes, I can see it today – made of a cotton fabric, with a navy background covered in white polka dots, it had a v-neck, a fitted top, long sleeves, a belt of the same material, and a fairly short (this was the age of the mini, after all) flared skirt. Down the front, and on each cuff, there were small fabric-covered buttons. She looked amazing.

Dad rose slowly from the table and caught her round the waist.

"You look like a million dollars!" he smiled. "Forty-one years old, and you're as stunning as the day I met you – and as slim," and he twirled her round, the flared skirt spinning around her. She laughed.

"Oh, stop!" she said. "I'd better get the breakfast on or you'll be late for work. I'm going to take this off again in a minute – I'll just wear it at teatime – but I wanted you to see it before you left," and she reached for and slipped over the top of the dress the apron she always wore round the house.

My father didn't arrive home from work until after 6, so it was late by the time we sat down to eat that day – potted meat sandwiches and green jelly, I recall: definitely a menu devised to please me. I'd insisted we wore party hats, and mum had chosen a dark blue one to match her new, wonderful dress. We ate and dad joked and we laughed, the radio playing quietly in the background. We were sitting at the table in our small dining room – only ever used for special occasions.

I vividly remember the news bulletin, and the pall that immediately fell over our birthday tea party. I can see mum slowly removing her hat as we listened to the words, before standing and beginning to clear the table like an automaton, even though we hadn't finished eating. She turned to my father and said, "My birthday will always be the anniversary of that poor man's death…"

I don't think, at nine years old, I fully understood what was happening, but I could see the effect the news had on my parents. They listened to the radio throughout the evening – we didn't yet own a television set – and talked in low voices. I went to bed earlier than usual, curling up with my book and my nightlight until mum came up to tuck me in and turn out the light. She sat on the side of the bed and stroked my hair.

"Don't be sad, mum."

Her eyes glistened as she smiled at me. Then she reached down with her right hand and tugged at the covered button, navy with white polka dots, on her left cuff. The thread broke, and she turned it over in her slim fingers before holding it out to show me.

"Eve, I'd like this to be the button you put into your box on your birthday this year. Will you do that?"

I nodded, but I didn't understand why.

"When you look at it in years to come, I want you to remember this. 22nd November, 1963. The day John F Kennedy was killed."

She placed it carefully on my bedside table, leaned over to kiss me, and then quietly left the room.

I never saw her wear that dress again.

Chapter Four: 1965

During the summer of the year in which I was to turn 12, we moved house. Dad had been promoted at work, and was to be based in a different office, which was situated in a town some distance away. He had more responsibility, a modest uplift in his salary, and my parents decided to 'flit', buying a house that was on the other side of my maternal grandparents' home, and a little closer to them in terms of travelling distance.

The house they chose was, in fact, very similar to the house they left, but it was in "a slightly better area" mum said, and within walking distance of the town, rather than in a village. So I said goodbye to Jackie-next-door, who was, really, my only friend – I was a shy girl who didn't find it easy to build relationships with my peers. I don't remember being distressed about the fact that I would probably never see Jackie again. It never occurred to me, for example, to ask her to give me a button, which I could pop into my wooden box on my birthday that year to help me to remember her. On our last day together, we sat on the stone bridge over the stream, swinging our legs as we always had, and when I felt it was time to join my parents, who were to follow the removal van in our Morris Minor, I jumped down, said, "Bye, then!" and walked home without looking back.

I'm unsure whether I realised that, even if we had stayed in the house where I was born, there was the possibility that Jackie and I would have grown apart in the following few years, in any case. I had passed the 11+ exam and won a place at the grammar school. Jackie hadn't, and was moving on to our local secondary modern. At primary school, force of habit had meant we spent much of our time together. We would both have had to make the effort to develop fresh friendships in our new schools. Even though we would still have been neighbours, perhaps as we moved into our teenage years, walking over the fields and sitting on the bridge swinging our legs and chatting desultorily wouldn't have been enough to satisfy us and to keep our connection alive.

The grammar school which I would now attend was in the town where we would be living, and I would be able to walk there, something which mum explained to me was a definite advantage.

"You'd have had to catch a school bus if we'd stayed in the village, Eve, whereas in our new place you'll be much closer to school and can even come home for dinner if you want. I think it's also a better school – it's mixed, for one thing."

The school I would have attended was a girls' school. I wasn't sure of the logic of equating a school which had boys with being better than a school without. But I allowed myself to be encouraged by my mother's enthusiasm.

I did enjoy the process of unpacking and settling into our new home, "building our nest", mum called it. The walls of my box room bedroom had been painted a pale lemon, and mum allowed me to choose the fabric for new curtains – sadly not from the catalogue, "Much too expensive," mum said, but from the local market. I selected (after much deliberation) a pattern with alternate yellow and orange flowers. In one corner of my new room my parents placed a corner table which had shelves beneath, and a glass top – bought second hand and rubbed down and painted white by my father. Mum sewed curtains for it in the same material as those that graced the window, so I could draw the curtains round the cupboard and the shelves were hidden from view. I loved it. And she even made me a small matching cushion to place on my bed, which I felt was the height of sophistication.

The house was situated in a cul-de-sac. There seemed to be no children my age in any of the neighbouring homes: the houses on each side of us were owned by elderly couples whose children had left home long since. There was one young couple across the road with a baby, and the house next door to them was occupied by a family which included two toddlers. Mum could see me weighing all this up.

"I know you'll miss Jackie," she said. Would I? "But you'll make new friends at school, and it might not be long before you're able to babysit for the families with younger children. That will be good, won't it?" she suggested brightly.

I gave her a steady look, but made no reply. I wasn't convinced.

The summer passed – quite quickly, it seemed to me. I'd always enjoyed my parents' company, and in the evenings we would read, or play boardgames, or watch television – a relatively recent acquisition. My parents enjoyed 'Z Cars', 'Emergency Ward 10' and 'Dixon of Dock Green'. I preferred 'Bewitched' and 'Tomorrow's World'. My father talked with enthusiasm about being able to watch the World Cup on television the following year.

During the daytime, while dad was at the office and mum doing her housework or sewing, I was often instructed to 'play out'. I don't remember feeling lonely, or bored. I wonder now whether it was because I was an only child that I was predisposed to be self-sufficient. I spent time alone in the garden, or walked to the local welfare park, as it was known, and sat on one of the swings, propelling myself slowly back and forwards sometimes for, it seems to me now, hours. I explored the surrounding area, too, though I didn't stray too far from home. I did walk as far as the school, about half an hour away, and stood at the locked gate peering at the buildings, and the playing fields beyond. Mum had taken me to the outfitters in town to buy my school uniform, my PT kit – it was called 'Physical Training' in those days - and a hockey stick, which I eyed uneasily, wondering what exactly I would do with it. I did like the idea of having a uniform, and wore it for the entire weekend after we'd purchased it, until mum said, "That's enough now, Eve. You'll wear it out before you even start," and she hung it carefully in the wardrobe to await the beginning of the new school year.

And then the start of term arrived. Dad took a photograph of me in my gymslip (navy), shirt (white) and tie (maroon and gold stripes), my navy cardigan and new maroon blazer, with the school crest which mum had sewn onto the pocket. The blazer felt a little too large, while my sensible shoes pinched slightly after a summer of wearing sandals, and the knee-high grey socks felt a little itchy. When I mentioned the tightness of the new shoes, mum said she was sure they would 'give', in time.

"See how you get on with them today, Eve. If they still feel snug at teatime, we'll fill them with wet newspaper and leave them overnight to see if they stretch a bit." As she spoke, she pulled a comb through my invariably tangled curls.

"The school rules say long hair must be tied back," she mused. "But your hair isn't really long – and it isn't really short. I don't think I could get it to stay in a ponytail – the curls would escape. It's as tidy as I can make it, Eve. If anyone tells you off today, we'll have a go at a ponytail tonight."

I looked at her with alarm; the prospect that someone might 'tell me off' for anything horrified me. She saw my expression and continued quickly, "I'm sure they won't, love – don't worry. Now, look, there's a spare button fixed to the label inside the lining of the blazer. I'll cut it off," and she did so, placing it carefully on the kitchen counter. "Perhaps that should be the button you put into your box on your birthday this year, to commemorate your first day at 'big school'!"

"Come on, then, princess," said my father, who had arranged to go into work a little later so that he could drop me off at the school gates on my very first morning.

"And I'll see you at dinner time," mum bent down to kiss me. "I'll make your favourite sandwich." She looked a little emotional for a moment – her only child already starting 'big school' – but then she gave herself a little shake and beamed at me. "Have a brilliant day."

School turned out not to be brilliant. But it wasn't terrible, either. It was just 'school'. I discovered that many of the children there knew each other from their respective primary schools, and they gravitated towards one another for security. The boys were quite boisterous. The girls seemed to whisper a lot in small gaggles. I always felt on the periphery, watching –

not exactly actively excluded, just not invited in. I had to be careful though – it only took one, "What are you looking at?" brusquely delivered to make me realise that my isolated existence could be perceived as odd or suspicious, and it was far better not to draw attention to myself.

Going home for dinner, and sitting eating sandwiches in the kitchen with my mother, meant that I didn't have to navigate the school lunch break, and of course I didn't have to brave the school bus. In lessons we were all occupied. Outside lessons – before school, after school and at break - I would find a quiet corner somewhere, and read. I made sure I always had a book in my satchel. Any book would do. I even worked my way through the Physics textbook, most of which mystified me, knowing that anyone who saw me doing so at breaktime would probably assume I was preparing for a test. I don't remember feeling unhappy. It was, simply, what it was.

A few weeks into my first term, I spent one Saturday morning with nana and grandad and, as I usually did on these visits, sat at the table with the button tin, making shapes and patterns, enjoying handling my favourites – there were several – and easily identifying the few new additions. By this stage, I could even spot what was missing. Nana would occasionally take a few out, to see if I noticed. "Where's the square brown one?" I would look up at her, and she would pluck it from her apron pocket and smile before popping it back into the tin.

As I arranged and sorted the collection in front of me, nana watched me from her chair by the fire. She often engaged me in conversation as I played, knowing that my fingers would continue to move as I listened to and then responded to her questions and comments. In some ways it was easier to talk when my eyes and hands were occupied.

"So, Eve. Tell me about your new school."

"It's all right."

"What do you like best?"

I was quiet for a while, thinking.

"I like my English teacher. I like reading."

"That's good. We'll buy you more books for your birthday – you'll have to tell me what writers you especially like."

"I don't think I know that yet."

Nana let that one go.

"Anything else you like?"

"I like going home for my dinner."

Nan looked at me for a moment, as I manoeuvred the buttons on the table, and didn't offer any more.

"And are there things you don't like, Eve?"

Again, I thought for a while before I replied.

"I don't like assemblies – they're a bit boring and they always seem to tell us off. I don't like the smell of the science labs. I don't like PT – it's cold on the field and the hockey ball is hard. I don't like the music teacher – he shouts and the boys laugh. I really don't like the girls' toilets."

That seemed to be it, for now.

"Do you have friends, Evie?"

I shrugged.

"Not really."

"Then what do you do at playtime?"

"It's not playtime at big school – it's breaktime. I go somewhere and read."

Nana was thoughtful.

"Can you go to the school library?"

For the first time, I looked up at her.

"I don't know. I haven't been in yet. I'm not sure exactly where it is."

"Well, you said you like your English teacher. Why don't you ask him - " "Her." "Why don't you ask her, then, to show you where it is, and ask how you can go about borrowing library books. Then when you want to read, you'll have somewhere warm and comfortable to go, and you'll have plenty of books to choose from."

I said nothing straight away, but as I moved the buttons and completed my desired pattern, I thought about her words, and the possibilities which opened up before me.

Nana had one last question.

"Eve – what do you think you might like to be when you grow up?"

It was a question I had thought about before – it was a question that adults of a certain age always seem to ask young people – but at that stage I had no idea. I shrugged, but then remembering my mother saying that shrugging and not replying was rude, I offered, "Not sure yet."

Nana rose slowly from her chair, her arthritic knees sore and stiff from sitting, and walked gingerly across to where I sat. She stood behind me, placing one hand gently on my shoulder, and she looked at the table in front of me.

"That is a beautiful design, Eve. I don't think you've ever created one quite like that before."

We both looked at it for a few seconds and then, as if it were a newly completed jigsaw, we each took a breath and then began to break it up, taking turns to place the buttons I'd used back in the tin.

On the half hour drive home with dad that evening, I reflected on this conversation, and wondered why I had never talked about school in this way to my parents. They invariably asked what I'd done at school, what I was learning, what homework I had, and I answered honestly. But I realised neither of them had a clear picture of what the experience of school was like for me – the picture I recognised my grandmother now had. I knew it was unlikely she would share this insight with my mother. They were always civil to each other, but they simply didn't communicate.

I did take nana's words to heart. At the end of my next English lesson, which fell just before break, I hung back, packing my satchel extremely slowly, so that eventually only Mrs Kitchen and I were in the room.

"Come on, then, Eve," she said with a smile as she shepherded me towards the door, the pile of books ready for marking filling her arms. "You won't have any break time with your friends at this rate."

"Could I ask a question please, Miss?"

"Of course you can."

"I wondered about the school library – are first years allowed to go in at breaktime, and can I borrow books?"

Mrs Kitchen gave a light laugh. "Yes, and yes! And I'm delighted you want to!"

"I don't actually know where it is," I admitted.

"Well, luckily, it's on the way to the staffroom, which is exactly where I'm going for my cup of tea. So if you want to come along with me, not only will I show you where it is, but I'll introduce you to the Sixth Formers who look after it at breaktime. And I'll show you how to get your library ticket."

And she did.

It was another month before I visited my grandparents again. On that occasion, I waited until I was sitting at the table, the button tin before me ready to be opened to release its treasures. With my hands still on the tin, I turned to my grandmother, who was working on her crochet in her usual chair.

"Nana?"

"Yes, Eve?"

"I know what I want to be when I grow up."

She raised her eyebrows and peered at me over the top of her glasses.

"Do you, indeed? And what's that now?"

I lowered my voice until it was almost a whisper. It seemed only fitting.

"I want to be a librarian," and turning back to the table, I removed the lid of the tin and plunged my fingers inside.

Chapter Five: 1969

The grammar school I attended didn't have a professional librarian. Mrs Kitchen, my first year English teacher, looked after the school library, alongside Sixth Form library prefects she appointed each year. These prefects wore a badge, a small navy shield with 'Librarian' in gold letters inscribed in a diagonal across it, which they pinned to the lapels of their blazers – black blazers in the Sixth Form, rather than maroon. I coveted these badges in a way I had never coveted anything before. The library prefects were almost always girls, I found; just occasionally a bookish, bespectacled boy made it into the group.

Most of those who frequented the library at break and lunch seemed to be quiet girls, like me. We smiled shyly at each other, acknowledging each other's presence, but we didn't speak, of course – library protocol forbade it, and I realised what a relief it was to diffident pupils that they had a ready-made excuse for avoiding small talk. There were boys in there from time to time – being in the library was one way of avoiding the boisterous playground games the vast majority of boys threw themselves into at break and lunchtime. There was a collection of magazines displayed on a stand – Mrs Kitchen periodically chose a selection from the local newsagent, and then she watched which magazines were popular and knew what to buy again in the future. The boys often gravitated towards the magazines, I observed.

The school library was definitely a sanctuary for me. I usually found my way there at break. Sometimes I sat at one of the tables and started my homework. Often I found an empty easy chair and settled myself with a work of fiction – I rapidly worked through the selection the shelves had to offer. Fortunately the school library services vehicle pulled up outside the school gates once each half term, and the library prefects had the privilege of helping Mrs Kitchen to select the new stock, so I made my reading choices from a regularly replenished collection. I was often so deeply absorbed in my reading that the end of breaktime bell made me jump.

I loved the library – the peace and calm, the order and the sense of everything in its right place. It was bright and comfortable. In the summer months the sun shone through the tall windows. In winter the lamps were switched on and the room was cosy and glowing. And it was always warm but never oppressively hot. It was the perfect environment for comfortable, undisturbed reading.

As I moved through the school years, visiting the library was the one constant in my experience of education. I was shunted into different form groups, had different teachers, tried new subjects. I was able to drop 'Domestic Science' – needlework and cookery – at the end of my first year in order to take Art in the second year. I had inherited none of my mother's flair for sewing. Our first needlework task was to make a green and white striped apron, which we would then wear in the following term when we started cookery. I was one of the small number of girls whose apron didn't sport a pocket, as I had worked so slowly that I never reached that stage. Cookery was a wash out, too – I remember taking home four inedible coconut macaroons and watching my mother trying to find something encouraging to say about them.

So giving up Domestic Science to take Art was a relief, though in truth I had no talent for Art either. The teacher, Mrs Williams, would stand behind me as I worked in my sketchpad, or at an easel.

"Interesting, Eve…" she would say before she drifted away. It was an early experience of the power of euphemism. I dropped Art as I moved into the third year.

But I wasn't hopeless at everything. I discovered a facility for languages – I enjoyed French, and did well in that subject, so I was allowed to take Latin in the second year and to pick up another language – I chose German - in the third year, and I learnt fast in these subjects. I looked forward to lessons in History and Religion, and Maths was bearable. The sciences never appealed, however – I was unable to get over my aversion to the smell of the labs, and dissecting a small fish in Biology in the second year was something of a low point: "Now who is going to be the first to find the swim bladder, ladies and gents?" Dr Woodcote's excitement was palpable. And Physical Training was weekly torture. Reaching the age of fourteen and being able to choose the options I wanted to take for O level was liberating – despite the fact that PT remained compulsory.

My favourite subject was definitely English. I loved the reading and the writing – though the discussion work we did was something I felt less comfortable with. I was disappointed not to be taught by Mrs Kitchen again, after my first year – no other English teacher compared to her, in my view – but I saw her frequently as she came in and out of the library, and she was always friendly and welcoming. And then, on one memorable day, she caught me at the end of break and asked if I needed to dash off home at 4 o'clock. If not, would I meet her in the library before I left the school?

"Yes, Miss. I walk home so don't need to get the bus."

"That's capital. I'll see you here, then."

I looked after her as she walked away. I couldn't imagine what she wanted to talk to me about, but I didn't think I could be in any sort of trouble – I had managed five years in the school without ever getting into any trouble. As I was now in the second year of my O level studies, I knew I wanted to stay into the Sixth Form and had decided that English, French and German would be my chosen subjects. Perhaps she wanted to see me about that?

I walked very briskly from my last lesson that day – determined not to be late for our appointment – and arrived at the library before Mrs Kitchen did. The door was open, but the library was empty. I stood by the magazine stand, looking at the latest selection. The range of magazines on offer had just been refreshed. I would always choose a book over a magazine, but I found it interesting to see what publications Mrs Kitchen thought might appeal to young readers.

And then Mrs Kitchen was standing behind me, watching me scan the titles on offer.

"I use the money from the library fines box to buy the magazines," she said softly. "I like to see what's popular, and what stays untouched. This time I bought a new magazine about football, called 'Shoot'. By the end of the week it looked as if it had been eaten, rather than just read... Word had definitely got round. But I'm not proud – I'll do anything to bring in a few new readers. I had to throw that copy in the wastebin, though!" Her eyes twinkled at me. "And better not say anything to anyone about the library fines box, Eve – I'm probably breaking some rule or other," and she winked.

She led me over to the easy chairs in the bay window. I sat quietly and watched her as she settled into her chair and turned to me with a smile.

"I can't believe it's five years since I taught you, Eve. It seems like yesterday."

I nodded, but her statement didn't seem to require a response, so I kept quiet.

"You must realise you are our very best customer, here. You come to the library almost every break – though not at lunchtime. I think you go home for dinner, do you?"

"Yes. I live quite close."

"You know, of course, that I choose a group of Sixth Form students to be my library prefects. They're really important to the smooth running of the library – I can't be here all the time, so I have to trust them to keep things operating smoothly when I'm not. They man the desk, issue and receive books, return the books to the shelves, keep order if they need to."

And they have badges... I found myself thinking. And they go into the school library van to choose new books. And they have Mrs Kitchen's special attention.

"I've only ever chosen Sixth Formers, Eve, but I've watched you carefully over the years, and I think you would make an excellent library prefect. I feel confident I can trust you. I know I could wait to the start of next year, of course – I hear you're staying into the Sixth Form. And I must say I'm very pleased to learn you're thinking of taking English among your A level subjects!"

I blushed, as I realised Mrs Kitchen had been talking to my form teacher about me.

"I just wondered whether you'd consider stepping into the role early. The only thing is you'd need to be around during some lunchtimes, but I've asked about this and you could bring a packed lunch if you wanted to. There's a small stock cupboard which doubles as a little office I use sometimes – I'd be very happy for you to eat your sandwiches in there on the days when you were on duty. You don't have to do that every day, of course. I have several library prefects so we operate a rota to spread the responsibility. I've also been thinking that it would be good to have a younger pupil on the prefect team, and especially someone who has been an avid reader over the years, so that when we make our selection from the school library service, there's someone we can trust to know what titles might appeal to our younger readers. Anyway, I don't need an answer today. Go home and talk to your parents about it, and let me know by the end of the week?"

Mrs Kitchen hesitated, and then leaned forward slightly.
"I think you can keep a secret, Eve."

It wasn't a question, but she raised one eyebrow as she said this, so I nodded.

"I'm not going to be around quite so much later this year. I'm expecting a baby..." – it was her turn to blush - "so I want a really strong, capable, prefect team to support Miss Withenshaw, who will be looking after the library for me until I return. You will all help her, I'm sure. I know that having you here, working with the Sixth Formers I've trained, will make the library prefects an excellent team. Have a think, and we'll talk again..."

I couldn't help it. I interrupted her – even though I knew how rude it was to interrupt.

"Mrs Kitchen – I don't need to think about it! I don't need to talk to my parents about it. I should love to be on the library prefect team and...and – thank you! Thank you for asking me, and for trusting me. I know I will love it, and I won't let you down, I promise."

I took a breath and we both blinked at each other. It was the longest utterance Mrs Kitchen had ever heard from me.

"And congratulations! The baby, I mean..."

And we looked at each other, and both of us smiled broadly.

When I got home, I was still buzzing with the thrill of it all. At some level, I think I did understand that, in the grand scheme of things, this wasn't such a big deal. To many fifteen year olds, this would have been, perhaps, a minor blip on the radar. But, to me, this was a significant life event.

I wasn't much later than usual when I walked into the kitchen, where mum was making our tea. Her back was turned to me as she busied herself chopping vegetables.

"Good day at school?" she asked, as she usually did.

"The best!" I exclaimed, before sinking into one of the kitchen chairs and dropping my satchel, with a thud, on the floor.

Mum went still for a moment and then she turned slowly to look at me.

"Eve? Whatever has happened?"

"Can I ask you something, mum?" I had been thinking about this on my walk home, and wanted to announce my news in a particular way, rather than answering her question directly.

"Of course you can – but, what's going on?"

"You know how, on every birthday, I put a button in my box – a button which means something special to me?"

"Well, yes – of course I know that. But what has that to do with - "

"I want to ask whether you think it would be OK to put in the button box something that isn't a button, but a fairly small button-size object that is precious to me. Something I want to keep, and to remember, forever."

Mum frowned a little, and said, "It's your button box, Eve, and you can put in it anything you want. It's the memory that matters. But what are you - "

"I want to put in my button box my library prefect badge. I'm getting it tomorrow!" And as I spoke I realised that I had never interrupted adults so many times in my whole life as I had done that afternoon.

"But I thought the library prefects were always in the Sixth Form – that's what you've talked about before."

"It is! They are! But Mrs Kitchen saw me today and said she wanted me to join the team now, because she trusts me, and I'm the best customer, or something, and she wants a strong team because she's having a baby and won't be around, and… I can't remember what else she said, but, mum, this is the best news."

"It is very good news, Eve. And I'm proud of you – and your dad will be, too. I know you will be really good at this, and you'll enjoy it. Did you say Mrs Kitchen is having a baby?"

"Yes. Miss Withenshaw will be in charge of the library while she's not here. I think that's a new teacher – she's never taught me. We have to help her, Mrs Kitchen said. Oh, and mum, I need to take a packed lunch so I can be in the library at dinner time. Mrs Kitchen says I can eat it in the stock cupboard."

I paused after I'd said this, suddenly remembering walking home every day to sit in our bright kitchen sharing sandwiches with mum. I knew Mrs Kitchen had said I didn't need to be in the library every lunchtime, but I wanted to be. Mum looked at me, and I knew she was thinking the same thing – it was an end to a routine we had both enjoyed for so long. But mum would never have said anything to detract from the joy she could see I felt, and she smiled and said, "From tomorrow?"

"Yes, please," and mum went to open the door to the fridge to see what she could put together for me to take to school for lunch the next day.

So my time as a school library prefect began, and I did, indeed, love it. Although there was a rota, I went to the library every break and lunch, and worked alongside the other prefects, helping wherever I could. I had a degree of humility which came from the fact that I was both new, and younger than the rest. But the six other prefects – Jayne and Kirstie, Anne and Theresa, Annette and Adrian – the token boy that year – were chatty and friendly, always encouraging and keen to help me learn. I felt part of a social circle for the first time in five years. And I wore my badge with pride.

The badge couldn't go into the button box until my term of office had come to an end – I knew that some prefects served for just one year, and others (perhaps the most committed?) served for two. Might I be able to serve for three, I wondered, in those early days. I couldn't imagine ever getting tired of the role, or ever failing to feel proud and honoured to have that responsibility. And putting the new and the returned books in their rightful places never ceased to be a profoundly satisfying experience for me. The Dewey Decimal System was a revelation.

Mrs Kitchen, now very nicely rounded, left for her maternity leave at Easter the following year. Mum gave me a parting gift to pass on to her, neatly enclosed in gift paper which was covered in a delicate pattern of lemon and pale green, and tied with a yellow ribbon. I didn't know what it was, so I was watching intently when Mrs Kitchen slowly unwrapped it, standing at the library counter at the end of her last day. Miss Withenshaw stood there smiling, too.

"Oh, Eve – they're beautiful! Tell your mother thank you so much!"

And Mrs Kitchen stood on the top of the counter a tiny pair of knitted baby shoes in soft white wool, each with a little strap across the instep, fastened with a shiny pearl button. And there was a small card inside, which Mrs Kitchen read, and then placed beside the shoes. I could see, in my mother's beautiful flowing script, the message:

'To Mrs Kitchen – Congratulations, and very best wishes.
And thank you,
Evie's mum.'

Chapter Six: 1971

My last three years at secondary school were definitely the most fulfilling. My O level exams went well, and I loved starting my A level subjects, English especially. I grew more confident as I matured, more forthcoming and a little less shy. When Mrs Kitchen returned from her maternity leave after the October half term break in my Lower Sixth year, she remarked on the change in me.

"Eve – you have blossomed! I knew you'd be a good library prefect, but I hear from Miss Withenshaw that you have, in fact, been exceptional. And Mr Manning tells me you are already proving to be a superb A level English student, too – you have a real gift, he says. I feel so proud of you!"

I blushed, but found my voice. "It's good to have you back with us, Miss. I've – we've missed you. And I'm pleased I've got the chance to say a proper thank you for giving me this role. It's really helped me."

"I'm glad to hear that. I'm afraid I'm only going to be here until the end of term, though. I love my teaching, but I think I loved being a stay-at-home mum even more, and I miss being with Susie all day. I can see Miss Withenshaw has done a great job, and we'll work alongside each other this half term, but I'd say the library is hers, now, rather than mine.

Anyway, what about you, Eve? Which A level subject are you enjoying the most so far?"

I grinned at her. "English, definitely."

"So, I know it's planning ahead a bit, but do you think you might do an English degree when you leave us?"

I hesitated.

"Actually, Miss, I'm thinking about Library Studies…"

"Well!"

"I love being a prefect, and I've been volunteering at the library in town on Saturdays. I'm learning a lot, and I can see myself in that profession. I know I could do a different degree - and English would be the one I chose if I did – and then go on to do a post-graduate qualification in librarianship. But the idea of concentrating on Library Studies for three years really appeals to me."

"Well, what have I started?" Mrs Kitchen gave a short laugh. "I still remember showing you where the library was in your first year here, and issuing you with your first library ticket!" She laughed again. "Anyway, you'd better get off to your lesson, and I have a meeting to get to. But it's been lovely to catch up – oh, and one other thing. Did I hear you've just moved house?"

"Yes – we're on the Thornicroft estate now." Another "slightly better area", according to mum, though it was still a small house, and I was still in the box room.

"I thought so. Well, we're only a few streets away. I wondered whether you'd consider babysitting for us from time to time? I need someone I can really rely on – Susie is the most precious thing – and I can't think of anyone I trust more than you, Eve. Would you consider it? We don't go out often, but there are times when we need to, or want to, and it would be reassuring to know we had a great babysitter we could call on."

"I'd love to. Thank you for asking me."

I felt two inches taller as I walked to my lesson. Would Mrs Kitchen ever really understand what a difference she had made to my self-esteem since we met when I was eleven?

I was in charge of the library desk that lunchtime – my very favourite part of the role. I was sorting tickets and making a list of overdue borrowing when the door creaked open and I looked up.

The tall girl standing in front of me was wearing a bright blue checked jacket with – I couldn't help noticing – the most beautiful covered buttons. I could see that the covering was made from crochet, which was unusual. The girl's long legs were accentuated by the slim-fitting black trousers she was wearing, tucked into high leather boots. Her hair was blonde, like mine, but long and straight, compared with my unmanageable curls. She looked stunning. And then she smiled and it took my breath away.

"Can I help?"

"I hope so." She had the trace of a foreign accent. "I'm here only for half a term, but I'm hoping I will be able to borrow books. Could I have a library ticket?"

"I might have to check with someone but – do you mind my asking, are you a student, or…?"

"Yes. I'm spending a little time in the Lower Sixth, I think you call it? Just until Christmas. My father is working over here for a few months and he decided to bring his family with him. I'm here to improve my English, and learn more about Britain, before I begin my Abitur studies next year."

"Ah – you're German!"

"That's right."

"I'm taking German A level. Maybe we could chat sometime – you could help me practise my German!" It was a sign of my increasing self-belief that I would even suggest such a thing to a stranger.

The girl laughed. "We do a deal - you get me a library ticket and I will have a conversation with you! My name is Birgit – Birgit Lindner," and she held out her hand to me to shake, not something I was accustomed to doing.

"I'm Eve. Pleased to meet you," I said, as I took her hand.

When I look back now I realise this was the start of my first proper friendship. Jackie-next-door and I had spent time together when I was small, but that was a relationship of convenience to some extent, and I don't think we had much in common. Building a connection with my fellow library prefects had helped me to feel less isolated in school, but I had never been out with any of them socially. I still spent most of my free time with my parents – we were as close as ever – and sometimes with my grandparents. I was almost seventeen, and I had never gone shopping with a friend, or out to the pictures (as we called the cinema), or even to the local café with people my age. On Saturdays I helped at the library alongside several motherly, middle aged women who were friendly, but not, of course, friends. My social circle was a dot.

And then Birgit came into my life. I gave her a library card and she gave me – what?

Conversation, first of all. We talked endlessly, switching between English and German, which benefited us both. She wasn't attending any of my lessons, but she knew she could find me in the library any break or lunch when she was free, and, for the first time, I paid heed to the prefects' rota drawn up by Miss Withenshaw and, if I wasn't on duty that day, I would join Birgit at the library door and we would go out together.

If the weather was fine we would wrap up well and walk outside – sometimes round the school field, arms linked and heads close together in intense dialogue about a whole range of subjects, moving between German and English as the mood took us. Birgit was well-informed and interesting. She was curious, too, eager always to find out more about what growing up in England had been like for me. In return, she told me much about her life in Nuremberg.

Sometimes we walked through the school gates – allowed to do that, as Sixth Formers, we would buy a drink and snacks from the local shop and sit on the bench nearby to eat as we chatted. If it was wet we would stay in school, sitting in a corner of the Sixth Form Common Room to continue our conversation.

Heads turned wherever Birgit went. She was allowed to forego wearing the Sixth Form uniform: grey jumper and skirt with a white shirt, black blazer – and still the maroon and gold tie - as she was to be with us for such a short time, so in school her colourful, stylish appearance was always cause for comment. Even when we were outside school and the absence of a uniform wasn't unusual, she was so striking in her appearance that she seemed to cause a stir. I was happy to exist in her shadow; I knew I wasn't unattractive, but compared with Birgit, I was monochrome.

For the first time I had a companion my own age. I asked to reduce my hours helping at the public library on a Saturday, just until Christmas. As this was voluntary work anyway, and they were grateful for any time I gave, it didn't cause a problem. So we caught a bus to the nearest city and drifted round the shops – Birgit, I remember, wore a soft grey leather maxi-coat with a fur collar, which I thought was singularly the most beautiful item of clothing I had ever seen. And everything she wore seemed to have attractive buttons – I shared my Button Box story with her at an early stage of our friendship. She laughed when I told her that one of the first things I noticed about her was the fact that she had bright blue crochet-covered buttons on her checked jacket. A little self-consciously, I showed her my button collection on one of her visits to my home, and she seemed to understand my interest and to appreciate the appeal, which meant a great deal to me.

I loved our Saturday shopping expeditions, although, in fact, we did very little actual shopping. We just looked, touched things, and compared our responses to what we saw. Then we would go to our favourite café at lunchtime, order Welsh rarebit and a pot of tea and feel sophisticated – though, as I pointed out, it was really only cheese on toast under a different name.

We also went to the pictures, Birgit claiming that it was quaint to call them that. I remember we saw 'The Go-Between', 'Play Misty for Me' (we swooned over Clint Eastwood) and the wonderful 'Death in Venice'. I even went to my first music concert. In early December – the Lindners' birthday present to me - Birgit's father got us tickets to see 'Lindisfarne' (with a little-known support act called 'Genesis') in the city. Birgit's parents dropped us off at the venue, and then went out together for a meal with Birgit's younger brother, Werner. They picked us up later, after the concert was over. We were euphoric and still singing 'The Fog on the Tyne'.

One amazing weekend I went with the family to London – I had never visited my country's capital city before. We went round all the tourist sites, including Buckingham Palace, Big Ben, St Paul's Cathedral and Madame Tussaud's. We strolled through Hyde Park, and queued up to see the Crown Jewels. We visited Harrods and Fortnum and Masons, where Birgit's parents bought Christmas gifts to take home to Germany. We walked through The National Gallery and the British Museum. And we went to the theatre – the first time in my life I'd done this. Birgit's father used an influential contact to purchase five tickets to see Agatha Christie's 'The Mousetrap'. It was just magical.

This was all part of Birgit and Werner's education about England – but I learnt as much as they did, I think. And I loved the company of this family. I found fourteen year old Werner charming – even though Birgit assured me he could be very irritating, and I liked Herr and Frau Lindner very much. I found all the Lindners friendly and easy-going, and I felt relaxed when I was with them.

Birgit claimed to like my parents too, and they clearly loved her from their first meeting. I don't think mum and dad fully realised, until it happened, that this was the first friend I had taken home - Jackie-next-door notwithstanding. It may have struck them for the first time how odd it perhaps was that it had taken me seventeen years to do so. I did feel a little awkward when Birgit first stepped over the threshold of our modest home, acutely aware of the contrast with the palatial residence – at least that's how it seemed to me – the Lindners were renting during their stay in England. And their house had central heating – something I had never experienced before. On the evening of my initial visit to that house I went home and sketched out a floor plan to show mum, reflecting on how much scope this residence would have offered me in my catalogue days – now a few years behind me.

"And it was warm, mum, in every room – even the bathroom!" Mum shared my wonder.

So the first time Birgit met my parents, I was conscious of the size of my home, and the relative chill of its rooms. At least the kitchen had been warmed by the oven, in which mum had baked a cake in honour of my friend's visit, and that's where we all sat. One of Birgit's many talents was putting me at ease, however, and soon she was laughing with my parents as we sat drinking tea, and she exclaimed over the delicious cake, and I didn't feel awkward any more. I was relieved that Birgit didn't need to use the bathroom, though. It was icy in there.

I wanted to take Birgit to see my grandparents, too – they were important people to me, after all – but my mother suggested I ask nana first, and, when I did, explaining who Birgit was, and why she was there, my nana grew quiet and thoughtful. When we heard my father's car pulling into the drive, nana walked me to the door and, standing outside, shivering in the chill air, she wrapped her arms around herself and spoke in a low voice.

"I'm very pleased you have a friend, Eve, and she sounds lovely. But I don't think bringing her here would be such a good idea."

I was puzzled, "I don't understand – "

"She's German, Eve," nana said softly. "I think it would disturb your grandfather."

"Come on then, missy!" shouted dad from the car, and I turned away.

When I got home I told mum what had happened. She just nodded slowly.

"I thought that might happen. Dad has never talked about the Great War, but he's always been sensitive about Germany and the Germans. Don't take it to heart, love."

But I was disappointed. I'd wanted to show off my friend, and found it hard to see how anyone could take exception to her – especially because of a nationality over which she had no control, more than fifty years after grandad's war had ended. I remembered now that the news that I was going to take German alongside English and French in the Sixth Form had received a muted response in my grandparents' home. Being still the even-tempered girl I had always been, I was predisposed to accept the situation rather than to argue.

And nothing could spoil the pleasure I derived from this friendship, or, at least, apart from the one cloud on the horizon - the fact that it would be short-lived. Birgit and her family were leaving at the end of term and returning home to

Nuremberg, where Birgit would resume her studies at the Gymnasium in the New Year.

"Could we write to one another, do you think? Pen pals?"

We were sitting in the Sixth Form Common Room while rain hammered on the roof, the week before term was due to end.

Birgit tilted her head to one side and thought.

"I should like that very much, Eve." Among the many things I loved about her was her slightly formal way of speaking. "I think you should write in German, and I will write back in English." Birgit took her learning very seriously.

"And might you visit England again? And could I, maybe, come to see you in Germany at some stage?"

Birgit leaned forward and looked at me intently for a few seconds.

"I think that would be an excellent idea!"

And I reached across and hugged her.

The last time I saw Birgit was the day after the autumn school term ended. It was a week before Christmas, and the Lindners were flying back to Germany the following day. It was cold, and we wrapped up warmly and walked in the park – Birgit wore her grey maxi-coat and I was in my old duffle. It was just before my 17th birthday, and Birgit knew all about the birthday button in the box tradition.

"So, I have something for you, Eve."

From the pocket of her beautiful coat she took the button she had chosen to give me – in fact she had customised it for me. It was one of the bright blue crochet-covered buttons from the checked jacket she had been wearing the first time I had seen her – the day she arrived at the library requesting a library card. But on top of the crochet she had carefully embroidered two letters.

"Be…" I read. "Be what, Birgit?"

"Be anything you want to be, Eve," she smiled. "But that isn't what I meant. Look again."

The letters were intertwined. A 'B' and an 'E', linked together.

Birgit and Eve.

She was my first love.

Chapter Seven: 1975

Babysitting for Mrs Kitchen – Ellen – and her husband Barney was a real pleasure. Susie was a delight, and it was good to be earning a little money as I made my way through the Sixth Form. I look back and smile now when I remember my earnings were 50p if I spent the evening looking after Susie, rising to 75p if I agreed to stay overnight. Many of my friends had paying Saturday jobs, but I stuck with my voluntary activity at the library each weekend, which I enjoyed and which I thought would be good experience for when I embarked on the Library Studies degree.

I could say "many of my friends", now. My time in Birgit's company had unlocked something in me, and as time went on I found it easier to build social relationships with my peers – my fellow prefects, first of all, and then with others in my A level classes. I can't say my life was a social whirl, but I did go out occasionally, especially on Saturday nights, and I was considerably less shy and awkward as the months passed. This meant that when I did take up my university place, I was able to relate to other students generally comfortably, although I did still enjoy my own company, and often chose to spend time by myself.

Mrs Kitchen – I never managed to call her 'Ellen', but I did, at least, bite back the impulse to say 'Miss', and somehow managed to avoid calling her anything at all - was a constant support. I remember sitting in her lounge one afternoon when I was home from university for the summer at the end of my second year. Susie had just turned four, and as I watched her playing on the hearthrug in front of us I thought of myself, at that age, discovering nana's tin of buttons for the first time. Mrs Kitchen was heavily pregnant, and resting with her feet up on the settee while we drank tea and chatted.

"So has Library Studies turned out to be all you hoped, Eve?" she asked. "No regrets about not taking English instead?"

I smiled. I thought of my fellow undergraduates, and how much more at ease I felt with the Library Studies group than I did with the more flamboyant English and Drama students when we met in the Refectory or the Students' Union.

"It suits me. I've learnt a lot, and it's confirmed that it's the job I'd like to do – not quite sure what type of library yet, but I've found libraries give me a sense of calm, and the idea of working in one has always been appealing."

"Why is that, do you think?"

"I'm not sure, really – but I think it's something to do with order, with putting things in categories and returning everything to its rightful place," I gave a slight laugh. "I like the systems, and the fact that if it's all properly organised you can find just what you want, no matter how much information you're faced with. I like the sense of control, I think. Being surrounded by books is restful. And the quiet. I really like the quiet…"

"And are you pleased you didn't choose a university closer to home?"

I remembered the conversation we had had at the time I was considering the choices I would put on my UCCA form. I had initially just assumed I would go to the nearest university – in the city of my Welsh rarebit lunches with Birgit and our trip to the Lindisfarne concert - and perhaps even live at home. But when Mrs Kitchen had asked me, as I got ready to leave at the end of an evening of babysitting, what my plans were, and I told her this, she grew quiet and thoughtful, before going on to suggest that if I lived at home, or studied so close to home that I fell into the routine of coming home every weekend, I might not be able to take advantage of what student life had to offer, including the building of my independence. Her words encouraged me to think again.

"You were right, I know," I tell her now. "I have enjoyed being in a new city, a big city, with all it has to offer. And I come home every few weeks – it's always good to see my parents and grandparents – but I do feel I'm more independent and self-sufficient. I think when I start looking for jobs next year I'll look in, maybe, a hundred-mile radius of home, but not right on the doorstep."

I had loved exploring the museums, art galleries - and, of course, the libraries – in this new city. And ever since 'The Mousetrap' I had been a keen theatre goer. My favourite theatre in my university city offered tickets for that evening's performance for 50p each if you were able to queue at the box office early in the morning. The seats were low banquettes round the stage, so you were thrillingly close to the action. I queued whenever the programme changed if I had a late start to lectures that morning and a free evening, and I had seen some wonderful productions. You were limited to two tickets per person, and when I finally reached the front of the queue and the woman at the counter smiled at me and asked, "Two?" I would smile back and say, "Just one, please."

"And how are your family?" Mrs Kitchen asked.

"Mum and dad are fine, but my grandfather is ill, I'm sorry to say. He's had chest problems since he was a young man – from not quite escaping the gas in the trenches, I think. And now he has some sort of respiratory infection and he's struggling to breathe."

Mrs Kitchen leant forward.

"Oh, Eve - I'm so sorry. I know you've always been close to your grandparents."

"They're staying with us at the moment. Mum wanted to help look after him, so..."

I didn't share with Mrs Kitchen the conversation between my parents which had taken place the last weekend I came home, after grandad's health had started to deteriorate dramatically, and it seemed possible that, at 83, he might not survive this infection.

"I want to bring him here," mum had said. "I don't think he'll have any peace with my mother in that house."

And dad had agreed.

I bent to pick up my bag, and took my jacket from the back of the chair I was sitting in. "Well, I need to get back. Thanks for the tea. It's been lovely to see you and Susie again."

Mrs Kitchen levered herself slowly upright.

"Thanks for coming, Eve. It's always good to see you, too. This baby shouldn't be too long in making its entrance, now. Do you think, if you're not needed at home, you might be able to come and look after Susie when Barney takes me to the hospital?"

"I'd love to do that," and I reached down to tickle Susie, who giggled up at me.

"And I hope things go as well as they can with your grandad, and that your mum is OK. Do give her my best wishes."

"I will – thank you. Don't come to the door. I can manage, and I think you should rest," and Mrs Kitchen smiled wanly as she sank gratefully back into the cushions.

I walked home slowly, and deep in thought. The atmosphere in our home was tense – everyone worried about grandad, but nana and mum's exchanges were, as usual, restricted to practical considerations and no one was talking about how they really felt – about fear, anxiety, or grief. I imagined mum talked to dad when they retired for the night – in whispers, so as not to disturb grandad in the front bedroom or nana, who was sleeping in my box room next to it. But who did nana talk to, I wondered? Might she talk to me?

A few years before, my parents had bought a small caravan, and every summer we toured different parts of Scotland. In between trips the caravan lived in the drive, and this is where I was sleeping this holiday, making room in the house for my grandparents. When I returned from my visit to Mrs Kitchen I let myself into the caravan and deposited my jacket and bag before joining my family.

They sat in the front room – my father reading the paper, my nana working at her crochet, and mum with a novel open on her lap, but her eyes were closed.

"How's grandad?" I asked.

"The same, love," said mum. This was becoming the stock response to the question.

"Can I go in and see him?"

"Of course you can. Just go in quietly in case he's sleeping."

I climbed the stairs and softly opened the bedroom door.

Grandad wasn't sleeping. He was propped up in bed, wheezing, and he turned his watery gaze on me as I came into the room. His laboured breathing made it difficult for him to speak, but he gave me a faint smile and a nod. I pulled up the chair that was placed near to the bed, a pillow folded into it to make it more comfortable for whoever was sitting there – mum had taken to sitting up with him for at least part of the night – and gently took hold of his hand.

He had always been slight in stature but he had shrunk in the last few months. The flesh was stretched on the bones of his hand and his veins protruded. I held it carefully and stroked it lightly. He smiled weakly at me, and then lay back and closed his eyes.

"I've just been to see Mrs Kitchen – you remember, my old English teacher. I used to babysit for her when I was in the Sixth Form. Susie is four, now, and there's another baby due any minute."

I spoke quietly. I knew he could hear and understand, but I didn't want him to feel he had to respond. We both knew he needed to preserve any breath he had for the hard work of inhaling and exhaling.

"She was the teacher who made me a library prefect when I was just starting the fifth year. I loved that job – I loved the badge! It went into my button box when I left school. And here I am, now, hoping to become a professional librarian. It's something I've wanted to do since I was quite young. I think it was nana who first planted the idea in my head."

I hoped he'd find my voice soothing. I picked up the book on the bedside table – one of his favourite authors. Mum had been reading to him.

"Shall I read to you for a bit, grandad?"

He gave a slight nod, and I opened the book and began where mum had marked the page:

"A chair scraped on linoleum, steps sounded, the transom above me squeaked shut. A shadow melted from behind the pebbled glass..."

I read softly until the change in grandad's breathing told me that he had drifted off to sleep. I quietly pulled the chair back from the bed, plumped up the cushion ready for its next occupant – likely to be mum - and let myself out of the room without disturbing him.

That evening, after nana had gone to bed, I sat reading in the front room where mum and dad were talking in low voices.

"You're exhausted, love," dad said. "Why not stay in bed all night tonight? I'll sit up with him."

Mum did look weary. There were dark shadows under her eyes, and her hair looked uncharacteristically lank.

"I don't like to leave him. He looks so frightened, sometimes. He gets this look in his eyes that makes me think of a trapped bird. It's as if he's pleading with us…"

"I know. I've seen it, too."

"But I am tired. If I sit with him for the first few hours, could we maybe swap places and you take over so I can get some sleep before the morning?"

"Of course I will. Just come in and wake me when you're ready."

"I'll go up now. Goodnight, Eve."

"Goodnight mum. I'm off to bed too," and I gathered my things, including my torch, and went out to the caravan.

Mum woke me gently next morning.

"Eve?" I opened my eyes. "Eve, I'm sorry. Your grandad's gone."

It took me a few seconds to wake fully and to understand what she was saying. I hugged her and we both cried for a few moments.

"When did it happen?"

"In the early hours – your dad was with him. He woke me to tell me and then we woke nana. I feel guilty that I wasn't there…" she breathed in deeply, with a sob, "but I know that's silly, really. Your dad says he just slipped away, so I don't think he would have known who was there."

We sat quietly for a short while, and then she said, tentatively, "Do you think you'd like to see him? The undertakers will be on their way but…"

"Yes," I said. "I'd like to say goodbye."

In the bedroom, grandad looked peaceful. He didn't have to struggle to breathe any longer. His watery blue eyes were closed. Mum stood behind me. I leant forward to kiss his cheek, and I stroked his hand, as I had done the day before.

I stooped to pick up the book, the marker still where I had left it, from the table next to the nightlight, which still glowed. And then I noticed the chair.

"Where's the pillow?"

"What, love?"

"The pillow, that was in the chair?"

"I don't know. It was there when I went to bed at about two, and woke your dad so he could take over. Grandad was sleeping, and I was fit to drop, but I remember smoothing the pillow after I got up. Dad must have moved it, for some reason. It doesn't matter, does it?"

"No, of course not. I think I'll go and sit with nana for a while. How does she seem?"

"It's hard for me to tell. She isn't really speaking."

We went downstairs, and I found nana sitting in the front room, the crochet on her lap but her hands still, staring into the fire which my father had just lit. Although it was summer it was a chill day, and my father would realise it might be comforting to have a fire. He was in the kitchen making tea, and mum joined him. I sat next to nana, and took her hand.

"Oh, nana. Is there anything I can do for you? Anything I can get you?"

She shook her head, but she smiled at me and squeezed my fingers.

"I'm all right, Eve. He's in a better place – somewhere where he doesn't have to gasp for each breath. But just sit with me for a while."

We sat and looked into the fire together. I'm sure she was thinking about grandad. I was, too, but - I was also remembering something that happened when I was about seven. We were still living in my first home, in the village, with Jackie next door. Jackie's family had a mongrel bitch who had just had a litter of puppies. She and I played with them endlessly, fascinated by them, their playfulness, their energy. There was one particular puppy that seemed to have so much more spirit and personality than the others – it was energetic and definitely the liveliest of them all. We called it Billy, for some reason, and I fantasised that I might be able to keep it, though my parents were very clear that this wasn't going to happen. And then one day Jackie's mum came to the door, in tears, holding a limp puppy in her hands. There had been an accident – we pieced it together from her broken phrases. She had moved the cardboard box the puppies slept in, trying to clean up and restore some order to the chaos in the house (Jackie's home was often quite chaotic). It was some time later when the family realised one of the puppies was missing. It was Billy, of course. And they found him trapped under the box, where he'd been deprived of oxygen for some time. He wasn't dead, but he wasn't Billy any more.

My father took the limp body from her, and looked carefully at it.

"He's brain damaged," he told her gently. "He won't survive."

Jackie's mother wailed again. Her husband was away, the children were distraught, and she didn't know what to do.

"Leave him with me," dad said.

And he took the puppy out into the garden.

I turned to mum.

"What will he do, mum?"

She came and took me in her arms.

"He'll do the humane thing, Eve. A difficult thing, that takes courage, but he knows it's the right thing. Your father will always do the right thing, and not just the easy thing."

I thought of this, as nana and I sat by the fire, remembering grandad. I would never know whether my grandfather had slipped away in his own time, or whether dad had done the courageous thing, taking the pillow and using it to answer the pleading in grandad's eyes. To bring him rest, and peace, and to save my mother further worry. I could never ask about it. I would never know whether mum was thinking what I was. But in years to come, whenever I handled the slim, smooth, white button from my grandfather's pyjamas which I placed in my button box that year, I would wonder.

Chapter eight: 1977

After I graduated, I was very fortunate to secure employment in the library of the university where I had spent the previous three years. I combined my day time work there with further postgraduate study in my own time – a diploma in Library and Information Studies - continuing to develop my skills in a way I found satisfying. Initially I rented a room in a flat owned by one of my university friends, Sally – she was from a considerably more affluent family than my own and her parents had given her the financial support to buy it. But after a year of saving up, combined with an interest-free loan nana had suggested, and had been very pleased to offer me, I managed to pull together the deposit and secured a mortgage to buy a small place of my own.

"Are you sure you want to live by yourself, Eve?" Sally asked, when I told her my plans.

"It's been great living here, but Jake is here more and more often, so I know you won't be lonely!" I smiled. I suspected Sally's boyfriend might well move in as soon as I moved out. "I hope we can still see each other, but I'm excited about owning a flat and making a home for myself."

I couldn't help thinking of mum's catalogues and my years of planning.

"Well, at least you won't be too far away," Sally mused. "And I know how self-sufficient you are. I don't think I could live all on my own, but I imagine you'll be fine."

I had found a newly-built apartment in a complex quite close to the city centre. It had two bedrooms – the second quite small, and I was debating whether to turn it into a study, with a sofa bed just in case I had guests. I was thinking of how it might feel to invite my parents to stay – to take them out for a meal, and perhaps even get tickets for the theatre. And I lived in hope that Birgit would come over to England at some stage. We had corresponded for years, but hadn't yet seen each other again. She had finished her studies, too, and embarked on a career in journalism, based in Munich. She had a boyfriend, Helmut, and they sounded to be devoted to each other. Once I was settled, I would ask whether there was any chance she, or they, might want to make the trip.

I felt anticipation bubbling up when I thought about my plans. A job, a home of my own where I could welcome those I cared about – I was making my way in the world.

I loved the process of turning the bare, pale-walled rooms into a comfortable space and putting my own stamp on the place. I liked the fact that this was a new-build and no one had lived in it before me. Mum made me curtains and blinds, and dad helped me to hunt for second-hand furniture that he could repair and refurbish. The fact that my funds were limited just presented an interesting challenge for me. I searched charity shops for pretty china and was always on the look out for homeware bargains. I could be patient and wait for some things, and my tastes were relatively simple. But I felt thrilled with each new acquisition. My father put up shelves in the living area, and I displayed my beautiful button box in pride of place.

I visited nana whenever I went home to see my parents, and she loved to hear about how my flat was taking shape and how I was gradually filling it with things that were useful, or beautiful, or both.

"I remember when we moved into this place, Eve – over half a century ago now. We had nothing, your grandad and I. But over the years we made this cottage into a home."

Since grandad had died, almost three years before, nana had seemed quieter, and more thoughtful. She moved even more slowly, her rheumatism troubling her, I knew, although she never complained to me.

"There is something I thought I'd like to give you, if you want it," she sounded hesitant.

"What is it, nana?"

"When we married, in 1920, my grandmother gave us a beautiful glass vase as a wedding gift. Foolishly, I thought it was too precious to use, and it's lived in darkness at the back of a cupboard for over fifty years. It strikes me now what a waste that was. I didn't want to risk damaging it, but that meant that I didn't display it and give us all the opportunity to appreciate its beauty. At least, I think it's beautiful – I suppose it might be too old-fashioned for you..."

I was intrigued.

"Where is it, nana? Can I see it?"

"You'd better fetch it – I don't trust myself not to drop things, these days," and she directed me to the corner cupboard in the front room - a room I only ever remember using when we visited on Boxing Day each year. As she had said, at the back of the cupboard, in the dusty darkness on the bottom shelf, there was a lovely, delicate, antique glass vase. I handled it carefully and brought it back into the living kitchen where nana was sitting by the fire.

I moistened a cloth and cleaned it slowly, inside and out. It was quite simple in shape, with a delicate pattern of ferns etched on the glass.

"I think it's wonderful," I said, as I set it on the table and we both looked at it.

"It wasn't new when it was given to us – I think it was something my grandmother had been given when *she* married, so it's been handed down through the generations. But if you do like it, and you think it wouldn't look out of place in your flat, I'd love you to take it. Just promise me you will use it – you'll put flowers in it and admire it every day, not stick it in a dark cupboard like I did."

"It's generous of you, and I'm sure it would look perfect, filled with flowers, in my flat, but...."

Nana looked at me as I hesitated.

"If it's a family heirloom, don't you think mum might like to have it, rather than me?"

Nana sniffed.

"As it's mine, I'd have thought I could give it to whoever I want. I don't think it's the kind of thing your mother would appreciate. But if you don't want it, you could just put it back where it came from."

I studied her for a moment. I had risked offending her, I realised. What *was* the problem between the two of them? I wondered again. One day I might be able to ask, but now clearly wasn't the right time.

"No," I said, carefully. "As you said, it's a shame to hide away something so lovely. I will treasure it. And I really hope you will come and see it – mum and dad would drive you over one day and we could have tea in the flat, so you can have a proper look at my new home. And I promise the vase will be full of flowers and displayed in all its glory!"

I smiled, and after a few seconds she smiled with me.

I took the vase back to my parents' house, and gave them a slightly edited version of the conversation I had had with nana about it. Mum just said, "It's very nice, Eve, and I know you'll look after it."

As soon as I got back to the flat, I placed the vase next to my button box, and the next day I bought a dozen long-stemmed yellow roses on my way home from work. It looked perfect, and gave me a little rush of joy every time I looked at it.

It was Christmas before I saw nana again. Dad brought her over to stay with us on Christmas Eve. I was back in my box room, as usual, with nana in the bedroom next door. I wondered, as I always did when she stayed with us, how it felt for her to sleep in the bed where her husband had died. She retired early that night, but her bedroom door was ajar when I went up an hour later, and as I passed I heard her call out faintly, "Eve?"

I pushed the door and went inside.

"Don't switch on the light," she said, as I moved my hand towards the wall. "Just come and lie here next to me for a few minutes."

I stretched out on top of the covers next to her in the darkness, and she reached out and took my hand.

"Are you all right?" I asked.

"I find it hard to get to sleep sometimes," she mumbled – I realised her teeth were resting in the pot on the bathroom windowsill. "I start thinking and it's hard to turn my brain off."

I said nothing, but assumed she might be thinking about grandad. So her next words took me by surprise.

"I was remembering Harold."

Harold? The name meant nothing to me.

"Nana?"

She took a breath, and when she spoke again I could hear the tremor in her voice.

"Harold was the man I was engaged to when the Great War broke out."

I had never heard of an engagement before nana met my grandfather. I waited.

"He was the great passion of my life, Eve. When he kissed me, I felt as if he was drawing out my soul…"

My grandmother, over eighty years old, started to talk to me about the intense love she had felt for this young man sixty years earlier.

"When he went away to fight, it was like I'd lost a limb. Like I was only half a person. He wrote to me – wonderful letters. I read them and could hear him speaking the words. I loved him so much – and he felt the same about me. I'd never thought I was worthy of that kind of love. I wasn't particularly pretty, or clever, or talented. But Harold saw something in me, that…"

I could tell she was crying softly in the dark. I squeezed her hand, and after a while she continued.

"He was killed on The Somme."

I could think of nothing to say.

"I felt like my life was over. The next few months – I was like an empty shell. At first the pain was – terrible, and then I stopped feeling anything, and the numbness was somehow even worse. It was like I was dead, inside…"

I wanted to say how sad and sorry I was, but the words seemed inadequate.

She took a deep breath.

"And then the war was over, and I met your grandad – injured and suffering, but alive. So we got married. But it was never like it was with Harold. And he didn't love me like Harold did – it wasn't the same at all. He loved your mother much more than he loved me."

And I detected it – that hint of bitterness in her tone.

"I just wanted you to know, Evie. I wanted *someone* to know."

I stayed with her until she eventually fell asleep.

She never spoke to me of Harold again.

And she never visited the flat, either. A few months later, in the spring of 1978, she collapsed in the garden – the garden my grandfather had tended so lovingly. Her neighbour, pegging out her washing, caught sight of nana's crumpled body and called an ambulance, and then rang my parents, who had only just had a telephone installed. They drove over to the cottage, but it was too late for anything to be done.

A few days after the funeral, dad dropped mum and me off at my grandparents' home on his way to work and left us to begin sorting out nana's possessions. We needed to decide what should be done with everything. Mum was dry-eyed, but clearly preoccupied. I didn't want to intrude – I fully understood that she would be experiencing a range of conflicting emotions.

After a couple of hours I said, "Let's take a break, mum. I'll make us some tea."

We sat at the table where I had arranged the buttons so many times.

"Did nana ever mention Harold to you, mum," I asked, tentatively.

"Harold? No – I don't remember a Harold. Who was he?"

"Oh, just someone she knew when she was a girl, I think – obviously not that important if she never spoke about him." I changed the subject. "Would you mind if we had a look at the button tin?"

I felt mum stiffen slightly.

"Why would you want to do that? Don't you just want to take it home with you, Eve? She would want you to have it, I'm sure."

"I'm happy to take it, but if you can bear it, I'd like us to spend a bit of time looking through it together. What do you think?"

Mum shrugged. I knew she felt uncomfortable – after all, this was something her mother had never allowed her to do.

I took the tin from the cupboard and brought it over to the table, gently levered off the lid, and started to lift a few buttons out.

"Nana's button tin isn't like my button box, really. Every button in my box" – there were two dozen of them now – "means something to me. I could tell you where each one came from, and why it's significant. But nana just collected buttons she liked over the years – from charity shops, or wherever."

As I was speaking I continued to select a few buttons from the tin and arrange them on the table.

"These are some of my favourites… What about you, mum?"

Mum watched me for a while, but then she reached into the tin, a little hesitantly, and started to select a few of her own.

"This is a pretty one…" she said. For a moment it felt as if she were the child, and I the parent.

"Yes – I like that one, too. And what about this one? And this?"

There was one special button I was searching for – a glass button I knew had come from my grandmother's wedding dress in 1920. I would keep it safe, and add it to my button box collection on my next birthday. I showed it to mum and she examined it closely. Over the next half an hour we sorted through the tin and each chose a dozen or so buttons that we particularly liked. There was something therapeutic about the activity, and I could tell that mum felt increasingly relaxed as we sat side by side quietly making our selection.

When we'd finished, I found two small plastic bags in the kitchen drawer, one for each of us, and we filled the bags with the buttons we had chosen.

"Could I take your bag as well as my own, mum? There's something I'd like to do with them?" Mum handed it over, without speaking. I took the tin containing the remaining buttons, too, and when dad picked us up later, loaded it into the car with other things we were keeping.

I went back to the city, by train, the following day. Near to my flat there was a professional framer – I had visited her when I wanted to reframe a second hand print I had found in a junk shop, and she had made a really good job of it. I went to see her a few days after I returned home and showed her the two sets of buttons.

"Yep, I can certainly do that for you, Eve. These are beautiful buttons! I'll mount them and frame them for you – it will take me a week or so. You want the two sets framing separately, you said?"

"Thanks – and yes, please. One set is for me and the other for my mother. They're from my grandmother's button collection. She's just passed away, and I thought this would be a way of remembering her, and something she treasured."

"It's a lovely idea. I'm sorry for your loss."

"Thank you. I'll call in next week and see if they're ready?"

As I walked home, I thought about mum and how she had, in the end, seemed to find the process of looking through the buttons quite soothing. I knew I could do nothing, really, to help to repair the relationship with her own mother, which had been dysfunctional for so long. It seemed as though it might all be bound up with Harold, my grandmother's grief and disappointment, and the fact that, somehow, grandad was second best in her eyes, and she had the conviction that she was second best to him, compared with the depth of love he felt for his daughter.

But I hoped that my mother would derive some comfort from the framed sample of the button collection. And I would display my own framed sample on a stand which I would place next to the antique glass vase - at that moment filled with multi-coloured tulips - and I would remember my nana, with love, whenever I looked at them both.

Chapter Nine: 1979

I'd been working in the university for three years, and living in my flat for two, when Birgit came to visit. She and Helmut were now engaged, and planning their wedding. She decided to come to England on her own to do some pre-wedding shopping; "My 'trousseau'!" She had said on the telephone, "which is Brautaussattung in German. Your word is so much nicer."

I had laughed. "English doesn't really have a word – which is why we have to borrow the French."

"Will you come shopping with me?"

"Of course I will – I will love it. Though you really don't need my help or advice, Birgit – you are much more stylish and have far better taste than I ever had."

"Do you remember our Saturday trips on the bus to the city when we were in the Lower Sixth?"

"I do, of course – your beautiful grey maxi-coat. We hardly ever bought anything, but we always enjoyed our..."

"Welsh rarebit!" Birgit spoke the words with me, and we both laughed.

"I am SO looking forward to seeing you!" I said. "Your letters always brighten my day, but to see you and talk to you will be blissful."

"I feel the same. Can you meet me at the airport?"

"I can. We'll need to get the train back into the city, but we can walk to my flat from the station at this end."

"I will so enjoy seeing it. You've talked about it so often I feel I have been with you every step of the way as you create your first home."

"And I will enjoy showing it to you. And showing you the city – including the shops. I might even do some research and find out where the best Welsh rarebit is to be found..."

I had relished living on my own, as my previous flatmate Sally had predicted I would. I never felt lonely or bored by myself. I saw friends – Sally included – and went out when I wanted to. I still enjoyed the theatre, and the cinema, and visiting exhibitions. But coming home to my flat at the end of each day, or in the evening after I'd been out, gave me a profound sense of satisfaction and peace. Everything was exactly as I'd left it that morning, except the flowers in nana's vase might have opened a little more fully, and there might be post on the mat. If there was an airmail envelope containing a letter from Birgit, it was an especially good day.

I also enjoyed receiving letters from my mother. Although we now had telephones installed in both homes, she had never really mastered the art of chatting on the phone. Whenever she rang me it was a brief, transactional call to make an arrangement, such as to check what time I would need picking up from the bus station on one of my (usually monthly) trips home. But her letters were wonderful – sharing her everyday news and giving me a taste of her life which was simple, calm, comfortable. She still ran her catalogue. She still made curtains. She had no desire to work outside the home, or to learn to drive, or, in fact, to change the pattern of her day-to-day existence in any way.

I realised that she missed me, and that writing to me, or receiving letters from me (I always wrote back within a few days of reading a letter from her), was the next best thing to seeing me and having a conversation with me. Dad never wrote, but mum often included, "Your dad says to tell you..." and I could picture the two of them sharing a pot of tea at the kitchen table, talking about what was in my letters and what mum would say when she replied. And when I thought of them, I could also see the framed collection of the buttons which mum had chosen from nana's tin, and dad had mounted on the wall of the kitchen – the room in which my mother spent most of her time, and where she would see it every time she prepared a meal, or washed up (while dad dried).

I knew when mum looked at the buttons she would think of me, and of her own mother. I hoped I could, somehow, serve as a bridge between the two of them, now nana was no longer with us.

Birgit had sent me photographs from time to time over the years, but even if she hadn't done that I would have known her immediately, even with her long, straight blonde hair now cut fashionably short and layered into feathers framing her beautiful face. She beamed at me and waved when she saw me at the barrier. She was wheeling a huge, expensive-looking, stylish suitcase (of course) and wearing a light fitted jacket over a flowing summer dress. I immediately thought of the words from Al Stewart's 'Year of the Cat', my current favourite LP, which I had played to death on my new hi-fi system:

'She comes out of the sun in a silk dress running like a watercolour in the rain.'

We moved towards each other and embraced as other travellers and greeters swirled around us. I breathed her in – was it my imagination, or did she have the same distinctive scent I remembered from when we had met as sixteen year olds nine years earlier?

I took hold of the handle of her suitcase and gave it a tug, expecting, from the size of it, that it would be heavy. And I found it was light. I gave her a quizzical look.

"It's practically empty, of course," she grinned at me. "But it will be full by the time I fly home!" That would be in three days' time. I closed my eyes for a few seconds, relishing the time that spread ahead of us. I knew it would pass in the blink of an eye.

And it did. I introduced Birgit to the phrase "shop until you drop", and we certainly managed that. Birgit helped me to choose my outfit for her wedding, and she put together a selection of beautiful things for herself – lingerie and nightwear and a selection of co-ordinating items that she would wear on her honeymoon in Italy. She was delighted with the choice this large city offered her.

I had arranged to take two days' leave from the university library, and we shopped and ate and drank and chatted – we talked, and laughed, so much. I knew myself to be a fairly reticent person, but being with Birgit had always released something in me. I recognised that our exchanges were well balanced; we each had plenty to say, but we also listened carefully to each other. Neither of us dominated and neither sat back passively. It was relaxing and energising at the same time.

We went out for a meal the first evening of the visit, and I took Birgit to my favourite theatre on the second night – which she loved. On Birgit's last night in England, I cooked for us and we ate on the tiny balcony of my flat, looking out over the gardens below, and the city beyond. It was a balmy evening, and we stayed there for hours, sipping white wine and talking in low voices. After we had watched the sun go down, I lit several candles and it was such a still night they only flickered gently as we sat companionably together.

"Are you getting cold?" I asked her. "I have a couple of wraps inside that I can bring out?"

Birgit shook her head, and she looked at me quietly and thoughtfully for a moment. I smiled back at her, and waited for her to share whatever was in her mind.

"So I have talked and talked about Helmut – how much I love him, and how excited we both are about our plans for the future. I really look forward to introducing you to each other when you come over for the wedding. I know you will like each other."

"I'm sure we will."

"But you have never spoken to me of anyone special in your own life, Eve. I don't like to pry, or to intrude, but I do wonder – is there anyone?"

I didn't reply immediately, and, when I did speak, I measured my words carefully.

"I have friends – male and female – people whose company and conversation I enjoy. I like to see them, though I'm also quite happy by myself, and I certainly feel the need to spend some time alone, perhaps more than many people do. I have a full life – I enjoy my home, my work, seeing my parents. There are many things I like to do, such as going to the theatre, and to galleries, and I read a lot. My life isn't empty, Birgit, at all, but..."

I paused, and she watched me carefully, waiting.

"I've never felt the need to attach myself to another person – romantically, I mean. I've never met anyone who has made me feel that way. Perhaps it's something missing, in me. I see those around me pairing up, and planning to share their lives with someone – like you and Helmut. I'm really pleased for you. I can see that you make each other so happy. But I'm not envious, and I don't wish that I felt the same."

Birgit nodded, slowly.

"So you've never been in love?"

Once, I thought, and perhaps I still was, as I watched her in the candlelight, but I knew I couldn't say that to her. It might make her feel awkward and uncomfortable. It might cast a shadow over this friendship, which was so important to me, and which gave me joy. So I just shook my head, and she didn't ask anything more. She just reached across the table and took my hand in hers.

"Well I'm very pleased that you're content, and that your life is rich and fulfilling, Eve. Who says that we all have to follow the same pattern? Be yourself, and be happy. Though it seems as if my secret fantasy will never come true..."

She paused, and I looked at her, aware that my pulse had started racing. When she didn't continue, I prompted, "Your secret fantasy?"

"My fantasy is that when you come to our wedding, you will fall in love with one of our friends – there are many eligible young men among them, all German – and it will be instantly reciprocated. Then you can marry and live near us in Munich, and you and I will have babies at the same time and we will be inseparable."

I was momentarily lost for words.

Birgit sighed, and smiled, "And now it may be time for us to go in. I need to finish my packing."

She was taking an early flight the following morning.

I would see her again in the autumn, when I flew to Hamburg and then by car to Nuremberg for the wedding. I was looking forward to seeing her parents, and Werner, now a young man.

And to meeting Helmut, who, all the indications were, deserved Birgit, if anyone did. And then we would resume our airmail correspondence, and it may be that our lives would diverge. I knew Birgit wanted children – "a big family!" she would say. But she was committed to her career in journalism, too, and talked of how she and Helmut hoped to manage it so that she continued her work. I had faith in her capacity to do whatever she set her mind to.

"But there is one thing I hoped we would do while I was here, and we haven't yet," she said, turning to me as I followed her through the sliding doors which led back into the flat. "I want you to show me your button collection, and talk me through the significance of each one from the last nine years. Where did you go after my clumsy attempt to embroider our combined initials?"

"Not clumsy at all!" I insisted, "but touching and wonderful!"

We sat on the floor together, and I spread out the two dozen buttons carefully on the carpet between us, explaining what each one meant to me and why it was memorable. Birgit laughed when she picked up the librarian badge which had been placed in the box for safekeeping the December after I had left school.

"I remember you wearing this, - you were so proud! I can see you the first time I met you, standing behind the library desk, this on the lapel of your black blazer..."

She then picked up the blue button she had embroidered, "Oh, maybe not as clumsily sewn as I feared...", my grandfather's smooth white pyjama button, the glass button from nana's wedding dress. She touched them reverently and listened to my stories. Her eyes were shining, I saw.

"Eve – this is such a wonderful thing to do. Something you will keep all your life, and you will add to it every year. The collection will always be as old as you are! I love it. I loved it when we were sixteen, and I love it even more now. Thank you for showing me," and she leant across and kissed me on my cheek.

The wedding, three months later, was, I think, the most enjoyable wedding I ever went to in my life. Birgit's and Helmut's families and friends were so warm and welcoming to this solitary English guest, and Birgit looked breathtakingly beautiful – the most stunning bride I have ever seen. I wore the outfit she had helped me to pick out on her visit in the summer – or, I should say, the outfit she had picked out for me, her taste being consummate and her eye for what would suit me faultless. And that December, on my birthday, I chose the spare button from that soft dress and matching jacket, in delicate autumn colours which brought out, Birgit insisted, the highlights in my hair and the green of my eyes, to go into my button box. It was a memento of a very happy day, and of my closest friend as she embarked on the next chapter of her life.

Chapter Ten: 1983

In the summer of the year in which I turned 30, something happened which altered the course of my life significantly. I was still working at the university library, still living in my small but comfortable flat, and my life had fallen into a predictable but, to me, soothing rhythm. I had joined a local gym and, every evening, as soon as I got home from work, I would change into my leggings, leg warmers and baggy tee-shirt and walk round the corner to spend an hour or so on the treadmills, bikes and rowing machines. The trainers who worked there knew me well by now and were always friendly and welcoming. Occasionally I would join an aerobics class, but generally I preferred exercising on my own, at my own pace. As I walked home afterwards I always felt somehow both rested and, at the same time, full of energy – whatever the exercise was doing for my fitness and physical health, there were most definitely benefits to my mental well-being.

It was June, and I felt a deep sense of contentment as I walked up the stairs to the flat after my hour at the gym, thinking about the lasagne I planned to heat up for my meal, a television programme I hoped to watch, the novel I was enjoying which I would curl up in bed with later. As soon as I turned my key in the door I could hear the telephone ringing.

It was my mother, though her voice was barely recognisable, as she sobbed on the other end of the line.

"Mum?"

I could hear that she was trying to bring her crying under control.

"Eve – can you come home?"

"What is it? What's happened?"

"It's your father – there's been an accident. He…" She was unable to carry on. I could feel the panic building within me, and it became difficult to focus for a few seconds.

"Mum – you're scaring me…"

"I'm sorry, Eve. There was a car crash – he was on his way home from work…"

"Where are you now, mum? Are you at the hospital? Is he going to be all right?"

"I'm sorry," she said again. "Eve - he died."

I hadn't yet learnt to drive. There hadn't seemed to be any point, living in the city and with the university library a short bus ride away. When I went home to see mum and dad I walked to the bus station, and caught the coach for a journey of just under two hours. Dad always picked me up at the other end. I tried to think clearly.

"It's OK, mum. I'll be there as soon as I can."

It wouldn't be OK, of course. In that moment I felt nothing would ever be 'OK' again.

"I'll just ring work to let them know I won't be in, and then I'll get the next bus and find a taxi at that end. Is there anyone who could come and sit with you until I get there?"

There wasn't, really. With no siblings and few close friends – dad had always been her best friend - mum was quite isolated. Dad's sister, Pamela, was geographically further away from mum and dad's home than I was. She, too, would be distraught.

"I'll be there soon, mum. I love you. Try to…."

Try to what?

"I love you too, Evie," mum sobbed. "Be safe." And she hung up the phone.

I looked down at my clothes – the baggy tee-shirt, the ridiculous leg warmers. I gasped as grief swept through me, and then I made myself take several deep, steadying breaths. I couldn't fall apart. Mum needed me to be stronger than that.

So I checked the bus timetable, got changed and packed a bag, and then rang Denise, my supervisor at the library, and told her briefly what had happened, and that I would need several days' leave to support mum through this and to sort out whatever we needed to do. Denise was shocked, and kind, but clearly at a loss for words – something I was to get used to in the weeks ahead. I was brisk and cut the conversation short – much to her relief, I'm sure – and then locked up and walked to the bus station.

Mum was completely devastated by her loss. Dad had only been in his early sixties, always active, and fit and well. He and mum had just started to talk about planning for retirement and the possibility of doing some travelling once dad had finished work. They were due to celebrate their ruby wedding anniversary in the autumn and we were planning a small party to mark the occasion. Dad was a careful driver – in fact he did everything carefully – but a lorry with brake failure had overshot a junction and ploughed into him. Dad had been killed instantly. The lorry driver was unharmed – physically, at least.

For the next few days mum and I did all we had to do – we spoke to the right people, generated the right paperwork, made the necessary arrangements. I was as calm and controlled as I could be, but inside my mind was whirring. What would happen when I had to go back to work? How could mum possibly cope on her own? I had had a telephone conversation with Aunt Pamela to see whether there was any chance that she could come over to stay for a while, but she and mum had never been close. It was her brother that Pamela had loved deeply, and she was struggling with her own loss. My aunt's reluctance was palpable, and I felt resigned as I hung up the phone.

We were able to schedule the funeral for the following week. We'd just arrived home after our latest visit to the undertaker to confirm the arrangements. I made us tea and we sat at the kitchen table, mum shredding a paper tissue as she stared into space.

"Mum?"

She looked up at me, distracted.

"Can we talk about what we should do between now and the funeral?"

She looked perplexed for a moment.

"What do you mean?"

"Well," I said slowly, "I need to go back to my flat and to work. Obviously I'll be back again for the funeral, but I don't want to leave you here on your own. Might you come back on the bus with me and stay in the flat for a few days? At least you'd have company in the evening, and..."

Mum had already started to shake her head.

"This is my home, Eve. I'll be fine," her voice wavered, but she swallowed and continued, "Please try not to worry about me. Do what you need to do, and I'll see you next week."

"Are you absolutely sure, mum? That you'll be all right?"

A ridiculous question, I knew. Mum just nodded.

"And then after the funeral..." I hadn't yet fully formulated my thoughts about what should happen next, but I knew that leaving mum to live here on her own, and my returning to the city, a two-hour bus ride away, to my flat, and my job, and the rhythms I had become so comfortable with, just wasn't an option.

Mum looked up as I hesitated, and then she said, "Eve, you can't make any decisions right now. We're neither of us in a fit state to do that. We both need time to think."

But I didn't need time. I'd already made up my mind.

Denise was understanding, but disappointed. I was a good worker, and we were a strong team.

"What will you do for work, Eve?"

"I'll find something. There are always libraries..."

"And your flat?"

"I've already seen the estate agent I bought it from. He thinks it will sell quite quickly. I know you think this is drastic, but I really don't think I have a choice. I can't leave my mum on her own. I need to be closer to home, at least. I've loved living and working here, I love this city, but perhaps it was time for a change, anyway. I'm almost thirty..."

Almost thirty, and giving up a job I enjoyed and knew I did well, a home where I felt safe and comfortable, and my independence, which I treasured, to move back home. But I loved my mother more. I felt her pain, and I couldn't bear to think of her by herself in the weeks, months and years ahead.

After the funeral I served out my notice at the university library, packed up the flat and put my furniture into storage. As the estate agent promised, the flat sold quickly. I walked away from my life in the city and moved back into my box room. And mum wasn't happy.

"You're my daughter. You're not responsible for me, Eve. This has to be temporary. I don't want you to put your life on hold to look after me for – what? The next thirty years? I'm obviously really unhappy at the moment, but I'm not completely incapable."

"I know, mum. I'll find a job, and once I've done that I'll look for a flat or a house in the right area, but I'll be nearer to you, and we can see each other more often – that's what I want. I love you, and miss you, and want us to be closer. And I'm going to have driving lessons, pass my test and buy a little car." I sensed mum stiffen at the word, but we needed transport, and this was the best way to secure it. I changed the subject. "More jigsaw?"

Mum and I had set up a jigsaw on the dining toom table. I'd tried to think of something soothing that we could do together, remembering how we'd sat sorting through nana's buttons on the day we were clearing her house and how therapeutic that had felt. There were a number of old jigsaws in my boxroom cupboard and we were working through them, sitting side by side in a companionable silence. It was calming.

It was cooler in the dining room and mum pulled on her cardigan as she moved towards the door. We worked quietly on the jigsaw for several minutes and then mum spoke. It was easier to talk about difficult things when our eyes were on the pieces and our hands were occupied, and I remembered conversations I had had with nana as I arranged her buttons during those childhood afternoons.

"It isn't that I'm not grateful, Eve. I know you worry about me being all by myself, and I do miss your father so badly..."

She swallowed, hard. "But you have your own life, and I feel uncomfortable that you've given up so much to be here with me. I was so proud of you, living and working away, having friends and interests, and being self-sufficient. Now it seems that you've taken a big step backwards."

"As you said, mum, it's only temporary. I will find work, and a place of my own. I'd love it if you wanted to move in with me – a new home and a fresh start somewhere else..."

"That's not what I want," mum interrupted. "This is my home, and it's where I want to stay. It's full of memories of your father, which are painful right now, but I can see they might be comforting in time. It will be lovely to see more of you, to have you nearer, but I want to see you living your life, and not putting it on hold because of me." She'd used the phrase 'putting your life on hold' before, I remembered, and it did feel like that – almost as if I were in suspended animation.

I moved to put my arms round her.

"We'll work it out, mum. I'll start looking for a job, and we'll take it from there."

I missed my father badly, but my sense of loss was nothing compared to hers. I could see we were both trying to be brave for each other, but at night I often heard her crying in her room.

Although she and I had always communicated well, there were things I couldn't share with her at this time. I was in a state of shock, I think, and grieving deeply, but an outpouring of my feelings seemed selfish, somehow. I did want to talk to someone, and, like my mother, close friends were in short supply. The one person I really wanted to talk to was hundreds of miles away. One day when I felt particularly low, I decided I had to make contact. It was early in the evening and mum was out doing her catalogue visits. It was cold in the hall, where the telephone was – dad used to joke that this was one of his strategies for keeping the phone bill down – so I wrapped up well, sat on the bottom stair and dialled the number.

She answered straight away.

"Birgit?" I started, and then I burst into tears.

We talked for an hour. At the back of my mind was the thought that I'd have to tell mum about the call and offer her something to cover the cost of it. But it was the best value therapy I could possibly have invested in. Birgit was wonderful. She listened while I poured everything out, and her empathy and concern for me were tangible. It helped that she had known and liked my father, and that she knew me so well. She just understood.

"I wish I could be with you, Eve. I want to hug you," she said, when I'd finished.

I gave a watery smile. "And that would be perfect, Birgit, but I know you can't be here right now."

Next to my bed in the boxroom upstairs I had a photograph Birgit had sent me only a few weeks before. It showed her identical twin daughters, newly born, lying next to each other and holding hands in their sleep. I thought it was the most beautiful photograph I'd ever possessed.

"I just needed to talk to someone, and you're the best friend I have."

"And I can say the same, Eve. When it is possible, we must meet, either here or there – or even somewhere in between. I will leave the girls with Helmut. Paris would be nice..."

I laughed properly.

"Paris would be amazing! But when you can cope with a visit, I'd love to come there and meet Luisa and Lotte – and see Helmut and your parents again. And I'd love to see what kind of a man Werner has become."

"Yes. We will do that."

And because Birgit said it, I knew it would happen.

"But first, Eve – what will you do?"

I paused for a few seconds.

"First I need to find a job. Another library, I think – I love the work. It just suits me. There are libraries everywhere, and I have experience and skills I can bring to the next place. I do need some independence – mum doesn't want me to live here, and she doesn't want to leave this house and all the memories it holds, which I do understand. So when I know where I'm working I can look to buy somewhere nearby. I have the money from the flat and all my things in storage. I need to make another home for myself, but a home near my mother. I just want to be closer to her, because she will be lonely, I know."

Birgit waited, but then prompted. "And what else?"

"I've already booked some driving lessons. As mum can't drive, I need to learn, to pass my test and buy a car, so we're mobile."

"And then?"

"I think then I'll feel I have some control over my life again. I can start to pick up the pieces, and help mum to do the same. I'll always miss my dad..." and my voice faltered for a second. I took a breath. "But I know he wouldn't want either of us to behave as if our lives are over, because his is."

"I do love you, Eve."

My heart skipped a beat.

"And I love you. Thank you for listening, for being with me through this."

"I am, and if ever you want to talk again, just call me. When we can, we will see each other." In the background, I heard a faint cry.

"You must go, Birgit, but thanks again. I promise I'll keep in touch. Bye..."

And after I'd returned the receiver to its cradle I sat hugging myself, sitting at the bottom of the stairs, and just pictured her, with her babies, nursing them but thinking of me, I knew, all those miles away.

And so the next six months passed. I found work as a librarian in a public library in a nearby town, half an hour's drive from mum's house in the orange mini I bought as soon as I'd passed my test. I bought a new flat close to my job, and mum and I found the process of decorating it, sorting out the soft furnishings, arranging my furniture and possessions and making it into my new, comfortable home a soothing experience. Putting it all together – it felt like doing a jigsaw on a grand scale. And we kept the jigsaws going, too. Whenever I called to see mum we would spend some time sitting side by side in the dining room, quietly fitting the pieces together.

I remember mum arriving at my new flat at the end of a day in which I had finally organised the last of my things in the different cupboards. There was a bus which took about 40 minutes, and mum insisted on making use of it - "You can't drive me everywhere, Eve!" I gave her a conducted tour of the flat, now everything had found its rightful place. At the end, she smiled and said, "My goodness, Eve – this is all wonderfully tidy!" and we laughed. It was, I realised, the first time we had laughed together since my father had died.

For my birthday in December, mum had arranged to have their wedding photograph from 1943 copied, and beautifully framed. It was black and white, and stylish: mum slim and stunning in a dress she had created herself, clutching a sheaf of red carnations ("I wanted roses, but we just couldn't get them") and holding proudly on to dad's arm; he tall and handsome in his RAF uniform, his hair gelled and his smile brilliant. When she gave me the gift, she also gave me something else – something she had kept for years, but passed to me now: a button from that RAF jacket, the latest and one of the most treasured items in my button box collection.

Chapter Eleven: 1986

Although the pace of life in the small public library where I worked was different from the university library – and the clientele very different – I soon felt settled and content there. All the staff were women, older women, of my mother's generation rather than mine, and they were, at least initially, maternal and even perhaps a little patronising towards me. But once they found that I was knowledgeable and capable, they began to respect my understanding and skills, and our relationship evolved into one of mutual respect and trust.

"I realise," I told mum, "that too often people equate experience with years on the planet. I'm younger than the rest of the staff by a good few years but, in fact, I'm probably the most experienced among us. I've just had to demonstrate that by being good at my job."

Mum smiled and squeezed my hand. We were sitting in my cosy, comfortable flat, which I loved. I found I didn't miss the city, after all – I was carving out a path for myself here, and being close to mum definitely brought me joy. She was adjusting to life without dad, and had even started talking about looking for some voluntary work which would give her the opportunity to develop fresh interests and to meet new people. At least she didn't have to find paid work - dad had a good life insurance policy, so mum was provided for, and didn't have financial worries on top of everything else.

However, she did feel the need to find something which would fill her days. "And I want to make a contribution," she said. "I'd like to think that I spend my time on something that makes a difference to other people. I'd like to help people."

My social circle continued to be relatively limited, I realised. Most of the regular visitors to the library were either elderly, or very young. We had a thriving children's section, and I enjoyed working in it. I was always happy to keep an eye on the little ones while their parents browsed the shelves to make their own selection, and I found I didn't have any difficulty in exerting a quiet authority. In a different life I might have been a teacher, I thought – perhaps if I'd just been a little more self-assured. I thought of Ellen Kitchen, who I still kept in contact with, and the impact she had had on my life. She and Barney had had three children. Susie, her eldest, was now in the Sixth Form, and Ellen had asked if I would meet her one day and talk to her about the university I had attended – it was one of the places Susie was considering applying to. Susie had met me at the library one lunchtime and we had enjoyed a coffee over a chat in a local café. It had been lovely to catch up with her and to see the composed and confident young woman she had become.

I also enjoyed helping the older men and women who came often to the library. Many were retired, and some were quite doddery, but they were almost all warm and friendly, and grateful for any assistance I could give them. I remembered from my time working in our local library when I was still at school that libraries are about so much more than books – they are a source of local information, a venue for events, a community hub. The principal librarian, Margot, was very willing to encourage any initiative I showed, and I was able to organise a poetry reading one evening, and to start a book discussion group which met monthly.

And I did begin to make a few friends – admittedly, not many my own age, and they weren't people I would see outside work, necessarily, but as I came to know our regular visitors better there were a number I found myself to be growing especially fond of.

George and Freda Buckley were in their mid-fifties. George had run his own business, and had clearly done very well for himself, as my mother would say. He had decided to take early retirement and had sold up and invested the profits. His wife, like my mother, had never worked outside the home. She had raised their two daughters – now grown and independent, one with a daughter of her own. In retirement, George and Freda relished the time they had to travel a little – they were becoming expert on the cruise circuit – and to enjoy the company of their friends and their family, and each other.

George had had a busy and active professional life, and, as he said, "I'm not quite ready for my pipe and slippers just yet..." so he was also keen to become involved in community events, supporting the poetry reading, and the book group, and volunteering as a governor in the local primary school.

"There are so many things you can do," he told me, "if you want to feel useful, and to make a contribution. I think one of the problems with retirement is that some people feel they've lost their sense of purpose. In our society we're too often defined by our jobs - when you meet someone for the first time in a social context it isn't long before you hear the question, 'And what do you do?' "

He turned to Freda and smiled.

"We love our life, don't we? We love having time, and choices. We love our holidays, and seeing the girls, helping out with Jenny, our grandchild. But we need a bit more than that if we're to feel happy. You have to feel life has a point to it."

Freda reached out and squeezed his hand.

"I understand that," I mused, "and it reminds me of a conversation I had with my mum at the weekend."

It was three years, now, since dad's death, and the conversations my mother and I had about the possibility of her finding some voluntary work were increasing in frequency. As mum said, volunteering might "get me out of the house more often" and bring her into contact with a wider range of people than she interacted with through her curtain-making and her catalogue work.

When I mentioned this to George and Freda, Freda immediately said, "Eve – why don't you bring your mother round for a meal one evening? We'd love to meet her, and George might be able to talk through with her some of the things he researched when he was deciding what he wanted to spend his time on."

I hesitated, wondering for a moment whether I should have talked about my mum to people who didn't know her.

"Well, I'm not sure – she's quite shy…"

But Freda simply laughed.

"We're not scary people, Eve! We can make her welcome and put her at her ease. And I love cooking – it will give me a good excuse to make something special. Please say yes. What about this coming Saturday – say, six o'clock?"

"Let me call her and ask what she thinks and I'll let you know."

"That's fine," said George. "We're coming into town tomorrow so we'll pop into the library and find out what she said."

And I watched them leave the library together, arm in arm as they invariably were, and wondered what my mother would say.

Mum surprised me.

"That's really kind of them, Eve. And if you like them, I'm sure I'll like them, too."

"If you're sure? I'll pick you up, and I'll buy some flowers and chocolates to take. They're only about fifteen minutes from you, but I'll come a bit earlier – say, 5pm? I finish work at 1 o'clock this coming Saturday."

"Why don't you come at 4pm, then? I'm itching to finish this jigsaw – we're almost there!"

We had an arrangement that mum wouldn't work on the current jigsaw without me.

As I hung up the phone, I thought how much brighter mum sounded these days. It would be good to go out somewhere with her, for her to meet new people – I thought she, George and Freda might become friends – and I felt positive about the idea of her doing some voluntary work which might also extend her social circle. Like me, mum was a quiet, private person, but we all need supportive relationships – mum, especially, now she faced life without dad.

Saturday evening went very well. The Buckleys' house was beautiful – a 19th century former farmhouse with a huge, well-kept garden, in which we sat out for drinks before we ate. Freda was a superb cook; she had poached a whole salmon, and created an exquisite dessert, and it was all delicious. I was driving so I limited myself to one glass of wine, but mum had several, and I watched her from across the table, her cheeks a little flushed and her eyes bright, as she chatted and laughed.

George and Freda were excellent hosts, skilful at making guests feel comfortable, and masterful at gently directing stimulating conversation. We all relaxed and opened up a little, I think. I found myself telling them about the button box, the jigsaws, and my love of putting things in order.

"I'm reading a novel at the moment, and one of the characters in it works as a 'Clutter Counsellor'. I looked it up, and it is a real thing, apparently. I think it could have been the perfect job for me," I smiled.

"I thought being a librarian was the perfect job for you, Eve," George said, and he turned to my mother. "Your daughter is amazing. She's gracious and helpful. She knows everything – or at least she knows where to find out everything. She's like a ray of sunshine in that library. When Eve opens the door, hope walks in!"

Mum beamed, thrilled, as always, to hear her daughter complimented.

"Hush, George!" said Freda. "That is all true, but you're embarrassing her. Tell us about the Clutter Counsellor, Eve."

"Well, people employ a Clutter Counsellor to help them to organise their lives – their paperwork, for example. Some people feel overwhelmed by things which pile up and they don't know where to start with putting everything in order – deciding what's important and what can be discarded, so they employ a Clutter Counsellor to do that for them. That's what happens in this book, at least! The Clutter Counsellor goes through everything and she sorts it into three piles – one pile to destroy, one pile to retain, and she organises that pile logically and files it so that they can easily find the important stuff when they need it."

"And the third pile?"

"The third pile she keeps as small as she possibly can, because those are the things she needs to ask her employer about. Do they want to keep it, or not? But she has to reduce this pile as far as she possibly can, because that's exactly what they've brought her in for. They don't *want* to have to make those decisions themselves. They want someone else just to do it for them." I leant back in my chair and took a sip of my wine to cover my momentary self-consciousness.

Freda and George sipped their own wine thoughtfully, but my mother leant forward.

"You're right, Eve. That would be a perfect job for you. You're systematic and extremely well organised, and you do, I know, love rationalising and ordering things. It's one of the reasons libraries have always appealed to you, isn't it? You fell in love with the Dewey Decimal System many years ago!" and she smiled, to show that she was teasing me gently, out of love.

George had talked about the different kinds of voluntary work mum might like to consider, and it did help her to clarify her thinking. On the drive home, she said, "I'm going to do two things next week. I'm going to call in at the charity shop, and find out whether they need any help – just think, Eve - all the buttons I'll be able to sift through!"

"A bonus! And the second thing?"

"I'm going to go to the hospital where your dad was taken after the accident. George explained to me that they have hospital visitors, they have a volunteer who takes round a book trolley, and they also have a cafe which is staffed by volunteers. He talked to me about all that while you and Freda were clearing the dishes. So I'm going to investigate the hospital, too."

She sounded energised, and I breathed more easily reflecting on how she seemed to be taking more control of her life.

"The Buckleys were lovely, Eve. Thank you for introducing me to them. They're kind people."

"They are – in fact, I think most people are, when it comes down to it. Maybe it's working in a library that gives me this world view that most people are benevolent! Public libraries attract good people, don't you think?"

"That could be the case. Will you come in when you drop me off, Eve? It isn't too late."

"Of course I will. Let's have some hot chocolate."

"Yes. And let's unpack the next jigsaw – there's a lovely one of famous sites in London which I think we will like. Hey – that would be another advantage of helping in the charity shop! Just think of the jigsaws that might be donated….I may be volunteering to serve in the shop, but I could end up also being one of their best customers," and she leant back against the seat, closed her eyes and smiled.

Chapter Twelve: 1988

My mother became friendly with Freda Buckley over the next couple of years and, through Freda, she met other women of a similar age. Although her group of friends remained quite small, she would arrange to get together with different women for coffee, or to go for a walk. She also joined the monthly Book Group that met at the library, and she worked one day a week at the charity shop and spent two days a week helping at the hospital, both as a hospital visitor, and serving in the café.

"I wouldn't say I'd expanded my horizons dramatically," she said one day as we pored over the latest jigsaw, "but they're certainly broader than they used to be." She smiled, and fitted in the last missing edge piece with a satisfied, "Yes!"

I hesitated before I asked the question.

"And are you happy, mum, do you think?"

Mum thought for a short while before she responded.

"I'm not sure 'happy' is quite the right word, Eve. 'Happy' is still something I associate with my years with your father. We were soul mates, I think – I know that sounds a bit corny, but I can't think of a better term. I'd say what I am now is 'content', and 'comfortable' – and I'm at peace with my life and how it turned out in the end."

"Mum - you sound as if your life is over! You're still a relatively young woman. You're attractive, and thoughtful and kind. Do you ever think that one day you might meet someone…"

Mum shook her head before I'd finished the sentence, and she sounded firm when she replied, "No, Eve. That part of my life is over. I'm enjoying making a few new friends, but I won't share my life with someone again – except in the sense that I share it with you. Now, shall we take a break from this and go and have a cup of tea?"

And then another sudden death changed the course of our lives again.

Although both mum and I felt we knew Freda Buckley quite well by this stage, neither of us were aware of her heart condition. Her family were, of course, and we later found out that the reason George had sold the business and entered into early retirement in his mid-50s was on account of his wife's deteriorating health. They wanted to make the most of their time together while ever she was fit and well enough – to travel, and to live the fullest life they could. No one expected that within a few years of their taking that decision, Freda would collapse in the bedroom after getting ready to go out for the evening. By the time the ambulance had arrived, she was beyond help.

"The very last words I ever said to her were, 'You look gorgeous!' " George told me, sobbing, the first time we met after the funeral. I moved closer to hug him.

George was devastated by the loss of his wife. Like my parents, George and Freda were a couple who would each say their spouse was their best friend, the centre of their world. Their daughters, Sarah and Melissa, were deeply shocked and overcome by grief – I remembered how that felt, and could empathise. They were both only a few years younger than me, and so around the age I had been when dad died. The first time I met them was at Freda's funeral, and they both looked at me blankly through their tears, not even registering who I was, I didn't think.

I talked to mum afterwards.

"As you and I have been through the shock and trauma of sudden death, you might think we'd know what to say and do to offer some kind of comfort and support, but any words seem inadequate, don't they?"

"Yes. There's nothing you can say that helps, or makes any difference, I don't think – especially at this early stage when the grief and pain are so raw. But at least they have each other."

Sarah and Melissa both lived locally. Each of them was married, and Melissa had a daughter, Jenny, aged about three. They were close to their father and he appeared to dote on them, and his granddaughter. At least he wouldn't be on his own, as I had feared mum would be after dad died. His daughters and their husbands had helped George with all the arrangements following Freda's death, and mum and I realised that here was a strong family unit on which he could draw in the weeks and months ahead.

George did turn to mum and to me, too, though. He came into the library more often than ever – he drifted in, looking a little lost, and he would find one of the comfortable chairs and sit with a book open on his lap – sometimes for an hour or more, without turning a page. I realised that he needed to have people around him, even if he didn't enter into conversation. I think he found that comforting. I would smile at him and touch his shoulder as I passed, and hope that helped a little.

Mum would walk up to George's house to see him from time to time, taking him a casserole, or offering to help with household chores. George had been a successful businessman, but he seemed easily overwhelmed by housework. Freda had taken responsibility for all of it. Mum suggested she help him to find someone to come and clean who might also do the washing and ironing. George must have mentioned this to Melissa, who rang mum the following day to say, a little tersely, mum thought, that she and her sister would sort that out for him, and mum needn't trouble herself.

"I expect the girls are still trying to come to terms with what's happened, and Melissa's suffering makes her sound brusque," mum mused. "She also insisted that she and Sarah were helping with their dad's meals and he wouldn't be in need of any more of my casseroles…"

"Was she rude, mum?"

Mum shifted uncomfortably.

"Perhaps a little, but I do understand, I think. They want to show that they're on top of this, that they can look after their father, and that he doesn't need 'relative strangers' – her term – to get involved. But you won't say anything to George about this when you see him, will you? I wouldn't want to cause any awkwardness."

"No, mum, I wouldn't dream of it. I suppose this is just something the family needs to work out for themselves."

But mum's words did make me thoughtful.

The next time I saw George, he arrived at the library shortly before we were closing one Tuesday, and I realised he was hovering to speak to me.

"Are you all right, George?" I asked, as I slipped into my coat and picked up my bag, recognising at the same time what a ridiculous question that was to ask a new widower.

He gave me a watery smile and a half nod.

"I wanted to talk to you, Eve – do you have a few minutes?"

"Of course I do," I injected as much warmth and sympathy into my tone as I could. "We might need to find somewhere to go – Margot is closing the library now, and it's a bit too cold to sit outside, I think. It's a little late to find a café that's open, and too early for the pub... Do you want to walk me round to the car park?"

George inclined his head and followed me through the door. Margot locked up behind us and gave me an encouraging smile before she turned for home.

"He's like a beaten puppy," I found myself thinking.

We walked to my car – still the orange mini – but George seemed reluctant to begin.

"Do you want to sit inside, and you can tell me whatever is on your mind?"

He nodded mutely, and I unlocked the doors.

Inside the car, the windows quickly steamed up as we sat there in the cold. George still seemed unsure about how to start. But eventually, he spoke. "Do you remember the conversation about the Clutter Counsellor?"

"Of course – the night you and Freda invited mum and me round for dinner. It was a lovely evening."

"It was – so good to meet your mum and to get to know you a little better." George cleared his throat. "I remember you telling us about the book you were reading and the job of one of the characters, and you said you thought it would be the ideal job for you."

I smiled. "I'm not sure how serious I was being, but, yes, I did say that."

"I think I need your services," and George turned to me with an earnest look on his face.

"What do you mean, George?"

He raised his hands in a hopeless gesture.

"The house – it's all getting on top of me. I can't cope with it all. Freda kept everything straight but now – I'm all over the place. I always told myself how capable I was – with the business, my hobbies and interests, the school governor work. But since Freda died..."

I sat quietly and waited for him to continue.

"The girls are willing to help, but they're both working, and Melissa has Jenny, too. Your mum suggested she'd help me find a cleaner – and I think I need a gardener, too. The garden was always Freda's domain. But Sarah pointed out that a cleaner might clean, but I'd still need to keep things tidy, and keep my papers in order, and I can't even seem to manage that. I'm just useless."

I resisted the impulse to interrupt. I think he just needed someone to listen.

"People probably don't realise this, but Freda did everything – paying the bills, booking the holidays. It started when I was working hard – she just took over everything that wasn't to do with the business, all the home stuff. Banking, insurance, and rates, and... I don't know where to begin. I need someone to help me. Sarah and Melissa don't really have the time. They also seem to get quite cross with me, and how hopeless I am. I can't say I blame them. I get cross with myself. I know you're busy too, Eve, but you're always so calm and competent. You are a master organiser, you're kind, and you'd be patient with me. I'd pay you for your time – I'd insist on that. But it would be such a comfort to me, such a help...."

And finally, he seemed to have run out of steam.

"I need you, Eve," George finished, simply. "You're my friend, and I need you."

A friend? Was I? Or a 'relative stranger', as his daughter would put it?

"I'm sorry you're so distressed," I said carefully. "Let me think about this, George." I really needed to talk it through with my mother to help me to clarify my thinking. "And I'll call you in a day or two."

George blew out a breath – in relief, it seemed. I hadn't said no. He hoped I would still say yes.

"Can I give you a lift anywhere?" I offered.

"No – that's fine. My car's at the other end of the car park. You'll ring me?"

"As soon as I've had a chance to think it all out."

"Thank you, Eve. Thank you," and he climbed slowly out of the car. He was only in his late fifties – not an old man, but he seemed to have aged twenty years since Freda's death.

"I suspect the daughters wouldn't like it," was mum's first comment when I explained what had happened and recounted as much of the conversation as I could remember.

"Yes – that's what I was thinking, too. But part of me sees that this is his choice, not theirs. He says they get quite irritated with him – 'cross' was the word he used. And he sees me as patient, and kind, I suppose."

"You are, Eve. You're also well-organised and systematic, and I think you'd probably relish the challenge. But how much time could you give to it? How might it work in practice?"

"Well, I'm not thinking of a regular commitment. I'm hoping that I can help George sort through the house, and support him to devise a filing system and some kind of calendar so that he can keep on top of his bills and all the paperwork, and build a routine for dealing with all of that – he is an intelligent man. He ran a business, for goodness' sake, so he must have these skills. He's just grieving, and so he's overwhelmed at the moment. If I can get him started, and then we – or his daughters – help him employ a cleaner and a gardener, then he might be able to cope after that. I would do it with him, not for him, and try to build his confidence and his capacity so that he doesn't feel so helpless."

"That sounds a good plan."

"I did wonder whether you might come with me so we could help him together?"

"When are you thinking of?"

"I have a week's holiday booked. I wasn't going to go away this time. I could certainly spare him a few days. He will insist on paying me – he made that clear. I've no idea how we work out a reasonable payment, but that's up to him to decide, I suppose. Maybe on the days you're not in the shop or at the hospital you could come along too? I think we'd need to give the house a good clean, first, and tidy the garden, and then go on to help him to rationalise his paperwork..."

I smiled a little, and mum laughed.

"Do you know when you say 'rationalise' your eyes light up?"

"I admit I would enjoy the challenge! But this is just helping George to get started and then to take control. I am wondering about Sarah and Melissa, though, and how they will respond. Should I talk to one of them before I agree to anything?"

Mum was thoughtful for a moment, but then she said, firmly, "I think that's for George to deal with, rather than you, Eve. As you said, this is his choice rather than theirs. If I were you, I'd just suggest that he might need to check how his daughters feel about it, because you don't want to make them feel uncomfortable, or pushed out, or something. You don't want them to think you're taking over. But after you've said that, I'd leave it to him – they're his family, after all."

"So it sounds like you think I should accept?"

Mum came across to me and put her arm round my shoulders.

"I think George would be lucky to have you. I'm happy to come along too, when I can, if you think that might help. I know you'll do a good job, and he'll benefit from your company and conversation as well as your phenomenal ability to rationalise! If you help him, he feels better and gets back on an even keel, and you enjoy the challenge, then everyone gets something out of it, and if his girls don't much like it, that's their problem."

I hugged her back.

"I knew you'd help me work it out. Can I use the phone and I'll let George know?"

And when I spoke to him he was so effusive and grateful, so relieved, I think, that someone was prepared to help him put his life in order, I felt very pleased that I'd said yes.

Chapter Thirteen: 1988

A fortnight later, I had my week's holiday from the library, and I'd told George I could spare three days to come and work through the house with him. As mum had suggested, I asked him to let his daughters know and ensure that they realised I wasn't trying to interfere or intrude – just to support. I emphasised that I recognised they were busy, with work and family, and I had some free time. I said I thought George should explain to them that he had asked me to do this as a friend, and I'd accepted because I recognised that he needed some help. At the same time I suggested he should perhaps explain that it was also a commercial arrangement - just as he would in due course employ a cleaner, he was employing me to use the skills I had and to provide a service he felt he was in need of.

I don't know whether George did talk to Sarah and Melissa – we didn't discuss it again. Part of me wondered whether he had the tendency not to face up to difficult situations, that the house and his finances had got into a state because he had ignored dealing with the day-to-day in the weeks since Freda's death. Might he be the same with his daughters, avoiding an uncomfortable conversation and simply hoping for the best? But when they visited they would certainly realise that someone had been there to help him put the house to rights, and I didn't think he would lie about who that was.

On the first day, mum came with me in the morning, as she wasn't due to go into the charity shop until after lunch. We loaded up the car with cleaning materials, as we were unsure what George would have in the house, and it took us a while to unpack everything we'd brought when we arrived. George stood in the porch, initially wringing his hands, until I suggested he help with the unloading. He scurried to the car to do that, looking shamefaced. Was it possible to train someone to show initiative? I wondered briefly.

Mum and I had decided beforehand that we'd spend the morning cleaning and, despite the size of the house, we felt we could make good progress in the time we had. We started by walking round the whole property. There were five bedrooms and three bathrooms, but George only used one of each. I decided I could set George to dust and later vacuum the unused bedrooms, which were ready for cleaning, but not disordered, while mum and I tackled the rest. Downstairs, the lounge, dining room, kitchen and George's study were all in need of considerable attention, as was the large conservatory at the back of the house. As we walked round, George moved desultorily around us, picking things up – a pile of newspapers, two empty mugs – and depositing them somewhere else (though not where they needed to be), and he kept apologising. After a few minutes, I looked him in the eye and said, "George, do you think you could make tea for the three of us, please, and then we can sit down and make a plan?"

"Yes, of course - whatever you think, Eve," and he scuttled off to do that.

Mum and I gave each other a steady look.

When George returned with the tea we all sat down together and I took a deep breath.

"First of all, George – please stop apologising. We all know that these are exceptional circumstances, and that there are particular reasons why things have slipped out of your control in recent weeks. That's why we're here, and you've asked us to do a job, which we can and will do. I know I can't tell you how to feel, but please try not to let guilt overwhelm you.

The three of us are going to work together on this. If you're OK with it, I'd like to ask you to do specific things to help. We only have a few days and after that, with the help of a cleaner and a gardener, you should be able to keep things in order – and we'll talk through a strategy for dealing with your paperwork, too. Does that sound all right?"

"It sounds wonderful, Eve. I knew you were the right person for the job. I'm so relieved."

"Mum can't be here all the time – she's working in the shop this afternoon, and she's helping at the hospital on Thursday, but we're sure we can do what needs to be done in the time we have."

George hesitated before asking, "But you will be here when your mother can't be?"

"Yes. I can give you three days of my time. I'm sure that will be enough – just to get you sorted."

"Thank you so much, and I'm sorry…"

I gave George a level look, and he caught himself and smiled a little ruefully. "What would you like me to start with?"

I gave him the spray polish and a duster and pointed him towards the little-used rooms on the first floor.

The three of us worked all morning, stopping for sandwiches around midday, after which mum had to leave. George had finished working on the bedrooms, and he sat at the breakfast counter watching while I worked in the kitchen. After asking me a couple of times what he could do to help, I said, "Have a break, George. I promise I'll let you know when there's something I'd like you to do."

He was silent for a few moments, and then he asked, tentatively, "What is that you're doing?"

I smiled up at him. "I'm polishing up your teaspoons with a scouring pad. They were quite badly tea stained. Look how they shine, now," and I held one up in the beam of sunlight coming through the window.

George smiled, though he looked bemused.

"How would you know to do such a thing?"

"I liked helping mum round the house when I was a little girl. I've grown up enjoying cleaning, and tidying, and putting things in order. It makes me feel satisfied and calm." I smiled back at him.

"And won't the teaspoons get stained again?"

I laughed.

"They will. So if they were mine, I'd clean them again the following week. I'm not sure whether this is something your cleaner will automatically do, when you've found one. Or whether you'd want her to." I shrugged. "But my nana always did it, so my mum did it, and now I do it."

George looked thoughtful.

"And when you have children one day, perhaps they will watch you and then they'll do it? And their children?"

This was a more personal conversation than George and I usually engaged in, and I just smiled, and said, "I'm glad you said 'children' and not automatically 'daughters'. It doesn't have to be women's work."

I was 34 years old. I might still have children, if I met the right partner. But as I had never yet found anyone I looked at in that light, it wasn't something I gave much time to thinking about.

"I'm wondering about your own home – your flat," George said.

George knew I had one, but he had never been there.

"I'm imagining it's always clean and tidy – it would certainly never get into this kind of state."

"Well, I am tidy. I like things to have a place, and I like to put them back into their place. But I do give it a clean once a week – all homes need that, I think."

I'd finished with the teaspoons, and I had started work tidying the cutlery drawer. George did use his dishwasher, and when he emptied it he clearly threw the cutlery into the drawer in a fairly random fashion. I separated out the knives, forks, spoons and general large utensils while I talked.

"Are you happy if I straighten your cupboards, George? They'll only stay straight if you commit to putting things back logically, but I just think it's easier to find what you're looking for if there's a system to it."

"I'm looking forward to having a system, Eve! I do spend too much time looking for things, I know. It frustrates me, and upsets me, too. Freda knew where everything was. Since she died...I seem to spend too much time looking for my car keys and my wallet..."

I opened the cupboard above the work surface.

"I saw a pretty bowl in here, before. Why not leave it on the table in the hallway? Keep your car keys and house keys in it, maybe? And your wallet on the table next to it? Then you can pick them up when you want to leave the house. You just need to remember to deposit them there each time you come in. Where are your car keys and wallet now?

"Not sure..." George gave me a rueful smile.

"It's all about systems, I think. We can decide together on the different systems that might suit you. You'll just need to follow them after that."

"You make it sound simple, Eve. You're a wonder."

By the end of the first day the house was clean and the downstairs cupboards were organised. Before I left, I realised I did need to ask George about Freda's personal things.

"George, have you thought about Freda's clothes, and jewellery, cosmetics, and everything? Do you have any plans for those things?"

The colour drained from George's face and he shuffled uncomfortably in his chair.

"I can't really decide. I know at some stage I need to sort it all out but I can't face it yet."

"That's understandable, and there's no rush. I can tidy and clean around it all as best I can, and I think when you do decide you want to do something with it all, Sarah and Melissa are the right people to help do that with you. Do you agree?"

George nodded, and looked down as his eyes filled with sudden tears. I sat quietly for a few moments and then I spoke gently to him.

"I do understand how difficult this all is. No one is trying to put pressure on you. You'll find your own way. I think we're done for today. Is there anything else you want from me before I go? I'll see you bright and early tomorrow. Mum will be with me and she's going to spend the day in the garden – the weather is looking to stay fine. I'll work on the cupboards upstairs tomorrow morning and then you and I can start on the study and the paperwork."

George looked up, his eyes still glistening, and he nodded and tried to smile.

The next day, while mum worked in the garden, I straightened the garden shed, and then I started on the cupboards upstairs. The last one I tackled was the large airing cupboard on the landing. George sat on a wicker chair while I emptied everything out and then we decided together how he wanted it organised – what could be at the back, and which things he used regularly and so needed to be at the front. There were a few things he agreed we could recycle. I folded and sorted and we chatted as I worked. He seemed considerably brighter than the previous day.

"I understand what you mean about logic and systems," he said. "And I do promise that in future I won't just throw stuff in the cupboards without any thought or care, which is what I realise I've been doing since Freda died. I know I need to stop that now, or all your good work will be wasted."

"You don't need to promise me, George. You're not doing this for me – but you can make life easer for yourself if you decide on where you want to put things and stick to it. It's up to you."

"I do feel calmer, you know. Just having a plan, and a sense of order. It's soothing."

"Good – that's what we're aiming for. Right, I think this is done. How does it look?"

"Brilliant. So what's next?"

"The study. We cleaned it yesterday, but I just piled up all the paper and it needs sorting, and some will need shredding, I think. This is real Clutter Counsellor stuff. What can go, what needs to stay, and how that should be filed."

"I remember, and the small pile of stuff you need to consult me over."

"You've got it. I can hear mum's come in – why don't you and she have a break and a chat while I make a start in there, and I'll come and fetch you when I need your opinion?"

"Sounds like a plan." George had a definite spring in his step as he moved downstairs and joined mum in the kitchen.

From the study, I could hear them chatting and laughing as I started to work through the pile of letters, bills, statements and documents of all kinds. It didn't look like George had done much with any of this since Freda's death and I sorted out to the best of my ability what needed to be acted on, what needed to be kept for reference, what could be disposed of. Listening to them in the next room I thought, not for the first time, of how well they got on, and how much they seemed to like each other. They were a similar age – mum just a few years older. I found myself wondering how it would it be if....

Mum insisted she had no intention of remarrying. George, on the other hand, I didn't feel was cut out for a solo life. He was far less self-sufficient than my mother, despite his years as a successful businessman. He needed someone to care for him, to be a companion, to share his life. I knew my mother was kind, caring, and she did derive satisfaction from looking after others. Might that be enough?

I gave my head a shake and went back to the paperwork. After a further half an hour, George stuck his head round the study door?

"Ready for me?"

"I think so. We need to look at the things that need attention, here, George, and make some decisions about the rest."

"Your wish is my command. It may be an odd thing to say, but I'm enjoying all this. I felt completely overwhelmed by it all, but you're starting to make me see it's manageable and not monstrous. You and your mother, I mean."

I smiled to myself as George quietly closed the door and took a seat beside me. I could hear mum humming as she moved upstairs.

The following day we finished everything off. Mum was volunteering at the hospital so George and I had the day on our own. Mum and I had compiled a list of what we considered we needed to do at the end of day one, and I worked through it now, crossing off everything we had accomplished. It was very satisfying. I talked George through it. We also discussed the steps he would take to find a cleaner and a gardener who would help him to maintain the order we'd managed to impose on the house and its grounds.

"It's doable, George – you see that, don't you?"

"I do."

George took my hand.

"Thank you, Eve. You've saved my life, I think."

I laughed and slowly withdrew my hand.

"No, George! We've just helped you to get your life back on track."

"I promised you payment, so want to give you this. You and your mother can decide how you want to divide it."

I looked at the cheque George passed to me and was momentarily stunned.

"George – that's far too much!"

George was, for once, very sure of himself.

"Not at all, Eve. You deserve every penny, and I won't hear a word of protest. Spend it on something that gives you joy."

"It's…incredibly generous. You honestly didn't need to... but thank you. We are grateful."

He beamed at me.

"I'd better go. I'll call at mum's on the way home."

"And I will call into the library and see you when you're back at work on Monday. In fact, as an added thank you, do you think you and your mother would like to come to dinner with me one evening next week? I'll book somewhere special and pick you both up?"

"Thank you – that's kind. I'll find out what mum's plans are and let you know."

When I passed the cheque to mum, she gasped.

"My goodness, Eve – that isn't what I was expecting."

"Me neither, but he was insistent, and I hate arguing about money, so felt I just had to accept graciously. He also wants to take the two of us out for a meal one evening. Would you be happy to do that?"

"Of course – he's good company, and he's lonely, I know. We have to let him show his gratitude, I think. I really hope this works and he doesn't end up in the same situation a few months down the line. What do you think?"

"I think he means it when he says he's determined to keep on top of things now, but we'll see. He told me how much calmer he feels when there's order, and that he feels in control again. I hope that might motivate him to try his best to keep a grip on things from this point. I keep reminding myself that he ran a successful business, so I do think his current incapacity is bound up with his grief and, as time passes, things will stabilise. I certainly hope so. Much as I find this kind of challenge satisfying, I don't want to be spending part of every holiday doing the same thing!"

I'd thought carefully about my next words in the car on the way over.

"I do think he will probably want to remarry at some stage, though. I'm not sure he's cut out for solitude. I think he just wants a companion, someone to guide him a bit and give him a sense of purpose and structure. Can you remember I told you about the conversation we had about needing to feel life had a point to it, when Freda was still alive? Just before you met them, in fact."

"I do, and you may be right."

"I was listening to the two of you talking and laughing together yesterday, when I was sorting stuff in his study, and I was thinking about how well you get on. You're just the sort of person he needs, I think. I know you've always said you were content to be alone, but..."

"Eve, stop," mum said, and she reached out to take my hand. "Don't you know?"

"Don't I know what?"

"We were talking about you – that's all George ever wants to talk about. He was making me laugh because he was so effusive about you and how wonderful you are. Eve – I've suspected it for a while, but the last few days have made this so clear to me. I'm not sure why we didn't realise it before. He really is grieving over Freda, and perhaps that stopped us seeing it, but…"

"Mum?"

"George is in love with you."

Chapter Fourteen: 1988

I couldn't stop thinking about mum's words. I didn't sleep well that night. On Monday when I returned to work I felt jumpy, knowing that George would appear at some stage: he had said he would, so I had no doubt he would keep to the plan. He arrived just before I took my lunch break – he knew when that was.

He had a jaunty air about him, was clean-shaven and smartly dressed – as he always used to be, I realised. He had a sense of purpose, I could see. He is an attractive man, I found myself thinking. I'm sure he will find another wife in due course, but, surely, not me, and certainly not yet?

"Good morning, Eve!" he said brightly, and then stopped and glanced at his watch, "Or – no. I'm wrong. It's good afternoon. How are you today?"

"I'm fine, George, thank you. How is everything at home?"

"Spick and span – I wonder where that phrase comes from? I promise I won't let you down, Eve..."

I decided to let that one go.

"I'm a new man!"

I smiled wanly.

"I think you're about to take your lunchbreak at this time, aren't you? I wondered whether you'd join me at The Farmer's Arms? They do a wonderful Lancashire hotpot. I'd love to treat you as an additional thank you for your sterling work last week." The look in his eyes was so hopeful, I couldn't hold his gaze.

"Honestly, George, you've been generous enough, and there's no need to keep thanking me. We did a job, and you paid us well." He looked momentarily uncomfortable, and I felt awkward, too, but over the weekend I had thought this over, and wondered whether if I could focus on the transactional, commercial nature of the arrangement it might help to put it into perspective. We'd entered into an informal contract, and we'd fulfilled it. Might that somehow depersonalise the whole process and help to put a little distance between us?

"And I'm sorry about lunch, but I've agreed to work through my lunch hour today, as we're short staffed." Lying didn't come easily to me, and I knew I was blushing, so I kept my eyes on the book I had been processing. I was grateful, at least, that Margot and the rest of the staff weren't within earshot. "So I just grabbed a sandwich in the back during my break. I'm going to be at this desk for the duration, I'm afraid."

I smiled quickly up at him to soften the blow, but he looked crestfallen. He had clearly been looking forward to our spending time together – he might even have already booked a table at the pub – and he seemed so disappointed, I had to glance down again.

"Ah, well, not to worry. It was late notice, and I know how much in demand you are. And we said we'd have a meal out later this week, didn't we – you and me and your mother. That will be lovely."

I knew we hadn't definitely agreed to this, but I just didn't see how I could reject that offer, too. At least if there were three of us, it would be safer. As I caught myself thinking that, it struck me that 'safer' was an interesting choice of adjective.

When I didn't speak, George pushed on.

"As the library isn't open on Sundays, and you can have a bit of a lie-in then, I thought that, if you and your mother are free, this Saturday evening would be a good time. I can make a reservation at The Last Drop – have you ever been?"

I shook my head.

"It really is something special. I think you would both love it, and I would be honoured to have two such attractive companions…"

It struck me that these were words he had planned and rehearsed.

"I can pick you both up - I don't mind driving, and then the two of you can have a glass or two of wine. If I reserve a table for 7pm, say, I could pick you up at 6, and your mum at 6.30?"

"I'll just need to check mum doesn't have something else arranged." Mum never went out on Saturday night, I knew. "Can I phone you in a day or so?"

The light in George's eyes dimmed a little, but he clearly wasn't to be deterred.

"Of course, Eve. As soon as you can, though – it's a place that gets booked up, and I really think you and your mum will love it there…"

He probably realised he was repeating himself, and his words petered out. Then he drew himself up again and gave me a brilliant smile.

"Well, I'd better be off – things to do, you know how it is. I'll look forward to your call soon." He gave a little bow, and I thought that, if he'd been wearing a hat, he would have tipped it as he turned towards the door.

I blew out my breath as the door closed.

I went to mum's straight after work and explained what had happened.

"I don't suppose you'd be prepared to say you're already committed on Saturday?" I asked, and mum actually laughed.

"Eve! Think it through! If I say I can't make it, he'll be thrilled, because it will mean he can just take you!"

My shoulders slumped.

Mum was thoughtful for a moment, and when she spoke again she said gently, "What is it you're afraid of, do you think?"

I shrugged.

"Oh, I don't know. Embarrassment, I suppose? Feeling awkward and uncomfortable? And I don't want to hurt him. Even just saying I couldn't go for lunch with him felt awful." I remembered the beaten puppy again. "He seemed so much more lively and positive than he's been in recent months. I hope he's turning a corner. I see that getting the house put to rights might be helping with this, but I really hope the spring in his step and the jaunty look in his eye isn't just because of me… He's been so bruised and battered. Am I going to add to his pain?"

Mum reached across and took my hand.

"George isn't your responsibility, love," she said softly. "If you're not able to return his affections, that isn't something to feel terrible about – or guilty. I do think he's falling in love with you, but there may be a way of just being his friend. You're not committing to anything by going out to dinner with him, especially with your old mother along!"

"You're not old..." I said automatically. "Yes, at least I won't be alone with him. Shall I ring him tomorrow and say yes, then?"

"They do say The Last Drop is an amazing place!" said mum, with a twinkle in her eye.

We did, in fact, have a very pleasant evening. George was lively and entertaining, and the three of us laughed a lot. The wine probably helped me to relax a little. Despite her natural shyness, mum was developing into someone who was socially quite skilled and good at putting people at their ease. She asked George questions, and of the three of us, he definitely talked the most, telling us about his life, his business, his travels. For the first time, when he spoke Freda's name he didn't falter, I realised. There was a sense of celebration, somehow, of the time they had spent together and the joy they had known.

George had picked me up first, and he dropped mum off first at the end of the evening. It did cross my mind that his choice of restaurant was geographically helpful, if he wanted a little time alone with me – it made sense to collect and deposit us in this order. He had been fairly quiet on the journey to mum's at the start of the evening, but after we had left mum's road to make the journey back to my flat at the end of the night, he was positively ebullient, perhaps bolstered by the successful evening, the laughter and the warmth of the conversation we had shared for the past three hours. This was a very different George from the man who had drifted into the library in recent weeks. He seemed to have regained his confidence and his energy. He seemed again like a man in the prime of his life.

Eventually we reached the flat, and he pulled up at the kerb, switched off the engine and turned to me.

"Do I seem different to you, Eve?" he asked, which felt for a few seconds as if he had reached into my mind and read my thoughts.

"You certainly seem – better, than you were. More..." I was trying to choose my words carefully, "...energised and hopeful, perhaps?"

"That's exactly how I feel. I think you know me, Eve, and you understand me."

Neither of us spoke for a short while. I wondered when and how I could open the car door without it seeming rude or abrupt, but I desperately wanted to get into my flat, to shut the door and be on my own inside.

"I know you said on Monday that I should stop thanking you for what you've done, but I just have to say this. I think you may not appreciate what a difference it made to have those three days with you – sorting everything out, but also just enjoying your company and your conversation. It made me realise something, Eve. I don't want to be on my own. I don't want to live on my own. I want someone to share my life with, to travel with, to spoil and pamper. Maybe even to start a new family with. I want – and need someone to love."

This was all moving much too quickly. I had talked to mum about my fear of embarrassment and awkwardness, and my anxiety about hurting George, but I didn't expect the evening to end with this. I felt as if things were quickly spiralling out of control.

"I know it's only a short time since I lost Freda. But Freda knew she could die early – it was something we talked about, and something we were prepared for, as far as it's possible to be prepared. She always said that I would – that I should – marry again. She didn't think I was cut out for the life of a solitary widower. She knew me and understood me very well, too. She and I even talked about the kind of wife that might suit me. We both thought... We both chose you, Eve."
I think I had stopped breathing.

"I've always liked you, and admired and respected you. Freda was fond of you, too. But over those few days, being with you in my home, I realised – this isn't too early. This is the right time. I love you, Eve. I absolutely understand that you don't feel the same. Perhaps you would come to love me in time, or perhaps not. But I think you like me, and you trust me. I will be a good husband. I could still give you children, if that's what you wanted, I'm sure. I would look after you and cherish you. Freda would approve – I know she would. Eve, I'm asking you to marry me. Please say yes."

I said nothing. I literally could not think of one thing that would be the right thing to say. It wasn't 'Yes'. But I couldn't just say 'No'. My thoughts about it being too soon after his wife's death were thrown into sharp relief by his comments about his discussions with Freda about what might happen after she had gone, and his conviction that this was a choice they had, in fact, made together. His daughters floated into my mind and then floated out again. What I really wanted, more than anything else, was to talk to my mother.

How many women, I wondered, in receipt of a proposal of marriage, immediately thought of their need to talk it through with their mother? Perhaps in Jane Austen's day, but surely not in the twentieth century.

George was still looking at me. At least, I thought suddenly, he hadn't offered me a ring.

I finally found my voice.

"George – I don't know what to say. This is sudden – I need time…"

"Yes, yes – I see that, and that's perfectly understandable," George said quickly. He sounded almost relieved. Perhaps, when he was anticipating this conversation, his worst case scenario was that I would run, screaming, from the car, and at least I hadn't done that.

"I can wait. Take the time you need, Eve. I love you, and I won't stop loving you. I will continue to love you, whatever you decide. I appreciate the difference in our ages, and that you might worry about what people will think…"

It wasn't that, exactly, but I wasn't sure how to explain the deep sense of shock I was experiencing, so I said nothing.

"But just take my word for it that if Freda is looking down on us now, she is smiling..."

That didn't help.

"I think I need to go, now, George. I'll be in touch, when... if... I'll be in touch."

I smiled faintly and, finally, reached for the door handle and climbed out onto the street.

"Do you want me to see you to the door?"

"No! No, thank you – it's just there. You can watch me let myself in from here. Thank you, George – it's been a lovely evening." That didn't quite sound right, but my automatic politeness was taking over. "Drive safely, and we'll talk again soon."

Once inside the flat, I fell face forward on my bed, and I stayed there, pretty much, for the next twenty four hours.

Chapter Fifteen: 1988

I did stir myself to undress and climb into my pyjamas at one point, and then I huddled under the quilt and, eventually, fell asleep, only to experience the most disturbing dreams in which Freda, more than George, loomed large. Sarah and Melissa put in an appearance, too.

I woke early and looked at the clock, calculating the earliest point at which a phone call to my mother was reasonable. I picked up my novel and read for a while, but my concentration was shot, and after starting the same page three times I finally gave up and laid it aside. I levered myself out of bed and went into the kitchen to make myself tea, which I took back to bed, and then I reached for the phone.

"Are you up, mum? I hope I didn't wake you?"

"Yes, I'm up, but still in my dressing gown. It's early, love. Are you all right?"

I found myself, suddenly, on the verge of tears, which seemed ridiculous. I swallowed and breathed steadily. If I sounded distressed, mum would be, too. I really didn't want to upset her.

"I'm OK, more or less. You remember our conversation about George, and me not wanting to hurt his feelings, and cause awkwardness and embarrassment?"

"Eve – what happened?"

"He proposed to me before I could get out of the car!"

There was a pause, and I knew mum would be thinking, and that she would choose her words carefully.

"That was unexpected – in its timing certainly."

"Yes."

"And you said…?"

"Very little. Just that I needed time to think."

"Well, that was a sensible thing to say. And what *are* you thinking?"

"I don't really know what to think!" I wailed, and then stopped myself and tried to breathe calmly again. "He said that he and Freda knew she might not live long, that she wanted him to marry again, because she didn't want him to be alone – and lonely. He said..." It struck me anew how bizarre this was, "...he said they'd talked about it, and they talked about me and – they *chose* me together."

"Goodness."

"I know. And he said he wanted to take care of me, and – that he would start a family with me if that's what I wanted..."

There was another silence while mum thought about this one.

"And is it what you want, Eve? I always thought you would make a wonderful mother, but it's a big responsibility and it would need to be something you were sure about, I think."

"I'm not sure about anything, mum. This is all so unsettling, and you know how much I like order, and calmness, and feeling in control..."

"Do you want to drive over here and we can talk about this face to face? Or shall I get the bus and come to you?"

"Thanks, mum, but I am all right, really. I actually want to stay here on my own and do some thinking. I want to curl up in my bed and stay in my pyjamas all day. Is that odd?"

"It's something you find comforting, I think. Well, ring me back if there's anything I can do to help. And – just one thing, Eve..."

"What is it, mum?" I prompted, as she hesitated.

"I know you like order, and routine, and all the rest of it. But I'm not sure that's the best reason for saying no to George."

"Are you saying you think I should say *'yes'*?"

"I wouldn't dream of telling you what to say, one way or the other, Evie. But give it some thought. If you do decide you want a family, we both know George is a good man and he would care for you and your children. He would be a good provider and a kind, gentle husband and father. If that isn't what you want, that's fine, too. But if it's just fear of disturbing the status quo which drives you now, I'd hate for you to make a decision you regret at some point in the future. That's all I'm saying."

I needed to digest all this.

"Thanks, mum. I do love you."

"And I love you, very much. And you know I will support you whatever you decide. But there is a decision to be made, and it needs to be made carefully and thoughtfully. Come and see me soon."

"I will. Bye."

I replaced the receiver, lay back against my pillows and closed my eyes.

On Monday, at work, I felt initially disorientated, but as I became absorbed in the different tasks that fell to me that day, I grew calmer and found I was able to think about things other than what George had said, what my mother had counselled and what I might say to them both in due course. The way forward still wasn't clear to me, and I was just starting to think that making a full list of 'pros' and 'cons' might help me to clarify my thinking, when I looked up and saw Melissa, George's elder daughter, enter the library holding her toddler Jenny by the hand. My heart suddenly started to pound in my chest. I gave her a wobbly smile as she made her way to the desk where I was stationed - a smile, I realised, that she didn't return.

"Eve," she said.

"Hello, Melissa. It's nice to see you."

Still no smile.

"Dad talked to Sarah and me last night."

"Oh?" I had no idea how to frame an appropriate response to Melissa's statement.

"Sarah and I wondered if we could call round at your flat tonight to talk to you properly. Might that be possible?"

My heart sank, but my customary politeness kicked in.

"Of course, if the two of you would like to do that. I get home at about 6. Do you have the address?" but Melissa had already turned away.

"We have it. We'll see you shortly after, then. Come on, Jenny," and Jenny, looking bemused, was led away by her mother.

As the library door closed behind them, I felt my legs suddenly weaken. I sank onto the chair we kept behind the desk – but rarely used - and tried to steady my breathing. Would it be ridiculous to ask mum to be there with me? I quickly decided that it would. I was 34 years old. I could surely manage this meeting, whatever they had to say to me. Should I ring George and tell him, or ask for his thoughts about what they might say, and how I might respond? I realised that until I had given him my answer – until, in fact, I had made a firm decision about what that answer might be – contacting George wasn't really an option.

I looked at my wristwatch – the 6 o'clock meeting was still eight hours away. How would I get through that time?

But, of course, I did get through it.

I called at the corner shop on the way home to buy a cake – lemon drizzle, for no particular reason - which I planned to serve with tea. That would be fitting, wouldn't it? I thought. I'd decided not to ring mum until after the sisters' visit, then I could tell her what they had said and we could talk through its implications. I decided that I would say the absolute minimum to them. What could I say? I didn't yet know what my answer to George would be, but it seemed disloyal even to share that indecision with his daughters. I simply knew that they would not be pleased about what had happened – Melissa's unsmiling face confirmed that, at least. And I assumed they would try to persuade me to turn George down – for one thing, Freda had only been gone a few weeks, and the unseemly haste would presumably seem to them crass and insensitive. I couldn't imagine that George would have shared with them that I was their mother's choice, as well as his.

I had spent much of the afternoon running through what George's daughters might say, and how I might avoid becoming enmeshed in any discussion. Perhaps I should have simply said no, when Melissa had asked if they could call. But what reason would I have given? Better, perhaps, to face up to what they had to say, and at least to listen, even if it was uncomfortable.

Later, I reflected that 'uncomfortable' didn't even begin to cover it.

While they sat in my living room, I made the tea and cut up the cake. I hadn't even asked whether they wanted tea, but had just said, nervously, "It's good to see you both. Please make yourselves at home and I'll fetch us some tea," and then retreated to the kitchen.

Waiting for the kettle to boil, I could hear their murmuring voices, but it was only as I approached the door, which I'd left ajar, with the tray, and prepared to push it open with my foot, that I could make out what they were saying. What I heard stopped me in my tracks.

"So, do you think that maybe the mother set her cap at him, and when she got nowhere the daughter tried her hand? And as she's young, and not bad looking, dad just turned into putty in her hands?"

"That's one possibility. Certainly when they were going through dad's papers they will have got a very clear idea about how wealthy he is. He's a catch, Mel – we both know that. What bothers me most is the thought that she's young enough to have children, and, if that happens, what about the inheritance that should come to us, and to *our* children in due course?"

"Surely dad wouldn't be interested in a second family at his age? He's a grandfather, for God's sake."

"But he's besotted! You heard how he talked about her last night. I think she has him wrapped round her little finger already. He would do whatever she wanted him to do. It's – disgusting, really."

I was rooted to the spot. I couldn't move, either forwards into the room, or back to deposit the tray on the kitchen counter. I wanted to stop listening, to cause a distraction – for a moment the thought of dropping the tray seemed like a possible way out of this excruciating situation.

"There is one other thing that occurred to me, Mel. How long have mum and dad known Eve?"

"A few years, I think – since she started working in the library. Why?"

"What if the relationship started while mum was still alive? What if..."

I couldn't bear it. I pushed the door harder than I planned to, and it swung back and struck the wall. I stood framed in the doorway, still clutching the tray with the tea things and the ridiculous lemon drizzle cake. They raised their eyes and looked at me and suddenly, I knew – from their raised voices, their steady gaze, and their lifted chins, that they had planned this, and had, in fact, intended me to hear every word.

"And then I just asked them to leave. And they got up and left. They'd actually done what they came to do. It was horrible, mum – I can't even find the words to explain how horrible."

Mum sat beside me, her arm round me, as I sobbed.

"Oh, Eve - I'm so sorry. What a terrible experience. I can only think that they are still so distraught about their mother's death that they're channelling all their anger and frustration in your direction and that's making them cruel. They're George and Freda's daughters – I can't believe that a kind, gentle couple like the Buckleys would produce such venomous offspring. But it's good that you didn't argue, or break down in front of them. You just got rid of them, which seems a dignified thing to do."

"Yes. The only thing I feel grateful for is that I managed to stay calm, and I didn't shout or cry or anything – at least until I got here!" I gave mum a watery smile.

"So what will you do? Will you tell George? Or I could tell him if you wanted me to?"

I shook my head.

"Whatever I decide, and whatever I say to George, I don't want to cause him any more pain than I have to. And I can't imagine how he would feel if I repeated their words to him. I think they both know that, and that's why they were prepared to say it. I suppose they could even deny it... I can't put him in that position."

"Has it confirmed your decision to say no to him?"

"Oh, mum – that's the worst thing of all. Do I turn him down because of what his daughters have said and done? So their strategy will have been successful? It was even worse than I could ever have expected – for them to say to my face what their objections or concerns were would have been one thing, but the way they did it – knowing I would overhear, and what they said about you, and..."

"Shush," said mum, as my tears started to flow again. "It's over now. It was terrible, but it's over. You're here, you're safe. Whatever you decide about George, you can see as little of Sarah and Melissa as you choose. But you will make your mind up – you won't be bullied. You're stronger than you think, Eve."

I hoped she was right.

The following evening, I was at home in the flat when the phone rang, and I stiffened. Might it be George? Or Sarah or Melissa? I'd spoken to mum briefly earlier so thought it was unlikely to be her. I considered letting it ring out, but then I gave myself a shake and picked it up.

"Eve!" the line crackled.

"Birgit! It's so good to hear from you!"

"And I have news - good news, Eve. Helmut is coming to London for a long weekend with work. Mutti has agreed to look after the twins, and so I am coming with him for a break. Can we see each other? Would you come down to London on the train and meet me on Sunday?"

I blew out my breath.

"Birgit – I can't think of one single thing I would rather do..."

We had the most wonderful day. We walked in the parks, we ate lunch in a little French bistro – "This is what it will be like when we meet in Paris, Eve – except we will be in Paris!" – and we talked and talked. Birgit shared with me the news that she was pregnant again. "The girls are five now, and they are delicious, but it is time. I feel it is a boy..." and I told her about

George – and about his daughters. She was suitably shocked, and outraged on my behalf. But she was more interested in the proposal, and what it might mean for my life, than she was in the girls' toxic reaction.

"You must do what is right for you, Eve. You have to look into your heart and decide what you really want. Not all marriages are about romance and passion..." My mother had said the same thing. "Relationships can work because of strong affection, care, respect. And if you do want children with this man, and perhaps grandchildren in due course, you can't let his spiteful daughters ruin that for you both."

On the train home, Birgit's words went round and round in my head. I did care for George, and I believed that he loved me. We could have a good life – companionship, comfort, developing mutual interests. Sarah and Melissa might never accept me, but this wasn't about them, after all. It was about George and me, and a possible future together.

And the alternative was a return to my ordered, solitary contentment. My mother – though, of course, she wouldn't be there forever; my work; my home. My few friends, like Birgit, and the interests that brought me joy. Life could be good, whichever path I chose.

The following Saturday evening, I invited George to the flat for a meal. I prepared the meal with great care, absorbing myself in the task to occupy my mind and to try to keep my nervousness at bay. George brought flowers, chocolates and an expensive bottle of wine. We chatted about inconsequential things, enjoyed the food and the soft candlelight. When I eventually rose to clear the dishes and then to turn on the lamps, George said, "Can I ask you to show me something, Eve?"

I turned to him with my eyebrows raised.

"I've always remembered you telling us about your button box. I'd love to see it."

I smiled back at him, and turned to lift the box down from the shelf where it lived, next to my grandmother's vase which I had filled with George's flowers. I returned to the table, opened the lid, and showed him the collection.

"Would you talk me through them?"

And, one by one, I picked out the buttons I had saved over the years – 34 buttons, one for each year of my life – and explained the relevance of each one, placing it carefully on the tablecloth – a swirling spiral of memories. George was mesmerised, attentive, fascinated by the stories and what they told him about me. He smiled and nodded and I suddenly realised that I was basking in his attention. It was the kind of attention I had only ever received from my parents, and from Birgit – from the people who had loved me.

When I had finished, we both looked down at the spiral of buttons, and then I looked up at him and smiled.

"Yes, George," I said quietly. "I will share my life with you."

Chapter Sixteen: 1993

George insisted on making a fuss as my 40th birthday approached.

"I really don't want a party, George," I warned him, "and certainly not a surprise party. Please, no."

What I really wanted was a quiet meal with George and my mother – my two favourite people in the world. What I really didn't want was a family celebration which included Sarah and Melissa and their families.

George's daughters had never forgiven me for accepting George's proposal five years before. They were civil enough when George was around, but if ever I found myself alone with one of them – or, worse still, with both of them – the snide comments and sarcastic digs continued unabated, and I never became immune to their power to hurt.

George was, as I knew he would be, a loving and solicitous husband, always concerned about my comfort, my well-being, and what might bring me joy. I couldn't share with him my concerns about Sarah and Melissa, as I knew it would deeply distress him. I avoided them as far as I could, which had actually been considerably easier than I might have feared.

George would have liked me to have given up my work at the library so that we could spend even more time together and do more travelling. But I was insistent that I loved my job and wanted to carry on working. I had, in fact, been promoted to principal librarian when Margot had retired, so I had more responsibility, which I relished, and even greater opportunity to use my initiative and develop our services in ways I thought would be well-received and useful in the community. I found I loved appointing staff, and then supporting them and helping them to develop; I had an unexpected flair for leadership, I discovered. Helping others to achieve their professional best was deeply satisfying to me.

But George and I did get away whenever we could, and over the past five years we had had some wonderful holidays, and I had seen more of the world than I ever anticipated. Best of all, George was very amenable to the idea of inviting my mother along whenever we could get her to agree to join us. The three of us got along extremely well, and we had enjoyed so many memorable trips over the last few years. I had managed to move George on from cruises – he persuaded me to try one, around the seas of Italy, in the first year of our marriage. I found the experience of being on the cruise ship far less palatable than George and Freda had always found it, although I loved the places we visited. I convinced George – without too much difficulty; he was an easy-going and receptive man – that travelling as a pair, or as a three, could actually be far more interesting and enjoyable than being herded around in a cruise ship party.

So I had a generous, agreeable husband, whose company and conversation I appreciated. My mother, now in her seventies, remained in good health and positive spirits. I found my professional life fulfilling. I loved the old farmhouse, and its beautiful garden. Making it into our home, rather than simply inheriting the home Freda had created, had given me great pleasure. If George's family caused me pain, I could find a way of living with that.

In the first few months of our marriage, there was one memorable day when George and I had looked after Jenny, who was then four years old. It was the first time she had stayed with us on her own. Melissa was expecting her second child, and had a hospital appointment. Her husband, Alan, was at work, as were Sarah and her husband Jonathan. I could tell that Melissa didn't relish the prospect of leaving her daughter with me, but George was a doting grandfather, and he was very keen that we should take care of the little girl. Melissa delivered the child to the cottage, and then she had driven herself to the hospital, promising to be back within a couple of hours.

It poured with rain. I made lunch and the three of us shared the meal – though we couldn't persuade Jenny to eat very much. We sat by the fire, where Jenny played with her dolls for a while, and then she began to handle the books Melissa had packed for her, picking each one up in turn but discarding it quickly. George tried reading to her, but she lost interest and wriggled away. He tried to entertain her, but the child couldn't seem to settle to anything and she became quickly bored and then started to whine for her mother.

An idea occurred to me. I went up to our bedroom, where I kept nana's button collection on the top shelf of the wardrobe - still in its original tin, with the picture of "Princesses Elizabeth and Margaret Rose" patting the corgi.

I brought it back into the lounge and set it on the table in the bay window.

"Jenny – would you like to look at this? I think you might find it interesting."

The little girl looked up at me and, when I said no more, she stood and came across to me. I lifted her up and sat her on my knee.

"The treasures inside this tin are quite small, Jenny, and it's important that you don't put any of them into your mouth. Do you understand that?"

I remembered my grandmother saying something similar to me, all those years before.

Jenny looked up at me solemnly, her eyes wide.

"I need to know you understand what I'm saying, Jenny. They're not to go into your mouth. Show me you know what I mean?"

Jenny said nothing, but she gave a nod.

"Good. Now some of these are very old, and quite delicate and precious, so you have to handle them carefully. Can you do that?"

She nodded a second time. I could see George watching us both from his armchair.

"So shall we take off the lid and have a good look at what's inside?"

I waited until Jenny nodded once more – and then I gently levered off the lid, for the first time in a number of years, I realised. Had I actually handled nana's tin of buttons since that day when we were clearing out my grandmother's house after her death, the day when mum and I had looked through them together, fifteen years before? I remembered packing up my flat in the days following our wedding, and placing the tin carefully into one of the removal firm's boxes. I took it out again when I moved into George's home and decided where I would keep it. But I didn't think I had opened the tin up at either stage.

The buttons, in all their glory, filled the tin, and Jenny peered in at the different colours, shapes and sizes. For the first time that afternoon, it seemed something had caught her interest. I lifted one of her small, pudgy hands, and guided it into the tin so she could feel the different textures, and let the buttons run through her fingers.

"What do you think? Do you like them?"

That nod again, but she also turned and looked up at me, and I saw the ghost of a smile on her face.

"We can take them out of the tin and look at them more closely. Are there any you especially like?"

After a few seconds of deliberation, Jenny reached in and extracted a small, black, shining button, and she brought it closer to look at it properly.

"That's a good choice, Jenny. It's made out of jet, which is precious, and it's very old. Much older than your grandad, in fact." I could sense George smiling from the other side of the room, but he didn't interrupt us. He just watched us, and listened.

Jenny, who could be quite a voluble child, I knew, was quiet and, it seemed, thoughtful as she played with the buttons. I kept her on my knee, and watched her carefully, as she lifted buttons out, arranged them on the table, and returned some to the tin. I chatted quietly to her about the buttons she selected – I knew the story behind some of them, and I speculated about the possible stories behind others. We must have been absorbed in this activity for about half an hour, I think, when I heard a car in the drive and realised her mother had returned. Melissa let herself into the house – both daughters always did that, as they had when their mother was alive – and she found us in the lounge.

The next thing I knew, she had swept Jenny off my knee and was shrieking, "What are you doing! Don't you realise they're a choking hazard!"

She was glaring at me, and I was taken aback by her vehemence.

George and I both started to speak at the same time.

"It's all right, I made sure…"

"Melissa, love, she's fine.."

"Do you have no common sense at all?"

I took a breath.

"Melissa – I explained really carefully that she wasn't to put any in her mouth…"

"She's four years old - you can't reason with a child of Jenny's age! You know nothing about children!" and she swept from the room, clutching Jenny, who was now wailing in protest. George followed her.

"Darling…" I heard him say in a tone of quiet protest.

I closed my eyes and steadied my breathing.

Did she really feel her child had been in danger, or was this all a melodramatic way of demonstrating my incompetence - another way of showing I was an unfit wife for her father?

I slowly returned the buttons to the tin, and replaced the lid. I thought of my four year old self - or was I still three? - being introduced to the buttons for the first time. I thought of how Jenny had seemed mesmerised by the collection, as I had been. And I realised that this was, no doubt, the last time she would see it.

I moved towards the fireplace and started to pick up Jenny's dolls and books, and return them to the backpack Melissa had brought with her earlier that day. I could hear Melissa's raised voice, Jenny's crying and George's placating tones from the kitchen. I doubted that there was anything I could do to win the approval, or even the trust, of George's daughters.

When George and I had a family of our own, I thought on that afternoon, Sarah and Melissa would hate it – I remembered what they had said that day in my flat, voices deliberately raised so that I would hear, about their threatened inheritance. But George and I would love our children, and when I wanted to introduce our son or daughter to the miracle of the button box, I would be able to do that. Responsibly, safely, but enthusiastically. No one would be able to take that away from me.

Now, on the eve of my fortieth birthday, I was reconciled to the fact that I would never have children. George was a gentle, sensitive lover, and our intimate life was pleasurable, though hardly passionate. But month after month, and then year after year, had passed, and I did not conceive. Finally, in my late thirties, I had said to George that I feared I was getting too old, in any case. I was disappointed to see what I felt was a look of relief on his face. I realised that he was prepared to father our children, if that's what I wanted, but that he himself didn't relish the thought of becoming a new parent in his early sixties. Could I blame him?

He looked at me now, with a quizzical expression on his face.

"So, tell me, Eve – what *would* you like to do to celebrate your special birthday?"

And suddenly, I knew exactly what the answer was.

"I'd love to go away for a long weekend, George. I can arrange cover from the library. I'd like mum to come too, if that's all right – I have spent my birthday with mum for the last thirty nine years, and I'd really miss her if we were apart."

"That all sounds perfectly reasonable. And where were you thinking of me taking you?"

"I'd like to go back to Nuremberg."

George smiled.

So I spent my fortieth birthday in the company of George and my mother, but also with Birgit and Helmut, Birgit's parents, her brother Werner and his wife and their three children, and Birgit's twin girls and her son, Jan, now aged six. So we were a family party, but the right family – a family I knew loved me and who I didn't mind at all making a fuss of me. Birgit and

Helmut had moved from Munich back to Nuremberg to be near her parents as they grew older. George and I had been out to see them all a couple of times – I was keen to introduce Birgit and George, as each of them had heard so much about the other. They liked each other, and watching them chat and laugh with one another gave me a deep sense of peace and contentment.

Before we left Nuremberg to travel to Hamburg and then to fly home, Birgit and I managed a short walk on our own. It was snowing, and we wrapped up well. For my birthday, George had bought me the most beautiful cashmere coat, a soft grey with a fur collar, and I wore that now. Nuremberg was ready for Christmas and looked beautiful in its coloured lights.

"So did you enjoy your birthday?"

"It was perfect. I couldn't imagine a better way of spending it - thanks for welcoming us, and for arranging for your parents and Werner and his tribe to be here, too."

"They all wanted to be. They love you too, you know!"

"It feels wonderful to be part of a large, warm family. I feel blessed in the relationship I have with my mother, but there have only been the two of us for so long, now. And George's family…"

I needed to say no more.

Birgit squeezed my arm gently.

"And have you come to terms with not having children of your own, do you think?"

I had shared my hopes, and then my regular disappointments, with Birgit over the years.

"As far as I can, I think. I have a good life, Birgit. Marrying George was definitely the right thing for me. I am lucky in so many ways, and I know that I need to appreciate my good fortune and not just focus on the things that I don't have."

"We all have to do that, I think!"

There was a pause as we walked on, our boots crunching in the snow.

"And have you chosen the button for your box? The fortieth one!"

"I have! There's a spare button sewn into the lining of this beautiful coat, and that's what I'll put into the box this year. I always want to remember George's gift to me on my fortieth birthday!"

"It is stunning, I agree. Do you know, I think it reminds me of something..."

I laughed.

"Me, too! It's the grey maxi coat you wore when we were 17. I always coveted that coat!"

"It's a wonderful gift – I saw the delight on your face when you unwrapped it. And what had George written in the card which made you laugh – can you tell me?"

"Of course! He'd written 'to the one who always makes my teaspoons shine'... It's something of a private joke!"

"He's a good man - and a loving husband."

"He is. He's made me happier than I could ever have imagined."

"I am so pleased – and thrilled that you chose to spend your special birthday with us."

And we hugged each other, before turning, arm in arm, and heading for home.

Chapter Seventeen: 2001

I was at work on 11th September, 2001, when the Twin Towers were attacked. It was a terrible, shocking day, on which we watched the footage on the library computers in a stunned silence. All those who came into the library as the afternoon wore on wanted to talk about it, and what it might mean – about how watching it happen made us think of a scene from a disaster movie, rather than something that we could understand as happening in real life, in real time, in a city many of us had visited. George had taken me to New York early in our marriage, and we had both loved it.

It was our late night opening, and I was torn between remaining open so that our visitors had somewhere to come and to talk, if that's what they wished to do, or to close early and allow the staff to go home and be with their families, if that's what *they* wanted to do. Iram, a young Muslim woman who worked in our administration support office, had quietly approached me as soon as the news had been released to ask if she could go home to pray, and I hugged her and she slipped away. No one else had said anything about wanting to leave, but in the end I gathered the staff together and gave them the choice – several accepted the offer to go home then, and a few remained with me until our usual closing time on that day.

"It's perfectly acceptable if we operate a skeleton service today," I told the ones who stayed. "Just be available to help people, or to listen to them, if that's what they want. Other work can be put on hold for now."

Our library was usually a calm and quiet place, but today the atmosphere felt different, and the mood understandably sombre.

I was thoughtful as I walked home that evening. I had rung mum from the library to check how she was, and whether she wanted me to drive round to see her, but she said she was fine. It was actually the evening she played bridge, and the three friends she was due to be with had suggested they all got together as planned, but just to talk, rather than to play the game.

"But will *you* be OK on your own, Eve?"

It was three years since George's death. I still missed him every day, and especially on a day like today when we would have talked it all out – he would have helped me to process what I was thinking and feeling, and he would have listened, and shown me how much he cared about me. But, as always, I was quick to reassure my mother.

"I'm all right, mum. A quiet night on my own will suit me very well, though I think I'll ring Birgit later on, just to see how they all are."

"That's a good idea. And I'm looking forward to our lunch at the weekend – but just call if you want to talk, or you want us to get together, before then."

"I will. Thanks, mum. I love you."

"And I love you – very much. See you soon."

My mother, who would be 80 the following year, was still a calm and capable woman. She had been a tremendous support to me during George's illness. It had been only two months between the diagnosis of pancreatic cancer and his death, at the age of 67. We had just celebrated our tenth wedding anniversary when he fell ill.

I wrapped up warmly and took my cup of tea out into the courtyard garden. After George's death I had sold the farmhouse and bought myself a ground floor flat near the library – it was good to be able to walk to work again. I had looked at a number of possible properties, but it was the courtyard garden of this one which had swung it for me. I sat outside whenever I could, watching and listening to the birds, tending the pots and the climbing plants, feeling the sun on my face whenever it shone.

I sipped my tea and thought back to those last weeks with George, and to the reaction of his daughters after the funeral: "You robbed us of our father – his time, his attention, his love!" Sarah had sobbed. At least the reading of the will hadn't caused conflict. When George and I married I insisted that he made clear in his will that all his investments, his savings, his stocks and shares should be divided equally between the two girls. The only thing that came to me was the house, but that was enough – all I needed, or wanted. I had sold it, bought the flat and invested the rest of the money. The income from that, my salary from the library and then my pension in due course, would enable me to live comfortably for the rest of my days.

I hadn't seen Sarah or Melissa since the day on which the will was read. Mum told me she had heard that Melissa and her family had emigrated to Canada six months after her father's death.

I wasn't unhappy. I still found my job fulfilling. I had, once or twice, considered moving to a different library, perhaps a larger one, which might bring new challenges. But in the end I had decided to stay where I was. I had a brilliant team to work with – all had joined us since Margot retired so I had had the opportunity to appoint them all myself. I enjoyed their company and felt invested in, and proud of, their professional achievements. I reflected on how young I had been when I started working there – the youngest employee by quite a few years. And now I was the longest serving and the oldest. Those years seemed to have passed so quickly.

I had hobbies and interests, and a few friends, though, like my mother, I had never enjoyed - or, indeed, wished for – a large social circle. I still considered Birgit to be my best friend, and, although we didn't see each other often, we kept in touch by email and spoke on the phone. I looked forward to ringing her later that evening and knew it might help us both to talk through the day's events.

I had never expected to marry, but I had been fortunate in my husband and, although ten years was too short a time to be together, it had been a very good decade. Even despite the tension emanating from the rest of George's family – which he was inevitably aware of, but which we never discussed – these were years of contentment and comfort, and I had no regrets. Now, at the age of 47, my life had settled into a particular groove, and I didn't anticipate anything would happen to disrupt that significantly. I pulled my shawl more closely around me against the early evening chill, and relished the prospect of my conversation with Birgit.

It was a month later when Tamara came to the library for the first time. I was at the desk, when she reached up from her wheelchair and placed 'Discovering Old Buttons', by Primrose Peacock, in front of me.

"For sure, that can't be a real person's name," she said, in a lilting Irish voice, and she smiled up at me. I registered green eyes and a shock of red curls. "I'd very much like to borrow this, if I may, but I've just moved into the area and don't yet have a library card. Is it possible to sign up, or register, or whatever the term is, and take a book home with me today?"

I smiled back at her. "As long as you have some proof of your address, that will be fine," I said. "And that's an interesting choice of book."

"Have you read it?"

"I have. I think I've read everything we have about buttons."

"Really? I don't think I've ever met anyone who is fascinated by buttons, like I am..."

"And I can say the same!"

Tamara held out her hand. "I'm Tamara. I'm a seamstress."

"I'm very pleased to meet you. I'm Eve – and I'm a librarian!" and we both laughed.

"Could you point me towards the other books about buttons you have here?"

"I certainly will. Shall we sort your library card out first?"

"That sounds like a plan. And would you be up for joining me for a coffee at some stage and we can talk buttons? And that's a phrase I've never had the chance to use before..."

The pace at which our friendship developed over the coming weeks was astonishing to me. Only with Birgit, with George and my mother had I felt so comfortable, so much at ease. Tamara worked for herself, making costumes on commission for theatres, for televised costume dramas and occasionally for films. Authenticity was important to her, so she carried out careful research before undertaking a new piece of work. She had a specially adapted sewing machine which she could operate from her chair, and it was wonderful to watch her at work – she was amazingly skilled and had such flair. Her hand sewing, too, was meticulous and magical, to me.

"Most of my work comes to me through word of mouth. You know? You produce something and it's well received, and people talk to people, and other offers of work come in."

"It also helps that you're incredibly talented, Tamara!"

"Well, I certainly have plenty of experience. And I love what I do – so I consider myself lucky."

And she did. I had never met anyone who was so positive, so confident and comfortable in her own skin.

When I knew her a little better I felt I could ask about the chair.

"A riding accident a few years ago. Pretty grim at the time, I admit. My legs are weak, but the rest of me works perfectly well," she said with a twinkle in her eye. "I do all right – I even go riding, from time to time, though it's a different kind of exercise when your legs don't work quite so well. It is great to be up on a horse, though. They're wonderful creatures. Have you ever been riding?"

"Never!"

"I'll take you one day."

"Tamara – I'm not far off fifty years old! I think it's a bit late for me to be taking up horse-riding!"

"Catch yourself on, Eve! You're fit and healthy. In the prime of your life, I'd say. You'd be fine!" and her eyes shone as she smiled.

Tamara was ten years younger than me. She had lived in Northern Ireland for most of her life, but had "fancied a change", as she put it, and had chosen this part of England as she had two younger brothers, Dan and Eamon, who lived in the area.

"You must meet them, Eve – they're a hoot!"

And so I did, and they were. I took Tamara to meet my mother, too, and the two of them quickly warmed to each other, I could see. Mum rang me later.

"She's lovely, Eve. And I'm so pleased to see you make another good friend."

"Yes – who would have thought it, at this time of my life. And that a mutual love of buttons would have brought us together!"

I had shown Tamara my box of buttons and explained the provenance of each one, including Birgit's buttons and the important part she had played in my life. Tamara showed real enthusiasm for my collection - and she was knowledgeable about the older buttons, sharing with me some things I hadn't been aware of.

"It's such a great idea, Eve. I have a friend who has kept a diary since she was a girl, and she now rereads her diary entries from 'this day in history' ten, twenty and thirty years ago, after she's recorded her current entry. It really makes me wish I'd had the discipline to keep a diary of my own. And I feel the same about your button box – why didn't I think of that and do what you've done?"

She was thoughtful for a while, and then said, a little hesitantly, "When is your birthday?"

"December - the 19th. Why?"

"Would you mind if I gifted you the next button for your box?"

"I'd be thrilled! Did you have something specific in mind?"

"I do. But I'm not going to tell you – it will be a surprise. Maybe I can take you out for a meal on your birthday – your mum, too?"

Already Tamara knew me well enough to realise I would want my mother to be part of any birthday celebration.

"That would be lovely. Thank you."

One evening towards the end of November, after several glasses of wine in my flat, our talk turned to the subject of Tamara's disability.

"Would you tell me about how your life changed after the accident?" I asked.

"Well, life in a wheelchair is interesting. You probably don't realise how wheelchair-unfriendly many places are until you're in one. And it's certainly true that people treat you differently. Your disability seems to make some other people uncomfortable, which is crazy, when you think about it. But in my case, it isn't just the chair that sets me apart."

I looked at her and waited for her to continue.

"Think about it. I'm a woman. I'm from Northern Ireland. I'm disabled..." she paused and looked steadily at me for a few seconds, "and I'm gay. I have the full bingo card, Eve. If you're prejudiced, take your pick..."

"But I'm not - "

"No! Sorry, Eve - I didn't mean if YOU were prejudiced. I just meant, if anyone is prejudiced, I could be a target of that for several reasons. But the idea of being a 'victim', or someone who's 'vulnerable', or 'disadvantaged', just doesn't sit easily with me." Tamara sipped her wine and looked into the fire.

"I've never known anyone less likely to feel sorry for themselves, that's for sure," I offered.

She grinned.

"You know someone asked me about equality recently, and what it meant to me," Tamara continued.

"And you said...?"

"I said it isn't about being treated the same as everyone else. But it is absolutely about being valued for who you are. I'm a woman, I'm Irish, I'm disabled, I'm gay. But none of those things define me. They're just all part of who I am - what I am. I'm so much more than that."

"You certainly are. You're wonderful."

"And so are you, Eve. I'm so glad that we found each other."

And one week later, my birthday present button from Tamara was a very old button – the oldest button in my collection, and older than anything in my nana's button tin, either. Tamara had come across it in the course of one of her professional research projects. It was very delicate, made out of shell. It was, I thought, probably the most beautiful button I had owned. Tamara packaged it in its own tiny box, to protect it from any possibility of damage. She handed it to me before we left my flat to pick up my mother and go for our celebratory meal. We were sitting side by side on the sofa.

"I give you this, with my love," Tamara said, as she passed the gift to me. And she kissed me.

Chapter Eighteen: 2003

"I'd like to take you to Northern Ireland for your birthday, Eve – would you like that?"

It was a Sunday morning in December, and we were enjoying a leisurely breakfast. We had converted the smaller bedroom to a sewing room for Tamara when she had moved in with me, as well as making other changes so that the flat was as accessible as possible. Tamara was happy working from her new base, but she had taken the decision not to work on Sundays so that we could always spend the day together. Often we went out for the day, perhaps visiting her brothers, or my mother, or driving out to enjoy Sunday lunch in a country pub. Sometimes we travelled further afield, exploring parts of England that Tamara was keen to get to know better. And sometimes we just stayed at home, lit the fire, read the papers, chatted and drifted and pottered, enjoying each other's company.

Tamara had turned forty that summer, and my next birthday was my fiftieth, so we had talked of doing something special. I knew Dan and Eamon and their families well, by now, and had met Tamara's parents on several occasions when they came over to visit, but I had never been to Northern Ireland, and I liked that Tamara wanted to show me her home.

"I'd like that very much."

"Shall we ask your mum, too?"

I was thoughtful.

"I'll talk to her about it, and we'll see what she thinks." I was acutely aware of the fact that, since she had turned 80, mum had become a little less confident about travel, especially if walking any distance was involved. Increasingly she spent time at home – the same home we had moved into when I was still at school. She listened to music, she read a good deal, she still sewed a little (though her curtain-making days were behind her) and she seemed reasonably content with her lot.

She had a small number of friends whose company she enjoyed. But we hadn't been away together for some time.

"I like my own bed these days, Eve," she had said, smiling at me.

She had been completely supportive of my relationship with Tamara, and was simply happy that I was so happy. I remembered the night of my birthday two years before, when we picked mum up to take her to the restaurant we had booked, and she had hugged me and whispered, "You're *glowing*, Eve!" and I realised that she knew exactly what was happening. After Tamara and I had announced our intention to live together, mum explained how pleased she was.

"When George proposed, and you were undecided about whether to accept, I remember being careful to try not to tell you what to do. But when you did say yes, I was relieved because I thought that…when I'm no longer here – no, don't interrupt me, Eve, I need to say this – after I die, I couldn't bear the thought of you being alone. Obviously, I intend to live to a ripe old age," she smiled, "but one day I won't be with you, and the thought of you with a husband, and perhaps children of your own, was comforting to me."

My childlessness still gave me a pang if I stopped to think about it, and mum knew how difficult those years of anticipation and disappointment had been.

"I am sorry that you didn't have children – as I know you are," mum continued, "and sorry that your time with George was so brief – he was a good man. But now you've found Tamara, and I can see so clearly how well-suited you are, and how happy you make each other. And so I feel, again, that sense of relief that you have someone to share your life with, and who will be there to support and sustain you when – well, you know what."

"I do understand mum. But it's hard to think about the day when you won't be with us."

"I know that, Eve. But I've actually come to terms with the fact that I won't always be around – it may be entering my ninth decade which has really brought that home to me! And death doesn't frighten me. I've had a good life and there's been so much to feel grateful for. I lost your dad too early, but will always feel I was blessed to have the relationship we had – and the love of a good daughter, too! Anyway, definitely time for a change of subject. I want to show you my latest jigsaw..."

So Tamara and I travelled to Northern Ireland on our own. We took the ferry from Liverpool to Belfast, and then I drove us to the small seaside town where Tamara's parents lived.

Tamara had talked of the beauty of her home, but I think I was unprepared for how stunning it was. The weather was cold, but fine and bright, and during the four days we spent there we drove along the coastal roads, and through the glens, stopping at various places she wanted to show me. The blue of the sky, the expanse of the sea and the rugged landscape took my breath away. I met several members of Tamara's extended family, and some of her closest friends. She and I spent time in the town's small harbour and then sat, well wrapped-up, on the sandy beach. Perhaps inevitably, visiting the place where she had been born and brought up made Tamara reflective, and she talked a lot about her early memories – both positive, and more difficult.

"Do you ever regret leaving?"

She shook her head.

"I do miss my parents and the friends who are still here, and it's just grand to come back to visit, but this is a small place, and not everyone turned out to be enlightened when it came to my sexuality. I think it's getting better now, but when I came out in the nineties I found it difficult in such a tight community. The first time I visited Dan and Eamon in England, I could see how liberating it could be to live among people who didn't know me, and my family going back for generations. I didn't feel the same weight of judgment. And they didn't know the Tamara from before the accident, and the difficult times I'd been through as I started to reshape my life. They didn't look at me with the same pity in their eyes. Coming to England gave me the chance to establish myself in a new place, and that, and meeting you, has helped me to find peace."

"It must have been hard for your parents when you decided to leave – and that must have made it difficult for you, too."

"It was. But they've been so supportive. They're like your mum. They just want me to be happy and I think they're proud of my independence and how I've carved out a career for myself. It's so important to me that they've accepted and respected my choices."

"They have been so welcoming of me – as have your friends. I'm so pleased you brought me. Are you getting cold? Shall we move on?"

"Yes – I am a little. Let's go back to the car. There's another harbour along the coast I want to show you. There's a great walkway the chair can cope with, and we can look out to sea and watch the ferry making its way over to the island. Let's come back in the summer and take the ferry out there. And there's an amazing ice cream place I'd like to share with you then."

I loved the fact that we were always planning for the future.

On our last night there, we went to the tiny local pub where we sat sipping our whiskey in front of the glowing peat fire in the snug, listening to the sounds of the fiddle player drifting through from the bar. I talked to Tamara of a conversation I had had with her mother while we were washing up together after tea.

"She told me about choosing your name, and the fact that some of her friends were scandalised that she chose a name they'd never heard before – and certainly not a traditional Irish name. She said she knew from the beginning that you would plough your own furrow – her words – and not be confined by others' expectations!"

"Yes! It's one of her favourite stories. My parents were certainly more conventional in their choices of names when Dan and Eamon arrived! What else did she say?"

"Just how hard it was for you after the accident, but how she was amazed at the strength you've shown since that time – she has huge admiration for you, you know – and how pleased she is that you've found your way. She is always so pleased to welcome you back here, though – she says 'the longest road out can sometimes be the shortest road home'. "

Tamara grinned.

"I've certainly heard *that* saying a few times in my life! And I'm so pleased about the button, Eve."

Tamara's mother, like my mother and her own daughter, was a keen sewer. She had heard of my button box, and had been eager to show me her own collection, insisting that I choose one from it as a keepsake, and I was able to select a button saved from one of Tamara's childhood outfits. That would be this year's addition to the box on my birthday.

When we left, Tamara hugged her parents hard, and I saw that her eyes filled, but she smiled through the tears and spoke of their planned visit to see us in the spring.

They hugged me too.

"Thank you for the warmth of your welcome!" I said, "I have loved being here."

"And thank you for loving our girl," Tamara's mother whispered to me as she released me from her arms.

And we began the journey back.

We had been home for a couple of days when we decided to go out for a meal, and we treated ourselves to a table at the classiest restaurant in the locality. We'd finished eating and were relaxing over what remained of our wine. I had just said something which made Tamara laugh, and she reached across and took my hand. I was becoming more comfortable with displays of affection in public places than I used to be – Tamara was demonstrative and, although I had always had a tendency to be self-conscious, I resisted pulling back in a way which I thought might hurt her feelings.

And then she said, "Don't turn and look, Eve, but there's a woman on the other side of the room who is staring at us, I think. Wait... she's walking across..."

I felt the warm pressure on my hand increase, and knew that Tamara was giving me a clear signal to be confident – in myself, and in our relationship – whatever this woman was about to say. I looked steadily into Tamara's eyes, and then I looked up, and saw Sarah.

She took in our clasped hands, the wheelchair, and the blush I felt rising to my face, but I kept hold of Tamara's hand, and I kept my voice steady as I said, "Sarah. This is Tamara. Tamara – Sarah, George's daughter."

Tamara gave a short nod. Sarah said nothing. I took a breath.

"How are you, and Jonathan? And how are Melissa and her family? I heard they'd moved to Canada. I hope she's happily settled."

Sarah looked taken aback at the questions. She glanced across the restaurant and caught the eye of the man she was presumably there with – and it wasn't Jonathan, I saw, as I followed the direction of her gaze.

"Jonathan and I are no longer together," she said.

"I'm sorry," I offered. "And Melissa – you must miss her?"

"Of course, I…"

She gave her head a sudden shake. This wasn't what she wanted to say. She drew herself up a little.

"I just wanted to ask – you're together, I assume?"

"We are."

"I knew you never loved my father."

There was a pause while I gathered my thoughts.

"It's true that what I felt for George wasn't romantic love. He knew that from the beginning, and he accepted it. I was extremely fond of him, and we were always kind to each other. We had a good ten years of marriage."

I swallowed, and was aware that Tamara was gently squeezing my hand.

"And I made him happy, Sarah. He had ten happy years with me. You know that, don't you?"

"He never loved you as he loved our mother."

"Perhaps not. But he was lonely and adrift without her, and I helped him through that. And he helped me, in many ways.

And now I'm with Tamara," and I smiled at her across the table.

Tamara smiled back, and then she looked up at Sarah, and her strength and self-assurance shone out of her. "Thanks for stopping by to say hello," Tamara said, and Sarah turned abruptly and went back to her companion. They exchanged a few words and left.

Tamara blew out her breath.

"Well, that was interesting."

"Do you know, I feel sorry for her. Thinking about it now, she lost her mother suddenly, then she lost her father, and soon after that her sister left with her family. Her marriage broke down, too, it seems. She's a sad woman."

"That's generous of you, Eve. From what you've told me she was cruel to you all through your marriage."

"She was, but she was unhappy, and perhaps still is. And I am very happy – which helps me to be forgiving! So let's pay the bill and go home."

As we made our way through the car park I realised I felt calm. The exchange with Sarah hadn't derailed me, and it certainly hadn't spoiled our evening.

"I'm surprised we haven't bumped into each other before, really," I mused. "This isn't such a big place."

"Perhaps she has seen you before, but has avoided you, do you think?" suggested Tamara. "I think it was seeing us holding hands which drove her to come across."

We were quiet as we reached the car and Tamara manoeuvred herself in and I put the chair in the back.

"I thought you were quite magnificent, by the way," Tamara picked up the conversation as we drove home. "You positively disarmed her with your charm."

"It's a strategy I've used in the library," I smiled. "If someone is rude, I find that if you are calm, and polite, and reasonable, they just run out of steam eventually. It's hard to sustain outrage if you don't get an aggressive response."

"Is that how you used to deal with Sarah and Melissa when George was alive?"

I shook my head.

"I was far too intimidated by them. It was always worse when they were together, and George wasn't around – and I tried to avoid being in that situation as far as I possibly could. But I also realise I am much stronger now – more confident, less cowed. Being with you is a large part of that, you know. You have made a huge difference to my self-belief."

"Well, I'm very glad to hear it!" Tamara grinned. "We are good for each other, aren't we? I was thinking that when I was at home. I've had my dark moments in the past, but I must say that since we've been together I've been on a much more even keel, and content."

"Yes. We're lucky, and Sarah clearly isn't. It isn't so hard to be generous, after all," and I pulled onto the drive of our home.

Chapter Nineteen: 2008

As the years passed, my mother grew physically frailer. Mentally, she was as alert and astute as ever. I knew other people whose ageing parents had retreated into the hinterland of dementia, and I felt very grateful that my mother was still the same person, that we continued to enjoy each other's company and conversation. I fell into the routine of visiting her on most days after work. We would sit in the kitchen drinking tea and chatting, and might spend a little time working together on her latest jigsaw, which mum still enjoyed, although her arthritic fingers were beginning to frustrate her and she would grumble about them as she handled the pieces. I would spend an hour or so with her before driving home to join Tamara for our evening meal.

Mum's mobility was deteriorating all the time; her legs grew weaker, and as a result she felt less confident walking outside the confines of her home and garden. She would potter among her plants outside, with the aid of a stick, and she would come out for a drive with me occasionally, but walking for any distance exhausted her, and she struggled with her breathing in a way which recalled my grandfather's respiratory problems.

The stairs in the house were also increasingly problematic, but mum was adamant that she didn't want to move. The thought that she might have to go into residential care at some stage distressed her. Even coming to live with Tamara and me in our ground floor flat was something she wouldn't consider. She did, however, concede to the installation of a stairlift, which made her life a little easier.

I broached the suggestion of a wheelchair one evening.

"It would mean I could take you out more, mum. You probably wouldn't need a motorised one like Tamara. I'm happy to push you – that might be good exercise for me, too! We could look into buying one at the mobility place in town. Shall we go and have a look at what they have at the weekend?"

"I'll think about it, Eve. I suppose it's vain of me to resist it, but I really don't feel like an old woman, even though I know I am! I think about what I used to be able to do, and how self-sufficient I was. It seems incredible to me that I'm now becoming so helpless."

I reached over and took her hand.

"I wouldn't say you were helpless at all. You're 86 and still living independently in your own home. You're mentally as quick as you ever were, and your eyesight and hearing are working perfectly fine. You are still very much my mum." I smiled at her, a little sadly.

She was quiet for a few moments.

"I do find myself thinking a lot about the past," she mused. "Perhaps that's what happens when there doesn't seem to be very much future – the past becomes so much more important."

"What do you think about?" I asked, hoping to get her to share some of her happy memories. But her response surprised me.

"I'm thinking more and more about your grandmother. And about my relationship with her over the years."

Mum looked up at the framed button collection, still hanging on the kitchen wall.

"You know I've never been religious, Eve. But I find these days I think about what might come next – whether there is some kind of life beyond death, and, if so, what that might mean. I wonder whether – in fact I fear, I suppose – I might meet my mother again 'on the other side', as they say…"

I found I didn't know how to respond to this. I squeezed her hand, and waited.

"I think about the conversation I might have with her. Whether I'd be courageous enough to ask her – and I know I never did when she was here with us - to explain why she was so cold to me over the years. I was very pleased that she was warm and loving to you, but I've never understood, or, probably, recovered from, the fact that I never felt loved by her."

I thought of my conversation with nana about Harold, the "great passion of her life", she had called him, and whether it might help my mother if I shared that story now. It wasn't an explanation, but I remembered at the time of my grandmother's death feeling there was some connection between this lost love and her relationship with her husband and daughter. But as I hesitated, my mother continued.

"I know it doesn't matter, really, and it's definitely something I should let go, but I find it preys on my mind. I don't think I believe in an afterlife. If there is one, and I had the chance to be reunited with your father, that would be blissful. Maybe that's why some people are so keen to believe in it. But coming face to face with your nana again..." Mum shivered slightly, and then turned to me with a smile. "Anyway, whatever the failings in my relationship with my own mother, I know how lucky I've been where my daughter is concerned. Now, tell me what you and Tamara are going to be getting up to this weekend." And the moment had passed.

We did visit the mobility place, and bought mum a wheelchair. I also persuaded her to invest in a 'grabber' to pick up things she had dropped, and a framed walker, for when her walking stick alone wasn't enough to help her stabilise. I helped mum into the car and loaded everything into the back, grateful that, after I'd met Tamara, I'd changed my latest mini – the last in a line of similar cars - for a considerably larger vehicle.

In the warm spring and summer days, mum and I made good use of the chair. There were several hours of daylight at the end of the working day, and we would drive out to somewhere where we could have a good walk, chatting all the time. On Sundays Tamara came with us – and she never seemed to mind that so much of our free time was now spent in my mother's company. I think we all recognised that the time was limited now, and so especially precious.

I talked to mum about organising some support from social services, and eventually she agreed to a daily visit from a carer who could call in mid-morning each day to check on whether she needed anything, to share a cup of tea with her and to chat for a while. As it became harder for mum to complete her own chores around the house – she was becoming increasingly breathless and had to stop and rest so frequently that every job she tried to tackle took ages – she agreed that I could help with her cleaning, washing and ironing. For some time I had been shopping for her, but now with the wheelchair we occasionally visited the supermarket together.

I never minded any of this. It was a labour of love, not a duty. I knew that as things became more difficult for mum, we would need to extend the support she had in place, but we would do whatever we needed to do. At the moment she was still able to get herself to bed at night, and up in the morning. I knew there would come a time when we needed to arrange additional carers to help her to do this. I was managing, for now, helped by the fact that Tamara was very supportive – emotionally and practically – doing much of what needed to be done in our own flat while I did all I could to help mum cope with living alone.

"I want to end my days in my own home, Eve," my mother had said to me at one point, holding my gaze steady.

Sadly, mum no longer had the manual dexterity to sew or knit, and I knew she missed this. She watched a little television, she read a lot, and she still had a few friends who called to see her. She had good neighbours next door, who I knew kept a careful eye on things. Tamara and I bought her a simple music system and she listened to her favourite classical pieces – by Rachmaninov, Vaughan Williams, Litolff.

"I still have things I enjoy, Eve," she said one day. It was a warm summer Sunday, and I had taken her out into the garden in the wheelchair. We had inspected her various plants – her garden had always flourished – and then she sat and tilted her face up to the sun.

"I'm not unhappy, you know. I have a lot to be grateful for. You, most of all."

"I'm pleased to hear it! I love you, mum."

"And I you, of course!" she smiled back at me.

The next morning I was at the library desk when Iram came out of the office and approached me quietly.

"There's a phone call for you, Eve. Someone called Mary Taylor?"

For a moment it felt as though my heart had stopped.

"Thank you, Iram. Could you keep an eye on the desk until Philippa arrives?"

"Of course I will. I hope everything is all right." She could see how pale I was, and I was aware my hand was shaking as I briefly touched her shoulder and hurried to take the call.

"Mary? It's Eve."

I listened to my mother's next door neighbour explaining that they had noticed mum's bedroom curtains hadn't been opened that morning. They had left it a short while but then knocked on the door. There was no reply, and they could hear no signs of movement inside.

"I'll be right there. Thank you so much for ringing me."

I grabbed my bag and coat, let Iram know I would be going out, but that our colleague Philippa should be there within the next half hour to take over the desk, and I dashed to the car. I phoned Tamara as I hurried through the streets and explained what had happened.

"I'll call a taxi and meet you there," she said.

"There may be no need - she could be fine," I replied, but the pounding of my heart told me how frightened I felt.

"No argument, Eve. I'll see you soon," and Tamara rang off.

I tried not to drive too fast, to steady my breathing and calm myself, though I wasn't completely successful. I parked the car at the kerb outside mum's house and ran down the path. My fingers were trembling as I fitted my key in her door. And then I was standing in the hallway, calling, "Mum?" in a tremulous voice.

There was no response, and I started to climb the stairs, feeling sick. I pushed open her bedroom door, and saw her, still beneath the covers. I knew.

I held her cold hand – too shocked for the tears to come, at first. I found myself slowly rocking, and then I was sobbing. The figure in the bed looked peaceful. Somehow it wasn't my mum. I found myself thinking, "Where IS my mum?" And eventually I knew – she was in my heart, and she was in my head – and would be in my memories while ever I lived. But she was no longer a physical presence in my life.

I looked around the room. Mum's clothes were neatly piled on a chair near the bed – on top, the soft grey cardigan she had knitted for herself some years before – still her favourite item of clothing. I moved towards the chair and picked it up, feeling its softness and then bringing it to my face to inhale mum's distinctive scent. As I walked back towards the bed I felt something beneath my foot. When I looked down I saw a pearly grey button, and realised that it had become detached from the cardigan at some point – perhaps mum had caught it on something as she undressed the night before. I picked it up and ran my fingers over its smooth surface. It felt like a message.

Tamara arrived at the house soon afterwards. She contacted the medical centre where mum had been a patient since she and dad had moved into their home, and a doctor came to certify the death. The firm of funeral directors we had used at the time of George's death came to remove mum to the funeral home. Tamara held me as we sat in the house in the gathering gloom; I was stunned and found it all difficult to take in.

In the weeks that followed the practicalities gave us both plenty to think about and decide. Making the arrangements for the funeral – a small, quiet affair – occupied me helpfully. There were arrangements to be made for the sorting of mum's possessions, the clearing of the house and its sale. I knew there would be a time when all that was over when the reality of the loss would hit me. I fully understood that losing a parent in their eighties is not exactly unusual, or tragic, but still I felt devastated.

On the night of 22nd November, the date when mum should have celebrated her 87th birthday, I lay in Tamara's arms and cried uncontrollably for some time, but eventually I calmed myself and we started to talk.

I told her what mum had said at the time when Tamara and I got together, seven years earlier – how pleased she was that I wouldn't be alone when the time came.

"I know there's a lot to feel grateful for – she wanted to die in her own home, and she did." My breath caught as I spoke. "The doctor said the stroke happened in her sleep and she'd have passed away peacefully – she wouldn't have been conscious of what was happening so she wouldn't have felt any pain or fear, though I hate the thought that she was alone. I always thought I'd be with her at the end. She had a good life and she appreciated that. And I feel so lucky to have had such a great relationship with her – I seem to know quite a few people who have a problematic relationship with a parent, as she did with her own mother. I'm glad I spent the last day of her life with her – we sat in the sun and chatted and I told her I loved her. It was a lovely day. She was my mum right up to the end – I know not everyone has that. So I feel that I didn't leave anything unsaid, or undone, where mum was concerned – there's nothing I regret, or feel uneasy about. So, given that her death was bound to happen at some point, there are so many positive things here."

Tamara said nothing for a moment, but just gently stroked my hair. Then she said, "I read somewhere the other day, 'Grief is just the other side of love'. "

"Yes. I can see all the positives, but still the pain is so intense. I miss her so badly – I'll just miss telling her things, and sharing things with her."

"I know."

And Tamara held me until, eventually, I fell asleep.

I put the framed collection of buttons my mother had chosen from nana's tin next to the framed collection of my own. And, when December came, the pearl button from the soft grey cardigan was added to my own button box.

Chapter Twenty: 2013

I had very much enjoyed my career, but found I was looking forward to my retirement. I had decided to finish at the library at Christmas following my 60th birthday. I was pleased that our directors had chosen Philippa as the principal librarian to replace me – I had appointed Philippa myself some years before, and had enjoyed supporting her as she grew in confidence and built her skills over the time we'd worked together. She would be assured in the role, I knew, and it felt good to be leaving the library in her capable hands.

I was keen to spend more time with Tamara at this point in my life, to travel a little more, and to have the opportunity to pursue existing interests and also to develop new ones. Because Tamara was self-employed, she was able to control how much work she committed to, and she was already starting to reduce the commissions she took on, in order to free up time too.

We started to talk about the possibility of moving. We had enjoyed living in the flat, but were ready for a change. Without my work, and without mum nearby, there was nothing to keep us in the area. Mum's house had sold easily, and we had invested the money. I still had savings from the sale of the home George and I had shared. With that and what we would get from the sale of the flat, we hoped we might be able to afford a cottage by the sea.

I had always lived inland, and a trip to the sea had been a special treat for me all my life. Tamara, having lived on the coast in Northern Ireland, missed it, I knew. The thought of living on the coast very much appealed to us both. So in the summer of the year when I would reach 60 and leave work, we decided to spend our Sundays driving to different places and looking for a possible future home.

I loved those Sundays. I would drive, and Tamara would navigate - something she was good at, and enjoyed. We explored a number of different seaside towns, some I already knew, and others that I had never visited before. We would always find a place for lunch - a pub, a bistro, a café. On the warmest days we took a picnic. And we talked, about all kinds of things. We'd always been able to move from the day-to-day, transactional exchanges to conversations on subjects that were more interesting, that made us think. On those hour-long journeys in each direction, over lunch, and as we looked round the different places we'd decided to investigate, I felt we strengthened the connection we had.

As we drove home at the end of one of these visits, I said, "It's a strange thing. We've been together for twelve years now, but on these Sundays when we've spent so much time talking about a whole range of things, I think I've got to know you even better."

Tamara grinned. "I feel the same. And it makes me so glad we're going to spend the rest of our lives together. Now we just need to find the place where we're going to spend it."

And eventually we did – a single storey cottage with a view of the sea, and access via the garden and a rickety wooden gate to the seawall which stretched in both directions. On the other side of the seawall were low dunes with their patches of marram grass, then the flatness of the beach and, beyond that, the North Sea in all its glory. The house had been empty for a while and was in need of significant renovation, but that presented us with an opportunity rather than serving as a deterrent. For one thing, we could make sure accessibility was a priority. The garden was overgrown, but it was a space with potential, and we both looked forward to transforming it over time.

While I worked my last weeks at the library, Tamara took on the task of liaising with estate agents, solicitors, the sellers of the cottage and the buyers of our flat. She enjoyed the challenge, and I was happy to leave it to her. She was organised, calm, and positively assertive when she needed to be. There were tense moments when we were unsure whether it would all work out as we hoped, but, like one of mum's jigsaw puzzles, we reached the point where the pieces slipped into place, and we moved in the spring.

There was so much to do – we needed to ensure the cottage was structurally sound, to replace doors and windows and to have a new kitchen and bathroom fitted.

"I'm back in my catalogue days!" I announced, with some enthusiasm. Tamara knew about my early obsession with order and organisation, with choosing and matching and placing, with creating a home from a floorplan.

"You're good at this," she observed. "That early training paid off, to be sure!"

We lived in mess and discomfort for the better part of six months, with workmen constantly trailing in and out – fortunately we found reliable ones who were glad of the work – and plaster dust everywhere. We had set up Tamara's sewing room as an early priority, and there were times when she felt the need to shut herself in there and get on with some work, away from the noise and the disorder, she said. But I was happy – as happy as I'd ever been, I think – directing the work, making cups of tea for the workmen and seeing our beautiful home take shape.

We left the garden untouched until the cottage itself was sorted, but once each day I would pick my way through it, down the uneven path and through the rickety gate to the sea. If Tamara came with me we would make our way along the length of the seawall. When I was on my own I would walk along the beach, by the water's edge. This became a daily ritual for me, whatever the weather, and as the wind blew and the waves crashed I breathed deeply and felt exhilaratingly alive.

And as I walked along the beach alone, I revisited my memories – time with my parents, my grandparents, with Birgit, with George, and of course with Tamara. I thought about the different homes and jobs I'd had, about what I'd experienced and what I'd learnt. I reflected on my interests, my small group of friends, the things that had given me pleasure over the years. And I thought about the things that had caused me pain. I remembered it all – I processed it all.

Sometimes I thought of my button box, and ran through in my mind how many of the sixty birthday buttons I could remember, and what their associations were. I realised how they charted my life story – the things that had mattered most to me over the years; the people who had been important; the memories I particularly treasured. I wondered how many more buttons would be added to the collection. I contemplated what I might like to happen to the button box after my death. It would become Tamara's of course, if she succeeded me – which I expected she would. Perhaps she would leave it to one of her brothers' grandchildren in due course. The thought of a young child playing with and enjoying the buttons certainly appealed to me.

As summer gave way to autumn, work on the house was eventually finished. We were both pleased with it and proud of our joint efforts. It was all we had hoped for – cosy, homely, comfortable, with everything to our taste. We then had the garden cleared, and relished planning out how we would make the most of the space. We looked forward to the spring planting.

We sat by the log fire one chill evening in late autumn, sipping wine and reading, just looking up from our books occasionally to exchange desultory remarks. After a while I became aware that Tamara was studying me.

"What is it?" I asked.

"I'm just thinking about you," she smiled.

"Well that isn't a remark you can leave there, is it? You have to elaborate!"

"I'm thinking that you really enjoyed your work, but you seem to have adapted to life after full-time work very well."

I thought for a moment.

"Yes. It's strange, I suppose, but I don't miss it. I feel grateful that I had a satisfying career for nearly forty years – I never found it boring or repetitive. I'm sure many people think of libraries as dull places, but that was never my experience. I suppose any job involving people isn't likely to be dull, because people are endlessly varied and, I think, fascinating.

So I loved it, but I think I love our life now even more. And what about you? Would you say that working on your own gets lonely sometimes, or has it ever started to feel mundane? Do you feel ready for a change?"

"No – I'm happy with how things are, though I can see myself gradually reducing the work I take on as the years pass. There are many other things I want to do now, I think. And my job has always been varied because each new commission brings its own challenges and new opportunities. I quite like my own company, so retreating to the sewing room for part of each day still suits me. But I really like that you're around all the time now, and we can spend more time together."

We lapsed into silence, and then Tamara spoke again.

"I've been thinking about Christmas. Do you have any preference for how we spend it?"

"I'd quite like to entertain, if you would – what about inviting your family over?"

Tamara gave a short laugh.

"Sometimes I think we're getting psychic. I was going to suggest we invited mum and dad over to stay for a few days, and then to see if Dan and Eamonn would like to bring the families over for Christmas Day. We couldn't put them all up overnight, but I reckon we could push tables together to seat everyone for Christmas dinner. We could manage the cooking between us, I think?"

"That would be perfect. I love our home and I'm going to love sharing it with other people in the years ahead, especially those we care about the most. It would be good to welcome your parents as our first overnight guests. I still remember how warm and welcoming they were when you first took me to stay with them."

"Grand. I'll ring them at the weekend and ask them."

"It is strange," I reflected, "having no family of my own, now."

"But my family are your family, Eve – you know that. They love you as much as they love me – I sometimes think actually more!" Tamara laughed. "You do still have living blood relatives, though, don't you? What about your father's sister you've mentioned to me before, and her family – Patricia, was it?"

"Pamela. Mum and I pretty much lost touch with them after dad died. Even the Christmas cards petered out eventually. I did write to her when I lost mum and she sent a note of condolence, 'from Pamela, David, Peter and Robin' – she had two sons – but there's been nothing since then. I should think she'll probably have grandchildren now."

"Did you send her a change of address card when we moved here?"

"I didn't – I never even thought about it, I have to say."

"Maybe you could write now, using the change of address as a reason to get back in touch. I do think family is important – don't you?"

I thought for a moment.

"I agree that my close family have always been really important to me – my parents and my grandparents. But Pamela and her family are strangers, really. I saw so little of them when I was growing up – even though Pamela was my godmother as well as my aunt. I haven't seen them at all for so many years – since dad's funeral. We don't know each other."

"And yet there's a bloodline link?"

"I'm not sure how much that means. But I will think about it, I promise. I'm certainly looking forward to seeing your family at Christmas. And working out how we can manage to seat them all comfortably in the cottage will be an interesting logistical challenge for me! I might even have to draw diagrams..."

In bed that night I thought about this conversation. I decided I would send a note to Pamela, and see if she responded. I would tell Tamara in the morning – her steady breathing told me she was already asleep. And there was something else I wanted to talk to her about too. On my daily walks along the beach I often chose to return to the cottage on the inland route, winding lanes which took me past a small and pretty church.

The last twice I had stopped and gone inside, and sat quietly in a pew looking up at the stained-glass windows and thinking.

I hadn't been brought up to practise any religion – my parents weren't observant, and the only times I had been into church, growing up, had been for weddings and funerals, or carol services and harvest festivals when I was still at school. But since my mother had died I had found myself thinking about religion, and about belief. I didn't really know what I believed, whether I had any kind of faith. But I did find sitting quietly in this church to be soothing and sustaining. I could see the valuable work that the church did in our small community, and felt a building desire to be part of that.

I wasn't sure what Tamara would think to this – she herself had been brought up within a strong Protestant family but she hadn't practised the religion for many years, and didn't appear to feel the lack of faith in her life. I knew she would always be supportive and understanding of anything I decided to do, but I suspected she would find it surprising. We would talk tomorrow, I thought, and I drifted off to sleep and dreamt of stained glass.

Chapter Twenty-One: 2019

"Should I be jealous? Paris in the spring with an old flame?"

I looked up at Tamara, but she was smiling, and I knew there wasn't going to be any tension here.

"Firstly, Birgit isn't really an 'old flame', as such. She's firmly heterosexual and nothing has ever happened between us – as I know you know. And secondly, if you would like to come with us, I know she and I would love it."

"I am teasing - as I know you know! You and Birgit need to catch up properly, and I would be a third wheel – no pun intended! You go and have a wonderful time, and I look forward to hearing every detail when you get back here."

Birgit and I had talked about meeting in Paris and spending a few days together for so many years. There were always good reasons why it didn't seem to be the right time – births and deaths and moves and all kinds of things that crop up to make you put plans on hold. But each of us had celebrated our 65th birthday recently, and so the spring of 2019 was the date when we were finally going to make it. I felt giddy about spending time with Birgit, and revisiting a city I loved but which I had not been to since I was married to George. And I loved Tamara so much but was glad that she was happy to leave us to it. Birgit and I had so much to catch up on.

The five years since we had moved into our home by the sea seemed to have passed so quickly. I had no trouble filling my days and engrossing myself in activities which brought me pleasure and satisfaction, and that included my involvement in the church community and my attendance at church services. Tamara would occasionally come with me, but she wasn't committed, as I was, and that was fine by both of us.

She was still sewing, though taking on fewer professional commitments now and spending more time on creative hand-sewing, including supplying occasional pieces for a local gift shop which sold them and took a small commission. It was a shop we both loved – tasteful rather than tacky – selling things like beautiful miniature wooden bathing huts painted in seaside colours, of which we had a fine collection displayed around our cottage. The woman who owned the shop, Millie, was a firm friend – one of several we had made over the last few years.

"I have some sewing for Millie which I need to crack on with while you're away," Tamara told me now, "so I certainly won't be bored – and you know I don't do 'lonely'. But Paris in the spring will be grand. It may well be something we should do together at some point in the future."

"That sounds like a plan. I'll scope it out this week and see what I think you and I might do while we're there. I'd better get on with the packing – I need to set off early tomorrow to get to the airport in time for check-in, so I should get everything ready tonight. I do feel a bit like a child the night before a treat. I have butterflies of excitement in my stomach and I may not sleep well tonight! And I'm 65, for goodness' sake..."

I could hear Tamara chuckling as I left the room.

Birgit and I had communicated reasonably regularly over the years. Since I had visited her and her family with George to celebrate my 40th birthday (a quarter of a century ago, I realised) we had met several times when Birgit came to the UK, and I had been out to Germany twice. In between visits we phoned, emailed and had the occasional Skype call. Birgit had always been my very best friend, and our bond had remained strong as time had passed.

She met me as I came through the barrier at Charles de Gaulle, looking stunning as ever – her fair hair now streaked with silver, she was still slim and stylishly dressed. We hugged for a long time, and laughed, and then cried a little, as we usually did when we met face to face after a long gap. And then we left the airport arm in arm and took a taxi to the hotel.

It was cold, but bright spring weather, and Paris was looking green and fresh. Over three days together we enjoyed excellent meals, did some shopping, went to a concert near the Arc de Triomphe one evening, enjoyed walking up and down the Champs Elysees at night marvelling at the mime artistes, and spent an afternoon in the Louvre. We drank coffee or wine in various cafes and bistros. We walked a huge amount – round the streets, in gardens and parks, along the Seine. And we never stopped talking.

As had always happened, despite my natural diffidence, whenever I was with Birgit she unlocked something in me, so that in her company my thoughts and my words always seemed to flow. It was partly because of the quality of her listening – she was always attentive and interested. I talked about Tamara, and life beyond work, my new-found involvement with the church, and life by the sea. I also talked about my mother's death and its effect on me still, ten years later. Birgit had come to England for the funeral, but this was the first time since then that we had spent so many hours together in conversation, and when she asked me how I felt, now, I had the strong urge to pour out things that I had only shared with Tamara. Birgit listened, squeezed my arm, understood and cared.

She told me about her family – both of her twins were now mothers themselves, and I loved hearing her talk about her three grandchildren. Her son, Jan, was to be married in the summer. Birgit's parents were both still alive, though increasingly frail. She told me of Werner – also now a grandfather – and his family. These were all people I loved, and it was so good to hear of their lives now.

"So do you miss your work?" I asked her – Birgit had had a fulfilling career as a journalist, and had only stepped back from that the year before.

"Sometimes, perhaps a little," she admitted. "But I see the sense of a slower pace of life now, and it is good to have more time for those I love. My parents need me more these days – and we help with the grandchildren as much as we can because Lotte and Luisa, and their partners, all have pressured jobs. I think I just have a different function, now. And you?"

"I loved my job but I haven't missed it, I have to say. Interestingly, the novel I read on the plane had a sentence in it that made me laugh and I thought, 'I must share this with Birgit!' ".

"What was it?"

"Wait – I have the book in my bag and I turned the corner of the page...I know that's a vandalism a professional librarian should be horrified by..." We stopped by the next bench and sat while I rummaged for it.

"Here it is. This is a good book by the way..." – Birgit and I always exchanged reading recommendations – "Here it is: 'If you can't trust a librarian, who can you trust?' It made me smile but then it made me think. I did feel I was in a position of trust and my work gave me the chance to help people – individuals and across the community. I did wonder whether without that responsibility in my life I would feel I lacked purpose. What would be the point of me anymore?" I gave a short laugh. "And it strikes me that perhaps my interest in the church is somehow related to that - needing to feel useful, and for life to have a significance beyond just pleasing myself all the time. I think community has always been important to me, even though I've always been a fairly shy and private person. Does that make sense to you?"

Birgit smiled and leaned towards me.

"You always make complete sense to me, Eve!"

Suddenly, I had a strong desire to say something to Birgit that I had never actually confessed before. I don't know what made me suddenly brave, but I found the words.

"You have made such a difference to my life, you know? You have given me comfort, brought me joy, helped me to become more confident. I remember so well the day you walked into the school library. I was smitten from that day – you were my first love, Birgit."

Birgit moved closer and rested her head gently on my shoulder.

"I know that, Eve. I have always known that. And I love you too, though not perhaps in quite the same way. I was concerned back then that our friendship might not survive a certain – imbalance? – in our feelings for each other. But I am so pleased I was wrong. It hasn't been a problem, has it?"

"No," I conceded. "I accept you for who you are, and you have done the same with me. And now I have Tamara, and we are happy."

"I see that. I was perhaps your first love, but Tamara is your great love…"

" 'The great passion of my life', " I murmured, thinking again of my grandmother. "Tamara gave me this ring for my last birthday."

"I saw it – it's beautiful. And you're wearing it on the traditional wedding ring finger, aren't you?"

"Yes. It's very special. Tamara designed it – she's so talented – and then got a local silversmith to make it to her specifications. So there's no other ring quite like it, anywhere. I love it. And it just seemed right to wear it on that finger."

"She is wonderful, I agree," said Birgit, and I thought, not for the first time, how appreciative I was that Birgit and Tamara liked each other so much.

"I did tell you how Tamara and I met, didn't I?"

"In the library, wasn't it?"

"Yes! Is it odd, do you think, that I first saw each of the two great loves of my life across a library desk?" I laughed.

"George, too? Isn't that how you met George?"

"Well, I don't remember an 'across the library desk' moment in quite the same way, but it was the library that brought me into George and Freda's orbit. But George was different. I was certainly fond of him, but it wasn't love, really. I can't feel guilty about that, because he always knew and accepted it and had made his peace with it."

"I do understand. So, Eve," Birgit sat up straight, and prepared to stand so that we could resume our walk. "We've talked of the present and we've talked of the past. What about the future?"

"Goodness – what a question!"

"Do you think about the future?"

"Only in the most general terms, I think. I don't expect we will move house again – we're settled and comfortable in the cottage, making friends locally, and, as I said, I have a strong connection to the church and to its congregation. It's different for Tamara and me in that we don't have children and grandchildren, as you do, so we don't have descendants, as such, though we are close to Tamara's brothers and their children, and Dan and Eamon will presumably have grandchildren in due course. I tried to establish contact with my aunt, my father's sister, and her family a few years ago, but sadly she didn't seem interested. So Tamara's family, and you and your family, are the people I am closest to. When I look ahead, I can't see any significant changes ahead – except for gradually ageing, of course. What about you?"

"The same, perhaps. We enjoy where we live, and our 'descendants' – I like your word! – aren't too far away. I know my parents won't be with us forever, and I understand how hard it can be when that happens. I make sure I relish every moment with them I can, now. Helmut still does some work, of course - he has resisted retirement, but there will be a time when he is too tired to carry on, and there is a sense that the older generation needs to step aside to make way for the next generation – professionally, I think."

"Yes – do you remember 'Lots of Candles, Plenty of Cake'?" I had sent Birgit Anna Quindlen's memoir when we both reached 60. It was a powerful evocation of what life can be like for women of that age, and the idea of a professional 'handing on of the baton' was one of the ideas it explored.

"I remember it so well, Eve! It has stayed with me. I loved what she said about how, if you ask someone how they feel about getting older, they start by complaining about their aches and pains and wrinkles. But then if you probe more – is that the right word? – they usually admit that they're happier now than when they were younger. They've grown into their own skin, she said."

"I think that's how I feel now. I'm more comfortable in my own skin than I've ever been – that's a phrase Tamara is fond of! But I think you're someone who has *always* seemed to be comfortable in their own skin, Birgit."

"Perhaps. I've been lucky in many ways. You have had more tragedy in your life, and some difficult times, I know."

"But somehow everything we experience is all part of making us who we are, don't you think? Even the tough stuff - maybe especially the tough stuff. And I don't have regrets. I don't wish I'd done anything very differently. I hope that doesn't sound smug."

" 'Smug' - what a delicious English word!"

And we started to make our way back to the hotel, to rest and change for our evening meal - our last one, as we were leaving Paris the next day.

We talked about lighter things over dinner. Birgit wanted to know all about the most recent additions to my button box collection, and I told her what I had chosen, and the significance of each.

"Sometimes when I'm walking on the beach I try to go through them all in my head - 65 of them now! It's like a mantra. Each one is attached to a memory - often, but not always, to a specific person. It satisfies my sense of order, somehow - something I've always been a little fixated about!"

"Your buttons, your catalogue days, your tidying, rationalising and list-making and your clutter counselling, your love of jigsaws - and your jobs in libraries - even from your schooldays. I see the pattern!"

I smiled at her across the table, and she raised her glass in the candlelight. "A toast!" she said, "To the button box of life!"

"To the button box!"

Epilogue

"So, I heard she's gone."

"Yes. She slipped away in the night, apparently. She made it to a hundred, but that was that."

"What do you think might be the cause of death?"

"I'd say probably heart failure, but it hasn't been confirmed yet. A peaceful end, at least."

"With no relatives, what happens to her effects?"

"She had very little with her. She had a ring on her wedding finger, though it didn't look like a wedding band exactly. It had obviously been there a long time and it was so deeply embedded in her finger – bad arthritis – they'll need to cut it off, I think, before the cremation. She didn't have much else on her, and nothing of value. She has property, they say, and perhaps savings - she was still managing in her own home, which is pretty amazing at that age, and given her poor sight. She had paid help, I was told – though no one who worked for her has visited her, so…. Word is that she left all she owned to the church in her will."

"What about that wooden box?"

"It's here."

"Did you open it?"

"Not yet. I was waiting for you, as we were talking about it last night. I thought we could open it together. When we know what's in it, we can decide what to do with it."

"Buttons!"

"Look at them – there are some beautiful buttons here, and so many. What's all that about, do you think?

"I suppose the box might be worth something – it is lovely. Look at the detail of the carving. Should we just tip the buttons out and take it to the charity shop, do you think?"

There was a silence, while they looked at the buttons, which the older nurse ran through her fingers, like so many precious jewels.

"I think it would be a shame to just throw them away. The colours, and the different materials they're made from – they feel… Look, there are brass buttons, and glass, and – do you think that's jet? There's one here in a little box of its own – it looks like it's made of shell, or something. So many, and such a variety. She must have been collecting them for years. There must be someone…"

"But who would want them? Do you know anyone who does hand sewing these days? Isn't it a lost art? Even people machine sewing at home seems like something from the distant past. Would these be of use to anyone these days?"

"I don't know about use, but… I do know who would love them."

"Who?"

"My granddaughter. She's five, so she's not of an age where you'd worry about a child choking on something like a button. She loves bright things. I think she'd really enjoy playing with them."

"Is it all right to take them, though?"

Her colleague stopped running her fingers through the buttons and closed the lid in a firm gesture.

"I'll ask the powers that be and find out. I just think it would be a shame for the buttons to end up dumped in the waste. This is a kind of treasure trove for a young child. I think the old lady would approve of the box and the buttons going to someone, no matter how young, who would appreciate it, you know. I'm certainly going to try. In the meantime, we need to strip the bed and get it ready for the next patient. We'd better get a wriggle on." And she set the box aside carefully, thinking of the small child whose eyes, she knew, would light up when she opened it.

Note: All the suggested questions below contain 'spoilers', so please do read the novels first!

Possible Book Club discussion group questions on 'The Dresser'

1. The narrative doesn't proceed chronologically. Did this work for you, and did it, in your view, add to the appeal of the story? If so, in what way?

2. The three main characters are clearly Alice, Laura and Jack. Was there one of these characters whom you found more interesting, credible or relatable than the others? Did you have a favourite section of the book and, if so, did your response to its central character have a bearing on that?

3. The book contains a number of secrets: Molly's drawer; James's affair; Tom's 'confession' to Jack about his love for Alice. What do you think the book had to say about secrets and the repercussions of the revelation of secrets?

4. The story also contains shocks and surprises, including Molly's death in chapter eight, and Laura's discovery of Maisie's letters in chapter fifteen. Did you anticipate either of these, and how did you respond to the turn in the narrative which each signalled?

5. How does the dresser itself bind the novel? Was this a convincing unifying device, in your view?

6. The idea of the strong village community is a feature of each section of the novel. What examples of the power of this community were you aware of? How convincing was the description of village life, did you think?

7. How were certain characters used to connect the different sections of the novel/time frames? Jack, Maisie and Joe, Eileen and Harry, and Ben Winters all appear in more than one section, and the character of Tom features

in the first and third sections. through his voice in his letters. What was the effect of this?

8. Jack's memories "both comforted and troubled him", and his relationship with Tom was very important to him. What did you think to this relationship and the significance of memory in this section of the novel, including Jack's constant rereading of Tom's letters, and his decision eventually to destroy them?

9. Did you find the chapter headings interesting? And what did you think to the way in which the Prologue and the Epilogue framed the novel?

10. Were there any other elements of the story which you particularly liked, or which you found disappointing?

Possible Book Club discussion group questions on '#OneWord'

1. Of the four main characters, Kay, Lily, Gabrielle and Sam, were there any that you found particularly easy to relate to, and why do you think that was? Were there any you found less sympathetic or credible? Again, can you explain why?
2. What did you think to the Prologue and Epilogue used to frame the story?
3. There were, as in 'The Dresser', a number of secrets, and subsequent revelations, in the book. Which did you find particularly surprising? Were the secrets generally convincing, did you think? Gabrielle says to Harry in chapter seven, "I do wonder whether we all have some things we don't share with each other, even though we're such good friends and we've known each other a very long time. Perhaps we all need our private spaces." Do you agree?
4. What would you say the book has to suggest about: friendship, family, and finding balance in our lives?
5. Was this essentially a story about *female* friendship, and is male friendship different, in your opinion? Adam asks Sam in chapter thirteen, "Do women *do* friendship differently from men?" What is your view?
6. There are a number of secondary characters we meet during the course of the year, including the women's partners, children and colleagues. Did you have any favourite characters among this group? Why did they appeal, if so?
7. "If she could live her life again, Lily reflected, she would make a number of different choices" (chapter two). Did the novel encourage you to think about the choices you have made in your life, or the choices of others?

8. Chapter twelve, where the four women all gather together in France, is the longest chapter in the novel, and it is predominantly dialogue. Did that chapter work for you? Did each character sound true to the picture of them you had built up as you read the earlier sections?

9. What did you think to the women's choice of #oneword for 2020? Were you thinking: 'Little do they know....'?

10. Were there any other elements of the story which you particularly liked, or which you found disappointing?

Possible Book Club discussion group questions on 'The Button Box'

1. This book, unlike 'The Dresser' and '#One Word', is written in first person narrative. What difference would you say that makes to the story?

2. The Prologue and Epilogue, again, frame the central story. How effective did you find that, here? The book could exist without that framing. Would it make a significant difference if the Prologue and Epilogue (which both use third person narrative) were omitted?

3. The novel charts Eve's life from her early years until her death. Did you feel her character developed in a plausible way? How would you describe how she changes as the book progresses? Could you identify with her in any way?

4. The idea of putting things in order runs through the novel. What were the main examples of this? Why is this idea significant, do you think?

5. Does the idea of the buttons (in her grandmother's tin, and in Eve's own button box) help to unify the novel? Consider, for example, the sorting of the buttons after Eve's grandmother's death in chapter eight, Birgit's response to the buttons in chapters six and nine, George's reaction to them in chapter fifteen, introducing Jenny to the button tin in chapter sixteen, and the fate of Eve's button box in the Epilogue. What is the significance of these episodes?

6. The pace of the narrative slows in chapters twelve to fifteen (1988). Why might this have been necessary? Did you find George and Eve's relationship credible: the fact that he proposes to her and that she accepts?

7. The book describes Eve's relationships with the key people in her life, particularly her grandmother, her

mother, Birgit, George and Tamara. Which of these relationships did you find most interesting, and why? What does Eve derive from each relationship?

8. Consider what the book suggests about the importance of family. There are examples of positive, and less positive, family relationships in the novel. How well did you think each type of family dynamic was explored?

9. What does the book have to say about ageing, for example in chapter twenty-one? Did that resonate? Which age group of reader do you think might best appreciate this novel?

10. Were there any other elements of the story which you particularly liked, or which you found disappointing?

ACKNOWLEDGEMENT

Cover photograph 'Phoebe'
by John P Berry

About the author

Jill Berry was a teacher, and latterly a head, who, after stepping down from headship, completed a doctorate and wrote a book about it: 'Making the Leap - Moving from Deputy to Head' (Crown House, 2016). Much as she enjoyed writing about education, she always wanted to try to write a novel, and started working on 'The Dresser' in the winter of 2019, just before the pandemic struck.

Covid gave her the time and space to write more, and between winter 2019 and the spring of 2021 she completed these three short novels. She offers them in one volume because they are short, and may be especially suitable for Book Club discussion for that reason. The volume includes possible questions for such discussion.

Jill lives in Newark with her husband, John, who has supported her fiction writing, as he supports her in everything.

Jill tweets @jillberry102. Please feel free to contact her on Twitter if you read any of the novels and have any feedback you'd like to offer. Thank you.

Printed in Great Britain
by Amazon

81813315R00304